SKIN

INEXTRICABLY TIED

Lost Touch Duet
in the Fangs With Benefits universe

Aveda Vice

Bad Bite LLC

Written by: Aveda Vice
Beta reading by: Gab With Purpose
Cover illustration by: Evertein
Cover design by: Designed by Vee
Map by: Abigail Hair

Also By Aveda Vice

Dedication

"Come back! Even as a shadow, even as a dream..."
— Euripides, *Herakles*

Author's Note

This book contains sexual situations. It is not intended for anyone under the legal age of adulthood. All characters depicted in sexual situations herein are over 18 years of age. This book is not to be used as an informational guide to any type of sex or sexual education.

Some topics within this book may be sensitive or disturbing to some readers. Reader discretion is advised.

For detailed information on the topics addressed, please visit the author's website or scan the codes below.

Skin

Inextricably Tied

SKIN

Prequel to
Inextricably Tied

SKIN

If Harbinger had kept the gloves on, it wouldn't have happened.

It was a simple job: lay her hands on a few objects and let their stories seep through her skin. See where the items had been before, who had touched them, what they'd done. Flood her senses with sights, smells, and sounds that weren't there any longer, all with a simple brush of her fingertips.

It's some divine cruelty that cursed her with the ability. She can imagine the gods, whomever they are, laughing at the banshee they created. Wailing about death wasn't enough, so they put a hair trigger in every inch of her skin.

Objects are easier to read: they don't carry as much as the living. Just show her flashes of what she needs before they settle into the back of her mind like a cramped storage locker. But when she touches people...they stick with her. Feed her their emotions endlessly, forging a connection between the two of them that can only be severed by death. She learned that the hard way. So, she wears the gloves.

She has it down to a science: cover every inch of bare skin in her black catsuit and skull helmet. Remove the gloves only when she needs to read artifacts. Report the findings. Put the gloves back on.

But something's wrong. She'd known as soon as the human unlocked the side door of the restaurant, gaze jerking behind Harbinger before he stepped back to let them enter. At the time, she'd chalked up his squirming to her partner's colossal gray presence, towering over them before he ducked to fit his wings through the door. Gargoyles are enough to strike fear into anyone, especially with the way Jasper Flint's brows stay knit above his monstrous maw. So she'd brushed it off; this was one of the least seedy places they'd been called to. She'd read the object, Flint would watch her back, they'd take the money and move on to the next person in need of a tracker.

Easy.

Flint's gruff voice grinds down her thoughts. "You said it was valuable."

Both partners stare at the ripped, soggy cardboard on the bar. Flint's lips press into a thin line, tight around the tusks extending from both rows of teeth.

"It — it is," the human stammers, edging behind the counter. "Well — the shipment is. This is all that's left after they stole the rest, and — well. You know how these things go."

"No. I don't." Flint doesn't hesitate, reaching for his keys, thumb over the button to unlock their vehicle.

"I'll read it."

His gaze shifts to Harbinger dwarfed beside him. He doesn't contradict her, but there's a tight twitch in the line of his jaw — the same one he gets every time she makes it harder for him to do his job and keep her in one piece. "It's not what we agreed to."

The human glances between them, unsure if he should be terrified or relieved. Harbinger maneuvers around Flint, flicking his bat-like wing out of the way before rolling up the sleeve of her suit.

"Welcome to the freelance biz."

She steps up to the bar, eyeing the cardboard before she pulls on each finger of her glove. Even after all these years, trepidation makes itself known in the squirming sensation of her stomach. Opening herself up to any number of things, making herself vulnerable, still terrifies her — even if only for a moment. But she flexes her bare fingers before lifting her palm over the bar.

There's a sharp inhale: the human, trembling like a sheet caught in the wind, honed on the bone white of her skin being swallowed by the pitch black of her fingertips. Residual stains from everything she touches, creeping further up her hands with time. There's a beat of silence before he jumps to an apology, and she can only imagine the deadly look Flint shoots at him...but nothing more. Good: they've had this conversation before. She'll handle it the way she chooses.

"It looks worse than it is," Harbinger murmurs, but she's focused on the object. It tremors, sending vibrations off before she can even touch it. Her hand hovers, fingers splayed, as if she might retract her offer, and then she lowers her palm to the surface.

All the connections spawn in a confusing rush, a thousand threads weaving together in her mind. She plucks a few strings before she follows the one she wants, letting the scene play out in flashes behind her eyes.

Boxes pulled from a truck, passed between hands as they're unloaded. They seem heavy, from the strain on the workers' faces, but otherwise, the people carrying them aren't bothered. Which makes sense, given they're only handling pallets of soda syrup — at least, according to the labels.

It's innocent enough. But...what she's seeing has to be a glimpse of the past, an image of what happened to the boxes as they disappeared. But none of the "thieves" are hurried or concerned, lounging against the truck and smoking as they chat. And the crates aren't being driven away; they're set outside a brick building. One that's an eerily similar shape and color to the restaurant Harbinger and Flint are standing in.

There's a more recent memory attached to the cardboard. A scene of the human at the counter, trembling as he tears a piece of cardboard off one of many identical boxes in a storage room. He stomps the scrap of cardboard into a puddle to give it a worn appearance, grinding it into the dirt.

Harbinger surfaces from the vision, eyes narrowed. "...what did you say you lost?"

The human hasn't stopped quaking, locking eyes with her before they both catch the dawn of recognition on the other's face. Her voice ekes out.

"Flint —"

Everything vanishes when Flint yanks her back against his chest, hardening to stone, and she clenches her eyes shut as the shots begin. Concrete chips, glass shatters, and a flurry of bullets rain against Flint's back. The gunfire comes from every angle, nicking past her helmet when his arms and wings curl tighter around her. The room moves past her, and she lands behind a bullet-ridden booth the moment before those enormous wings send napkins scattering through the air.

And then there's screaming. Drowned out by an inhuman roar, claws slashing the bar in half, blood splattering across the checkered floor beneath her. Weapons clatter to the ground, and the shrieks and gasps of pain finally fall silent. Her heart scurries to escape her chest, panic pumping through her blood until a goliath shape blocks out the fluorescents in the ceiling.

Flint shifts out of the rock armoring him, covered in little more than scratches...save for the sprays of blood coating his old scars and discoloration. A hand extends to her — but guilt stops it, soaking even deeper than the gore. His red eyes flick to the naked length of her skin curled against her chest. He doesn't have to ask; when he meets her eyes, he knows it's too late. That in all the carnage and chaos, the one thing she remembers most is the moment Flint's bare hand closed over hers.

Adrenaline wears off. His emotions swell like a tide inside of her, and she vomits across the floor.

For the next three days, she avoids him. A nearly impossible task when they're at the beginning of a week-long travel stint — made even harder by the fact that she can now feel his every emotion coursing through her.

The first day is hell. It's been years since she touched another person, and she remembers why, gripping the edge of the motel bed when the feelings overtake her. Flint keeps his distance. The only sign of him is the takeout left outside her door when he returns from a day of appointments she's missed: all her favorites, made as if she'd ordered them herself.

Day two is manageable. More exhausting than anything, and she keeps a wet towel over her eyes, burrowing into herself to avoid the swell of his everyday irritation.

That's how she stumbles across it. Purely an accident, while she's still dizzy from having someone else's emotions inside her, begging to be felt. A tiny flame buried beneath the armor of his concern, his worry, as he tries to keep a lid on everything else. She inspects the light inside her and feels a flicker of yearning deep in her chest, one that makes heat pool in the pit of her stomach.

It's subtle. Wouldn't have even noticed it if it hadn't drawn her in...because it reflects her own. Shedding new light on her memories of exhausted nights after tracking, slipping into motel rooms next to each other. A reminder of the glances he's gotten of the sunken places in her face, the back of her neck when she removes her helmet. Intimacy and affection burn stronger in Flint than any other emotion — except the guilt that swarms him.

The pain of someone new inside her system is waning. Only made worse when she fights it, so she tries to settle into it. Accept her new read on him like a snug blanket...which isn't hard when his presence is warm and certain, draped over her shoulders without weighing her down. Enough that on the third day, she manages to pull herself out of bed and into the passenger seat of their SUV, slumping behind her helmet.

"Don't say shit. Just drive. *Slow.*"

There's only a moment of silence before the ignition cranks, and they hit the road again.

It's a long day. She barely remembers half the shit she touches, floating nebulously while Flint tersely handles all their conversations. It's harder to deal with his emotions with so much less space between them, but all things considered, he's doing quite the job keeping a rein on them.

By the time they get back to the motel, it's dusk, and she's able to think of more than his presence for a few minutes at a time. They've nearly reached their rooms before she senses it: the shift in him, pointed in her direction. She jams her keycard into her door.

"You can feel it," he interrupts.

The light blinks green. She could press down the handle and slip into her room, ignore his statement...because it's not a question. But Flint has never been one to let her escape the things she needs to face.

"How I feel about you," he finishes.

Eyes bore into her back. He *knows* she can feel it. She's explained it to him enough in those late nights at diners, swirling cold french fries through ketchup and refilling coffee cups. The way people feel to her, when she touches them, could send her to her knees. All their emotions flooding into her at once and never draining back out. Once someone's there, sewn into her mind through a brush of skin, they're there for life — or at least, as long as she's lived it thus far. They grow quieter the longer she goes without them, the more distance she puts between them, but they never leave. Always lingering on the other side of her consciousness.

She says that's why she has commitment issues. She doesn't think it's a joke.

Flint clears his throat, maintaining a respectable length of space between them. "I apologize. I never wanted to burden you with it."

"It's not your fault."

"It is," he says flatly. Not that there had been much of a choice. It was either live with his feelings or bleed out on a restaurant floor.

"Well, it's fine," she shrugs. "It's — small, anyway."

Those eyes heat the back of her neck, and she feels the tiny flare of him in her chest growing — not into a raging flame. Just warmth spreading through her, the truth of his feelings when he isn't holding them back. A different kind of flush spreads across her cheeks, and she has to duck her eyes from his when his voice levels her.

"It's not small."

As quickly as it appeared, he tamps down on the feeling again until it's little more than an ember. "But I'm sorry, regardless. I'll do my best to contain it. And once we wrap up this week, we can find you another partner."

The sudden jerking fear in her body is all her own — and somehow, that's worse than any feeling he's shared with her. Dealing with this shit is bad enough on a good day; the thought of facing it without Flint makes her want to scream.

Instead, her voice croaks out. "You don't have to do that..."

But he doesn't argue the point before he turns to his door, reaching into his pocket when the words burst out of her.

"— do you want to come in?"

Both of them still, but she doesn't walk back the offer. A drink bottle knocks its way out of the vending machine below them. They both wait: to see if he backs into professionalism or if she changes her mind.

She doesn't.

After a long moment of silence, he nods and squeezes through the doorway behind her.

Cheap motels aren't made for his stature — hell, *nothing* is made for his stature — and she has the sudden thought of his big body draped across her queen-sized bed. Cold sweat pricks on her neck, but she removes her coat and tosses it on the back of a chair.

"Thought maybe we could order in...unless you're really eager to sit in a fast food dining room this evening."

Tusks lift when he smiles. "I'm not."

Only in the safety of her room does she remove her helmet, freeing the deathly black of her hair, streaked through with white almost as stark as her skin. It's nothing he hasn't seen before — at least, on rare occasions. Through the cracks in bathroom doors, in the quiet of hours-long drives, from the couch when their motel stays have only one bed.

Removing the helmet at all requires trust that he won't touch her — that he'll keep his distance. And he always has. But there's something in his eyes when he turns away, doing his best not to stare...and for the first time, she can feel exactly what it is.

A swell of twisted pain, the yearning she recognizes when he sees her skin pulled tight over her bones. The dark space under her milky eyes, cheekbones hollowed out, a strange skeletal amalgam of before and after. Half alive, half dead, tied between two worlds to be able to see what moves between them.

But his feeling isn't revulsion. It spreads through her chest like a deep sigh, a pining relief, a sight that's been missing from him that has finally returned.

Before she can question it, Flint bears down on the straining ache, and it extinguishes inside her.

They order a smattering of grease and carbs and eat over the cramped table, sinking back into discussion of their cases. That's always the safest bet: the route they choose most often until it's dark out, when the conversation winds to other topics. Childhoods and goals and past relationships where they always linger a bit too long. Tonight, though, there's a different weight; it fills the silence when the ice shifts in their empty drinks.

"Why do you think they ambushed us?" She tilts back her cup

of watered-down soda.

"Because you've been catching onto them. Getting too close to uncovering something they don't want found. It sounds like they're connected to the crime ring you've been picking up on." Flint stretches, and the chair creaks beneath him. "Fortunately, they didn't have a full understanding of your power. I'm sure they were as surprised as anyone when you spotted their lie on a soggy piece of cardboard."

Her eyes flick back to his, but he doesn't meet her right away, turning the tiny plastic fork over in his hands. There isn't anger on his face — not quite. But his scowl is knit with a different sort of resentment that hovers in the air. She waits to see what it is...and it comes.

"For someone who has to take so much precaution...you can be so fucking *reckless*."

The truth of it stings. Her layers of clothing, the helmet, the extra sheets she brings to motel rooms, all to keep her from encountering a rogue surface. Meanwhile, she'd been thoughtless at the restaurant, putting them both at risk because she hadn't weighed the consequences. She can imagine his frustration now more than ever: he's given her accidental access to his every feeling, yet he's still left in the dark about what she's thinking.

"Consider it job security."

But it's her failed attempt at levity, and he shakes his head, tapping the fork on his takeout container. He wears half a smile, but there's something heavier weighing down the corners. "You'd think after this long, I'd have a better idea of where your head's at...but I don't."

Her eyes drop to the table. It's a little twisted: how much she keeps hidden when she can see the deepest parts of other people. What an advantage she has — knowing what they're feeling, what they've done — even if it comes at a price.

Maybe that's why she does things without thinking: so inundated with outside thoughts, she can't be completely sure which are hers. So overwhelmed with external emotions, she doesn't ever reach for her own. They both wait in silence for her to find the words she wants to say — or at least, something close enough.

"...I'm sorry I said I'd read it."

Even though Flint was correct in his evaluation, he doesn't let it linger between them.

"It wouldn't have mattered. The guns were ready. They'd have been just as happy shooting our backs walking out the door."

"Still..." An unsettling guilt squirms through her. They've been partners for more than half a decade, learning to read these situations. To read *each other*. The thought that her negligence might have cost far more than sharing his emotions is distressing. "*I* might have agreed to do it, but *we* didn't."

A tiny smirk twitches at the corner of his lips. "If I'd really wanted you out of there, you wouldn't have had time to get the glove off."

Strikingly, suddenly, she's hyper-aware of the gloves she's wearing now. How they cling to her fingers, stretch and bend, and the thought that reverberates in her is the distinct lack of memory for how his skin felt. She remembers the moment: the crushing grip over her wrist before he yanked her against his chest. But she doesn't remember the *feeling*: the texture, the temperature, the way her skin tingled at the first brush. Selfish thoughts turn bitter in her mouth: that the ambush forced the two of them together but didn't let her keep the one feeling she greedily wants to remember. His hands are clean now, claws sheathed away, but she remembers the blood dripping off of them.

"Does it bother you?" She shifts in her seat. "That you had to kill them?"

A wilder fire flicks to life in her stomach, in his eyes, burning red like fury.

"It bothers me far less than the alternative."

Heat swells in both of them, stirring like some ancient

sleeping giant, before he cuts it off at the source and stands to gather their trash. "I should go. Let you get some sleep. You're still recovering."

Her head bobs, but her heart's not in it, more frantic and panicked than any of the emotions coming from him. She grasps for something, anything more. "What if you stayed?"

He stills. She doesn't move, willing the rapid thrumming of her heart to slow before he hears it.

"...what if I did?"

The air conditioner kicks on. She tries not to focus on the placid lake of his emotions, his strain to hold them back from her. But she feels her own, nestled somewhere deeper, and wonders if this is a mistake. A boundary they shouldn't cross. A way to take a knife to every thread that weaves them together.

Her boots find the floor. She breaches that border between them, but he sinks back into his chair. Maintaining the distance, always standing by for a flash of her regret. But there is none when she eases toward him. Sidles up between his knees, and his legs open further, like she's meant to be there. Her gloved hand lifts to the broad line of his jaw, finding where it connects to his neck, then traces back down to the place where his tusks extend.

There's a pull in him, but he doesn't move. Lets her take her time before she breathes it out: "You can touch me."

Another moment's pause before his heavy hand is skating up the fabric on her leg, brushing against her thigh, chaste and so painfully intimate she wants to cry. He goes no higher, just keeps his fingertips light against the curve of her knee, tracing slow and infinite patterns until she lifts her hand to the horns jutting out from either side of his temples.

They're almost eye-level, and he never tears his gaze from hers — save for when she tightens her fingers around the base of his horns. His eyes close. And it's somehow the softest and deadliest look she's seen when it pierces straight into her.

Can't remember the last time she allowed herself to get this close: no mask, no barrier between their faces. Loses herself in every line between his brows, every scar carved onto his face, every visceral detail she's missed since the moment they met. When he opens his eyes again, the red of them is glowing.

His hand engulfs hers completely, hovering over the end of one gloved finger before he takes the fabric between his. Guides it loose, then moves onto the next, waiting for a waver of her hesitation. But she's watching him, locked under the gentle grip he has around her wrist until he drags the glove off.

He holds his palm beneath hers. An offering. Her black fingertips dip, drifting closer to the smoky color of his skin, both holding their breath like there's no air left in the room.

It's surreal, the thought that she could feel her skin against someone else's after years of infinite precaution against it. Avoiding anything that might force her here, to be this close...but he already exists within her. He can't get any closer than he is.

Their fingers brush, and a gasp rips out of her. He flinches — but doesn't move. Lets her drift, ghosting against his palm and sending a ripple of want through her at every pass. Even with nothing but her face and fingers bare, she's an exposed nerve, trembling every time he touches her.

The places they meet feel like tiny starbursts, amplifying all the emotion he tries to keep hold of. She sinks into his lap, held aloft by thick thighs beneath hers, the arms encircling her waist. But that's all they do, her pressed to the hard planes of his chest and the curve of his stomach, breaths rising and falling against each other.

They might stay like that forever, because Flint won't move without her, and her own unsettling need spikes so much higher than the one she feels from him.

"You can *touch me*," she pants. She's thought about it. Not in any daylight hours — not when she could help it. But her mind always wandered when his work slacks stretched over his muscled thighs. When he shifted out of his ruined jeans at the end of a long mission.

Arms tighten around her waist, but he speaks through gritted teeth. "I don't want to — take advantage of the connection."

The ache in her gets louder. "*I* want you to."

Finally, her hips dip close enough to wind against him, drawing a sharp breath out of both of them. "I promise you..." she begins, nails digging marks into his shoulders, and she revels at the feel of skin under hers. "I barely feel anything from you. *Frustratingly* so. It's like you don't even —"

"Is it?"

There's an uncertainty in his eyes before he loosens the control. Uninhibited desire seeps into her, rushing through her body and straight between her legs.

"*Fuck.*" It's enough to have her on edge, like one small touch could set her off, but he doesn't move. So painfully, gloriously, *horribly* still, and she can't think past their arousals bound together: hers spiked and impatient, his embracing and softening all its edges, so tight she could combust.

She gets a hand between her legs, eyes shut, sweat pricking. "Can I —? I can't — think —"

"*Yes.*"

She doesn't wait for more, circling her clit through her clothes and jolting immediately off the edge. Nearly arches out of his grip with the force of it, but he holds her tighter, letting her orgasm sweep her out and under. Through the blinding haze, his desire grows stronger, like watching her come apart in his arms has done nothing but sharpen his arousal.

It's a high she can't come down from: the sudden, spontaneous release paired with being this close to anyone. When she finally manages to open her eyes, he's watching like he's never seen her before. Like she's somehow remade right in front of him.

Heat blots her cheeks. "Sorry."

"Don't apologize."

Her heart keeps rapid time under her skin, but she can see

more clearly, bare fingers hovering near the buttons of his shirt. There's a swath of steel-colored skin, purple in the dim light, and a gunpowder trail of lust ignites inside her. One bare finger traces the opening. Flint sucks in a breath, but his hand comes up to close around her wrist, careful to stay on the fabric.

"We need to talk first." He senses her resistance, because he squeezes. "At least establish some guidelines."

"Yeah, you love guidelines." Her gaze dips to his mouth, and she feels him getting lost in it before she pulls back enough to see his face. All his undivided attention makes her body clench...but the discussion is non-negotiable. Sighing, she leans back on her elbows against the table. A smirk flits across her lips as he does his best not to be distracted.

"Let's hear it."

"I'm the only person you can touch?" he clarifies.

She considers it and winds into him. "Only person I'm still in contact with...including my last girlfriend."

Thick fingers flex over her hips, but he doesn't stop them from moving. "And what do you want from this? Exactly?"

Surely there's a responsible answer somewhere, but it's impossible to find when she can watch the way their bodies slot together. How her legs barely fit around his waist. How his hands engulf her body. How his eyes engulf her.

"I want..."

She loses the rest of her words, using her leverage against the table to drag herself along his cock. He grabs her sharply, keeping her suspended in two enormous hands. Their eyes meet, fire against fire, and he holds her to the flames. It's enough to force her to find words. Not enough to set her mind straight.

"I want you to fuck me. As much as you can take."

There's a deriding sound from him, and she rolls her eyes. "Fine: as much as *I* can take. Until I forget what I've been missing the past seven years."

This time when she shifts her hips, he doesn't release her.

"And is this because you have no other options?"

"I have other options; I can find someone I've touched before." But those options are backtracking, going somewhere she's already been, finding exes or crossing paths she's long since moved past. Her palms press up on the edge of the table, bringing her closer to his mouth. "I just prefer not to."

Despite the heat that's sparked between them, a different gravity settles into her. When she speaks, her voice is quieter, gaze drifting to his lips to avoid his eyes. "I don't trust anyone else to do this with me."

There's a bob in his throat when he swallows. When his voice finally comes, it's a deep rumble from his chest. "My emotions might overwhelm you. Even when I'm holding back."

Her grin is sharp. "I don't think you'd be worried about that if you could feel mine."

"But I can't feel yours," he reminds her, curving ample fingers against the small of her back. It archers her toward him, lifting her until she's drifting toward his lips. "...so you're going to have to tell me." Tusks frame both corners of her mouth. "You're going to have to do a lot of talking if we do this, Harbin."

The words are secondary to the way he's drinking her in. His eyes trace her features, searching for more answers...or devouring the sight of her bare face. Her mind is lost on the way his lips curve, so he squeezes her tighter, rooting her back to reality before he speaks. "I'm going to ask you for a color. At any time. Probably more than you'd like."

Her huff of air blows a strand of hair from her face.

"And you should use them, even if I don't ask. Red means we stop, and I give you some space. Yellow means we slow down, and I try to control it. And green —"

"— means go." Her mouth slots against his, and it's her own desire that fills her like a dam breaking. Flint loosens the hold he has around her waist until she can press fully against him. She's nothing against the barrel of his chest, and still, he handles her delicately. Enough of that: her teeth drag into his lip, and she feels pain lancing through him before he grips her ass in his hands.

"What do you like, Harbin? In bed?"

A grunt of annoyance escapes her. He doesn't let it slide.

"I told you you'd have to talk."

There's little she can do but answer, spiraling her hips against him. He allows it — for now. But she doesn't miss how he keeps both hands ready to stop her.

"I don't know…" Shame spreads across her face, as if making herself spontaneously orgasm in his lap was less embarrassing than this. She's out of practice: hasn't had to verbalize anything about her desires in so long. "I, um…"

Memories flip past her eyes, distant and futile, a slideshow of all the other interactions she's had. Her solo fantasies are closer to her tastes: the thoughts she uses when she's alone, touch-starved and needy. Maybe she's a masochist for how often she's thought about it. Fabricated some new species who was immune to her powers and envisioned what she would do if given the chance.

"It's hard to say, because I couldn't…"

Thick fingers work their way up under the back of her hair. Each tiny touch makes her shudder, blinking through her brain and taking out any other thought she has. He notices and stills his touch so she can formulate words.

"I couldn't trust anyone; the risk was too great. So I did what I could: me on top. Tied them up." She coughs. "A few glory holes."

Heat spreads across her cheeks at the image of doing that with him, but his expression is as honed and focused as always. There are none of those risks this time; this is an *opportunity*.

"But it wasn't the same." Resentment edges into her tone. "Not touching doesn't work for me. *Strangers* don't work for me."

She knows this is a line neither of them had ever planned on crossing. That they were content to keep their attractions separate, self-contained and inactive…for the partnership. But now both their wants mingle in her, a vial for the chemical reaction of desires eating through the isolated vessels they've kept them in.

"So the better question..." Flint murmurs, guiding her hips to work over his length. A sound unlike any she's made slips out. "...is what you *want* in bed."

Bare fingers grip the thick cords of his shoulders. There's an answer somewhere; she knows there is, but the hint of his arousal mixed with hers has her wet and slick and caught on the thought of stretching over his cock.

"...you want to be controlled?" He hasn't stopped drawing patterns against her back that jump through her like lightning. She takes too long to answer, and he slows the way he moves her.

"Color?"

"Green." She grits it out, forehead pressed to his. "Please keep talking. Fuck..."

He winds her against him in a figure eight that feels absolutely filthy. "You always had to be in charge. Set your safeguards, make sure you were protected..." A heavy thumb presses against her clit when his voice lowers. "Do you want me to take over for you?"

Another sound gets strangled in her throat, and she's moving on her own, seeking the friction of him beneath her. Tightens her arms behind his neck, the outline of his dick scraping her through every layer of fabric.

"*Yes.*"

It's like a starting gun. He lifts them both toward the bed with no effort, never pulling back, lowering her to the sheets when he holds himself above her. His gaze is too much. Too intense. So she squirms beneath him, huffing a laugh that's more breathless than she means it to be.

"You can throw me around, Flint." Her fingers find the front of her catsuit, struggling to work herself out of it. "You don't have to be gentle."

A smile stretches behind his tusks, and he moves her hand, slipping the buttons out of their holes for her. Flicks a claw out from one of his fingers, tracing over the fabric around the hardened peak of her nipple. A tremor runs through her — not just at the way he glides the suit down her body, lifting her ankles on the tips of his fingers to unhook her boots. His eyes peruse her, tracing over the small swell of her breasts, dipping down to her stomach, each bone pronounced despite the curves of fat and muscle. A reminder ingrained in her body, of the way she walks so close to death — but his devotion brings her unmistakably *alive*.

"Baby…" His voice is laced in a way she's never heard it. Not the brusque, hardened responses she's used to. Almost…pitying. Like she has no idea what she's in for. "I don't have to be rough to control you."

Eyes clamp shut when the pads of his fingers trace up the backs of her bared calves. Her fingers flex, desperate to reach, to grab, to stop, to pull him closer, something forbidden only days ago.

She doesn't realize he's stopped easing her legs apart until he speaks. "Color?"

Breath comes shallow through her nose, trying to untangle her thoughts when his skin on hers feels like vines circling her center. "Green?"

"I need you to look at me when you say it."

Finally, she pries one eye open. The sight of him, broad and massive, kneeling between her thighs makes her stomach knot. Still, he waits.

"Green," she breathes again.

His weight shifts on the bed, and she reaches for his shirt, twisting her fist into the shoulder. Like her body's separate from her mind. Like it wants something she hasn't let herself think about for years. He lowers himself, dragging his open mouth to the inside of her knee. It pops like warm champagne under her skin.

"You don't have to," she stammers. "We can just…"

But Flint winds their fingers together, pressing her wrists back down to the bedding.

"You're not in control anymore, baby."

It's not quite chastising, not a reprimand, but a reminder all the same. The hands around her wrists squeeze once, like he knows they'll stay in place...and then he's trailing back down the curve of her arms, inside her elbows, the outline of her waist. "And I want to see the way you look coming on the end of my tongue. Color?"

It knocks the breath from her. "Green."

"Good girl."

Her toes curl. Legs twitch. She tries to still them, but he stops where he's lifting her hips in one hand, watching her with hot, narrowed interest.

"You like that?"

Thighs tremble on either side of his face.

"You like when I tell you how good you are for me?"

A whine breaks through her, head tipping back to escape the ferocity of his gaze. The words twist deep in her stomach, winding hot and bright until she thinks she might break. It's the first time since she touched him that she lost him. Drowned out his emotions with the swelling need of her own, the surge of her desire swallowing his whole. But she feels his mounting again, as if watching her writhe under his praise stokes his arousal.

Frission races over her skin, hovering on the expectation of his fingers dragging off her last piece of clothing. But it doesn't come — and as she lifts her head, to understand where he's gone, his mouth presses hot and open between her legs.

Sheets twist in her fist when he rolls his tongue over her clit. Fabric clings between her thighs, tugging against her with a friction that's warm and wet and obscene.

"Flint..."

She fights to keep her hips from rising to meet him. He lifts his eyes, drawing a lazy loop with his tongue.

"Color?"

A vulgar sound hisses through her teeth. "Green." His hum rumbles against her, and then his mouth is back, tusks scraping the inside of her thighs. There are no thoughts, just her hips rolling and desperate for more, but he's slow. Methodical. Keeping her stilled with a hand splayed over her stomach.

Frustration rips out of her. "What color is — above green?"

The question pulls his mouth off of her, but there's no relief, thumb replacing it with tight circles. "How do you mean?"

The mattress dents under her heels, but it doesn't make him move. "What color — gets you to go faster? Because I need…" Breath pants out of her, but he's so fucking patient, only enough pressure against her to make her moan. Torturous patterns continue, and he pulls the fabric of her underwear tighter against her.

"What do you need?" He says it like he knows exactly what, but he won't move, won't give more than the gentle pressure on her clit until she screams. "Use your words, baby."

"I need your mouth on me. Nothing between us, just — skin."

For a petrifying moment, she's scared he'll keep her on the edge, make her tell him how badly she needs it until she's a babbling mess. Then the growl builds in his chest, and he yanks her panties down her legs.

"Good *fucking* girl."

Her body clenches, but then he's pressing his mouth bare against her, and she feels like light scattered through a mirror. He laves his textured tongue against her, infinite sensation jolting through her body from every bump and ridge. She tightens her thighs against him, tugging the sheets half out of place when he tilts her hips up to meet him.

"You can touch me."

He turns the words she'd used back on her. She's vibrating, trembling, breath catching when she looks down at the sight of him. His tongue is thick and ribbed, curling and arching her off the bed. But he's watching her while he mouths against her, something more than lust in his gaze.

She knows she can touch him. In the logical part of her brain, the part that knows she's already crossed that line, but the thought of it — of his horns beneath her fingers, of tugging him closer, feels so intimate. Even more than feeling his emotions — like it's giving away a glimpse at hers.

He drags his tongue between her folds and presses into her before he pulls back, enough to breathe over the trail he's left. "Color?"

"Green," she trembles, and he reaches for her wrists, keeping his eyes trained on her expression. Unwinds her fists from the blankets, lifting them off the bed before he presses another slow, filthy kiss to her cunt.

"Color?"

Her attention wobbles. "Green." He guides her arms lower, one immense hand enveloping both of hers to tilt them toward his head. Fingers slip around his horns, and she grips them at the base before he lifts a brow at her.

"...green," she finally answers, and he lets go of her wrists, lowering his mouth back down to her. Her grip is still loose...but the look in his eyes makes her tighten. Lips brush back and forth against her pussy, dragging up to her clit before he slips off the top and urges her hips to move. To fuck herself against his mouth.

"Take what you need from me."

It's so raw, so carnal, the slick slide of skin on skin. Shorts every nerve-ending she has, making her a mess of stimulation, of him kissing her open like he doesn't need anything else. Her eyes snap shut at the same time her fists grip around his horns.

"Yellow."

He doesn't move. Barely breathes, but she can feel his presence between her thighs, and she aches when he speaks.

"Is it too much?"

A sob threatens to break through her, voice cracking when her hips fight to find his mouth despite herself. "It's too *hot*."

There's a moment's pause before he chuckles, breath ghosting against her clit, but he pulls back enough to let her breathe. "Tell me when you're ready."

He can't get far with her fingers circled around his horns, and her body's moving before her brain finally admits it. All the frenzied need inside her is her own; Flint's arousal is only a steady ripple making tiny waves.

Finally, she lets out a breath. "Green."

There's a nod against her hands, and he fits a palm under her ass, lifting her hips toward him. Shifting his shoulders, hooking her knees behind them, a slow process meant to ease her in...but the muscles in his neck flex, and there's heat in everything.

"You're doing so well with your colors, Harbin."

Approval notches itself deep in her stomach like an arrow ready to fire. The pads of his fingers brush against her thighs, sending little sparks to the base of her spine.

"Now...I'm going to put my mouth back on your pussy. And I want you to fuck it just the way you like. Can you be a good girl and do that for me?"

A whimper streaks through her, thighs clenching against his jaw, and she can't bear to look at him. Knows what she'll find: the tenderness burning over the tiny, hidden cinder of control. One he's kept out of sight, letting the flames lick higher until she's sweating. There's no uncertainty in him now; he knows he can get exactly what he wants with a soft word, like she'll do anything he asks. Like he isn't even concerned about it. All those barriers between their skin didn't keep him from figuring her out. All those years of being partners, close but not close enough, showed him far more than she realized.

The wet heat of his mouth closes over her clit, and she's gone. Shocked out of her thoughts, gasping for breath. Arching off the bed like the arrow of want has been replaced by a bow that threatens to break. He kisses her slow and open, that thick tongue teasing inside her, the same way he could...and she can't stop herself. She holds his horns, pressing heels against his back to drag herself closer. Red eyes flash, but he doesn't speak — just grips her hips harder, tilts her further, letting her chase her release against his mouth.

"That's it, baby..." His voice muffled by the way she drags across his lips, his eyes skating over her body when she makes helpless circles with her hips. She whines when he pulls back again to breathe against her clit. "Gods, look at you..."

"*Flint.*"

He finally stills himself, only claiming as much skin as she allows, but his fingers splay wider to envelop both her sides in his hands. The image is obscene: her half-lifted, chest arched, hair sweat-slick and splayed behind her. Completely bare to someone else when she hasn't been in years. And him, still clothed completely — the only sign that he's affected are the wrinkles she leaves in his dress shirt.

Her hand clamps over her mouth. She comes with a cry, hips stuttering in his hands, still keeping a vice grip on one of his horns. It almost sounds like mourning: weeping at the touch of someone else, of *him*, and fighting to muffle the sounds.

He doesn't stop. Lets her ride it out against his mouth, smearing herself against his lips, his tongue laving until even that's too much. She pushes on his head, and he pulls back to leave the lightest kisses against the inside of her knees, the curve of her hips, the juncture where her thighs meet her body. Her chest heaves for nearly a minute before he speaks.

"Color?"

Her voice is patchy and hoarse when she finally finds it under the rubble he's left her in. "Green."

A contented noise rumbles out of him, but he makes no move to pull away from her — keeps pressing idle kisses against her skin. It's still surreal, feeling someone else bare against her. Feeling *him* against her. She presses up onto her elbows, nearly toppling over before he gets a hand under her back.

"I want more." Her hungry demand.

He keeps a steady hold on his emotions. "We don't have to."

"I know." Her fists twist into his shirt. "*I* want to."

She seals it with her mouth over his, sighing at the taste of her on his lips. Of her on someone else. He holds her close, tight in his arms, and every point of contact sets off another string of synapses through her body.

He pulls back, and her gaze drifts to the bulge in his slacks. But when she moves for his belt, he catches her hand easily in one of his. She tries again — and again, she's caught with the same huge hand.

Her eyes flash. "What, turnabout isn't fair play?"

A smile cracks across his face, but he only lifts her arms, dangling her over the mattress. At his mercy, if he decides he wants to touch any inch of her skin. It should terrify her, to be so defenseless against it. Her heart thuds against her ribs — but it's a different feeling, knowing Flint's the one that holds her captive.

"You're not ready."

There's a moment of silence before she barks a laugh. "Who knew Jasper Flint was a sex god among men?"

Something flickers through him when she speaks his name, but it settles, every inch of his emotions unruffled. "It's not arrogance; it's logic. It's been a long time for you..." His eyes follow a trail down her body, reinforced by both her wrists clasped in one of his hands. "Size difference notwithstanding."

"I can take it."

But he doesn't move, the tips of his wings nearly cresting the ceiling. "You will," he agrees, and the promise sends a shudder straight down through her shoulders. "But not yet."

Her tongue clicks to counter, but before she can, he quiets her with a finger over her mouth. "I'll work you up to it. I promise." The pad of his finger presses against her lips, and his eyes flick back to hers. "Open."

So simple...but it shoots between her legs, a whimper boiling up, and she knows she won't contradict him. Her lips part, flat of her tongue gliding out against him, looking up beneath her lashes. He hisses a breath before he presses down, spreading her mouth to fit.

"Wider."

Her jaw shifts. Lips circle him, and she hollows her cheeks the same time his arousal swells in her.

"*Perfect*, baby."

Sounds like a prayer, like he would worship her if given the chance. But he withdraws his finger, keeping her wrists held when he guides his other hand down her body to slide against her clit. A groan slips out of her, and she's not sure if she's trying to get away or so much closer.

"We should talk about protection."

Her mind is elsewhere when he speaks, fuzzy with static every time he circles her, when he eases against her with just the right pressure. The concept of contraception is so foreign, so unreal. It doesn't take long for him to notice and pull away.

"I'm not...on...anything." Can't remember the last time she took a protection potion. Can't remember the last time she needed to.

Flint nods, but he's still watching her, considering something behind his stone facade. "I have a condom. But just so you're aware: I haven't been with anyone since the last time I was tested. And I had a vasectomy...quite a few years ago."

His fingers are soft on her hip, dusting back and forth. But not distracting: a comfort. Only then does she realize the wall he's built between them to keep his emotions at bay. To prevent any influence on her decision. She reaches for the well of him inside her, to see what he's thinking, but he keeps the bricks between them in place.

"— I don't want you to wear it. I just want — your skin." Nothing but him dragging deep, buried in her heat and waking every inch of her...

It's enough to hijack her thoughts again — but not his. His fingers keep their motion, but his mouth twists, thick brows furrowing.

"Actually…" The words come slow, like he's weighed them in his mind. "I think I should wear it. Not that I don't trust your judgment, but all of this is new…for both of us." He leans forward then, holding his mouth off of hers, the corner of his lip tilting. "And I don't think I'll be able to keep a hold on my emotions if I feel you bare around my cock."

Her breath hitches, but he lifts his brows. "All right?"

It takes a moment for her to nod, and her stomach constricts when he pulls away.

"For now…" he murmurs, "we need to get you ready for me."

Sweat shines across her collarbones. "Is that not what you were just doing?" Her voice trails off when he drags his finger to his mouth, lapping up the remnants of her with his tongue.

"Eating your pussy was selfish. That was for me."

It's ludicrous, the thought that getting her off was a self-serving act. But he shifts his weight back onto the bed, leaning over her body while that large finger circles her clit.

"This…" The tip presses between her folds, teasing inside her, and she feels like she could crawl deliciously out of her skin. "Is to make sure you enjoy my cock as much as I enjoyed making you come on my tongue." With a slow press, he edges his finger in to the first knuckle, and it's dangerously close to the biggest thing she's ever had inside her.

"And I won't know you're ready until you're past the point of begging."

The words come through a tunnel on the other side of how it feels spreading around him. But he pulls away, and her frustration boils over, splashing out of her throat with a groan. He doesn't give in: guides her to her knees to face the mirror on the wall. It's a vision from something dark and gothic: a girl like a skeleton, the portent of death, skull painted across her face. And the beast behind her, wings too large for the frame, eyes glowing red in the dark. The devil leans over her shoulder and guides her idle hands.

"I want you to show me exactly what you like."

Words might as well be a whip for the way her body tenses, rigid and hot and too aroused to think straight. More infuriating is his patience and how well he keeps his emotions tamped down.

She reaches behind her, tugging on the buttons of his shirt. "I'd like you to take this *off*."

He snags her hand, her futile attempts little more than a fly buzzing about his head. "Not yet. It's too much skin."

She whines at the tiny contact, the firecrackers his hand sets off around her wrist. "Fuck, it's not — *enough*."

But he waits and watches. Stone-still and silent, a testament to his true nature, as impenetrable and unbreakable without his rock armor.

The impasse breaks, and she dips her hand between her thighs. It's already slick, and he knows it. Has felt it, drug his tongue through it, known her in ways no one has in so long. But before she lets the thoughts guide her, he eases up behind her, pressing his clothed chest to her back.

"Show me what you like...and use my hand."

Everything he does strikes too close to something she wants, sending sparks flying. He knows too much...has seen too much of her, somehow, when she's the one who's supposed to have a better read on him.

But she finds her footing and meets his eyes with the foggy pools of hers, reaching back to drag his arm across her chest. It covers half her body, muscles hard and weighted where they press against her. Requires both her hands to maneuver, closing all his fingers until the thick middle digit points up between her legs.

He could cup her completely in one hand. Grip her and lift her, but he doesn't move — makes her guide herself to the tip of his finger. So she pays him back in kind: makes him wait, stirring her hips in slow circles until the burning ember of his eyes grows brighter in the mirror. Entrancing, the way his gaze follows her, how her nails drag down his arm. How she holds his wrist still, wrapping her fingers around the last knuckle...how she stretches to fit over him.

The contact quakes through her, only kept upright by the strap of his arm. He holds his weight off of her, but he's a ghost against her back, across her chest, submerged inside her with a flaring arousal as she works herself lower.

A tiny sound spills when she sinks halfway. There's no stopping how her head rolls back against his shoulder. Weak, wanton, lips parting and finding his eyes when a plea fights loose.

Arousal surges deep in her stomach — but not from her. He loses the grip on his want when their eyes meet. When she gives him that hopeless look and lays all her weight on him. Even like this, she can see his jaw tense, reaching deep within himself to staunch the flow of emotions. And then her hips find a new path, grinding back against him, circling into his lap where he's hard for her. That sends a spiral of his desire through her so tight it makes her gasp, and she throbs around his finger, even when he forces her forward and holds her there.

"It's not about me." It's a warning against her hair, but she hears it break into a snarl — one that promises even more than he's given her.

"I know…" Even when he holds her fast, she tries to work back against him, debauching his words on her tongue. "I'm selfish; that's for *me*."

But the momentary lapse is over, his arousal locked down once again, until the need between her thighs is all her own. A chuckle gusts across her neck, and she shudders, but his mouth is out of reach.

"That's ambitious, Harbin…" Mocking compassion snakes into his voice, and she knows better than to meet his eyes in the reflection — and still, she does. "You haven't even taken a whole finger yet."

It burns her cheeks, and both their eyes cling to her body in the mirror, following the way she strains to grind her clit into his palm. Arched and writhing with his thick hand between her thighs, two knuckles slick and disappearing inside her. She wants to take more. She needs it, and if this is what it takes to have him...so she spreads her knees, clutching his wrist when she sinks lower and groans a string of curses.

A furious desire swells from him. "That's my *fucking* girl."

It races through her, winding her down against his palm until she's taking him to the hilt. The other fingers of his hand curl, slotting against the juncture of her thighs, framing where she fucks him in the filthiest way. It lights the wick at the end of her orgasm, a steady spark eating its way toward her release, and he grips her chin to keep her eyes lifted in the mirror.

"Come like that."

She bites back a sound, but Flint doesn't let her stop. Takes his time to ready and ruin her, and she's already too hot with the scraps he's given her.

"Color?"

She curses, trying to build her rhythm against him.

"Fucking — green!"

Then he releases the floodgates on his emotions. Pours every ounce of his arousal into her, honed straight to her clit, tusks scraping against the back of her neck. She clutches at him, legs trembling when the ache crescendos to a howling peak.

"Do what I tell you."

She comes with a start, clinging to his arm. There's a curse low against her throat, somewhere outside the veil of her orgasm, and another snap of arousal sinks its teeth into her.

"Flint..." It doesn't stop him. Doesn't change the new rhythm he's started at all, fucking his finger up into her, and a whimper builds in her throat. "I want more."

There's no acknowledgement. He keeps working her over in long, slow strokes that make her feel every stretching inch. He doesn't respond. Doesn't make any motion to stop, and she moans.

"Flint." Hardly threatening with all the cracks in her voice, debris shattered next to the solid boulder of his chest. Even as she

wars with him, her hips meet each motion, a pitiful excuse for standing her ground. "Give it to me…"

"Color?"

Damn that — *fucking* word. The corner of his lips tilt in the mirror, but that's the only thing that changes, and it daggers frustration through her.

"Flint, I'm begging. You said —"

"That," he moves out from behind her, lowering her suddenly onto her back, "is not begging. Not for me."

There's no moment to fathom it before his finger is on her clit, jolting her out of her body.

"Have you ever begged for anything, Harbin? Anything like this?"

She's suspended, body ramrod straight, as if she'll topple off the edge if any single thing beneath her shifts.

"Have you?"

Her eyes cinch shut. "No." Her body is a battlefield, thoughts clashing with the painfully slow tension in her abdomen.

"Color?"

"I want your cock."

"*Color*, Harbin."

"*Green*, fucking — more green than this!"

There's a smug little smirk against her knee, but Flint gives no mercy, using his hand to overstimulate her. "Do you want me to tell you how to get what you're after?"

"Yes." Even as she says it, she knows she doesn't want the answer. He's occupied, drawing idle circles against her clit for so long she thinks he's forgotten.

"You said you want my cock." Finally, he speaks — and she isn't sure if it's the way he's burying one finger in her cunt that makes it sound like a riddle. "You need to *need* it."

A groan wrenches out of her when he sinks his finger to the hilt, filling her completely, and it overwhelms her as much as the first time. Her brain is taffy, pulled in a thousand different directions, all leading back to how easily he speaks.

"It's written in everything, Harbin. Your whole body's tense: your shoulders..." From within the mess of blankets, he pries her hand out, pressing it back to the mattress. "Your fingers in the sheets...your thighs." He swats one with the back of his hand before a second finger edges up against her entrance. "Your jaw."

Her teeth grind together. She tries to breathe, to release some of the pent-up energy, but the bindings around her chest don't loosen. His second finger edges closer, spreading her over just the tip, and she fights for a breath.

He stops moving against her, stills the hand working her open. "You feel everything else: the things you touch, the people who haven't left you. Every residual emotion...but I need you to tell me yours."

Impossible. Her tongue prepares the word before he even finishes, but he curves one finger, nudging against the spot deep inside her. "I told you you were going to have to talk..." The well of his arousal begins to rise, pushing her up toward the surface, hurtling too quickly to hold onto. "I meant it, Harbin. Tell me what feels good. What you *feel.* Let yourself need this..."

And as she's gasping, adrenaline coursing, pupils blown wide — he rips his desire away, tugging the rug from underneath her. It drops her like a stone until she's plummeting back through open air with nothing to land in but her own emotions.

His voice echoes in the emptiness. "And know I'll give it to you."

It hollows her mind. Wipes her, for a moment, of every other thought and memory and feeling that isn't hers. Only when she returns to the mosaic of her body, surfacing through the trails so many others have left within her, does she realize how blissfully, brilliantly blank those few seconds were. A haphazard groan escapes when she realizes he's worked his second finger halfway in.

"Can you do that for me, Harbin?"

No. How can she, when she's so focused on everything but herself? She doesn't know how to feel things any more — not anything that's her own. Emotions are work. Business. Weightless things she picks up and carries that are so much heavier than they should be. Foreign objects that appear inside her and never leave. Things she holds for the moment she needs them before she shoves them down and avoids them again.

How can there be anything in between?

But she feels his emotions warming her chest, little more than a reminder that they're there. That he is. The rest of her body is a cavern, a vessel to the feelings she's kept long-buried inside her. Shrinking, sifting, water expanding to fit its container.

Yet if she focuses on them and nothing else, on letting her feelings flow into her, flooding her limbs and chest...her body starts to unwind. To release the tension that was keeping her at bay from herself, trickling open as her knees ease apart, back finally sinking into the mattress. She tries to swallow the heady cocktail of feelings. None of the words she has are right — not quite. But she gets close.

"I feel...hot. Impatient."

But that doesn't spur him into action, fingers stilled inside her, so she exhales and reaches toward her emotions again.

"...afraid. Not because of the size, really. Or you."

He doesn't speak. Lets her sort through her feelings, sifting through the sand of everything else to find the ones that are completely hers.

"There's something...thrilling. About being able to touch someone. Like the possibilities are laid out in front of me, and I can't see the end."

Even now, it swells in her throat, but she brushes aside any connection that 'someone' has to 'you.' There are so many other feelings to think about, and she finds the pool of her desire and delves deeper. Lets it rise above her head.

"Feels like your mouth is —" It cuts off in a curse, because she can imagine the start of his smirk forming, and that's enough to career her thoughts off course. " — going to be an unfortunate daily distraction."

A laugh ghosts against her ankle. In her descent, she'd forgotten how close he is, how he gives off an aura inches away. It brings her desire coursing forth, and she lets the feeling take hold of her tongue and loosen it.

"Feels like…as soon as you touched me tonight, something else started. Not something from you. Something in me…that's awake."

A kiss presses to the juncture of her thigh. "Such a good girl." It zings through her, zipping to her core, a mix of pride and heat and need.

"Green," she breathes before he can ask. Flint doesn't make her wait, starting new strokes inside her, tongue rolling against her clit. Both fingers slot completely inside, and her body threatens to tense, to pull her up from the waves, but she forces herself to relax. To sink, letting herself be wound up with each motion.

Pressure builds. A slow nudging against her abdomen, growing insistent until every other feeling becomes shallow in its wake.

"Flint…" Her voice strains, still clipped, trying to hold back — but she doesn't. "Flint…"

His name tastes sinful in her mouth, hunger winding through her at the sound of her own desperation. Her hips shift, edging toward him, fingers grasping for his hand on her thigh.

"Flint, please."

Her eyes shut, but not to block it out — to let her feel it, capsize into it, let herself be swallowed whole. He keeps pushing, and she keeps reaching for him, finally closing the distance between desire and her body. They come surging together, entangled, until she can't reach her thoughts through the desperate torrent.

"Please. *Pleasepleaseplease*, I need it —"

She fucks herself over his fingers, taking him as deep as she can, and this time, they both gasp at the way he fills her. The way he *could* be filling her.

"I need your cock, Flint, please, anything, just — *please...*"

Doesn't care how pathetic she looks. Everything is open, drawn out from somewhere that she hasn't touched in so long.

"Flint — I'm —"

But she can think of nothing else. No words, just vibrant flares of skin against skin, colors and patterns she isn't even sure she knows that replace all the syllables slipping through her fingers.

"Wh —" But it doesn't make sense — nothing does, not under the torment against her, and a forsaken whimper rips out of her throat.

He rises toward her mouth the same time the well of his desire rises in her. "That's *exactly* it."

The kiss drives her out of her mind until she's keening, tugging at his shirt, afraid he's forgotten what she asked for. But of course he hasn't. He pries himself away to produce a condom packet from his bag on the floor. It's larger than any she's seen, but thrumming promise replaces any flicker of fear. She won't admit he knew what he was doing working her up to it like this. Still, when he undoes the buttons of his shirt, watching her eyes trace down the expanse of his bare chest and the round of his stomach, desire darts through her.

It's no secret he's vast, built like a shield, scars and coloration marking the pewter of his skin. Her breath catches at the girth between his legs when he works out of his clothes...but there's no disguising it when he eases her back, slotting between her thighs and rolling her on top of him. She starts to argue, but he squeezes her wrists against his chest. "Less skin to start. Trust me."

And, unequivocally, she does.

He fists the condom on, guiding her up onto her knees until his shoulders span the width of the bed. There's no pressure from his emotions — only the ones she's unearthed still swirling around inside her.

One of her hands half-circles his length — and there's the glint of his restrained desire when her fingertips brush against him. So she fists over him, making him hiss, before she sinks around the head of his cock.

Their groans collide, tight and fractured, her fingers pressing down against his chest. She's barely taken any of it. Her eyes clamp shut when his fingers ease between her thighs, gliding against her clit.

"Color?"

Her mind jerks in a thousand directions, but he doesn't stop his touch — and she sinks lower, spilling a string of curses out on one breath. She gets a glance at her stomach and moans at the slightest bulge of his cock under her skin. His emotions swell before he tries to tamp them down, gripping her hips, driven to distraction. Lust wreathes through her, and she watches where they meet, shifting to bring herself to his head and sink lower again.

"Harbin…"

Can't decide if there's a warning in his tone, but she keeps riding, taking him deeper with every stroke. Both of them groan at the stretch, but it feels — "So good." Waves of their arousals lap against her, inseparable and endless. He tries to still her, but she finds his mouth, baring teeth into his lip. Takes him almost to the hilt, so painfully slowly that the gasps between them could be mistaken for pain — but she finds words on the tail end of a breath.

"Green, it's green, it's so — fucking *green*."

Finally, he's satisfied, skimming a hand up her chest to envelop her entire throat. Fingers brush her jaw, the jut of her cheekbones, and he doesn't take his eyes off of her when she leans back and starts to move. Arousal struggles against the restraints he's placed on it. Thrashes low in her abdomen when he fills her completely, and a breathless smirk crosses her face.

"Having trouble?"

The rise and fall of his chest moves her. Even when she guides fingertips against the knit in his brows, fitting her lips with a pitying smile. His desire twines up with a tiny bit of indignation, and she grins.

"Are you green, baby?" Her hips work in slow circles before she drags her chest against his. "You look like you might need a breather."

There's only a flicker of warning before he's turning them, pulling out and pressing her back into the mattress. Blocking the light out with his body, outlining the essence that leaves everyone they encounter quaking: glowing red eyes, wings expanding toward the ceiling, terrifying enough to keep evil away. It steals her breath, and when it returns, it's as hot and heady as her thoughts of him.

"Having trouble?"

He twists the words back on her. She fights against his hold when his desire licks like flames against her stomach. Keeps her still with one hand on her hip, and when she tries to slip out of his grasp, a tiny smile crawls up his face.

"Reckless, Harbin." And then he's feeding his cock back into her with a clench of his teeth and her groan. "Always *fucking* reckless."

She's too loud for the thin walls. They both clamp a hand over her mouth, sound vibrating against his fingers, trying to stay focused when he starts slow strokes into her again. His other hand finds her ankles, pressing her knees back to her chest until she's splayed open, losing a string of thoughts with each thrust.

"Is this too deep?" He doesn't stop moving. Doesn't stop touching her, doesn't stop his arousal binding up with hers. All she can do is moan, like he's splitting every connection she's ever made except for the one of him inside her.

"Is this too fucking deep?" Buried to the hilt, grinding deeper, bending her legs until he finds that constant pressure against her clit. When she doesn't answer —

"I'll pull out, Harbin."

"*No!*" Can't imagine anything worse — not when the searing

heat of wanting him is the only thing melding her together. Nails leave tracks down his arms where he holds her open, voice breaking on a sob. "Don't you — *fucking dare.*"

His hand closes over her mouth again, laugh dark against her throat. "Fuck, you have to be *quiet*."

Then, of course, he does his damnedest to make sure she isn't. Drags his tongue over her breasts, stirring his hips inside her until her tears slip against his hand. Everything is torturous, each moment of his restraint leading to this: to him taking her apart on the end of his cock. He watches every shudder, heightened against every inch of skin, overwhelmed and overstimulated, but it's still — not *enough*. Her words are muffled when she weeps.

"Please, I need — to touch more —"

But he shakes his head, pressing her knee back into the mattress, soothing a tear away with his thumb. "Not until you come."

It whets his emotions, throbbing where they bear into her. No amount of whimpering stops him grinding against her clit, building her to the peak where he wants her. She breaks, shatters, sounds slipping against his mouth when he kisses her open with his tongue.

Pounding comes from the wall behind the bed. They both still, eyes tilting toward the headboard while her mind recoils.

"Told you to be quiet."

Her foot lands weakly against his chest. "Don't make it so good, then."

A hand catches her ankle. "You still want more?" His eyes follow the trail his fingers take against her calf, smirking when they tremble. "Can you *take* more?"

She stretches her arms over her head and doesn't miss the way his eyes trace down her body. "Yes."

Fingers glance over her calf, the barest hint of claws before he sheaths them again. How can someone so built for strength, for instilling fear, be so gentle with her?

And still, completely intent on devouring her.

His hips wind deeper, pressing a gasp out of her before he withdraws completely. Already, she misses the feeling of being filled and crushed against him.

"How do you want it?" Tusks scrape under her jaw, against her clavicle, his shoulders shifting like a prowling beast above her. "Harbin?"

It's a taunting sound. She tries to think through the haze of her arousal, to remember what she'd begged for moments ago.

"I want you — behind me."

Simple enough. But instead of turning on all fours, she lifts on her knees to face the headboard.

"They'll hear you," he warns.

"Not if you keep me quiet."

A dark look passes over him, and she takes the opportunity to arch her ass back toward him. He doesn't stand a chance; there's only a second before he cages her with his body, poised over her back and guiding her hands to hover over the headboard.

"Do you want to touch it?"

It's a risk...but it's not a common surface, not a piece that carries many residual memories. She nods, and he lets her palms make contact before she's gripping it with a shuddering moan. Every touch that's been there is curled with arousal, and they flood into her, giving her visions of everyone before: white-knuckled grips, nails scraping, teeth digging into lips and shoulders. It takes a few long, heated moments to realize he's clamped a hand over her mouth, chuckling breathlessly in her ear.

"You have to be *quiet*, Harbin."

She nods, even as she has no plans for it. He loosens his grip against her lips and nods toward the headboard.

"Keep that still. Don't let it knock against the wall, no matter what I do to you." His rough tongue trails a long stripe up her neck, and she already feels herself failing. "Or I'll stop fucking you. Understand?"

Everything in her quivers. But he doesn't move without an answer, so she nods — until he lowers his hand from her mouth.

"You'd better just keep that there."

Amusement flecks his tone. "You can't keep quiet for even a minute?"

He gets his answer when he traces the head of his cock against her entrance, teasing against her clit, and a whimper trickles out.

"Covered it is."

Good thing, too: she moans into his grip as soon as he starts to sink inside, working her hips back to take him deeper. Sparks ignite where his chest brushes her back, and she feels like she's going up in flames.

"You want me to slow down, you bite me. Got it?"

Blood roars in her ears. She manages a nod, keening at the feeling before he buries himself completely. Skin muffles both their sounds, trapped against his hand or her shoulder, until he takes the first thrust. It's slow, rocking out until his head tugs at her entrance — and then he's driving into her again. Even at this pace, the headboard nudges the wall, a tiny motion that she can't hear — but he clucks a sound of disapproval against her throat.

"Getting reckless, baby..."

She fumbles to keep her weight against it. Behind him, she can hear wings expanding, beating in the air when he rocks his hips into her. A groan slips into his palm, but she does her best to follow his instruction, shaking with the effort of keeping the headboard still. His pace increases — only a fraction, but it's already enough to send the bed bumping against the wall. He slows, and she panics, making contentious sounds before the slick fingers against her clit silence her.

"I'm going to have to fuck you so *slow*." It's an admonition, but it doesn't feel like one when he drags out of her inch by inch. "Just like this. To make sure you can follow our agreement."

He taunts her with her earlier negligence, and all she can think about is how languidly he moves to ruin her. Desire drips and simmers deep in her stomach. It's all too much, winding back against him, hands slipping against the wall. The bed thumps once, and he curses, pausing deep inside her.

There's no sound but their breathing. No knocking or murmurs from the other side of the wall, so he guides his free hand over both of hers and slots them against the headboard.

"You stay right there." He rocks slowly into her again. Doesn't ease his weight off of her hands, because she can't be trusted to follow orders. "Keep it against the wall for me — just like that." Another experimental shift of his hips, but with his weight against it, the headboard doesn't move.

"That's a good girl."

Every nerve inside her is alive, brushing against his skin, and she gives a moan into his hand again. Their sounds are slick and filthy, and the shadow of his wings falls over her against the wall. This is how they must look to everyone else: the guardian, grim and terrifying, always just behind her. The thought winds itself tight and burrows hot between her thighs.

"You're taking this cock so well for me."

For me. The rhythm he's set increases, honed and fixated, like he's hunting down her release. Stark colors of their bodies contrast, her black and bone-white fingers under the marbled gray of his hand, the two of them laced together. It drives her perilously close to the edge, and she shuts her eyes when his arousal seeps into her again.

"You want to come for me?"

All she feels from him is the distinct need to make her fall apart one more time. His arousal screams louder, howling, screeching through her until she sees the edge of her climax coming faster than she can prepare for. Whimpers barely contained by his fingers, but he doesn't stop any of his motions: not his hips. Not his palm over her mouth. Not his fingers twining between hers on the headboard.

"Then *do it*."

That's what breaks her: every inch of skin they're touching. The added pressure of his chest against her back that makes it feel more like she can breathe. And then she's wrecked, coming apart and losing the fight to keep herself on her knees. He catches her in his arm, stifling her sounds, but there's no one to help him when his gnarled growl becomes too much to hold onto. He buries it against her neck the same time he sinks completely inside, finally giving over to his release, and that's nearly enough to make her come again.

There are no more sounds from the other side of the wall. Just their panting breaths, the mewling she makes when he withdraws, and his deep, rumbling laugh against her shoulder. They lay across the bed, blanket twisted beneath him and her spread lazily across his chest. Fingers trail through her hair, one of his hands large enough to massage her entire scalp, and she moans into his skin.

"That good, huh?"

"It's been so long," she groans, and he continues, scratching his claws in patterns that make her euphoric. But that's not the only thing his thoughts are on. She can read it in more than his emotions: his breathing slows, body tightening, and she moves her chin to her arms to look up at him when he speaks.

"This complicates things."

"I was planning to ignore that."

Flint tugs on a strand of her hair, and she swats idly at his hand.

"And I don't want to be presumptuous..." he continues. A laugh snorts out of her, but he smacks her ass, smile slipping up between his tusks. "But you seemed to enjoy yourself. Quite a few times."

Retaliation grinds her hips down against him, and she's rewarded with the burgeoning flare of his arousal. But he stills her with a heavy look, and she stops her movements...for now.

"If I'm the only one who can touch you..." And he does, gliding fingers down her sides, following the path that makes her skin flare. "Then I want you to know I'm more than happy to do this again. As much as you want."

One broad hand grips her ass. His finger drifts lower until it brushes back and forth across her clit, the barest touch that has her mind reeling. She wrestles between the way her hips want to take him inside her, and the part of her that knows this is more complex.

"I'm not expecting anything from this," he continues, halting his movements. "We're still partners first — not even that, if you need the space. But…" A teasing circle starts against her pussy, and they lock eyes before she seats the tip of his finger inside her. This close, they can both see the shifts in their expressions: eyelids fluttering, nails digging into his chest, lips parting against each other's.

"Maybe you need a guard who can do more than just protect you."

She takes him deeper, sinfully slow, until she's fucking herself in leisurely drags. It's a feeling she wasn't sure she'd capture again: naked and pressed all along skin, basking in arousal until it's overtaken by her own. He urges her closer, stealing the gasp off her tongue with the curl of his when she asks.

"You want to be on call for orgasms whenever I want?"

Hips roll, dragging his hardening length between her thighs until she can grind against it. The grip tightens around her waist, and her moan is muffled by his mouth and the pinprick of emotion that feels like more than lust.

"What are partners for?"

INEXTRICABLY
TIED

ONE

Flint

Harbinger is going to wreck him.

Flint barely has the SUV in park before she tugs down the zipper of his slacks, single-mindedly focused on taking care of the hard dick she's been teasing.

They're late for a meeting. Granted, it's with the Orena Investigative Division, so neither of them minds a lascivious detour. But their front windshield isn't tinted, and this fast-food parking lot is more cramped than Flint would like. Across the asphalt, a pair of nyads usher their children into the restaurant without a glance toward the SUV, but Flint still presses his tusks against his fist. His elbow digs into the door as Harbinger takes him into the wet heat of her mouth.

"Harbin..."

His cock muffles her hum. It's an intoxicating sight, the massive stone-colored swell of his length disappearing between her lips. She gives no sign of stopping, spitting over his head until it's slick enough to wrap both her skeletal hands around it.

When her lips stretch around him again, Flint's grip tightens on the steering wheel. "That can't be comfortable."

Harbinger edges him into the back of her throat until he curses. She pops off with a flourish. "You're right. Would be much better in my ass."

Flint scrubs a hand down his face. "For fuck's sake, Harbin..."

But she isn't deterred, knocking her skull helmet to the floor and clambering over the center console into the backseat.

Flint doesn't have that luxury. No affordable vehicle accommodates his gargantuan gargoyle stature. Instead, he adjusts his dick back into his pants, shoving off his seatbelt and squeezing out the driver's side door. He scans the area as his bat-like wings stretch, one hand running through the graying temples of his black hair. There are a few empty cars in the lot, plus a couple of people arguing as they prepare to drive off. Flint nods cordially as they pull away before two hands are on his shirt, tugging him into the back of the SUV.

He locks the doors behind him, pulling up the divider to the front seat before he lets Harbinger distract him. Bone-white skin peeks through the front of her black catsuit, undone all the way between her thighs. All her bones protrude, pronounced among fat and muscle, skeletal features carved into her flesh. Her banshee body is somewhere between living and death that Flint wants to drag his mouth over.

She pins him back against the seat, her slight form against his colossal one, pressing against the round curve of his stomach when she fists him out of his pants again.

"You act like you've been deprived," he taunts.

"I *was*," she insists, "for seven years."

Before Flint accidentally touched her bare skin and became the only person who could get this close. Before him pulling her to safety ruined her plans to keep the world at arm's length. Before they became more than partners, and she became privy to his emotions.

He guides both her hands in one of his, dragging up and down his cock. Frustration twists into her shoulders and the sweat above her lip as she tries to stroke faster. Classic Harbinger: always running, running, running, diving headfirst, never slowing down.

"Flint..." She grits through her teeth, but he keeps both her hands trapped against him. It takes all he has to keep his red eyes trained on her. To not let his dick twitch between her slick palms.

His horns brush the ceiling as his head tilts. "Do you need something?"

He can't fight a smirk at the way she's torn between watching his eyes and the precum beading where their hands tighten around his head. His dick barely fits in both her hands. Still, she grips him tighter until he hisses.

"You gonna make me beg?" Harbinger mutters. "We're already behind schedule."

Like she gives a fuck. And still, she tries to use it against him, to force him to move, to have him diving headlong into the rush with her. Flint doesn't change his pace, resting his other arm behind his head like he has all the time in the world. "I don't mind telling the whole Orena Investigative Division that we're late because you needed your pussy stretched out."

Harbinger groans. "*Fuck* the OID." Her opaline eyes find his again. She's practically salivating at the sight of his head disappearing between their fists. "*Give it to me.*"

"I gave it to you last night."

Her laugh stays on her lips, voice hoarse when she manages to speed her hands. "What, are you rationing me? Giving me dick once a week until a new shipment comes in?"

"I should." Flint lifts his hips, fucking into their melded grips. "You need a break once in a while." The chiding slips between foreplay, where she's less likely to disregard it. "This size difference isn't a joke."

Harbinger lifts to her knees, lip tucked between her teeth. "I promise you..." Her skeletal face hovers in front of his, her hands still trapped beneath his claws. "I'm always wet enough." She stirs hips against his hand, brushing the bare skin of her stomach against his cock until she shudders. "You can check, if you want to make sure."

Innocence drips from her pout, but Flint knows better. His eyes narrow...and still, he can't keep his gaze off her mouth. "Let me get the lube."

"We didn't use any the first time."

"Because someone was impatient."

"Someone's impatient now, too." Her clit brushes his knuckles, and the car fills with the sound of her gasp. "Color?"

Flint can't deny her. Even if he wanted to. Even if they were in the middle of the OID, her hand on his thigh, her dangerous mouth begging to have him. The only thing that could keep Flint off of her is a threat to her life. *Which there isn't,* he reminds himself. He cuts his eyes out the window to make sure —

Then Harbinger's cunt slips against his fingers, and their groans shred through the quiet.

"Told you," she breathes. They both focus on their hands stroking over him, dragging his cock between her thighs. "Color?" Harbinger prods again. It's the system he instituted. Red to stop, yellow to slow, and —

"Green." His finger flicks against her clit to make her curse. "Maybe I should fuck you like this." Flint doesn't give away the ache she always causes in him. The one he tries to tamp down on so she doesn't feel it. "Make you grind that little pussy against my hand until you get what you need." He strokes both their hands up to his head, and she's almost close enough to sink around his cock...

But not close enough.

He covers his cockhead with their fists again. She whines her frustration, and Flint clicks his tongue as she tries fruitlessly to climb into his lap.

"Flint..."

He can't help but laugh at the warning in her voice. Lowering his mouth, tusks brushing her chest as he pushes aside the fabric and swirls his rough tongue around one of her nipples. Finally, he releases her fingers from the cage of his. "Fine. You want to ride?"

She's halfway in his lap before he finishes. He holds her back with a clawed hand around her waist, digging a sizable condom from one of the bags in the trunk.

Harbinger squirms in his hand. "We could leave the it off, you know."

Flint grunts his distaste, tearing into the packet and slipping the condom over his girth. "Not for the first time in a *parking lot*."

Harbinger's gaze clings to the sight of him, no less aroused by the barrier. "That's your hang-up, not mine. It's not like we need it."

She tries to slot her hips over him, but he keeps her suspended as he reaches for the bottle of lube in the center console. "It shouldn't be just my hang-up. You feeling my emotions complicates things; you know that. That kind of skin-on-skin contact could overwhelm you."

Disappointment flickers across her face, but she slows her movements. A hint of guilt rises in him, but they can't be that careless. Not now. Not here. Their eyes meet before he promises, "We *will* do it. Soon."

A softer smile settles onto Harbinger's lips before she leans close, reigniting the heat in his stomach when she drags herself against his cock. "Then I'll take what I can get for now. *Please*."

Holding out is futile for both of them. Flint squeezes lube into his hand and fists over himself, those same slick fingers dragging between Harbinger's thighs. She sinks halfway over his dick like she's starved for it, and Flint's head knocks back against the seat as she clenches around him.

Working her way down, taking another inch as her hand braces against the window beside her. Black and white hair unwinds from her braid, static lifting it on end. "*Fuck*, it never gets old."

Flint could stay like that — halfway inside her, letting her take what she wants — but Harbinger is determined. She needs *more*. Catsuit slipping off her shoulder, she sinks to the hilt.

The sight is intoxicating. Distracting. Around them, the backseat is humid and sticky, feeling much smaller than it had when they were both in the front. Flint's gaze flicks to the tinted windows, checking the perimeter of the vehicle before Harbinger's fingers pull his chin back.

"Am I boring you?"

She punctuates the words with another lift of her hips before she buries him deep again, both their eyes rolling back. He claws against her suit. Every sound is lewd, hot and slick, sweat and desire when Flint keeps her hips pinned to him and winds deeper.

That's his answer; Harbinger is anything but boring.

She fumbles for something to hold onto, cheek smearing against his when she pants. "*Gods*, more. Fucking *please*."

Everything about her is frantic, taking all he gives like she's outrunning death, and all Flint can do is try to hang on. To shield her, to slow the hectic motion of her hips, to keep his senses heightened while she does whatever she can to sever his attention.

It's a constant battle of wills; him trying to keep her alive, and her careening out of his grasp.

He remembers the moment they first touched. The bullets pelting his rock armor. The terror on Harbinger's face. The blood he had to spill to save her.

He had to.

He *had* to.

Harbinger's too exposed in this position. Flint rolls her underneath him, stretching her back out against the seat, his wings struggling to unfold over the headrests. A look passes over her face. Something like awe before her smirk settles. "Knew there was a reason you sprung for the big backseat."

As if his mind had been anywhere near here when they'd

started tracking leads seven years ago. His hand splays against her stomach, engulfing her torso, his rocky gray skin contrasting against the white and black of hers.

All he can do is wind his hips into her. Her boot slips against the glass behind him, hands flying to the door above her head when the skin of her stomach bulges to accommodate him. Her eyes shut on a whimper. "Why is it so hot?"

"Because you like making room for me." His hips jut against the bottom of her thighs. "You like having me in your stomach. You like your body being half made up of my cock, don't you?"

The thought makes her moan, leveraging against the door to meet his thrusts, breasts bouncing with the motion. She doesn't tear her gaze from where their bodies meet. Where she stretches around him. Where he grinds against that spot deep inside her. With every thrust, he fucks out her stilted groans, picking up the pace until he's the only one who can speak.

"You'd take it if it was even bigger, wouldn't you?"

Harbinger bites the sleeve of her suit until Flint gets a thumb against her clit. Her hips stutter. Her whimpers heighten. Flint smirks. "'Cause you'd take anything if it meant you could have this dick. Isn't that right?"

Shudders rack through her, head craning back against the door as she screams. Waves of her orgasm clench around him, hot and tight, almost enough to send him over the edge with her. He clamps a hand over her mouth, enough to muffle the sounds as his gaze darts to the parking lot.

No one pays the rocking SUV any mind.

Once Harbinger quiets, he pulls his hand back from her ragged breaths. He smooths a touch against her thigh, withdrawing before she digs her heels into his ass.

"Keep going."

It would be easy to pull out of her grasp...but the warmth of her body is so inviting, windows fogging with their breaths as he runs a claw down her sternum. "I don't need to —"

Her grip around him tightens. She bolsters up on her elbows with a growl, as if she's the imposing gargoyle. "If you don't fuck me 'til you come —"

It's enough for laughter to rumble out of his chest. Then he delves in deep again, pressing a moan out of them both. The SUV shifts on its wheels with each thrust. A blissful grin slips across Harbin's face, fingers trailing through the condensation on the glass. "You're rocking this whole fucking car."

Flint doesn't stop. Doesn't slow, dragging out completely before he's buried again, and Harbinger's strangled curses stifle under the low rumble of his voice. "You wanted it deep, didn't you?"

It's filthy, her pussy spreading over him, his cock slick with her desire. She reaches between her legs, but he pins her hand back against the door. "You want to come again?" A claw retracts on one of his fingers, circling her clit. "Greedy little thing." There's no hiding the softness in his voice, but he presses her further, working into her in time with his circles. "Tell me."

She squirms in his grip until his motions tighten to that perfect rhythm. Her body strains to reach for him. "Yes, I'm fucking greedy, I want it — fucking deeper."

A smile breaks across his lips. "That's my fucking girl." He hardly has to ask before she's arching, helpless, needy. "Then give me another one."

Only like this can he get her compliant. Open. Willing to do as he asks. To let him direct her, protect her, to squeeze out her lawlessness until she's a puddle beneath him.

All that chaos ricocheting inside her as he swallows her moans, her fingers digging into his shoulder. His tail coils around her leg, and she clenches around him.

"Yes, fucking — use your tail. Wrap it around me."

There's temptation to let go, to give her exactly what she's asking for, but it's too dangerous. He can't. Not when he could lose control. When the mace shape sprouting from the end of his tail could hurt her...or worse.

When he retracts it, she groans her frustration, but he doesn't stop rolling into her. Dragging their bodies together, beating hearts and staggered breaths filling the space. "Come on." His teeth scrape her neck. "Do it again for me. Come again, baby. Give me another one."

Now, he lets loose on the hold he has around his emotions. When she's so strung out on desire, he can let everything else slip into her, too: his devotion and doubt and desperation. All the things he tries to keep buried, pouring out of him and into her.

It's a flood of him delving inside her, and he can tell when it hits. When her eyes widen, neck arching, body writhing beneath him as she comes apart again.

That's what pushes him over. Her fingers curling in the back of his hair, mindless words passed from her mouth to his. He rocks in deep, buried between her thighs when his release takes him, his low growl vibrating up the column of her throat.

The SUV stills. Sweat plasters them both together. A tiny laugh bubbles out of her, stray hairs clinging to her face over the warm blood in her cheeks. "I have a feeling the OID is gonna know why we're late."

"I told you..." Flint pulls slowly out of her, both of them groaning at the loss before he ties off the condom. "I'm gonna tell them exactly why we had to stop."

His lips tug up past his tusks as she nudges him with her boot, resecuring the buttons on her catsuit. Flint works himself back into his slacks, shifting up off the seat, pants pulled taut against his thighs as he tucks in his button-down.

Harbinger moves up to her knees, draping arms over his shoulders. "I think you needed that even more than me."

Her taunting teeth in his pointed ear are enough to make him shudder. He works his belt buckle back into place, checking out the window again. "How do you figure?"

Her brows hike when he glances back to her. Point proven.

"You've seemed distracted the past few weeks. Even while I was sucking your dick."

Shame swells in his cheeks. He tries to hide the emotion, even as he knows she can feel it. "For good reason. Neither of us want to go through what happened at the restaurant again."

It's an excuse. A way to rationalize how on edge he's been since that day. In Flint's dreams, he still sees it; their client squirming behind the counter. Harbinger's brows knit in confusion. Then the panic in her eyes as she called Flint's name the second before gunfire started.

No matter how quickly he'd pulled Harbinger to safety, it was a big dose of luck that kept them from bleeding out on the floor.

Harbinger's voice cleaves into his thoughts. "Should I, I don't know, learn some acrobatics to keep you entertained?"

"No! Gods…" Flint scratches at his beard. "It has nothing to do with you. Or…I guess it has everything to do with you."

He rests back against the seat before he looks at her. Harbinger isn't offended, tuned into him the same way they've been since they began this partnership. It eases some of the tension in his neck. "I know we've been careful since the restaurant. Taking the jobs with the lowest risk —"

"And the lowest pay."

He winces. It's true. But Harbinger moves closer, draping her legs over his lap and resting her arms on her knees. "I'm giving you a hard time." She picks at a thread unraveling on the inside of her suit. Shit: they'll have to replace or patch it soon. Another expense. "I know I was resistant when you suggested we take lighter work, but, I mean, hell. I'm not exactly chomping at the bit to get shot at again."

Flint twists the end of her braid around a claw, following the strands of white woven through the black. Horns honk in the distance as a car runs a red light at the intersection. It draws his focus — even now, in the midst of their discussion about his distraction. He tries to keep his eyes on Harbinger, despite his body's nagging reminder to make sure they're not in danger.

"But we're running low on cash," Harbinger finishes. She tries to understand Flint's concern, but a sigh escapes. The two of them have made ends meet for years, but getting picky with their cases means their finances have taken a hit. Flint's being overcautious. He knows he is, but that doesn't make it any easier to take risks for a bit of money. It's not a simple thing to put them — to put *her* — in danger.

Unfortunately, Flint's definition of 'potentially dangerous' has grown in the months since the restaurant.

"It's just..." Harbinger won't quite look at him. "The slightest thing sets you off now, Flint. Meeting in a secluded area? No thanks. Object too obscure? Try again. Paying too much? Next. Like your mind's already whirring through worst-case scenarios before we make first contact."

She's not wrong. Lately, the smallest uncertainty grows into an intrusive thought for him. Harbinger has been patient. Understanding. But it's no secret their funds are drying up. They skip lunch more often than not, sporadic nights spent in the backseat of the SUV instead of a motel room. Hell, money's the reason they agreed to today's meeting in the first place.

Not that Flint loves the idea. The OID has been on his back for years, and the way he fought back at the restaurant shined a spotlight on him. The bullets and shell casings, along with the restaurant's malicious ties, were enough to clear Flint...

For that crime. Who knows what else the OID has dug up in the time since? Things from Flint's past he isn't sure how Harbinger would take.

"Maybe the OID will have something for us," he sighs. Harbinger's skeptical look says it all, but they both know they're running out of options. She plucks at the fraying string again, lifting her eyes to his.

"At least we're together."

It warms his chest. Words spring into his mouth — things he

hasn't been saying, things he *wants* to — but Harbinger's eyes widen like she feels it.

"We'd better get going." She swings her legs off his lap and climbs back toward the passenger seat, leaving him alone.

It's always hardest after sex. When her body's so close, a warm reminder of how much he has to lose. They've been partners for so long, but this added physical layer is new. Fragile. He told her the first night that he didn't expect anything, and Flint can't risk what they've built just because he wants more than he thought he did. Especially when Harbinger pulls away any time the feelings swell in Flint.

He gets a handle on his emotions again, pushing out the door and back into the driver's seat. Harbinger slumps as the ignition cranks, flicking to a rock song on the radio.

"Let's get this over with."

TWO

Flint

They're fifteen minutes late by the time they pull up in front of the OID building, an intimidating concrete structure at least ten stories high.

Flint checks the clock on the dash: *sixteen* minutes late. Which is extended by the checkpoints and haranguing they go through before they're left in a meeting room on the ninth floor. Harbinger's helmet reflects the fluorescents as she slouches back in her swivel chair, Flint standing behind her.

After a few minutes, the door swings open on Agent Tamneth, a blonde elf with a sour disposition on his pale face. Tamneth does his best to appear professional, chin lifted as he slots sunglasses into the pocket of his suit jacket. "Harbinger. Flint. Nice to see you again."

"Wish we could say the same."

Harbinger's helmet muffles her voice, but there's no mistaking her words. Tamneth prickles, but he knows better than to look to

Flint for any help. Flint doesn't even lift an eyebrow. Tamneth brushes past the tension, sinking into the chair across the table. "Thank you for meeting with us today."

"Your voicemail didn't leave much of an option." Harbinger examines her gloves. "I believe the word 'warrant' was used."

Tamneth flicks his watch face toward him as he shuffles paper on the desk, a subtle reminder of their punctuality — or lack thereof. "I know it's been a while since our last encounter —"

"You mean when you called me a con artist in front of the courtroom because we testified for the defense?"

Tamneth smooths a hand back through his hair before he locks his fingers on the table. "What else would you call it when you take people's money and tell them what they'd like to hear?"

Harbinger's head tilts as she hums. "I prefer the term 'freelance-seer.'"

"I understand our working relationship —"

"Get to the fucking point."

Even without Harbinger's abilities, Flint can read her. The irritation spiking from her shoulders, arms crossed over her chest. Flint does nothing to make her distaste more palatable, his eyes narrowed across the table when Tamneth speaks again.

"Instead of remaining at odds, the OID would like to work together."

"Quite the change of tune from 'con artist.'"

Tamneth does all he can to keep his tight smile in place. "Even if I question the validity of your 'abilities,' the OID is willing to make certain concessions for this case."

"What case?"

Tamneth pulls papers from the folder before him, turning the pages so Flint and Harbinger can read them. "These are non-disclosure agreements. We have something we'd like you to look at. With your...'powers.'"

Flint scans the document. Harbinger keeps her eyes on Tamneth. "*What case?*"

Tamneth doesn't budge. "If you sign these agreements, we can share that information with you."

Even reckless Harbin is skeptical. Flint doesn't hesitate. "We're not agreeing to anything until we know exactly what you're asking us to do."

Tamneth sighs, steepling his fingers. "It's for the Raymond Reid case. Suspected kidnapper, torturer, serial killer —"

"Reid?"

Flint's stunned. Harbinger's posture changes, helmet tilted toward Tamneth like he may give something else away.

"He was all over the news earlier this year when you arrested him." Flint remembers the images of an unassuming white human, glasses, receding brown hair. Exactly what you'd expect.

"We suspect Reid's been active for a few years, but his movement increased exponentially in the nine months before his capture. His victim count is likely between fifteen and twenty-five adolescent girls."

"Teenagers?"

Tamneth pulls a round of images from the folder, an array of young girls from various family photos. Toes digging into sand at the shoreline, teeth sticky and stained with candy, first car keys dangling from fingers. All smiling.

Flint's stomach twists.

Harbinger turns a picture gingerly toward her. "And you think they're all...dead?"

Tamneth gives her a hard look. "It's very likely. They all tend to fall into the same population: thirteen to seventeen, white, human or human-appearing."

"Wow," Harbinger drawls. "That's the one demographic you care to look for. And you still haven't figured this out?"

Flint fights the tug in his chest. It's tragic, but he knows what Tamneth is doing. Playing on their heartstrings, trying to soften them for whatever comes next. Whatever favor the OID has to ask. "If you know all of that, why do you need Harbinger?"

Tamneth leans back in his chair, as if it pains him to admit it. "We've found plenty of circumstantial evidence tying Reid to the crimes; witness accounts and recordings placing him in the vicinity of each girl's last known location. But we haven't been able to recover any of the bodies. No trophies, no DNA, nothing concrete."

It lances through Flint. He knows Harbinger can feel it, but neither of them reacts save for the barest tilt of her helmet. Flint's voice is level. "What are you asking us?"

He knows how the OID operates. The things they ask without thought, without consideration. The selfish demands they make of people. An ember of rage starts to flare inside him when Tamneth speaks.

"We want you to use your abilities on Raymond Reid."

"You're out of your goddamn mind." A threat rumbles through Flint's voice. "Absolutely not."

For once, Harbinger doesn't give it a second of consideration. "I've told you a hundred times, it doesn't work like that. With living things, I get the present. Emotions. With objects, I get the past. Memories. I can't make them cross. And I'm not getting tied to a fucking serial killer forever. Besides," her fingers press to the table, "banshee abilities are still considered hearsay. We have you to thank for that. If that's why you brought us here, you're wasting all of our time."

"We thought you might say that —"

"Then why would you fucking ask?" Flint snarls. Tamneth holds up both hands in surrender, trying to quell their indignation.

"We have to try." Tamneth looks exhausted, but Flint can't scrounge up any sympathy for him. Not when the OID has brought so many of these problems on themselves with shoddy tactics, racial profiling, and internal misconduct. "These girls' families have no answers. Reid hasn't talked since we arrested him. He lawyered up right away, and our leads have dried up. Without any physical evidence, it's going to be next to impossible to get a conviction."

"She's not reading him."

Harbinger rests a glove on Flint's wrist. It's the only thing that makes him realize his red eyes are flaring. That he hasn't breathed since Tamneth suggested it.

"I'm not reading him," she confirms. It loosens a bit of the stress strapped across Flint's chest. "If that's all — "

"Wait." The situation is slipping through Tamneth's grasp much faster than he anticipated. His teeth grind as if he hates to admit it. "There is another option."

Flint huffs a breath. "Your 'other option' had better be real fucking good after that stunt."

Tamneth's gaze cuts between them. "We've acquired an object of Reid's. We'd like you to read it."

Harbinger's eyes narrow. "And what is 'it,' exactly?"

"It's magical. Something we haven't seen before. We can't be sure exactly what it does."

"Where'd it come from? Why don't you bring me his car keys or something?"

"Raymond Reid was meticulous. Very private. Maliciously clever: we have no record of him needing glasses. We suspect he used them to appear more mild-mannered. When we arrested him, his house was spotless. Every inch clean, no trinkets or personal effects or much furniture. It's as if he has somewhere else to store things, but there's no other property on record, no storage unit, no family. We never recovered his vehicle. Our forensics found no traces on anything."

"Then where'd you find this object?"

Tamneth's eyes are cool on Flint. "We recovered it from a private stash Reid kept hidden in his home. This was the only object there."

Harbinger mulls over the possibility, but Flint doesn't need to. "It doesn't matter. She's not doing it.

Tamneth eases to his feet. "Now, wait —"

But Flint's ready to shut Tamneth down when Harbinger's hand closes over his. She doesn't look at him, which means one thing. Flint's stomach drops.

She speaks before he can. "You'd have to pay us. A lot. Double what you're thinking."

"Harbinger —"

"We could compel you," Tamneth challenges. "Charge you with impeding the investigation, obstruction of justice. Reopen the restaurant investigation..." Tamneth's eyes cut to Flint. "And a few others."

Flint doesn't let his expression shift. Harbinger leans across the table, helmet winking in the fluorescents. "We can sit in a jail cell for a few days. It won't get you any closer to solving this case."

Tamneth's jaw clicks. "Fine."

"Put it in writing."

Flint moves between them. "You can't be fucking seri-"

For the first time, the edge in Tamneth's voice sticks in Flint's thoughts like a briar. "If Harbinger reads this item for us, we're prepared to compensate you both."

Every alarm bell in Flint's mind clangs. Harbinger keeps her helmet toward Tamneth. "Can you give us a moment alone?"

He straightens his papers before he steps out of the room. Harbinger doesn't turn to Flint until the door clicks shut. Flint doesn't give her a chance to speak first. "Absolutely not."

"Hold on..." Her gloved hands lift in an attempt to placate him. She knows this is ridiculous. It stokes his indignation.

"No, Harbin! Are you joking?" It's only once Harbinger places a hand on his that he realizes he's shaking. From rage, or fear, he isn't sure. A cup trembles at the other end of the table before he withdraws his hand and tries to calm himself. "You can't risk gods know what for the fucking OID because they can't handle an investigation."

"I wouldn't be risking it for them. I'd be risking it for the girls."

Pain shuts Flint's eyes, shallow breath scraping in his chest.

Of course she sees it that way. Of course Tamneth has gotten to her bleeding heart, the one she hides before she rushes into danger. She's so intent to keep everyone out of harm's way before she flings her body at the nearest problem without a care for what it means for her.

"I know you want to help." Flint opens his eyes and meets the reflective sheen of her helmet. Gods, if he could see her face...if they could talk, maybe she'd understand. "Will you open your visor? Please."

He tries to keep the strain out of his voice, but from the way her body tenses, she hears it. She unhinges the skeletal jaw of her helmet. The jawbone falls open to show her face, eyes following him when he leans closer.

"I know you want to help," he repeats. "But it's not — " He exhales through his nose, but Harbin doesn't interrupt, mouth pressed in a thin line. "They don't know what this object is. And I know you want to do right by those families, but you can't help everyone to your detriment. You don't know what this would do to you. How it might hurt you. You remember the restaurant..."

Her gaze shifts away from him. He doesn't hold that day against her; he's told her as much. But he hasn't forgotten, less for what danger it put him in and more for her. How easily she could have been hurt. How quickly her life could have ended.

"I know what happened at the restaurant was a little reckless," she acknowledges. "But this is different."

"How?"

"Because it's not putting you in harm's way. Because they already have Reid in custody. We've been looking for something low risk with high reward, and there is..." Harbinger swallows like it pains her. "Nothing higher than OID money. And if we don't help them, those girls will never come home. We both know that. You said it yourself; the OID doesn't know how to handle an investigation. They're out of ideas. This is one thing we can do — one thing that's safe. One thing that can get us the money we need."

"But it's not worth it if you're at risk!"

"I'll be fine." She smiles gently.

"You don't know that."

"I do: no object has ever harmed me, not even magical ones. No lasting effects. Hell, I might not be able to get anything off of it, anyway."

Defeat swarms his chest. His shoulders fall. "I don't like this, Harbinger."

That's finally enough to slow her. For her to take one of his hands between both of hers. "I understand." Her fingers trace the back of his hands: chipping, discolored, and scarred from years of protecting her. "I've been trying to take things easier. To go slower. We've been cautious for months, but I can't..." She takes a deep breath, eyes slipping shut. "I can't leave those girls out there alone. Someone has to care about them. What's happened to them. Someone who can do something. I can't do nothing if I can help."

He hates it. Strain is evident on his face, through the threads of his emotions flowing into her...but he can't control her. Can't keep her, can't contain her if she wants to do this. It's her choice. Her ability. Her body. Finally, he sighs.

"Fine."

But it's not, and he does little to tamp down on the turmoil swirling inside him. Maybe he's selfish for wanting to keep her as close as possible — as *safe* as possible — but he can't help the relentless uncertainty in his chest.

Her hands stop moving over his. Voice soft, crawling past the edge of her helmet. "You don't have to come with me."

As if it were a choice. As if leaving her on her own would ever be an option. "Of course I'm going with you." His eyes harden on hers. "But if we do this, we do it our way. You let me set the terms. Agreed?"

She nods.

It'll have to suffice.

Flint lifts his gaze toward the door. "You can come back in."

No doubt Tamneth's been listening, but he waits a few seconds before he opens the door again. Harbinger clicks her helmet back into place, and Tamneth stands at the end of the table.

"If we do this, you pay double our asking price," Flint begins.

"Of course," Tamneth agrees, "And —"

"I'm not finished." Flint lifts his hand. "All of it gets deposited into our account. *Today.* If we incur any ailments from this work, you pay for our medical services as long as they're necessary."

"That's —"

"Non-negotiable."

After a moment, Tamneth's eyes narrow until he nods. Flint leans back, wishing the weight would slip off his shoulders. "Draw up the contract, then. We'll start once the bank confirms the money is in our account."

Tamneth gestures toward the door. "Then follow me."

THREE

Harbinger

Even if Harbinger weren't privy to Flint's emotions, he wears them on his face. The glare he levels at Tamneth is poisonous enough that Harbinger wonders if they should keep an antidote on standby. She's glad she's not on the receiving end of it.

But the feeling Flint reserves for her is worse. A knowing sadness radiates through his steps as they follow Tamneth down the corridor. Flint keeps his focus on their cell phone. He's not surprised this is the path Harbinger has chosen to take, but he is disappointed, which is worse than anger or fear or any other emotion that rattled around the conference room. It's enough to make her second-guess herself. To consider turning on her heel and flipping the OID off as they disappear out the door.

But they can't do *nothing*.

She knows what Flint would say. *Yes, we absolutely can.* But Harbinger can't. Can't leave those girls out there alone. Can't leave their families in the wake of tragedy. Can't leave them with no resolution, stories untold, mysteries unsolved.

Banshees hang between life and death, slipping through the Veil and brushing against the ether of what was and could have been. If Harbinger can't use her power for good, then what's the point? What use is this fucking ability if she can't help?

Even if the girls are dead.

She and Flint need something that'll pay without putting them in danger. It's a compromise; one she doesn't love making, but a risk she has to take nonetheless. Flint will have to get on board. Never mind that they don't really know what touching this thing will do to her, but Harbinger has to believe it's safe enough.

She'll touch this object. Tell them what she sees. Move onto the next.

Flint stuffs the phone back into his pocket. "The money's in our account."

She thinks he breathes a little easier. Maybe she's lying to herself.

They come to a stop in front of a metal door as Tamneth holds out the NDA's. Flint inspects them for a second time — a third, when Tamneth gets huffy — before they sign. Tamneth swipes his badge against a digital panel.

The door unlocks. Harbinger gives Tamneth a wide berth when she steps into the stark white room. It's vacant, save for a small, clear box on the lab table. Harbinger's head tilts before she steps closer.

"Harbin…"

She looks back at Flint, meeting the worry in his eyes.

"You don't have to do this," he murmurs. "We can still leave."

His emotions rise within her, a mixture of doubt and guilt and frustration. But she plasters a confident smile on her face before she realizes her helmet blocks it. "Don't worry," she soothes. "It'll be fine."

Thank the gods their connection goes one way, and he can't feel her mounting uncertainty.

Tugging on her fingertips, she pulls off one glove as Flint's hand stretches out to take it. With murmured thanks, she steps toward the table, leaning to get a closer look.

The object looks like a scrap of black fabric, no bigger than the pad of her finger, but it's odd. A mixture of states of matter: solid, liquid, gas. Its colors shift like a shadow, adjusting when Harbinger changes angles, vanishing like smoke or blending into the corners of the case.

She calls over her shoulder. "You're sure you don't know what this is?"

"Correct." Tamneth waits by the door. "It's the last thing we recovered from Reid. No one has been able to determine what it does."

The box unlatches, flipping open to expose the object held against the bottom of the case like a specimen. A creature with its wings pinned. Flint's swirling unease heightens her own, but she pushes past it, the black markings on her fingers drifting toward the object.

She sucks in a breath.

Flint starts to protest.

And then, her fingers touch down.

Her mind is sucked away. Submerged, pulled deeper, like the heavy tug of a drain. She's not underwater. She's elsewhere, surrounded by swirling black shadows, fog creeping across the edges of her vision. Everything is hazy, oil smeared over a camera lens, a murky quality that seeps over her like dread.

It's unlike anything she's touched. No web of interconnected strings zig-zagging through events. There's nothing she can follow, no way to categorize what she sees. It's not like she's touched an object at all.

More like something *alive*.

But it's nothing like touching Flint. Every part of this is subtle, lapping against her like a tide rising on the beach. Slow, gradual, until it could envelop her. Until it could drown her. Until it could swallow her whole.

There's movement beside her.

She tries to follow it, but it's like slogging through mud, buried in a dream, an abstract of the world she knows. She tries to make out the shapes in the distance, white noise swelling in the space around her.

Something breathes down her neck.

Harbinger jerks back, cleaving the connection and stumbling as she gasps to the surface. Back in the real world, room tilting, her head lolling back before she comes to. Flint's broad arms keep her off the floor, his voice rushing into her ears.

"What happened?"

Her heart races against her ribs. She searches for Tamneth's face. "What is that?"

He shouldn't know the answer. *No one has been able to determine what it does.* But his eyes stay trained on her, monitoring her reaction...

Like an experiment.

He makes no move to answer. "What did you see?"

Flint tucks her closer to his chest. "Give her a fucking minute!"

Nausea roils in her stomach, head swimming at the sudden influx of sensation. Black spots bloom in her vision. She clicks her helmet open, gulping for air as her legs wobble beneath her.

Flint's hand is steady across her back. The need to vomit slowly passes. After a moment, Flint guides her to her feet, and Harbinger steels herself against Tamneth.

"What is that?"

He doesn't bother to look surprised any more, face settling into a cold expression as he motions to a pair of armed guards down the hallway. "It's a night terror."

"A what?" Surely she misunderstood. Her jaw tightens, mind whipping in a new direction. "So you knew the whole time. That's why you called us. It wasn't some 'object' you found."

"It's new technology we're testing. We extracted it from Reid's mind." Tamneth jerks his chin toward the box on the table. "That's a piece of it."

Harbinger can't fathom it. Why would the OID develop tech like that? Her mind whirls from the sensation, hands holding her helmet straight as her body tries to regulate.

"What did you see?" Tamneth insists, stepping closer. Her head jerks up the same time Flint does.

"Oh, fuck off."

She takes her glove from Flint's hand, trying to jam it back over her fingers.

"So you did see something." Tamneth's eyes are dark. Flint rises to his full height behind Harbinger.

"You paid me to read it," she seethes. Flint made sure to negotiate that loophole. "Not tell you anything about it. And I'm sure as shit not going to now. This is why I don't trust organizations. *'Something Reid had stashed away.'* Fuck off!"

Tamneth tilts his head. "Technically, Reid did have it stashed away...in his mind."

The look Flint gives should be enough to send Tamneth running. Unfortunately for all of them, he doesn't know when to leave well enough alone.

Harbinger's about to tell him as much when a strange feeling tugs in her chest. Experimental. A line of rope disappearing into the dark with something at the other end.

"Oh no."

Flint turns back to her, worry surging next to something else. Some*one* else.

Harbinger's throat tightens. "I'm connected to it."

It takes a moment for Flint to understand. "You're..." He whirls on Tamneth. "You said it wasn't alive!"

Tamneth's glare slices toward Harbinger. "It's not! Not by any normal metric. Doesn't need to breathe. Doesn't have a pulse. Doesn't eat or sleep."

Flint grinds his teeth. *"But?"*

"But," Tamneth continues, "it is sentient."

Harbinger steadies herself on the table. Just like that, she's bound to an unknown variable. Something that doesn't feel like anything else she's touched. Something that's not the dead weight of an object, nor the constant ebb and flow of another person.

And she's stuck with it.

Forever.

A sickening feeling churns in her stomach. Déjà vu, a cracked egg spreading over her mind, tiredness dulling her senses before the brush of invisible fingers across the back of her neck.

"So you used her." Flint's anger whistles like a tea kettle. "Without her consent. You've tied her to this *thing* for the rest of her life, and you don't even know what it does!"

Tamneth lifts his chin without the decency to look ashamed. In fact, he looks a little proud. "It's a small price to pay to protect the public."

Flint closes the space between them, clawed hand raising, but the guards lift and cock their weapons toward Harbinger.

"Careful, Mr. Flint." Tamneth's voice is low and level, an eerie knowingness in his expression. "I'd hate for your temper to get the best of you again."

Again?

Confusing emotions string through Flint when he looks at her: fury, shame, biting nostalgia. But all Harbinger can make out is the tension through his shoulders.

Slowly — *slowly* — Flint takes a step back. There's no use fighting back here. Not when they're deep inside OID headquarters, surrounded by weapons and false claims and political pull. Harbinger clenches her fingers around Flint's forearm, to stay close. "Where's the rest of it?"

Tamneth lifts a brow. "The rest of what?"

"The night terror. You said there's more. That it's *sentient*. Where's the rest?"

Flint's body is still tight with rage. "Harbin, forget it. Let's —"

"I can't," she whispers. Her fingers dig into Flint's arm, voice just loud enough for him to make out. "If I'm connected to this thing, I need to know what that means."

There's a long moment before they both turn back to Tamneth. Harbinger locks her helmet visor back into place, and Tamneth steps back to allow them through the door. She keeps a hand on Flint's elbow as he tries to calm the bitter hatred spiking through him.

She can't think about it. Can't focus on what this means, because if she does…

There's a subtle pull on her consciousness.

What the fuck? *What the fuck?* She's been so careful to keep these connections at bay, and now, this thing…

Who knows what this means for her abilities? Her body? Her life? She nearly lurches over a trash can, desperate to expel this disturbance, but it's not that easy. It never has been. She's never gotten to choose who and what has access to her.

Only once Flint steadies her does she realize she's leaning into him. She gives her best reassuring squeeze, but he's too wound up to relax.

She just *had* to read this object.

Of fucking *course* she did.

Tamneth swipes his badge against another panel, and a pressurized-door unlocks. "The cuffs we have on it should prevent it from changing shape. It's restrained to the chair."

Flint stops Harbinger in the doorway. "Why is it *restrained*?"

Tamneth forces his eyes away from Harbinger. "During the course of our study, we've lost a few agents."

Flint is incensed. Harbinger's head falls, eyes slipping shut, trying to breathe through one blow after another.

A night terror. From a serial killer. Melded to her for the rest of her life. Able and eager to kill.

It can't be real. Like Harbinger is pulled from her body, floating above herself, watching as Tamneth stands rooted in his righteousness and Flint fights down his helpless anger.

Pick it up. Then put it down.

It's a phrase she hasn't thought in so many years, the mechanical way she learned to cope with her powers. She can still picture it. Smaller, skeletal hands holding her gloved ones. Knees trembling outside a tall wooden door. Milky white eyes staring back, set into a face mirroring her own.

Pick up the object. Read what they ask for. Then every feeling it gives you, every horrible thing you see, push it away.

Pick it up. Then put it down.

Harbinger clings to the thought of that awful wooden door, the distant squeeze of fingers around hers.

Then, with a slow breath, she opens her eyes and steps into the containment chamber.

FOUR

Harbinger

An empty chair is cast in shadow in the middle of the room. Confusion clouds Harbinger's thoughts, still trapped in her memory, until her eyes focus on the darkness enough to make out an arm. A leg. An almost-human shape strapped to the chair.

He's dark in varying shades, shifting from pitch black to dim gray. Fire-like wisps flicker at the top of his head, like the black flame of a candle. Around him, the air gives off static. Harbinger can make out the line of his shoulders, the lithe expanse of his chest, all tapering to his waist. Metal straps hold his throat and ankles to the chair, thick handcuffs locking his wrists together in his lap.

She knows it's 'him,' because he prods at their connection until he catches sight of her. His eyes have no pupils, just two glowing yellow slashes that match the gash of his mouth when he smiles.

Flint edges in front of her, but the creature doesn't make a move for them...not that he could. Instead, his gaze lingers on Harbinger's skull helmet behind Flint's elbow. When the terror speaks, a chill rakes up the backs of her knees.

"Sorry for staring, sweetheart, but you look like death itself."

His cadence is smooth, unperturbed, no audible tell that suggests he's a prisoner against his will. But there's a haunting quality to his voice, like a distant thud. A flicking tongue. An object moved in an empty house.

For a moment, Harbinger's glad Flint stepped in front of her, but the way the night terror watches them replaces the iciness of the room with prickling heat.

"Have we met?" Interest swirls in the terror's shadowy depths. Harbinger forces her voice level.

"I'm Harbinger. This is Flint."

The creature laughs, a distorted sound that makes her skin crawl. "Oh, *yeah*." His gaze licks over her, and the pull on their connection grows tighter. "I know you."

Flint stiffens. The creature catches it the same time Harbinger does, and his lip twitches. "You can call me Agony."

Harbinger's brow hikes. "Original."

"I thought so..." Agony's glowing tongue toys with their names. "*Harbinger* and *Flint*."

Tamneth stays on the edge of the room — of fucking course. When Harbinger turns back, Agony is sizing Flint up.

Flint does nothing to hide his distaste. Agony isn't put off in the slightest. "Big, aren't you?"

Something about that twists in Harbinger's stomach – but they have to stay on track. "The connection: you feel it, too."

Agony turns to her again, giving an experimental pluck on their bond. Harbinger stops it, like grabbing a vibrating wire. Phantom sensation travels up her arms, as if she did grab...something.

Intrigue blooms in Agony's expression. "I'd love to know how that works."

"I touched part of you. In the other room."

Black flames on Agony's head flare higher. He shoots Tamneth a vicious look. "They like to cut off little pieces of me as keepsakes. Isn't that right?"

Tamneth doesn't answer. Agony returns his attention to Harbinger. "They've been poking and prodding me for weeks. Didn't even take me to dinner first. Horrible manners."

"Seems to be a habit with them," Flint says coolly. Agony beams up at him.

"Bet you'd never treat me like that. You're a real gentleman, aren't you?"

Harbinger cuts in. "What do you know about Raymond Reid?"

Agony stretches as much as he can, draping back against the chair, as comfortable as a cat in the sun. "Only what they tell me. He's been taking girls. Killing them. Vicious stuff. He wasn't so tough during my time with him."

"How do you mean?"

Agony splays his fingers, as if it's obvious. "*Night terror.* I tormented his sleep. Chasing the fear, the pain..." That tongue slips out again. He clicks it to the roof of his mouth with a pop. "That's what I like. I don't know what went on outside of his dreams."

Harbinger scowls. "So you have no recollection of what he did during waking hours?"

"Not unless it showed up in his sleep. And, if we're being honest..." Agony leans forward against the restraints. "Killing girls would have been a fantasy for him, not a nightmare. I never got a look at any of that."

Tamneth scoffs behind them. But Harbinger saw *something* when she touched Agony, growing clearer the second before she pulled herself out. A vision taking shape on the horizon. If she could spend more time there, now that the connection's already forged...

"Harbin."

Flint keeps an eye on the gears turning in her head. She tilts her helmet toward the door. When Tamneth tries to follow them, Harbinger holds up a gloved hand, tempted to land it across his face. "You? Stay."

She and Flint find a sitting area down another hallway, empty save for a fake potted plant and a couple of chairs. She turns to him with purpose.

"I have an idea."

Flint sighs. "I already hate it."

Harbinger pushes up to stand in one of the seats, close enough for Flint to hear her. "The connection is there," she confirms. She can't dwell on it. *Put it down.* "It's not like touching another person, but it's not nothing, either."

She made the decision to go through with this, but Flint's guilt lingers regardless. She waves it away. "It's not your fault. I'm...it is what it is." Nausea begins to swell if she thinks about it too deeply — so she doesn't. "But I don't like the thought of the OID having possession of something that's attached to me."

Flint's eyes narrow. He knows where she's headed. "What do you mean?"

"You heard what Agony said. They've been experimenting on him for weeks; they're sure as hell not gonna stop when we walk out of here with middle fingers high. I don't want to find out what the connection feels like when they torture him...or worse."

Deep inside herself, she reaches toward a jagged hole in her chest, overgrown and vacant where a connection had once been.

She can't do that again.

And Flint can't disagree with her, but this solution stares them down like the muzzle of a gun.

"We have to take him," Harbinger finishes.

"Are you —" Flint scoffs a breath, looking around for some support, but there's nothing but ringing telephones and whirring copy machines. Flint leans back toward her. "You want to take him, and do what?"

"Look for the girls."

"Gods, Harbinger." He massages his jaw, clamped from gritting it again and again.

"You said yourself the OID does shoddy investigations. There's no way they're going to find those girls. And then, what, a serial killer goes free?"

"We can't take some unknown creature with us," Flint hisses. "Who knows what he's capable of? The OID hardly knows! And lest you forget, he came from that *serial killer* you're so worried about."

"That doesn't mean —"

"That night terror has *killed people*, Harbinger!"

"Can you blame him?!"

Flint's lips part. He doesn't find a response, because he's done the same protecting her, *would do* the same again if he had to. Almost did when they learned what Tamneth had done to Harbinger. When he experimented with her body. When he forced this on her and told her to live with it.

They both know how someone reacts to that.

A tide of shame rises in Flint, and Harbinger's regret swells to meet it. "I didn't mean —"

He stops her with a gentle hand, gaze cast off down the hall. "Like you said. It's complicated."

Strained silence separates them before Flint speaks again. "But you're asking me to let you put yourself in danger." His emotions plead and press up against her, like he's run out of ways to fight this. "To put *me* in danger."

Harbinger sinks down to rest against the back of the chair. "You're right. I didn't..." She winces. "I didn't think about it like that."

Uncertain fear twists through her ribcage. Finally, Flint speaks again. "We have to take him."

There's no way around it now that Harbinger's tied to this creature. But it doesn't feel like a victory once Flint has pointed out what little thought she gave to this. They can't leave Agony here, but bringing him along adds its own danger.

"We can figure something else out."

"No..." Flint shakes his head, searching for another out before he sighs in resignation. "You're right. We can't leave something — some*one* tied to you with the OID. But the question is, how do we get him out?"

Leave it to Flint to find practical applications for her wild thoughts. He bows his head in thought, murmuring ideas to her until they settle on a plan.

Tamneth's head jerks up as they approach the containment room again. He meets them in the corridor, pulling the door shut.

"Are you ready to —"

"She's not touching him again." Flint doesn't give Tamneth a moment to suggest it, to weasel his way into something advantageous.

Tamneth's eyes roll. "Now, hold on, Flint —"

"No."

"I understand your hesitation." Tamneth tries to laugh. To sound amenable. "Trust me, I do —"

Flint doesn't have to use his massive frame. Doesn't even move, just lowers his voice to a level that rumbles through the walls and sends a frigid snap down Harbinger's back. His eyes burn with each pristine word.

"You have no idea what you've done to her. What an incalculable risk you've taken. What that creature is capable of, or what the lasting effects will be."

The words aren't just for Tamneth. The point of Flint's emotions angle toward Harbinger, shining a spotlight on what she's done. He tries to hold it back, but fear cuts from him like an undercurrent, leaving him raw and exposed.

Harbinger swallows her guilt. "Flint's right. I'm not reading him again. Not until we know more about how he works or what he can do." The dreamscape comes back to her, making her fists clench, apprehension creeping into her shoulders. What she'd seen was fathomless and unknowable, laced with foreboding. What else might happen if she goes back there?

Tamneth fumes, brows knit until they converge. "Going to be difficult to get anything out of it if you won't look."

Harbinger resists the urge to punch him. "It's 'him.' Have you tried asking him?"

"Of course. It won't tell us anything, either. Says it doesn't remember. That it wasn't 'awake.'"

Harbinger tilts her head, as if she's considering the thought for the first time. "What if we take him with us?"

Tamneth's shock is palpable. "Absolutely not. The night terror is unpredictable."

"Oh, now it's unpredictable?" Flint's hatred for the OID outweighs the rest of his worries. "What happened to all the 'trials' you ran? The cuffs being secure?"

"Yes, but —"

"So you were willing to risk Harbinger for information — *scraps* of information, mind you — but us taking your prisoner is a step too far?"

"It's a danger to the public."

"Or you're on your last leg to make things right after you fucked up the investigation."

"That's not —" Tamneth splutters. "You can't trust this thing."

"We don't trust *you*." Flint barrels straight into negotiations, not giving Tamneth a breath to cut in. "So you'll pay for all expenses: lodging, travel, meals —"

"That's not —"

"I'm not finished. You pay us a flat fee up front, no matter what we uncover. No matter if or when we decide to pull out. And no one from the OID has any part in our investigation." Tamneth blanches at the sharp kick through his line in the sand. "They don't travel with us. They don't interrupt us. You give us what you have, case files and evidence, and we'll take it from there. We check in once a week. Otherwise, you stay out of our business."

"I can assure you, our agents —"

"Non. Negotiable."

Tamneth's glare cuts to Harbinger. She doesn't help him. He tries again.

"We can't allow you to disappear across the country unchecked. There has to be a representative from the OID with you."

"You fucked up," Flint answers. "You hired us to save face. You need us a hell of a lot more than we need you, so take your pick. Hand the terror over, or we walk."

Tamneth's mouth pulls into a thin line. He doesn't contradict them.

"We leave tomorrow afternoon," Flint finishes. "Make sure the money's in our account, and the terror is waiting for us."

They leave Tamneth without another word, a wisp of shadowy feeling stirring inside Harbinger. When the partners make it back to the parking lot, Harbinger pops the SUV's passenger side door open before she realizes Flint is watching her.

"Look, I'm sor-"

"What did you see?" The SUV squeaks when Flint leans against the hood. "When you read him."

Harbinger taps the connection inside her. It sounds hollow, like a pebble knocked down into a cavernous hole, echoing as the rock skips and falls into the depths.

"It was like a dream." Dreams she's had for longer than she cares to remember: the stone slab in the water. The house she won't go near. She shakes them out of her thoughts. In the vision with Agony, everything was distant. Blurry. Dark. Already, the image slips away from her like a nightmare she can't hold onto. "There was something there. Something moving. Pieces I couldn't make out."

"And the connection?"

Her brows knit. Flint waits for her answer.

"It's not the same as ours. It's not like a floodgate; it's more like...a pathway."

Flint's expression is unreadable. He keeps a tight lock on his emotions, even when she says the words he doesn't want to hear. "I have to go deeper."

Flint huffs. "He's dangerous, Harbin."

"No more than a serial killer on the loose."

She hoists herself into the passenger seat. Flint stays on the pavement. "This isn't a joke."

His voice is different. Heavier. She pulls her helmet from her head, resting it in her lap. "I know," she acknowledges. She has to. "But this is the only way we're going to solve this."

Flint's gaze tilts back toward the upper floors of the building, lost in his own stream of thought. "You can feel it coming off of him: something twisted. Evil."

The same feeling she had in the vision. She tugs the seatbelt across her body, swallowing down fear and guilt as she tries to give Flint an easy smile.

"Lucky I have you to protect me."

FIVE

Agony

Killing them will take an entire minute. Maybe a minute-and-a-half.

The gargoyle will be harder — literally. Especially with that protective streak where the banshee is concerned. Agony will have to get rid of him first. When he least expects it, before he has a chance to roll into a rage at whatever Agony does to his little partner.

Agony's still not sure what the banshee did when she touched him. But now that she's been inside of him, Agony wants another taste of that *delicious* feeling.

She saw something when she touched him. Herald. Hark. *Harbinger* — that's her name. Unlike the agents that played with him like a lab rat, Harbinger was the first to see something when she brushed against him. The first to experience more than the surface-level of his being. The first to avoid his uncuffed tendrils wrapping around her throat.

A lapse that will have to be corrected.

Because she did more than see; Agony felt her slip inside. Out of all the people he's disposed of — the lab coats that drifted too close, the microscopes and magnifying glasses that leaned in a little too far — none of them got a glimpse at his essence. None of them saw the dreamscape.

And Agony wants a little more alone time with this banshee who can get under his shadows.

Not that he created the dream world inside him. He took what was supplied by his host, shuffling the places and people and things into some horrifying combination to leave Reid in a cold sweat. It took a bit of experimentation to see what would disturb Reid, but Agony had it down to a science.

Not that Reid remembers his night terrors. And Agony doesn't have a clue what went on in Reid's waking mind, especially now that they're separated.

The woes of a performing artist.

In any case, Agony's not sold on getting rid of this pair, the gargoyle and the banshee. Not yet, anyway. Killing in a nightmare is easy. Almost accidental. But the physics of the real world seem different. More tangible. Permanent. And these two did get him out of lockdown. Really, Agony should be thanking them.

But maybe he'll get bored. See what he can do to the gargoyle's throat.

The partners have piqued Agony's interest. Not enough to keep him compliant, of course. He's not going back to that sterilized building. At the first opportunity, he's getting the fuck out of here. If someone gets in his way? That's their problem. They can deal with the consequences.

Unfortunately, the cuffs around his wrist are doing a spectacular job of keeping him contained. He has to admire the craftsmanship, the research that went into them. Those scientists learned a thing or two after losing a dozen of their comrades, which is more than he can say for the partners. The homemade cage around the backseat of this SUV will be little more than toothpicks once Agony's not locked in this physical form.

They pull over at a gas station off the highway thirty minutes down the road. The gargoyle pulls Agony from the backseat, ignoring any attempts at conversation as Harbinger rounds the back of the car.

It's a curious thing, watching her work. Pulling off her glove and drowning out the sounds of traffic with her power's nearly-imperceptible buzz. Black marks creep up her fingers as she reads the handcuffs locked around the shadows of his skin.

"Looks like you took a dip in me," he sneers.

She does her best to ignore him, but there's a telltale tug in the center of Agony's being. A burning coal in his stomach. A feeling that comes from her, passed through the link between them. But she smothers the coal, focusing on his cuffs again and trying to ignore the fact that they stand eye-to-eye.

"No tracking device," she finally murmurs. "That would've been smart."

"You can see why they didn't think of it," the gargoyle grumbles.

They load Agony back into the SUV. He kicks his feet up on the cage between them. The gargoyle — Rock. Stone. *Flint* — tenses in the front seat. Harbinger's helmet stays trained on the eighteen-wheelers parked on either side of them. "Did we lose the tail?"

Flint's eyes flick to the rearview. Agony grins. Flint tears his gaze away. "Yeah. They followed the bugs."

Harbinger's touchy trick revealed three tracking devices on the SUV's undercarriage, planted this afternoon as the partners retrieved Agony. Now, those trackers are riding along underneath three separate vehicles headed in the opposite direction.

Clearly, the scientists underestimate this woman's ability.

Once the SUV pulls back onto the highway, most of the drive is spent ignoring Agony. Harbinger reads through the case files, touching her bare fingers to the few bits of evidence. With each one, her scowl deepens.

"Nothing incriminating. This is all they found? Where did this guy keep his stuff?"

Agony tries peeking over her shoulder, but she stuffs the box back to the floor. Boredly, his eyes rove the car's interior for anything interesting.

Leftover cup. *Fine.*

Broken sun visor. *Sigh.*

The driver's manual. *Gods.*

But his persistence is rewarded by the keys in the ignition, a dangling leather patch painted with a worn purple flower.

"Cute keychain." He scrutinizes Flint. "It suits you."

Flint glares at the road. Harbinger glances toward him. "When you told the OID we'd check in with them every week..."

Flint snorts a laugh as he types into the GPS. "Yeah, we're not fucking calling them."

Agony's feet twitch to an unheard beat as he looks out the window. "Got a driving playlist?"

They both ignore him. *Boring.*

"They have to know we'll head to Reid's house first." Harbinger's voice filters through her helmet. "They'll catch up to us there."

"Maybe." Flint checks mirrors as he changes lanes. "But they won't know when. We'll stay a couple hours away and keep an eye out for another tail while we're there."

Scenery whizzes past the windows. It's different than Agony's used to. Not just the landscape of concrete, cars, and buildings. Everything in the physical world is more focused, vibrant, solid, not the dreary overcast that permeates dreams.

Even Harbinger's dreams. She didn't get much sleep last night. She doesn't realize how much her touch connected them, but Agony was there as she slept, when the OID building cleared out and left him in the dark.

There was a new trail in his dream world. Off the beaten path, leading Agony to a place he'd never seen before.

Even when he couldn't quite make Harbinger out, he could feel her, a steady energy focused on things Agony didn't recognize: a dais in a pool. A suburban house with the door cracked open. A restaurant with checkered floors.

His presence unsettled her more than she cares to admit. He can sense her wariness through all those protective layers, past the catsuit and gloves and helmet.

And Agony wants more of that: more pain. More fear. More shivers.

As they drive, she moves to lift her helmet off her shoulders, but she stops as if she thinks better of it. Above the collar of her suit, Agony can make out the bone-white skin of her neck. A tendril of black hair peeks out beneath the helmet.

"Don't stop on my account," he grins. "That can't be comfortable."

"Neither is riding with a night terror in the backseat." She turns back to the road, Flint bristling beside her. "I'll survive."

Perhaps.

"I'm happy to relocate." Agony rights himself, leaning his forehead against the caging between them. "Squeeze between you two. Or you can sit on my lap." His smile swings to Flint. "Both of you." Cuffed wrists tap against the cage. "Just have to take a few things off first."

Flint doesn't look his way. "Not a chance."

Agony's mouth hovers against the grate behind Flint's neck. "You let me know if you change your mind." Flint's wings twitch as Agony reclines. "You know where to find me."

"Instead of being a nuisance," Harbinger retorts, "tell us what you know about Reid. The casefile says he didn't get along with many people."

"Would you expect a serial killer to get along with people?"

"He *tried* to, but his coworkers found him annoying. His sales weren't very good, but he acted like they were. Thought he was the smartest person in every room." Harbinger's helmet scans the document. "He was a printer salesman."

Agony's eyes roll. "Riveting."

Flint checks the mirror again. "Means he doesn't know how to take no for an answer."

"He sold to middle and high schools, which was the last place a lot of the girls were seen." Harbinger looks back to Agony. "So tell us what else you know."

"Would that I could, little death."

Flint glares in the rearview. Agony's attention drifts out the window, imagining a stick figure running beside them.

"You have more information than I do. I only got random shit from his life to torture him."

"So how were you made?"

Agony wonders if Harbinger narrows her eyes behind that helmet. If her brow furrows. If she keeps her expression schooled. What it would take to get a reaction from her.

"Couldn't tell you," he answers. "But technically, I was made to torment Reid. I'm a hero."

Flint snorts. "Unlikely."

"I've paid my debt to society." Agony lounges back across the seat. "Didn't see you torture a serial killer for years."

"Didn't stop him from killing those girls." Flint's words lash toward the backseat. His grip tightens on the steering wheel. "Maybe you caused it."

Harbinger's helmet ticks toward him. "Flint."

Flint doesn't apologize. But he does flick on the turn signal, gaze lingering over his shoulder longer than it needs to. "Make sure his cuffs are still locked."

Agony holds up his wrists before Harbinger can turn. "What, don't trust me?"

Neither of them answers.

Agony keeps his eyes on her, waiting for another glance at the pallid curve of her neck. "What's with this banshee business, anyway?" The light of his face reflects in her helmet, smile curling.

"Don't tell me you touched me for business, not pleasure."

It's impossible to see how his words affect her, but an undercurrent skips through him. Barely noticeable, submerged, rippling to the surface of their connection.

"Business." She turns her face away, helmet catching Agony in her periphery. "And not intentional. I've never read something like you before."

He gasps. "I was your first?"

"We need to stop somewhere," Flint interrupts. The puzzled current from Harbinger snaps, her focus back to the present. Back to Flint. "We should eat before it gets late. Find a motel that's not too seedy before it's dark."

"Fuck it." Harbinger kicks her boots up on the dash. "We've got OID money now. They can spring for someplace with room service and a suite."

For the first time, Flint glances willingly toward Agony. "They said you don't eat."

It's not a question, pulled out of Flint like a forced pleasantry. Agony loves the sound of it.

"And you're going to believe the OID? After they lied to you?" Agony clicks his tongue in disappointment. "I didn't want any of their bland shit. I want to try sushi. I'll let you feed me."

Flint fights a sigh as they take the next exit. Harbinger scrolls on the cell phone — one they share between them, by the looks of it. After a few swipes, she hums to herself. "They have pre-made sushi at the grocery store."

"Come on," Agony boos. "You want my first time to be from there?"

"They have it at the gas station, too."

Agony groans.

Under his breath, Flint grumbles to Harbinger. "We don't have to get him sushi. We don't have to get him *anything*."

Agony narrows his eyes, but Harbinger keeps tapping on the phone with a shrug. "Well, now I'm in the mood for it, too."

Flint's lip gives the barest twitch of a smile, enamored. Agony lifts his brows, and Flint catches it in the rearview before he glares again.

SIX

Agony

After they pick up the food, the hotel they choose is immaculate. Arches lit, a doorman gesturing guests into the lobby, ceilings vaulted twenty feet higher than necessary. Harbinger leaves them in the SUV while she checks in. Agony almost has Flint answering in multiple syllables when she pops open a side entrance.

The partners don't turn their backs on Agony in the suite, with its curving couches and views of the city. Flint cuffs Agony to a chair in the main area, ankles locked against the legs with a strap across his chest. Agony's tempted to fling himself onto the floor for some action, but Flint captures his attention instead, moving from one room to the other and flicking on the lights.

"Paranoid?" Agony calls.

"Attentive." Once Flint's satisfied they're safe, he adds a portable lock to the front door.

Agony nods to himself. "Paranoid."

Harbinger sets their food on the table, tugging restlessly on her gloves before Flint sidles up beside her.

"You don't have to." His voice is barely loud enough for Agony to hear, only understood from the strange frequency Agony gets from Harbinger. "I can keep him in a separate room."

But Harbinger places her hands on the sides of her helmet. "I've already been inside him." It almost sounds like she's trying to convince herself, in a flash of rebellion. "What's a little peep show?"

Her disheveled braid falls out when she pulls off the helmet, black hair shot through with a ribbon of white. She wrestles with the long neck of her catsuit, popping the high collar buttons before she sets the helmet on the couch. Her back stays to Agony, but in the far mirror, he gets a glimpse at her reflection.

Skin impossibly white next to places sunken and darkened like a skull. Under the hollows of her eyes, beneath her cheekbones, on the end of her nose. The pattern of her skin is skeletal, but bone protrudes through fat and muscle. She blinks white eyes, clouded as if there's a veil over them, trained on someplace no one else can see. Between life and death: the place Agony comes from. The place she sank into with him.

For the first time, Agony wonders if he needs to breathe. "Wow…"

"Don't be a dick." There's a deadly point on Flint's words, the kind that sharpens when he talks about Harbinger. For a lingering moment, she meets Agony's eyes in the reflection before she smooths out her hair.

"You do look like death." Agony smiles. "Like you could kill me." His fingers flex under the restraints. "I love that in a woman."

Despite her scowl, the corners of her lips tip up. "Play your cards right, and you might find out if I can."

She pulls back a chair at the table. Only then does Agony realize Flint is staring between them before he takes the seat across from her. They rip paper from chopsticks, plastic cutlery stuck into piles of rice and hibachi as Harbinger tears open packets of soy sauce.

"Is this a hand-feeding situation?" Agony rocks in his chair. "I'm not opposed —"

"We'll feed you once we're done." Flint takes a bite with the enlarged fork he brought himself, as big as a kitchen spatula. "Unless you want to stick your face in it."

"Don't threaten me with a good time."

Despite Agony's charm, Flint and Harbinger settle into conversation. It's tempting for him to draw their attention again, but there's something enticing about their relationship. Night terrors fade into the background of dreams, but with the two of them, Agony's sure it would have happened anyway. Their voices are weary from hours on the road, but there's softness in both their hardened faces. In Harbinger's smile when she teases Flint. In Flint's eyes when she taps through the phone. They talk in coded language, vague references Agony isn't able to understand.

He doesn't need to know what they're saying to pick up on everything else.

There's a barrier between them. Nothing physical: more like an idea. One that Agony felt last night as Harbinger slept. The wall between them is something she erected, and Flint presses against it, reaching around but never crossing it. Always aware of the boundary, the both of them. It's obvious when Flint rests his hand against the table, close enough for Harbinger to touch...but she pulls her fingers away, eyes back on the casefile, discussing the next town they should hit.

Flint dabs at his mouth with a napkin, covering a wounded look. "All right, terror. You're up." He reaches for the food, but Harbinger stands instead.

"I'll do it."

Agony smiles. "Scared I'll bite his finger off?"

She gathers the plastic tray, sitting back against the edge of the table. "I'm more concerned for *you*."

Flint smirks behind her. Agony lays out the flat of his tongue.

Pink streaks across her cheeks, but she maneuvers the chopsticks and lifts a piece of the roll into his mouth. Agony drags his tongue over his lips before he swallows.

"Satisfactory?" she asks.

His eyes fall shut when he hums. "Worth being strapped to a chair for."

"So do you actually need to eat, or are you just being annoying?"

"Don't know." Agony chews the next piece she offers. "I don't think I need to eat. Or breathe. Or have a pulse. But I learned everything from Reid — his human body. Sometimes it just happens, like a reflex." Agony's gaze locks on Harbinger's, and that coal stokes to life in his stomach again. "And I like to taste."

He finishes off one roll, but when he pouts, Harbinger moves onto the leftover pieces of hers. It's almost enough to make Agony feel bad for what he's about to ask...

Almost.

"So what's your story?" Agony looks between them as Harbinger picks up another piece of food. "You two fucking?"

Flint stiffens. Harbinger jerks a hand under the sushi before it slips. The silence goes on too long, and they both realize it.

Agony smirks.

"Do you want to starve?" Flint grumbles.

Agony meets Flint's eyes like two swords clashing. "I'm just *asking.*" His voice is saccharine. "It's nothing to be ashamed of. All that time on the road in compromising positions must make things...tense."

It's stifling. There's not even the sound of their breath in the room any longer. Chopsticks perch in Harbinger's hand, but she doesn't move toward Agony. "What makes you think that?"

Agony doesn't mention her dream. The depths he's already come to know her. "It's radiating off of you. Hey, I won't tell. I'm sure you don't let it interfere with your work." His smile grows. "After dealing with the OID, I'd want a way to blow off steam, too.

And I'm sure whatever the hell you've got going on is better than torture."

Tension knots through Flint's shoulders. Harbinger's fingers clench, and Agony feels a wave of her guilt breach their connection. "Stop talking so I can feed you."

Agony tilts his head. "Sore spot?"

Harbinger shuts him up by shoving another piece of tuna into his mouth. Every time he swallows enough to speak, she shovels more in.

Clever girl.

On the final bite, he shifts his mouth toward her, knocking the chopstick to the ground. "Smooth," he teases. Flint does his best to focus on the casefile and avoid the glaring chasm Agony has exposed.

With a resigned sigh, Harbinger kneels for the chopstick — and Agony laces his handcuffs around her throat, yanking her back between his knees.

Now the big boy pays attention. Flint grips the table, ready to push to his feet, but Agony clicks his tongue and pulls tighter. Harbinger gasps, gripping at the metal digging into her throat.

"Now, you two, let's not be hasty."

It's intriguing the way Flint's mind works. His eyes flick between Agony's hands, the chain against Harbinger's throat, Agony's wicked eyes. There's panic, sure, but also the trained techniques of someone who's done this before. Someone who knows better. Someone who prepares for the worst and still looks surprised when it rises up to greet him.

Agony twists his wrists. Tightening the chain, but not enough to cut off Harbinger's air. He lifts his brows to the look on Flint's face. "That doesn't look like just partner panic."

Fear pounds between them. Harbinger looks toward her gargoyle savior, trying to fit her fingers between the cuffs, but Flint is trapped by the fear of what happens if he moves.

The dread is heady. Intoxicating. Blood dripping in the water, and Agony poises to strike anywhere he can land his teeth.

Then Harbinger pushes off the ground, plunging back into Agony and toppling his chair. Submerging in him, dreamscape swirling around them as she scrambles for footing.

Then Agony's back slams against the wall, chair dangling from the chains around his legs and chest. Flint's hulking body blocks the rest of the room, clawed hand crushing Agony's throat.

Flint presses harder. The drywall cracks.

"Do not. *Ever*. Touch her again."

Flint's growl vibrates the end table, lamp teetering close to the edge. Agony's eyes brighten, setting Flint's furious face awash in a yellow glow.

"Come on, you can do worse than that." Agony's tongue slips out, laving against Flint's hand. *"Tighter."*

Something in Flint begs to be set loose. To lose control, to slam Agony into the wall over and over. Agony wants to draw out that danger. To see it, taste it, run his tongue over the fear and terror spiking beneath the vicious rage.

But Flint doesn't rise to it. He raises his hand until Agony can't look anywhere but his face.

"If you so much as let the *thought* of harming her pass through your empty fucking head — if I even suspect you're *entertaining* it…" Flint's breath is hot on Agony's face. "I will make your nightmares look like a fantasy. I will rip these pathetic shadows to pieces. I don't need the OID to do it for me."

Agony wants more. Wants to tap into Flint's anger waiting for someone to stoke it, but the embers in Flint's eyes fade. His breathing slows. He drops Agony to the ground, chair stuttering back on four legs.

Already, Flint's back to Harbinger, softening the gruff scrape of his voice as he looks over her neck. "Are you okay?"

"I'm fine." Her eyes stay on Agony, fingers rubbing the circle of her throat.

"That was a cute trick you pulled," Agony jeers. "Using your power to overwhelm me. That was clever —"

"Shut the fuck up," Flint snarls. It's almost enough to goad him again, to draw him into losing it. Instead, he yanks a washcloth from the folded linens and stuffs it into Agony's mouth. It has the desired effect; Agony can't work the rag out between his lips, and Flint's shoulders finally relax.

His touch is so much gentler as he inspects Harbinger. The claws that were clamped around Agony's throat now retract, tracing the bones protruding at Harbinger's collar. Small bruises already start to form. Flint looks torn between wrath and remorse before he finally lets his hand drop back to his side.

"You should go to bed. I'll watch him."

"But you've been driving —"

"I'm not going to leave you alone with him." Flint brushes her hair back into place. "And I don't need as much sleep. I'll be fine."

"I'm not going to be able to sleep, anyway." But she gives in, shooting Agony one last glare before she disappears into the bedroom.

The look she gives him isn't hate. Well: not *just* hate. Agony can't decipher her baffled expression when he reaches for the strands of their connection. Flint sets up on the couch across from the dent in the wall, between Harbinger's bedroom and Agony. Agony's sneer slices across his face. "You can't protect her everywhere."

"Try me."

So Agony does. But he doesn't get a chance to delve into Harbinger's dreams, disrupted by Flint any time Agony looks a little too relaxed. The chair loses any sense of comfort after the first hour. Agony's physical body took more of Flint's beating than Agony's used to. He's stiff and sore, rolling his neck and shutting his eyes to escape Flint's venomous hatred.

Agony doesn't need Harbinger's dreams to know she's not sleeping. The line between them is frantic with static, pins and needles of restlessness as she tosses and turns. None of them sleep.

Flint doesn't take his eyes off of Agony. Doesn't seem to blink until the sun peeks through the curtains, giving Agony all the attention he instigated.

It's a long night. Longer morning. And the day's just getting started.

SEVEN

Flint

Flint couldn't have slept if he wanted to. Not after Agony got that close to Harbinger, as if he'd been planning it since the second they touched. Flint needs to be more careful. More rigorous. Add double fail-safes to the links in Agony's chains, check the knots twice to be sure it's safe.

Because if anything happens to Harbinger…

This whole thing was a bad fucking idea, a slippery slope that has them careening toward certain death. Bringing the night terror was a mistake, but Flint let Harbinger talk him into it. Gods only know what the alternative would've been. Harbinger in agonizing pain while the OID experimented on the night terror with no way for Flint to help her. Or worse: Harbinger going on this harebrained mission by herself, left at the mercy of that thing.

There's no way Flint would let that happen.

He should have been more careful at the OID. Shouldn't have taken the meeting in the first place. Should have known they'd force Harbinger and him into a corner. Should have gotten her out of there as soon as it happened.

But he let his intuition lapse. Again.

It's her decision.

The reminder is true, no matter how much it pains him. Psychometry is her ability. Her body that's affected. Her choice to bring Agony, even if there wasn't much choice to begin with. But it's not just her that has to deal with the consequences; Flint's anxious need to keep her from harm means he's suffering for it, too.

He's on edge from lack of sleep, keyed up on anxiety and the tossing and turning from Harbinger's room. Last night was the first time they haven't shared a bed since the restaurant. The thought twists on his chest, and the gap between them that he's tried so hard to close stretches out again.

Maybe it was the lack of his presence that kept her from sleep. In any case, her brows are knit when she emerges from the bedroom, circles darker beneath her eyes.

"Breakfast?" Flint pushes his glasses back up his nose.

"Not hungry." But she sinks into a seat at the table, tearing into the cereal bar he requested from room service. His lip quirks.

She's distracted as soon as she takes the first bite, gaze leveled across the room at Agony. But she doesn't look horrified. Doesn't look scared: not completely. More like she's inspecting the edge of a cliff, judging how much power she needs to put behind her jump.

Flint's skin crawls.

Agony's attention to her, Flint understands. The terror is an asshole. He wants something to hurt, and Harbinger's captivating all on her own.

But why the hell is Harbinger so interested in Agony?

It's nothing.

It has to be nothing.

Surely it's nothing.

"You ready?" Harbinger's voice slices through Flint's thoughts as she pulls on her helmet, hoisting their bags onto her shoulders.

Flint double-checks the room before he jerks Agony a bit too roughly by the neck, pulling him down the stairs as the elevator doors close on Harbinger. No way Flint's trapping her in a confined space with the creature who tried to kill her. But in the few minutes it takes them to meet downstairs tightens the anxiety in his chest. Only once he sees Harbinger loading their bags into the trunk of the SUV can he breathe easy.

Well. Eas*ier*.

"You know, I —"

Flint stuffs the slipping rag back into Agony's mouth, shoving him into the backseat. Handcuffs clink against the new chain wrapped around Agony's middle as Flint shuts the door. Harbinger lifts on her toes to close the trunk. "I can drive."

Flint shakes his head, taking a few steps away from the vehicle. Harbinger follows behind, and Agony's eyes follow her.

Flint wants to black out the car windows. "We have to take him back."

Harbinger is unreadable beneath her helmet. Fingers twitch at her side, but after a moment, she pulls back the skull visor to reveal her face.

"I can't do this every night," Flint continues. "And there's no way I can sleep knowing what he might pull. Doesn't seem like he sleeps at all."

"Maybe he's nocturnal." Harbinger glances over her shoulder. Shockingly, Agony doesn't smirk. Out of character with what little Flint has learned about him.

And Flint doesn't want to know more.

"We're going to Reid's house today." Flint tears his gaze away from Agony. "We'll find more clues than we can get from the night terror, and then we'll take him back to the OID."

Harbinger still doesn't meet Flint's eyes. Disquieting heat prickles up his neck, but there's nothing to be jealous of. This night terror is a threat. He came from a killer, and he's no fucking better; he's a killer himself. There's nothing there for Harbinger to feel but hatred or fear at what Agony almost did to her.

And yet...

"Flint..." Her voice is low when she turns back to him, wariness in the white of her eyes. Like she's going to tell him something he won't like. Like she's going to say they should keep this creature.

Flint braces for impact.

"I don't think he was going to hurt me."

It takes a moment to register, because Flint must have heard wrong. He puffs out a breath, the closest thing to a laugh he can manage. "He had metal wrapped around your *throat*."

"Not around," she corrects, and Flint tosses back his head at the semantics. "It was shocking more than anything. It didn't really hurt. And when I went back into him, I could feel it. What he was thinking. What he was feeling. It wasn't anything about harming me. He was curious about you and me. Our...relationship."

Flint tries not to flinch at the way she says it, like it's a creature that followed her home.

Yeah. I'm curious about that, too.

But Flint has to laugh. He has to, because it's the most ridiculous thing she's ever said, but no sound comes out of him. All he can do is stare, as if she's suggesting stripping down and rolling across the lot in her bare skin.

"He's not from this world," she tries. Making excuses. "He doesn't know how things work here. All he has to work off of is Reid, and only the gods know how fucked up that is. Agony didn't even know if he could eat."

"He tried to *kill you.*"

"I don't think he did."

Flint throws his hands in the air, pacing away from the car. He wants to circle the parking deck, take a lap around the building. Maybe he'll come back to this conversation where Harbinger makes a shred of sense. "He's evil. You can't domesticate him."

"I know how it sounds." Her voice is slow. Measured. Leaves Flint feeling absurd for wanting to protect her. For wanting to get rid of the thing who had her throat in a chokehold hours ago. "I know what I felt. And we need to finish this job so we can get that payout."

"We don't have to finish it! We got payment up front." But it's not a solution. The OID isn't going to let them take the money and run. The muscles in Flint's neck tense, jaw ticking when he turns back to face her. "No amount of money is worth this."

"Maybe not," she concedes. "But it's worth it to bring those girls back to their families. To show that someone cares. To give them some closure."

It doesn't faze her, the thought of her life being snapped away. It means nothing. Does nothing to her. Like it wouldn't permanently alter the foundation of Flint's life.

Living is an afterthought to her. Barely a consideration.

"Harbinger, we can't do that if you're *dead*!"

"Can't you just *trust me*?"

Her voice echoes off the stone columns of the deck. Agony's eyes burn a hole in Flint, bringing the rage from last night to a boil again. Harbinger flinches as it swells through their connection, and Flint tries to swallow it down. He can't lose control again. He can't be as depraved as Agony.

He fights to protect Harbinger. He doesn't fight out of anger.

"I know how it sounds, Flint. I know I don't have the best track record for not being reckless, but I'm telling you what I saw. What I felt. He couldn't fake that."

"We don't know that!" Panic rises in Flint again. He lowers his voice, stepping closer to her. "We don't know anything about this thing or what he can do to you."

"It's always about me."

Her voice is quiet. Flint tries to settle his emotions clamoring out of control. He hates it. Hates letting go of the anxious grip he has on a sense of safety. Hates the thought of Harbinger risking anything to make someone else's life easier.

"You do everything to protect me," she murmurs. She doesn't meet his eyes. "I know that's your job, but you can't be hypervigilant about everything. You can't keep *everything* outside some ten-foot bubble around me. You're going to exhaust yourself — *kill* yourself — trying to keep me safe. I can't avoid every single thing that might hurt me. Some things I have to fucking deal with."

But he *can* keep everything from her. It's exactly how he handles his feelings for her. Tamping down on his emotions, never bringing them to the surface, never asking for more. Never seeking what he wants.

Because it would be asking too much from her.

Maybe she's right. Maybe protecting her is wearing on him. But there's no other choice.

If Harbinger won't protect herself, who else will?

Anguish seeps into his voice, a fatigue that he's been fighting back. "Don't you care about what this could do to you? What it may have already done?"

Something flickers behind her eyes. "There are more important things than what happens to me."

"Not for me."

It's an impasse, both of them deadlocked on either side, a stalemate they can't negotiate their way out of. They watch each other until she swallows, glancing back to the car. "Let's just go to Reid's house. Maybe we'll find what we need, and this conversation won't matter."

Flint doesn't argue what they both know. This fundamental difference in their priorities will rear its ugly head again.

It's always going to matter.

Harbinger has lacked care for her wellbeing for years. Flint was surprised she took on a bodyguard at all, but never before have they been so completely at odds. Never before was she so willing to throw herself into the line of fire in the hopes that somehow, they can do something.

But the girls are dead. And as much as the truth pains Flint, no amount of evidence or final resting places or vengeance will make that fact easier to live with.

Maybe Flint's selfish for wanting to stop Harbinger. Maybe he's wrong for it.

He doesn't give a fuck.

They can't keep arguing in circles. It's the only thing he can hope for, that the house will tell them exactly what they need, and they can get rid of Agony.

Doesn't mean the cracks forming between Flint and Harbinger will seal back up.

They drive for hours. It's not hot enough to keep the AC on, so silence fills the space. For a moment, Flint considers pulling the rag out of Agony's mouth for some noise, but he's not that desperate.

Harbinger finds a rock station on the radio. One jarring enough to amplify how they aren't speaking. She keeps her helmet on for the entire ride, visor turned out the window when the offramp's sharp turn knocks her against the door.

Flint passes Reid's house the first time. There's something foreboding in its presence, like the cloud cover is a little grayer above the roof. It's set back along a dirt road off of an old two-lane highway, overgrown with weeds, not just from months of being left on its own. The wooden trellis beneath the porch has come off its nails, vines climbing from bushes toward the roof.

By now, there's no more crime scene tape. *MURDERER* slashes in spray paint across the garage door as the gravel behind the house crunches under their tires. Flint pulls Agony out of the backseat and removes the gag, but the terror doesn't wisecrack. He watches the house, like he's waiting for it to move. A breeze rustles through leaves dying on the trees.

"There's something wrong about this place," Harbinger whispers, as if lifting her voice will disturb something they can't see. There's a sense that something is wrong. *Was* wrong.

Flint speaks gruffly to Agony. "Do you recognize this place?"

Agony's eyes flick over the building, but they don't land anywhere for long. "Vaguely. There was something like this in the dreamscape, but it wasn't..." He searches for the word. "It wasn't the main stage. It's not where Reid's thoughts spent most of their time."

Flint doesn't know why he bothered to ask. Agony will string them along with false clues and red herrings until they're spinning their wheels. The three of them step onto the covered porch, steps thudding across the wooden slats. Kudzu winds around gutters and railings, blocking their view to the street.

With the side of his hand, Flint smears a hole through the window's dust and debris. Inside the house, there's nothing but darkness.

Emptiness.

Silence.

EIGHT

Flint

The interior of Reid's house is bare, drag-lines in the carpet from random pieces of furniture. Dust motes float through the air, winking in the pockets of sunlight that make it through the windows. Flint shoves Agony down onto the patio furniture on the porch, looping his cuffs around the metal before Flint checks the rest of the house. It's a one-story ranch with a few other rooms, and they're all the same: small, dark, empty.

Flint makes room for Harbinger to continue inside before he unchains Agony from the porch. Agony stretches when he stands. "Your wings puff up when you're jealous."

Flint elbows him over the threshold. "Be careful what you touch," he murmurs to Harbinger before he thinks better of it. Memory simmers in the back of his mind.

Can't you just trust me?

She moves through the dated kitchen toward the garage. "Here first?"

Flint waits for her to step down onto the concrete before he foists Agony with them. Agony's whisper cuts through the quiet. "You two should think about couple's counseling."

Flint's grip tightens on Agony's neck until he hisses.

Harbinger moves toward the edge of the garage, empty without so much as a spot of oil. She removes her glove and clicks back her helmet, kneeling to press her hand to the floor.

"You think —" Agony starts again. Flint hauls him to the other side of the space.

"I don't want you talking unless you recognize something. So, do you?"

After rolling his eyes around the room, Agony shakes his head. No use lingering, then. As Harbinger works, Flint moves Agony back into the kitchen. "Anything?"

"It's the same room, no matter which way you turn me." Agony traces a finger along the cabinets. "It's familiar. Might have been a background. But I told you, this isn't the main location."

It's frustrating that both Harbinger and Agony have an idea of what they're looking for. Visual cues, feelings, things Flint can't cling to. But that's not why he's here. He's here to protect Harbinger and keep Agony in line, at least until they can get rid of him.

Harbinger returns from the garage, wiping her hand on her catsuit. "A lot of traces of OID members crawling through here, bagging and tagging. I didn't get a hint of the girls or anything malicious in there. But there was something…" She moves through the kitchen, skating the counter with her bare palm as her brows knit. "On the wall, there were holes puttied over, sanded, painted. I wouldn't have noticed them, but when I touched them, I saw some sort of weapons' rack used to hang there."

"Hunting rifles?"

"Yeah, but also a tranquilizer gun? Some kind of feathered darts, blue and yellow." Her fingers trace the cabinets the same way Agony had. "They were newer. Reid removed them before the OID cleared the house. They didn't know it was there."

Flint's brow knits. "What kind of vehicle did Reid have?"

"An off-roader. Pretty serious for someone who lives off the highway."

"Unless he spent time outside the city. This house looks unlived in: overgrown outside, spotless in."

Harbinger turns to look at them. "Where's the closest place you'd need a vehicle like that?"

"The Break. Only place for a hundred miles with terrain that rough." Flint shifts his weight, floor creaking beneath him. "But you don't waltz in there. The geography would make it a pain, even with the right vehicle. None of the packs there would want Reid in their territory." Flint glances to Agony. "This is the quietest you've been."

"Well, you told me to 'shut the fuck up,' in no uncertain terms." There's a lift in Agony's voice that's almost playful. His eyes follow Harbinger around the room. Flint's about to turn him away when Agony speaks again.

"I don't know if anything happened here, but something has permeated. The carpet, the walls, the same way the smell would stick if someone had been smoking for years."

"Something like what?"

"I don't know..." Agony's eyes slide toward Flint, deadly light searing through them. *"Evil."*

Harbinger finishes touching the cabinets, the floors, the dishwasher with clicking knobs instead of digital buttons. She shakes her head. "Nothing. I got some inklings, but no traces of the girls."

"What do you see, exactly?" Agony's eyes light her face in the shell of her helmet. Flint keeps a tight grip on his chains. "It's not what you saw when you looked inside me, is it?"

Harbinger's gaze flicks to Flint. His jaw is tight, antsy, ready to tell Harbinger not to answer — but she does. "I see what happened on these surfaces. OID agents sweeping the place, Reid prepping meals or sorting through mail. I can't feel his thoughts or emotions. The memories play like a movie."

She passes toward the back bedrooms, closer to Agony than Flint would like. He keeps Agony in the living room, guiding him around the last remaining furniture to see if anything sparks recognition: beaten-up couch, mismatched armchairs, rickety television stand.

"Anything?" Flint asks.

"An overwhelming boredom I may never recover from." Agony kicks at the hearth in front of the fireplace. "Wait —"

Flint tenses, but Agony makes no attempt to escape, leaning toward the wooden mantle on the chimney. It's inconspicuous. Plain. No detail that stands out among the rest of the room, but it draws Agony toward it.

"I remember this." He reaches out a hand to brush along the wood, following the whorls and knots.

"What about it?"

"I don't know." There's a knot of frustration in Agony's brow, as if he's actually trying to remember. "It wasn't important." He presses his fingers to the wood "But it was there, in the background."

"So something happened near it?"

"Maybe." Agony feels along the seam between the mantle and brick. "The dreams did, anyway. But it wasn't here, in this house. The chimney was somewhere else."

"That's not exactly helpful. Or possible."

Agony works against the mortar. "I can only tell you what I saw. Things from your world showed up in the dreams, but they were all distorted. Fuzzy. Washed out." There's newfound bitterness in his tone, a snap that gives away his irritation. "I don't provide the props; I just set the stage."

A chunk of brick tumbles to the ground. The hole it leaves is no larger than a ring box, but it's empty. Flint grips Agony's biceps to keep him still, but Agony feels along the inside of the hole, like he's not sure what he's looking for.

"Expecting something?" Flint leans closer.

Agony's shadows ripple. He tilts his chin enough to meet Flint's gaze over his shoulder. The slashes warm Flint's face, but not as much as Agony's eyes dipping to his mouth. "Apparently not."

Flint can hear his breath. Doesn't realize he's clutching Agony tighter until he pulls away, leaving a reasonable amount of space between them. There's no way it's true. How could Agony not remember details from his own world? There's no use wondering. There's nothing Flint can compare this creature to, and Flint's own dreams are as nebulous as Agony makes his out to be. Still, that can't be all Agony remembers. There has to be something.

"Did you hear that?"

Flint follows Agony's gaze toward the hallway. Surely Agony's looking for another chance to cause chaos.

"Hear what?" Flint keeps his voice gruff, but a chill creeps up his spine. Agony's fucking with him, trying for distraction so he can make a break for it. But Agony doesn't move.

"Something broke."

"Don't play with me, terror."

Agony doesn't look away from the hallway, focused enough that a dim glow from his eyes spreads along the walls. But —

It's not from Agony.

Something crashes through the front window, sending flames across the carpet.

"Shit!"

It spreads too quickly for Flint to contain, scorching a hot line between them and the corridor. He grips Agony with one hand as the living room rapidly fills with smoke.

"Harbinger!"

There's no response. Flames race to the base of curtains, too fast to be normal fire. Rainbow colors shimmer in the blaze as it spreads across the ceiling, eating through the drywall in a flare of multicolor.

Phoenix fire.

"Fuck!"

Flint has to move. To make a decision before the flames engulf the building. He has to get Harbinger.

He has to get Harbinger.

"Uncuff me."

Agony's voice jerks Flint from his thoughts. "Are you out of your goddamn —"

"Uncuff me!" Agony rattles his chains. "I can go through the shadows. I can pull her out that way."

"You're joking." Flint doesn't have time for Agony's plot to escape, but Agony's insistent.

"Uncuff me!"

"No!" Flint roars. "Enough!" He can't move through this much phoenix fire in his stone armor. And Harbinger —

Fuck.

Flint lifts Agony under one arm, smashing the mace of his tail through the front door before it's engulfed. He lunges through the flames, dropping Agony on the porch, eyes skirting over the windows. He has no idea which room she's in. No idea where she is. Desperation claws at him to batter straight through the nearest pane of glass, but flames lick up the inside of each one.

Fuck. *Fuck*.

"There!"

Agony leans over the porch railing, pointing down into the yard. Something black has skidded through the grass, leaving a line dug into the mud. Flint can barely make it out through the smoke pouring from the house, but sunlight reflects off of the visor.

Harbinger's helmet.

He turns back to the broken windows, searching for a hole — and finds one, shattered glass twice the size of Harbinger's head with flames dancing behind it.

It's the only choice he has. Flint's skin hardens to a stone shell, tail slamming through the glass, wood screeching as he splits the window frame to fit inside.

Smoke blocks all the light in the room. Flint can't see in front of him, hardened skin already heating as the flames whip at his body.

"Harbinger!" His throat is hoarse and crowded with ash, but he can't stop. Can't leave without her. Can't let anything happen to her.

A beam cracks in the ceiling, raining sparks down around him. Hysteria constricts the little room left in his throat. He presses deeper into the house, searching for any sign of her.

He can't lose her. *He can't lose her.*

"Flint!"

A gloved hand grabs onto his. He pulls Harbinger to his chest, lifting her off the floor and cradling her against him. The way he came is impossible to find, no sign of the outside world through the wall of fire. Thick plumes of smoke billow through the doorway. Harbinger buries her face against him, fingers curling over his pounding heart.

"Flint..."

Despair thrums through his veins. The stone casing of his body heats too quickly. Before much longer, it'll melt her suit to her skin. There's no way out. Except...

His eyes lift to the ceiling, covered in flames and smoke too thick to see through. There's no telling how the roof is constructed. If there's an attic. If the fire has spread there as well.

But they have no other option.

Flint shifts his wings out of stone, hissing when flames waste no time burning through the thin membranes. He kicks off the ground, clutching Harbinger tight, ducking his head to ram through the ceiling. Splintered wood scrapes down the line of his wings until it pierces him. He bites back a groan, gripping claws into the beams around him, but he doesn't stop.

Flight is impossible with the stony weight of his body, but

finally, there's nothing but sky above them, tainted and diluted with smoke. The base of Flint's wings groan in protest. One begins to tear, pain shooting through him as he encloses Harbinger in his arms and plummets toward the yard.

Their crash drags a ditch through the grass as Flint's back skids along the ground. He coughs up soot, throat burning and sore when Harbinger presses up on shaking arms. Her singed gloves cup his face as he shifts out of his armor.

Both their chests heave, faces streaked with ash as her eyes search his. "I'm ok," Flint wheezes. She collapses on his chest, clutching his neck until both their breathing evens. He's tempted to stay like that, swallowing gulps of fresh air with Harbinger safe on his chest, but a voice cuts through his peace.

"How heroic."

Agony's presence strips away the last bit of comfort Flint has. An ache seeps through his wings, making him wince until he cranes his head enough to see the damage. Harbinger hisses.

"Oh, Flint..."

"I'm fine." But as he says it, he knows it isn't wholly true. His wing isn't lifting right, a parachute with slashes cut through it. Harbinger's hands drift over him.

"And your legs..."

In the distance, sirens draw closer. Agony lifts his eyes toward the highway. "Great fun, you two. Straight out of an action movie. I'm gonna take my leave."

Even in Flint's wounded state, he's too fast for Agony, whipping out a hand to jerk Agony's ankle and send him sprawling across the ground. Agony struggles to get back to his feet, but Flint's grip doesn't budge.

Harbinger climbs off of Flint's chest, and he manages to get to his knees with a sharp inhale. "Let's go."

"We need to take you to the hospital."

Grimacing as he rises, Flint lifts Agony with a hand on the back of his neck. "No." Blisters form on his feet, wings angled oddly behind him as he limps toward the car. For once, Agony doesn't try to dart away. It takes a moment for Flint to realize he's putting some of his weight on Agony — and Agony's taking it.

When Flint shifts all his weight to his own feet, pain rushes immediately back.

Harbinger grips her ribs in the same place Flint's body is throbbing. "Flint, we can't heal this without —"

"I'm not leaving you alone. Not with him." His chin jerks toward Agony. "And I'm not sticking around to deal with an investigation. If we check into the hospital, the OID will hear about it, and I don't want to deal with them."

"He has a point."

Agony's voice startles both of them. As soon as they look his way, his smile turns infuriatingly lazy. "I wouldn't trust you alone with me, either."

Before Flint can tighten his grip, Agony rushes on. "And if any witnesses mention a massive gargoyle, they'll have no trouble finding us in the burn unit."

It's the first intelligent thing Agony's said, but Flint still huffs. "Us? You were making a break for it not thirty seconds ago."

"I adapt."

The sirens grow louder. Harbinger checks over Flint's injuries before exhaling a scream through her teeth. "Then I'm driving."

Flint doesn't argue, hauling Agony into the backseat before he hoists himself into the passenger side. Harbinger adjusts the driver's seat almost completely forward before cranking the ignition. Then she curses, hands slamming the top of the wheel.

"My *helmet*."

A plastic sound echoes from the backseat. "Got it."

And there it is, perched next to Agony. Harbinger gives him a guarded look before she puts the car into gear, kicking up rocks as they peel away from the blaze.

NINE

Harbinger

"It's fine," Flint assures her. "You're not hurting me."

Harbinger puts the needle and thread through his tattered wing again. His face doesn't flinch against the mattress, but pain spikes through their connection. She holds the needle between her lips, reaching for scissors from where she straddles his ass. "There's no use lying when I can feel it."

A hint of a smile crosses his lips. "It's not as bad as getting the injuries, I promise."

Remorse swirls in her stomach. She ducks back to the task at hand, minding their connection to know when she pulls the stitches too tight. After a few hours, she's bandaged Flint as best she can. The apothecary was hesitant to give Harbinger all the medicine she asked for, but after a nice tip from their OID funds, the pharmacist bagged the vials and jars without a word.

Healing is another beast, especially if Flint is intent on doing the heavy lifting of their partnership. Thankfully, he doesn't put up a fight when she picks up dinner, but he does insist on being the one to feed Agony.

As she clears their dishes, the cell phone on the counter vibrates. *OID calling*. Again. She silences it as breaking news blares from the television.

"Is that about us?"

"The fire." Flint's big body sprawls across one of the queen beds, next to Agony bound to a rickety chair.

Video flashes across the screen. Black smoke rises from the charred remains of Reid's house as firefighters gather around the sopping mess. Then Reid's face fills the screen.

Agony's head tilts, searching for something until he realizes Harbinger and Flint are staring at him. "Aw, don't look at me like that."

Then the TV jumps to a crude sketch of a massive creature with muddled green skin and fangs.

"Police are looking for this man, a person-of-interest in the arson."

"Pretty sure that's supposed to be you." Harbinger jerks her chin toward the screen. Flint scans the image with distaste.

"Lucky I wasn't with you when we checked into the motel."

Luck has nothing to do with it. They've been in this business long enough to know when to plan ahead. Finding a cheap motel was the first order of business. No paper trail. No curious front desk clerks. No questions.

"We'll have to lay low for a few days. Which is good, since *you* need to heal." Harbinger cuts off the TV before the broadcast wraps, sinking down on the edge of the bed as Flint makes room for her. "Shame they want to talk to you when we have no idea how it started."

"Could be someone pissed at Reid." Flint winces as he props his back up against the headboard. "Wouldn't be the first defacement to his house, not that I blame them. Where we parked, it's possible no one knew we were in there."

"Still seems dangerous to light a house on fire, even if it is for revenge"

A strange emotion twists through Flint. By the time Harbinger turns to ask him what it is, he looks past her. "Rationality probably doesn't play a big part in it, especially if it was one of the girl's families." His voice is soft, lost in a thought Harbinger almost follows before his brows knit. "Phoenix fire, though: I can't get past that."

"It's not that hard to come by."

When Agony speaks, Harbinger and Flint look toward him. He lifts his brow. "What?"

"Why do you say that? That it's not hard to come by?"

Agony's face is blank. "Because it's not?"

"Why do you think that?"

His eyes tilt toward the ceiling, like he's wracking his brain. "I'm not sure."

Flint sits up straighter. "Did Reid use phoenix fire?"

"I don't know." Agony's gaze drifts as he considers it, reaching back through the depths of his mind. "It was in the dream near the end. Reoccurring. Why?" He looks between them. "*Is* it hard to come by?"

"Nearly impossible," Flint answers, "if you're doing everything above board."

This adds a new dynamic to what happened, unearthing a thousand more questions. Flint and Harbinger dive back into conversation.

"You didn't see anyone at the house?"

"Not when we pulled up. Not when we left. Obviously I was distracted at the end, but..." Harbinger tosses a roll of gauze between her hands.

"Does Reid have someone on the outside? Did he send someone to torch his house to hide evidence?"

"But why would he? I didn't find anything. And why would he destroy it now and not before the OID took everything? Was there something left that he didn't want them to find?"

"Or something only you could find." Flint rubs a charred patch of his beard. "But how would he get in contact with someone?" He glances to Agony. "Do you know how Reid was getting phoenix fire? What context, how it was used, why it was familiar to him?"

"No."

Flint makes a disgruntled sound.

"Look," Agony snaps, "the details are distorted. It's like you trying to remember dreams after you wake up. My job was to torment Reid when he was asleep. That's it." Agony clinks the cuffs around his wrists. "I could tell you more if you take these off."

Flint barely lets him finish. "Absolutely not."

"Then you're gonna have a hell of a time finding out what happened to those girls."

Agony knows it's a sore spot, glancing toward Harbinger for support. Flint follows his gaze with a pang of betrayal. How could Agony think he stands a chance of Harbinger agreeing with him? Although, he has a point...

But she won't go there. Not when things are too precarious; they nearly died. Flint's still healing. She waves it off. "Forget about it."

Relief sighs into her from Flint. Agony doesn't hide his disappointment, but there's no way to tell if he's speaking the truth. It makes sense, but it could be a ploy. Agony learned all he knows from Reid: lying, manipulation, violence. Conniving his way out of his cuffs to kill them would hardly be out of the question.

Especially since last time, he didn't need to be out of his chains to try.

"We need to figure out a new direction to take. We can get in contact with the ferry into the Break to see if Reid traveled that way. If he didn't take the main route, though, there's no telling where he went, if he was in the Break at all. Besides that, it spans hundreds of miles. We can't search the entirety of it for clues."

"Maybe the Timber pack knows something." Flint tugs on the

bandage around his wrist until Harbinger swats his hand away. "I can leave a message for them when we call the ferry outpost. Probably be a while before they get back to us, though, depending on the next time they make a visit to town."

With a sigh, Harbinger drops back on the bed. "The OID's stored evidence had nothing on it. Reid's house is gone. Which leaves us with…"

Her traitorous gaze jumps to Agony. A smile flits across his face, but she can't say it. Can't suggest that she's thinking of slipping back inside him. Flint will never go for it. He cuts in before Agony can make another sound.

"We'll talk to the girls' families. The OID botched the investigation already. Who's to say they didn't miss something with them?"

They do have a massive stack of casefiles. "What if they don't want to talk to us?"

"I wouldn't blame them. But if we explain we don't work for the OID, maybe it'll be easier. Our goal is finding their children. If they don't want our help, then…" Weight settles into Flint's eyes as he shrugs. "That's completely up to them."

Harbinger's mind spits out a thought that she immediately strangles.

You could always go to the C-

No. Fuck no. That's a last resort.

The bed frame creaks as Flint adjusts his position, breathing past the pain in his ribs. "And to think, this was supposed to be a risk-free job."

Harbinger worries the inside of her lip enough to draw blood. "We can stop." Bandages cover Flint's feet, swollen skin and ragged blisters draped in gauze. Because they took this job. Because she insisted. "We can take the money we have, and we can leave."

She can't look at Agony and the heat of his eyes on her skin. Watching. Waiting. Flint can't hide the temptation as he considers it, tilting his face up to the ceiling before his eyes slip shut.

"No. We'll keep going." He returns his gaze to Harbinger, some unknown nostalgia tugging at him. "We've made it this far, right?" He tries for an easy smile, but everything about Flint has gravity. Weight. Weariness. "What's the likelihood we get burned alive again?"

She doesn't want to consider it. To jinx it. To put those words into the universe when she knows better than anyone what forces are at play between their physical world and elsewhere.

Like the feeling of Agony probing her thoughts. His attention is a spotlight so bright she can't see past it, can't reach past it to read him. Nothing like Flint, whose emotions are straightforward even when they're dampened. Flint is clear, undisturbed water with the barest of ripples. But Agony's a dark, murky lake, stretching further than she can see. No telling where it ends, how deep it is, if it's connected to someplace else.

Or some*one* else.

The abyss stares back into her, as if their connection goes both ways. Like he can feel her, delve into her, run his fingers over her thoughts until she shudders. It's eerie, being tied to someone and still so out of tune with what they're thinking. Being on the receiving end of her abilities is disconcerting. And giving Agony a look into her feels somehow more dangerous than anything else she's done.

With a twitch of her head, she jerks away from the straining connection and turns back to Flint reclined against the headboard. Flint, who's safe. Flint, who she understands.

"Can we…"

There's too much space between them. Too many bandages, too much skin, too much loss thrumming from her thoughts, from the house, from everywhere they still have to go.

She needs something more.

There's no shame when she slots her thighs on either side of Flint's hips. He stiffens, so aware of another presence in the room.

Agony, the person Flint has to build a wall against. Or maybe Flint's building a wall around Harbinger to keep her away, hidden, protected…trapped.

Since the day Flint touched her, she's been spoiled. After so many years without another person's touch, she felt disconnected from her body, adjusting to the lack of intimacy. It couldn't be a part of her life. She accepted it, knew she could never have that comfort again. Someone's arms wrapped around her, finding her mouth with the heat of theirs, holding on too tightly to let go.

Flint's touch was an accident. Overwhelming and powerful, her head pounding and stomach rolling for days, but she can't bring herself to regret it. Not when she can touch Flint so easily now, the slightest brush of his skin easing the frantic pace of her heart. Little moments swell with emotion when he brushes fingers over her hair, his thighs pillowing her when she sprawls across him.

Even now, he cradles her cheek in the palm of his hand, tracing claws across her scalp like he knows where every hair falls into place. "What do you need?"

It's too much. Feelings well up inside her until they muffle every other connection, every worry, everything between them that they can't solve. All she can focus on is desire. "I need to be close to you."

Now Flint moves without thought, pulling her to his bandaged chest, barely flinching when she settles against him. She closes her eyes. Breathes. Presses her cheek against the thud of his heart. "Not just like this."

Confusion twists through him when she pulls back enough to meet his eyes. Then she takes his hand, guiding the claws out of her hair, tracing down around the curve of her breasts and scraping her nipple through the fabric until it stiffens. Until Flint groans. Until she gasps. "I want you to touch me."

Flint sucks in a breath the same time Agony does. Both their eyes jerk toward him.

"Don't stop on my account." But the humor in Agony's voice is heavier, dipped in something darker, burning through the pit of Harbinger's stomach.

Flint hesitates, brushing hair back from her face. "I need to keep an eye on him."

So worried about keeping her safe when she's asking, *begging* for the connection she needs. He's focused on Agony. Keeping Agony at bay. Ensuring Agony doesn't get close to her, when she would take that risk if it meant getting close to Flint.

"I don't care if he sees." Her fingers dust down the line of Flint's jaw until his eyes fall shut. "Because you're the one who gets to touch me."

A battle rages behind Flint's eyes...before he wraps his hand around hers to guide it away. Rejection sinks into her stomach, splashing like a rock until all the heat between her thighs fizzles out.

"I don't want to be distracted," he breathes. "And I don't know how much I can do —" Bandages tighten when he flexes his fingers. "Like this."

Any movement sends pain lancing through him. It makes sense, but her lips still twist to keep from trembling. Why does she care? It's sex. One time. It doesn't change their partnership. But every feeling inside her — from Flint and her and Agony — sends cracks beneath her surface, screaming with steam like she might burst.

"What if..." Flint holds her cheek in his palm, bringing her eyes back to him. "You touch yourself the way I tell you. Right here." He grips her ass, grinding her along his thigh. Wet heat sizzles to life in her core. "Would you like that?"

Already, she's jerking apart the buttons of her catsuit before Flint clamps a hand over hers. Agony jumps in.

"I'll shut my eyes!"

But Flint leans toward him, gripping the back of Agony's chair and spinning it toward the wall. Flint turns back to Harbinger.

"Good?"

Agony answers instead. "Great. Can't see anything."

Flint snorts his distaste until a smile ticks onto Harbinger's face, buttons slipping from the clasps on her catsuit. It drifts over her shoulders, draped over her breasts, framing the skin she always keeps hidden. Flint waits for her to finish, but she doesn't move except to trail her fingers up the deep V of her suit. Her grin grows when Flint's narrowed eyes flick to hers.

"Someone's taking her time."

"I kind of like this." She grinds over his thigh, mouth taunting him out of reach. "Big, bad bodyguard isn't in control anymore."

She lowers her lips, then drags her tongue along the thick line of his tusk, obscene when she swirls her hips in the loose grip of his hands. Arousal spikes in him as he chuckles, sinking back to a deeper incline. With a scowl, she chases his mouth until he's the one smirking.

"I told you before…" His talon traces down the line of her suit, outlining her breasts. An involuntary shiver rockets through her, feeding the easy line of his smile. "I don't need to be rough to control you."

The shift in his demeanor is palpable. Broad shoulders splayed across the headboard, giving her all his attention. Not distracted by work or danger or Agony, whose shadowy flames flicker a little higher.

"In fact…"

At Flint's voice, Harbinger jerks her attention back to him, biting a whimper in half when he flips open a clasp of her suit with a claw. "I bet I could have you do exactly what I want without touching you."

The thought cinches deep in her stomach. Flint pouts to mimic her, dragging his talon up to her mouth. She parts her lips without thought when he guides his finger inside.

"But you wouldn't like that, would you, baby?"

This time, she can't fight the sound, writhing against his leg as he brushes the pads of his fingers against her jaw. Every touch ignites her. "Because you want me to touch you, don't you?" He withdraws the finger from her mouth, hand closing delicately around her throat. Never pressing tighter. Keeping her lovingly caged. "Because why?"

The heat is unbearable. Each touch is never enough for her, and still, it's so much. Filling her with Flint's desire, teasing out her own until her clit aches from wanting him. He brings his mouth close, brushing lips against hers, so painfully sweet she wants to cry. He answers the question himself.

"Because it's mine."

If there's a sound from Agony, it's covered by Harbinger's groan, hips stirring until Flint's eyes leave a scorching trail down her body. Laughter rumbles out of him, low and hot. She's scared she's left a wet spot on his leg, pitiful and needy, when he instructs her. "Touch what's mine. Play with that pussy for me."

Her fingers jerk at the remaining buttons of her suit to get against her clit, shuddering when his tusks brush her mouth as he growls.

"Make my baby's pussy feel good."

She circles herself with two fingers, leaning into his palm encircling her throat.

"One finger. Just your clit."

A groan slices out of her, rife with irritation. She lifts her chin to look at him, curling her hand into a fist until only the middle finger is left against her clit. A smile darts across Flint's face, but he lets her get going again before his voice cuts her off.

"Slow."

She tests his limits. Maintaining the same sharp speed until she finds the rhythm that makes her hiss, honing on her clit with a tight pattern. Her haughty look doesn't go without notice, but Flint doesn't move. Doesn't tighten his grip. Doesn't let his brows sink into a scowl. Just lowers his voice to little more than a whisper.

"If you don't slow down, I'm gonna lay you on the other bed

and make you beg for my attention."

The words jerk her to a halt. "Please don't —"

"Then all you have to do is listen." His head tilts, finger trailing over her bare skin, leaving a scorching path. "Is that so hard?"

It's pitiful how she nods. Forcing her fingers to a glacial pace, doing nothing more than teasing. That's exactly what Flint wants, and she hates to admit he's right. That all he needs are soft, well-placed words to have her desperate to do exactly as he says.

"That's right, baby."

Everything about him is big, a shield against anything they might encounter. But like this, his body is luxurious, letting her stretch and strain against him, laid out across his chest and draped over his thigh.

As close as she can get.

His hand still cradles her throat, keeping her head from lolling back. Agony does the same in the corner of her eye, head resting back against the chair as he focuses on the ceiling.

He looks tense. Twisted tight, like the sounds of Flint and Harbinger are doing things to him.

But right now, all that's coming out of Harbinger are squeals of frustration. "Come on…"

"I said slow."

"I'm not moving my finger." She finds her loophole, keeping her wrist locked in place as she winds her hips toward it. Flint's unamused, but a light flicks into his eyes. Harbinger already aches with regret.

"I guess I can't blame you." He brushes back a strand of her hair. She wants to beg for mercy. "Got to take whatever you can get, huh? Since you don't get to be filled."

Fuck, she hates it. Craving the wholesome stretch that comes from Flint working himself inside her. Making room for himself between her legs, in the back of her throat, never as rough and reckless as she wants. Always careful, even when he's splitting her open. It makes her body burn.

"But I could…" She reaches between his legs where she knows he's hard, but he stops her wrist with a click of his tongue.

"No, you can't. You want me to rest, right?"

Fuck her logic. Fuck her trying to be reasonable. She wants his dick, and she wants it *now*. But he's intent on torturing her tonight, guiding her hand back between her legs, drawing circles with her finger at her entrance.

His hand withdraws from her neck. "You can have one finger inside."

She slumps forward, cursing into his shoulder. As if that's close to what she needs. As if it's a gift and not an unbearable tease. Still, she sinks over her middle finger, muttering beneath her breath. "It feels like nothing."

Flint's laugh rumbles beneath her. "I doubt that very much. You've been spoiled getting this dick whenever you want." He tilts her chin up with a talon. "Haven't you?"

TEN

Harbinger

Flint's simper makes her squirm, a lash of meanness that she laps up every time he gives it to her. Unpredictable, a contrast to every other way he speaks to her. Now he's pitying, mocking in the sweetest way.

"Maybe I should save my cock for special occasions. Is that what you need me to do?"

Her hips jerk against her paltry finger, slotting another inside as she groans. "*Please* don't take it away."

"But I have to, Harbinger." Flint reaches between her legs to withdraw her second finger. "Because you hate listening to the rules. You always want to break them. You have to learn to be patient. To have some restraint."

She drags her teeth into his shoulder and earns a sound in response. "You're actually *fucking* killing me."

"I would never do that to you." His lips press soft and sweet to the crown of her head while he tortures her to the edge of sanity. "But we have to see if you can follow the rules. If you show me you can tonight, maybe I'll give it back to you next time."

She groans, pitching backward, nearly toppling off his lap. Flint keeps a hand around her waist.

"Get your lube. And a toy." His lip twitches. "Pick whichever you want, but I have a feeling I know which."

He eases her off of him, and she trips on her own shaky legs, stumbling down to her knees by her suitcase. The orc dildo's not as big as Flint, but given the years she spent unable to touch anyone else, she got a lot of use from it. It should have been a hint to where her head was at when she ordered the largest model they had four years ago.

There wasn't a gargoyle replica back then. Flint's grin has been insufferable since she confessed that she'd checked.

But a toy is nothing compared to the real thing. The distinct line of Flint's arousal shows through his sweats, and she salivates at the thought of getting him in her mouth again.

Agony's fists clench against the arms of the chair. Flint catches it with a smirk before he shows Harbinger where he wants her.

"Oh, come on," she scoffs.

But Flint isn't joking, tapping a half-bandaged claw against the headboard.

Her arms fold across her chest. "We don't have the best history with headboards."

Flint looks wicked. "I'd argue we have the *best* fucking history."

That brash audacity makes her knees weak, one hand skirting out to steady her on the TV stand. Gripping the dildo around the shaft, she holds Flint's gaze as she steps up onto the bed. Doesn't matter that he's sitting, his face barely a foot below hers. She's the one trembling when he instructs her.

"Get it wet. I want it sloppy. I want to hear every time you take it."

She clicks open the lube, drizzling it over the length of the toy. Once it's slick in her hands, she slams the suction cup against the headboard right next to Flint's ear.

He gives a flick of his brow.

She'll have to do more than that to get to him. One of her fists twists over the toy's massive girth before she adds her other hand, stroking with her palms v'd underneath. Just the way he likes.

But Flint doesn't look at what her hands do. Doesn't pull his gaze away from hers until she drags her sloppy fingers between her thighs.

"Wet enough?"

His smirk stirs her stomach. "You tell me."

The toy hangs deliciously heavy from the headboard, dripping and ready. The thought of Flint like that makes her clamp her teeth. "Can't you just fuck me?"

"No."

Bastard. He's enjoying this too much. He tilts his head toward the toy.

"Now show me. Show me why I should take that pussy next time. Why I should give it exactly what it's begging for." The heat of his eyes bores straight between her thighs. "Why I should remind you that it's mine."

A strangled sound comes from Agony. Harbinger glances between them, afraid the reminder of his presence will ruin the moment. But there's a smug set to Flint's mouth, the kind that tightens the lines in Harbinger's body. The kind that makes her want to smear that mouth between her thighs and beg exactly like Flint said she would.

"All right over there?" Flint asks.

Ever casual, Agony hums his assent, but he's straining. Warring with the same tension in his body as Flint's emotions surface into Harbinger. Restraint, jealousy, possession blooming deep in her stomach. "Now," Flint turns back to her. "Fuck it."

There's only one way to follow his orders when the toy is this close to him. A way that requires her ass against the headboard, draping a thigh over Flint's shoulder as she works back. A glory hole without the hole, with Flint acting as the wall.

He planned this.

Fucker.

But she won't back down. Not when Flint's finally dipping into this delicious pool of playing fast and loose. Harbinger turns her back to the wall to match him, but Flint's not done giving orders.

"Take your suit down to your knees. Don't take it off."

Her gaze cuts to Agony. From this angle, he can make her out in his periphery, eyes twitching toward her.

She could move. Press back against the headboard, take herself out of his line of sight, but heat coils in her at the thought of stripping down out of his reach. Of toying with the mysterious creature she can't understand. Of teasing the person that drives Flint mad. Of playing with fire.

And then, Flint's voice snaps, making both of them jolt.

"Keeping your eyes on the wall?"

Agony's gaze slips smoothly back to the painting in front of him. "Yes sir."

It's intentional, Flint directing her where to put the toy, keeping her on the brink of Agony's vision. A reminder of who she belongs with. Belongs *to*. It trills through her.

Deliciously torturous, and not just for Agony. His eyes flicker, on the verge of catching Harbinger behind him. The thought of him seeing her bare sends sparks along her skin. She pulls her arms from her sleeves, trailing fingers down the dip in her waist. Tight fabric clings to her ass before she works the suit over her hips and drags it down her thighs.

Flint curses a breath. Agony wavers, tempted to twist his head and get a look, but he doesn't. Only lets the sides of his eyes tilt toward her, enough to see her curves in blurry focus.

She takes her place against the headboard. Both she and Flint face the room, her eyes narrowed on him beside her. He smirks. "Don't knock the headboard against the wall, will you?"

She fights a smile, pressing her ass against the headboard as she reaches between her legs for the toy. "I can't stand you."

Talons skirt along her hips as she tries to steady herself, but in this position, there's no way. Flint reminds her of it, hiking her closest thigh onto his shoulder, her calf draped down his chest as she tries to work the toy inside her.

It nudges between her folds. Her chin drops to her chest, weight settling onto Flint. He taps her leg until she meets his eyes.

"Watch me while you take it."

Teeth drag into her lip when the toy sinks inside. Her head falls back, but she focuses on Flint as she takes each inch, lifting and sinking lower again. Arousal stirs in Flint at the way her eyes widen, noises strangled in her throat, eyelashes fluttering.

She only has the toy halfway inside before Flint squeezes her thigh on his shoulder. "Stop there."

Her hands scramble for something to hold onto. "Gods, you're *killing me.*"

Flint drags his lips against her hip, down into the crease that meets her thigh, sinfully slow and teasing. Once her standing leg is quivering, he pulls back. "Now fuck it 'til you come."

Past her whimper, she takes aborted strokes along the toy to stretch herself over the middle. Every circle of her hips sounds filthy, muffled by the sounds of her heavy breathing, headboard nudging the wall. Flint's mouth is hot and open against the outside of her thigh. His lips leave a trail of synapses firing, heightening her arousal with his as she groans in frustration. "It's not deep enough."

"Too bad: make it deep enough."

Her catsuit strains against her knees, keeping them close together. It's agonizing to be unable to sink to the hilt, to not have Flint, fucking herself on this poor substitute while he mocks her.

And still, it's enough to wind her closer to release, lube dripping down her thigh. Flint catches it on a fingertip and smears it back across her clit. Her body jerks, but then his hand is gone, brows lifting as if she should know better.

"I told you…" His teeth dig into the flesh of her thigh. "To make my pussy come."

Every word is level, measured, unbothered, and Harbinger wants to scream. He got her addicted to it — to *him* — the first night he touched her. He knows exactly what he's doing now. Her frantic fingers find her clit as she tries to sink deeper, but Flint's grip on her ankle against his chest keeps her off balance.

"Half of it," he reminds her, dragging tusks against her hip before he bites into the swell of her ass.

Her eyes clench shut, fingers fumbling to find that pattern against her clit. "Oh my fucking *gods*…"

Flint's smirk curls against her skin. "It's just me."

Nothing compares to the slow drag of his mouth, sending sparks wherever he touches her. She comes like that, heel digging into Flint's chest, both her legs shaking, one hand gripping for his hair. He keeps her upright, looping kisses against her thigh, ribbed tongue dragging against the skeletal patterns of her skin. When her eyes open, it's to him looking up at her. Reverent. Devoted. Enough to make her knees weaker than the orgasm.

Agony pants in his chair, like he's the one that came apart. Flint doesn't let Harbinger rest, easing her off of the toy and back onto her feet before he turns her to face the wall. She presses her breasts against it, trying to keep her thoughts straight, lascivious memories from its surface trailing through her. "What are you…?"

Flint lifts his shoulder in invitation. "Climb up."

She laughs, but his face is blank. It wraps a rope around her desire and tugs it toward him.

"Get on," he demands. Flint jerks his chin toward the suit clinging for dear life to her legs. "And take that off."

It's torture. There's no other explanation. So she returns the favor, leaning down toward his mouth as she strips off the rest of her suit. His self-control is infuriating. Admirable. All he does is lower his lashes as she bites her lip.

When she straightens to face the wall, he gives her no warning.

Nothing more than a hand on her ass as he lifts her in one palm.

Her fingers scrabble against the wall, trying to find purchase as he guides her bent knees to either of his shoulders. It's dicey, threatening her balance when she moves, but Flint bears her weight with his hands locked around her hips.

Even with his injuries, moving her is barely a task, muscles corded through his neck and arms. Her fingers dig into his hair to steady herself against the hypnotizing lock of his eyes. Like she's a bunch of grapes dangling over his mouth, waiting for him to take a bite.

"Do it, Harbin." He keeps her legs spread open, face between her thighs, breath ghosting her clit. "Ride my face."

Her legs wobble at the sight. "I can't," she grits through her teeth. Flint won't accept any excuses.

"You can. Remember your colors?"

She pants, resting her forehead against the wall. "Yes."

"Tell me."

Her eyes clench shut. "Green is go, yellow is slow, red is stop."

"Are you green?

"Yes."

"Then you have to let go."

The words scrape deep, a heavier meaning that she can't look at. The bond between them cinches. She curls her fingers against the wall, grinding down toward his mouth.

"You know…"

Agony's voice jolts through both of them, drawing their attention. Flint doesn't let her fall.

It almost seems like Agony's melted. At least, as much as he can while chained to the chair. His eyes stay focused on the portrait before him. Dark flames lick across his head, voice scraping out like he's swallowed smoke. "Hotel art is an unappreciated medium."

If she could think of anything but Flint's tongue, she might laugh. But Flint's brows knit. Not in annoyance: in competition.

The coil in her stomach notches tighter.

Agony continues, the dark flames atop his head flaring higher. "You can see anything you want in it."

Flint turns back to Harbinger, brooking any argument. "Ride my *fucking* mouth."

Both her hands against the wall, relying wholly on Flint to keep her upright, she sinks down.

"That's my girl," Flint murmurs against her clit. "Look how good you ride for me, baby."

There's no hiding it. He can see it all with her perched above him. Her breath quivering, legs spread achingly wide, his tusks teasing inside her thighs. His eyes flick up toward her. She sinks lower, dragging against the widest part of Flint's tongue, smearing over the ribs.

"This, for example..." Agony's voice curls like a snake. "The flowers." His tongue slips over his lips. Hot and deadly, making Harbinger's legs tense. She shouldn't be thinking about it. Shouldn't be thinking about *him.*

"Every petal spread," he muses. "Could run your fingers over them. Between..."

His voice trails off in a moan the same time Harbinger's does. Flint laps against her clit until it's slick enough that she slips down his chin.

"Flint —"

His mouth is excruciating, teasing her clit until it *aches.* Her nails dig tracks into the wallpaper. Flint doesn't stop. Not until his tongue buries completely inside, Agony's panted breaths mixing with hers.

Flint drags her off his mouth, keeping her hovering above him, lips inches from her clit "Whose is it?"

"Yours."

He presses on her ass, encouraging her to move, to fuck herself against his tongue.

"Like I could..." Agony squirms in the chair when Harbinger

whimpers. Flint teases circles against her, letting her use his mouth. Guiding her hips in stirring motions, her breasts bouncing with each thrust, trapped above him.

"Who does this pussy belong to?" Flint growls

"You." She doesn't try to clamp down on it. Neither does Flint, as if he wants their neighbors to hear. Wants *Agony* to hear. Wants Harbinger's every sound amplified.

She's so close. High on the adrenaline of being held aloft, of Agony this close to seeing them, of being tormented and never quite given what she needs. And Flint's textured tongue, marking every inch of her cunt, melding over her clit when she stretches her arms up the wall to find something to hold onto.

Then Flint's floodgates open. Pouring his emotions into her, arousal and possession and protection screaming straight to her clit. It's electric when he touches his tongue to it, making her hips stutter as he snarls.

"Whose is it?"

"Yours! It's yours, it's all fucking *yours.*"

His eyes burn into hers before he buries his mouth against her. "Then *tell him.*"

And she does, screaming through her release, fingers scraping into the wall as Flint's horns gouge the wallpaper. He's the only thing keeping her steady. When she comes down, Flint takes his time pulling his mouth off her. Eating until she's shaking, quivering, pleading with him to stop while her hips keep rolling over his tongue.

His chest rises and falls when he pulls her down, trailing claws against her scalp as she tries to think of anything past this. Atop Agony's head, the flaming shadows return to wisps, his eyes leaving bright spots on the blooming picture.

ELEVEN

Agony

By the time there's movement behind Agony, his head hasn't stopped swimming.

"I'll watch tonight." Sounds like Harbinger's still breathless, too. Agony's tongue drags over his lips.

Flint tries to argue, straining like he's pushing himself upright, but the movement stops.

"Yes," Harbinger insists. "You need to heal. And you stayed up last night." There's a smile in her voice when it echoes off a different wall, as if she's turned away. "You're not even going to be able to protect *yourself* if you're exhausted." Fabric rustles, like she's trying to trap him in bed by tucking in the sheets. "You can sleep between us. I'll keep watch from the other bed."

"Wake me every hour," Flint grumbles. Glaring red eyes come into focus in the plastic reflection over the picture as he rolls to face Agony.

Flint is tense for minutes after until his breathing slows,

settling into sleep. Harbinger completes her nightly ritual, flicking on the television as she searches for her toothbrush. Once her weight settles into bed, Agony takes the chance to speak.

"Possessive, isn't he?"

Her sounds stop, frozen. Flint's reflection doesn't move. Without seeing Harbinger, without a glimpse of what she's doing, Agony can feel her. Her breath held like she's trespassing, sneaking into someplace she knows she isn't allowed. A rush of adrenaline sweeps into her, and she ducks under the sign warning her to *Keep Out*.

"Not until you showed up."

Agony's head tilts dreamily. "You're welcome, then."

There's the barest hint of a laugh before she stops it. She shouldn't be finding humor in the thing that tried to kill her.

"You don't question your abilities, do you?" he asks. There's no response. Agony didn't expect one, sinking down in the chair. "You see what you see, and you know it's true. Not much room for error."

"Yes..."

"'Yes, but...'?"

There's a snap in her voice. "There's no 'but.'"

"Sure there isn't."

He pictures her stewing from across the room before her voice surprises him. "There *was* no 'but' before I touched you."

Agony's smile widens. "That sounds like the beginning of a love story."

She groans under her breath.

It could end there. She could cut off the conversation, leave them in silence for the rest of the night...but she won't, he has no doubt. Daring little thing.

"I never questioned what I saw, because it's always been true. With objects, I see the past. With people, I see the present. With you..."

The bed creaks under Flint. They both freeze, but he doesn't wake. Harbinger's voice lowers.

"I don't know if what you show me has ever happened. Ever will happen. You're so Between. Not real, but not imaginary. Not alive, but not dead."

"Like you?"

There's a pause. "Like me." And then, after another long moment: "You've been in my dreams."

It's not a question, so Agony doesn't answer.

She presses further. "Well?"

"Turn me around."

"Are you connected to me, too?"

"I'll tell you if you turn me around."

She scoffs. "Well, that answers that." But there's an open space at the end of her sentence, an uncertainty that Agony leaves to linger in the air. It thrills him, how he can anticipate her. How she's glancing at Flint, making sure he's undisturbed before her socked feet touch the carpet.

There it is.

Footsteps grow closer behind him until her presence engulfs him, like sinking into a warm bath. His eyes shut before something hard and plastic presses against the base of his neck.

"Pull any shit, and I'll beat you to death with this room phone. As long as it takes."

When she turns him, his grin is radiant. It's a shuffle to maneuver him without getting too close, but soon, he's met with Flint's dozing form. "What did you give him?" Agony murmurs as she crosses back to the other bed.

"Healing potions to fight infection. But it's hitting him harder than expected." Worry crosses her face, flecked with shades of remorse. "He needs the rest. If he doesn't take it willingly, his body will make sure he does."

She props herself back against the other headboard, one pillow stuffed behind her. It's different than the motel linens Agony expected. Her case matches the pillow pressed to Flint's chest as he curls around it in sleep.

"You bring your own bedding," Agony notes.

"Have to." Harbinger slips her feet beneath the worn gray of her sheets. Her shirt is oversized, but he can make out the bare skin of her legs, the column of her throat under the low-slung collar.

"So you don't have to wear the suit to bed."

The shirt pools up toward her thighs when she shifts, revealing the shorts underneath. Agony drags his eyes up to hers, but she looks away, back to the casefiles splayed before her. Agony lifts his chin toward her pajamas.

"That his?"

She doesn't look up. "Start answering my questions, or I'm gonna turn you back around."

Right: their deal. "Yes, there's some connection. No, I'm not sure what it is."

"You don't seem to know much of *anything*." She flips over a notecard, emphasizing the words again. "But you *have* been in my dreams."

The corner of his lips turns up. "That's sweet, darling."

She moves to stand. His hands jerk up in surrender. "Ok, ok!"

Clattering chains shatter the quiet. Both their eyes dart to Flint. Agony holds the breath he doesn't need. The line of Flint's brow knits, teeth grinding. Then he rolls onto his other side, settling Harbinger's pillow against his chest. Neither of them moves until his breathing evens out again.

"Yes," Agony whispers. "I've been in your dreams."

"How much?"

"Enough to see what your mind goes back to."

Her eyes harden, but she doesn't concede anything. "Then why do you keep looking?"

"I like seeing you scared." Dark flames curl wickedly up his face. "It's what I do."

Her eyes narrow, but she doesn't seem put off by it. Doesn't continue the conversation either, returning to her notes as the TV hums. Now she's unfocused, lifting a piece of paper between her fingers, hovering before she remembers to set it down.

"You've touched Flint too, right? You two are connected?"

Harbinger's eyes slide to Agony before she picks up another notecard. "Yes..."

"What does it feel like when he dreams?"

Her fingers flick back and forth over the card's edge, hesitant to answer. Like she's giving something away that she shouldn't. "It's more and less." A self-deprecating laugh escapes at her poor description. "Emotions are more refined in dreams. Less detailed. Classic, discernible blocks compared to the shades and degrees when someone's awake."

That's how she feels to Agony, when he dips into her sleeping mind. She clicks open a pen, scrawling across a sheet of paper. "In Flint's dreams, happiness is yellow. But when he's awake, sometimes it's amber, sometimes it's gold, sometimes it's honey."

When she glances toward Flint, her face softens, as if this is one of the few moments he's this relaxed. This free of worry. This content.

"The medicine definitely has an effect. Usually, he can't fall asleep for hours." Her eyes flash to Agony. "So don't get your hopes up. But when he does sleep, it's never well. I don't know what he dreams about, but more often than not, it's..." Her brows knit. "Unnerving. Full of anguish. Bitter."

But she can't ask him about them, Agony suspects, because that would mean addressing the feelings that arise in her own dreams. Already, she darts past them, edging back to safer territory.

"He doesn't hold back emotions while he sleeps. I don't think he can. But he keeps such a handle on them when he's awake that his sleeping feelings can be overwhelming. Ebb and flow with no rhyme or reason. At least, none that I can see." She knocks a stack of notecards against her knee. "I feel the reaction, but I have no idea what caused it."

"Do you prefer that? Having access to his emotions without a filter?"

"What? No." The words leap from her mouth. Agony lifts his brows as pink warms her cheeks. "I know why he controls his emotions," she explains. "I know he wants to keep from overwhelming me." Teeth dig into her lip. Agony's eyes follow it. "But it's like he's holding something else back. When I only get a piece of whatever he's repressing, it's almost worse, because I know there's something that he's not saying. Something he's trying to spare me from."

She turns her attention back to the documents, but her focus is elsewhere. "And it's not fair for me to bring it up, because most people don't have this sort of insight. I'm invading his privacy. So he hides his feelings, and I pretend like I haven't felt them, and we both..." She exhales. "Lie to ourselves. And each other."

"Have you told him that?"

She leans back from the piles of cards. "No."

Agony does his best to cross his arms. "Do you ever address your *own* feelings?"

"I get enough of other people's emotions. I don't need to slog through mine." She shakes her head, shuffling the cards together. "And I'm not interested in advice from someone who was born, what, two days ago? Not to mention the horrendous people skills."

"My entire purpose is to pinpoint what distresses people. And I've been out in the world for at *least* a week, thank you."

She won't tell Agony much more than that. The rest of the night passes under the buzz of the TV, her notes scrawled across paper between pockets of conversation that break off any time Flint stirs. When the morning news begins, Agony rocks in his chair. "You should turn me back around."

Cards scatter across the floor when she fumbles to her feet. "Shit. Right." She tiptoes across the space, warring with guilt when sunlight starts to creep up Flint's body.

"Don't worry," Agony purrs as she turns him back to face the wall like she's been tampering with evidence. "It'll be our little secret."

TWELVE

Agony

There's some kind of syndrome — Agony can't remember the name — where prisoners develop affection for their captors. Or maybe it's captors sympathizing with their victims.

In either case, he's sure it's fake. But it does lead him to wonder exactly what's happening in these motel rooms.

Harbinger and Flint are captivating. Alluring. Entertaining enough to pass the hours, even if Agony has no control over what happens in this real world.

If he did, things would move a lot more quickly. And he'd add a lot more sex. When Flint and Harbinger hunch over the casefiles for the thousandth time, Agony imagines a knock on the door to disrupt the plotline. An introduction of a new character. A resurrection of someone assumed long-dead. A sudden shift to another environment.

But no knock comes, except when their food is delivered or housekeeping offers extra towels. And, in a way, that mundane blip is surprising for someone used to nightmares.

Dreams don't follow logic. Patterns rarely extend for more than a few nights, which becomes predictable in its unpredictability. The real world has very different patterns, ones that Agony can use to surmise where the day will take them.

In this arc, for example — the "Flint needs a few days to heal" arc — Harbinger spends much of the nights watching television. Or, looking at the television, at least. Because her mind is elsewhere, gaze flicking over to Flint at random intervals. By this point, Agony faces the room full time, so he can see whatever show she's not-watching. He becomes familiar with the other paintings on the walls, as well as the newspaper puzzles Flint begrudgingly hands him after breakfast.

Flint doesn't sleep long. But with the medicine, he does sleep deeply, which leaves time for Harbinger and Agony's stilted conversations. She stays on her bed, flipping through case notes, and Agony treads carefully. Speaks softly. Asks questions to catch her off guard. If he lets the silence stretch long enough, she doesn't realize she's divulging until it's too late.

But that sounds sinister. And Agony isn't trying to trick her into anything...probably. Hard to say, when he's not quite sure what's "appropriate." The Reid case is fair game for discussion, although it leads to Harbinger quizzing him about things he can't answer. Broaching the topic of Flint is a minefield. Some questions soften all the lines in her face, while others make her clam up for the rest of the night. And Agony is relatively certain that telling Harbinger he wants to see, not just hear, the way she looks when Flint fucks her is risky.

Or maybe Agony should go for it. Those nights with Flint asleep between them, it almost seems possible. Harbinger's scowl heats when Agony smirks, a blade fresh off the iron, fingers playing absently with the edge of her shirt. When Agony asks something she hasn't considered — or something she doesn't want to — there's a rewarding, surprised look in her eyes.

He fantasizes about it more than once. Imagines Harbinger

stalking across the motel room, slipping under his bound arms and against his chest. All that skin she never shows grinding torturous circles into his lap, hair slipping out of her braid when she makes good on the threats to shut him up.

Never mind that Agony's fantasies usually end with Flint catching them and making them pay for their indiscretions by fucking them both into the sheets.

Agony should get back to planning their demise. Given the chance to get Harbinger under his hands again, though, he's not sure if he'd rather give her a final death or a little one.

Most surprising of all is how Flint allows Agony to participate in their conversations. A necessity, since they're all trapped in a tiny room together, and Flint won't let Agony out of his sight. But it's not to be nice. Agony realizes that when Harbinger smooths burn ointment over Flint's chest, pressing against his side in the bed...

It's so Agony doesn't forget that the two of them are together.

Flint heals for a few days. Harbinger cleans and dresses his wounds. On the news, the search for Flint's lookalike dies down in the wake of public appreciation. Turns out people enjoy seeing a serial killer's house burned to the ground.

Who would have thought?

As soon as Flint is well enough to travel, they find a different hotel room every night. They return to swanky suites once they're far enough from the arson, and their days find a new pattern. Visit the families of the missing girls. Leave Agony alone in the backseat, until the day he tries to kick out one of the windows. They lose any OID tails on their way to a new hotel, settling in to scan through another chunk of the casefiles.

"What I don't get..." Harbinger flattens a nearly-empty folder. "Is how the OID never followed up on some of these."

Agony works through a crossword puzzle with a giant marker, his Flint-approved writing utensil. Harbinger places her hand on a stack of folders brimming with paperwork. "Some of these follow protocol: interviews, transcripts, evidence logs." Her hand moves to a smaller stack with far more folders, but far fewer files. "And these have — what, a page or two each? There aren't pictures in half of them. There's no consistency."

Flint looks up over his glasses. "Which one's the most recent?"

She rifles through the stacks until she comes to a smaller folder. "This one: Evolet Albrun. She disappeared around the time they arrested Reid." Harbinger drops the paltry pages back onto the table. "No picture. Classified as a runaway. Looks like the OID scheduled an interview with the parents and never followed up." Harbinger unlocks their cell phone. "If we leave early enough tomorrow, we could get there before dinner."

"Did the ferryman into the Break get back about Reid?"

"Yes," she sighs, zooming into the map. "He said Reid didn't look familiar. Since there's only one ferry that holds a couple cars, we can rule it out. I still asked him to get a message to the Timbers, but he said there's been a lot of commotion recently. No telling when they'll get back to us." Harbinger shifts her attention to the sparse information in the girl's file. "I'll have to talk to the parents alone." Her eyes narrow on Agony. "Since we can't take you in. Or leave you alone for an hour, apparently."

"It's for the best." Flint takes the phone from her hand, setting a new alarm when a call comes through. *OID*. He swipes it away. "The three of us on their doorstep would be overwhelming, at the very least. And if you show them what you can do, it might be easier for them to talk to you. The OID's already burned them. Can't imagine they feel trusting."

Before sunrise, the three of them are on the road. It's a trek to the Albrun home, but eventually, Flint pulls up to the curb on a side street and double-checks the address. Cottages crowd the neighborhood, connected by stepping stones through a massive garden. Colorful smoke twists from chimneys, an amalgam of talismans decorating thresholds behind elders who call to children picking petals and fruits.

Flint leans over the steering wheel. "Evolet's a witch?"

With a jerk, Harbinger hops out of the passenger seat, slamming a plain black helmet over her head. "The OID didn't put that in her file?"

It's like an airlock when the door shuts behind her, her black-clad form moving down the garden path. Flint and Agony watch her, as does the rest of the neighborhood. She does her best to give a small wave, stopping at the bottom of a set of steps where the front door pulls open.

A man with pale, freckled skin shakes a neighbor's hand before they both descend off the porch. The man — must be Evolet's father – waits as Harbinger removes her helmet. Her mouth moves, and the neighbors in the garden murmur. After a long moment, he steps back to offer her the open doorway.

Flint exhales. Agony reclines across the backseat, propping his feet on the opposing window and its poorly-patched cracks. "Sure you can make it an entire hour with her out of your sight?"

It's a reward when Flint rolls his eyes, resting his elbow on the window sill and running a hand through his beard.

Agony whistles. "Never know what's going on behind closed doors."

"I don't think the family of a missing girl is doing much besides grieving and looking for her." The words are sharper than Agony expected. Still, Flint's eyes cling to the front of the house. "Harbinger will be fine."

"Almost convincing." Agony slips arms behind his head, tapping his toes. He considers not saying anything else, but Flint's fingers worry against the leather keychain. It's going to be a long hour. "I was kidding. Bad joke. She'll be fine."

"Can we not?" Even with the extra sleep Harbinger's given Flint, he's tired. Grumpy at the best of times, from Agony's estimation, and healing took more out of him.

Perfect time for an escape.

But Agony doesn't make an attempt...for some reason. He's

tired from the drive. Wants to annoy Flint. Too many variables. Flint's thermos steams with coffee, wisps rising and disappearing like spirits.

"How much do you know about her?" Agony murmurs.

"This shit again?" Flint rolls his neck to crack some of the tension. "More than you."

Agony hums as irritatingly as he can. "I wouldn't be too sure about that."

Try as he does to hide it, Flint's fists clench. "And why is that?"

"We've had some late-night conversations. Harbinger's a big girl." Agony's tongue rolls lecherously over the words. "Trust me."

Now Flint's claws curl completely around the steering wheel, digging into his palms. Agony's sure he's going to lose it, but instead, Flint growls. "I know plenty."

Such conviction. Agony almost believes him, but Flint's eyes flick out the window, warring with that uncertainty.

Got him.

"Your wings are puffing out again."

"We've been partners for seven years. You get to know each other pretty well in that time."

"I'm sure you *talk*." Agony emphasizes the word. "But how much do you really know? Past the surface-level, the shop talk, the late-night storytelling. Where does she come from? What happened before she met you? What does she know about you?"

"We've talked about our pasts." But there's that tic in Flint's jaw again. The one that appears when Agony gets close to something he shouldn't, a cat pawing a vase. "We know what's important. We know enough."

"How does she feel about her connection to me?"

"We haven't had a moment alone since —"

"How does she feel about *your* connection?"

"She..." But the sentence dies in Flint's mouth. His voice is as soft as Agony's ever heard when it finally comes. "It's overwhelming. Painful. I can't imagine she enjoys it."

"Have you asked her?"

"Do I need to?"

"I'm noticing a trend with you, Jasper." Flint's eyes dart to the rearview. Agony shrugs. "I checked your ID."

"Do not —"

"Everything you do is to protect Harbinger. To keep her safe. To keep her happy." He lists them off on his fingers. "You take the late-night shifts. You keep her away from me. You strangle every little feeling you have that might distract either of you."

Flint doesn't argue. Of course he doesn't; it's a point of pride for him. "It's my job."

"Oh, come on: it's not your job to bury every emotion that might complicate things. Even if it was, that's not why you're doing it. I may have been born last week, but I wasn't born yesterday."

Flint's shoulders tighten. "You don't understand."

"I understand you're scared you'll break her. You wrap her in safety nets, keep everything at a distance — including you." What started as an easy way to push Flint's buttons has spiraled into something else. Something that tugs on Agony's mouth to speak, his words getting ahead of him, heavier than all the carefree ease he's used to. "Harbinger's not the only one handling things with kid gloves."

Flint scoffs. "Harbinger is perfectly capable —"

"Then act like it."

"Like you did at Reid's house?"

It's an abrupt shift. For once, Agony's stunned into silence. An alarm pounds through him, even as he swears he doesn't know what Flint means. "What are you talking about?"

"You told me to set you free so you could save her. You pointed out her helmet in the yard. You made sure we made it out of the fire. Seems like you *care*..." Flint's infuriating, perfect tongue lingers on the word. "About her, too. Somewhere in that abyss of a heart."

Does Agony have a heart? Who knows. Who cares? With a

shrug, he lets his eyes drift out the window. "Night terror, remember? I like seeing fear, and offering to save her was an easy chance for escape. Can't blame a guy for trying."

Flint clicks his tongue. "Come on: that doesn't hold up." Now *he's* the picture of breezy while Agony starts sweating.

"As flattered as I am that you want me to take care of your *partner*, that's a fantasy." Agony forces a smirk across his face. "One I'm happy to partake in the next time you drive her away."

"You trying to start shit?" Flint twists the keys in the ignition, reaching for the radio knob before Agony blurts.

"When you touch her, I can feel it."

Flint's hand hovers over the dial. "What do you mean?"

"The other night, when you two were..." Heat notches at the memory. "I could feel things. Not just from hearing it. Which..." Agony sucks in a breath. "You two could make a career out of that. But even without seeing, I could tell exactly what you were doing."

"Like what?"

There's a challenge in Flint's voice. Like he expects Agony to back down. Like it's a dare. Like Flint wants to hear the words, forbidden and wanton, from Agony's mouth.

Their eyes stay locked in the mirror. "When you curled her hair around your finger. When you unhooked her buttons and brushed against her skin. When you made her come on the end of your tongue..." Agony's eyes slip shut. "It felt like it was happening to me."

The molten red of Flint's eyes shift, hot magma beneath the surface. "If this is your attempt to get me to stop touching her —"

"It isn't." Agony doesn't trust his mouth. Doesn't trust his mind, either, so he says it as simply as he can. "I don't want you to stop touching her."

He can't make out Flint's expression, stoic and unreadable. Maybe the thought disturbs him...

Or maybe he thinks it should.

A car alarm goes off. Flint and Agony jump, but it's just a toady creature fighting with her key fob. When it finally shuts off, she pulls away, staring at the SUV as she passes. Flint doesn't speak again until the other car disappears, as if someone could overhear.

"I won't stop touching her. And if you get off on it too..." Flint doesn't look at Agony again. For some reason, it stings. "So be it."

A spike of heat rushes through Agony. Provocation is his only recourse. "You like knowing I feel every ripple of pleasure your partner does?"

Flint's eyes stay trained on the house. Always working. Always composed. "I don't even think about you."

Agony trails a finger against Flint's neck through the grate until he flinches. "Lately? I'm *all* you think about."

THIRTEEN

Harbinger

It's easier when Flint's with her, the reassuring timbre of his voice like white noise under a weighted blanket. It sets the families more at ease. Or at least, it calms Harbinger, because when she's on her own, her words feel like sand slipping through her fingers.

Evolet's father leads Harbinger through the entryway of their cottage, holding up a hand for her to wait. She tucks her helmet under her arm as she tries not to look at anything too long, as if she's intruding.

You are.

The house feels odd. Bright colors out of place, vibrancy muted by grief. There's a lack of something. Someone. Coats squeeze together on the hooks, and a bright teal jacket clings to the last one. The right size for a sixteen-year-old girl. When Mr. Albrun returns, Harbinger follows him into the living room, giving the jacket a wide berth.

A woman sits on the couch. She looks the same age as Mr. Albrun, early forties with skin a shade lighter than his. When

Harbinger enters, the woman smiles softly, then pushes up suddenly from the seat. "I'll get you something to drink."

"Oh, no, that's ok."

Mrs. Albrun settles back onto the couch as her husband takes his seat beside her. Harbinger does her best to smile.

"It's nice to meet you. I'm Harbinger. And I'm going to record this, if that's ok."

Mr. Albrun takes his wife's hand. Harbinger sets her phone on the coffee table before she sinks down into an armchair, helmet perched on her knees. To their credit, the Albruns appear only mildly interested in the skull pattern of her face. Instead, their attention is held by the end table crowded with picture frames.

One is decorated with glued-on seashells, lovingly sloppy with child's craftsmanship. At its center, a young girl with ginger hair squeals as she pulls a fish into a boat.

Harbinger realizes how quiet it's gotten. How long she's been staring. She shifts her gaze somewhere else.

"You can look." Mrs. Albrun lifts a different picture from the table beside her. The frame has inlays for multiple portraits, but some don't quite fit, cut out and squeezed together. There are three children, two girls and a middle boy with glasses, grinning in first-day-of-school backpacks or leaning together in summer shorts. The eldest wraps her arms tight around both her siblings' as they make faces for the camera.

"Is that Evolet?"

"Yes, Evie. She's always been a good girl. A good sister." Mrs. Albrun's mouth quivers, like she can't decide between a smile or a sob. "People don't look at the pictures any more — not the ones when she was younger. I wish they would." Her fingers trace the curve of Evie's chin, marking the same indentation Mr. Albrun has.

"I wish people would talk about her, like before." Mrs. Albrun sounds far off, like she's talking to herself. "Not the questions or about what happened. Evie is such a big part of our lives, especially when she was — here. We said her name hundreds of times a day and never thought anything of it. *'Evie has rehearsal this afternoon. Evie tried to dye her hair. Evie forgot to take out the trash.'* Mrs. Albrun looks like she wishes Evie could forget it again.

"People don't say her name any more. 'Her.' That's what they call her now. *'Any news about Her? Have they found anything of Hers?'* But mostly, they don't want to bring her up at all. Like it'll hurt too much." Mrs. Albrun presses her lips to Evie's face before she sets the picture back on the table, keeping her eyes on her daughter. "It hurts worse not to talk about her."

It's too familiar. Harbinger perches on the edge of the seat, gloved hands clasped before she's able to talk past her swelling throat. "Is Evie a witch, too? I don't mean to assume —"

"Yes, she is." Mr. Albrun brightens at that. "Very good with plants. Terrible at cooking." That makes both the Albruns laugh. "She's talented with the medicinal side: healing spells, salves, ointments. Wouldn't trust anything she asks you to eat, though."

"I'm guessing you have?"

"Oh!" Mrs. Albrun swats her husband's leg, smiles warm at the memory. "For a holiday, no less. She wanted to try her hand at baking. We should have let her have a practice run. When she set that poor cobbler on the table — she said we were all being dramatic, but after she tasted it…" Laughter bubbles up between them. "She decided we had a point."

They settle contentedly before Mrs. Albrun looks to Harbinger again. "Thank you for indulging me. I know you're not here to recount my memories."

"Well, in a manner of speaking." Harbinger finally sets her helmet on the floor. "I know my showing up here is surprising."

"You're a banshee?"

Harbinger nods. A cloud shifts over the Albruns' expressions.

"So you think she's —"

"Not necessarily. Banshees don't only deal with the dead. I understand it can be confusing, but we — banshees — all have different abilities. It's more about seeing what's Between. Things that defy real-world explanation, using senses most creatures don't have."

"Senses like what?"

"Like —" Harbinger blows out a breath toward the ceiling. Fuck, she's no good at this. "Sorry. Let me start at the beginning. Your daughter — Evie — has been missing for some time."

"Four months."

"And you reported it to the OID."

"Yes. We've hardly heard from them since." Mr. Albrun scowls. "Do you work for them?"

"No." Disgust jumps out before Harbinger can stop it. "I'm a private investigator. The OID asked for help with another case, but we — my partner and I — took over instead."

Mr. Albrun watches Harbinger closely. "What case?"

She's not used to this, exposed without her helmet, her expressions readable. Teeth drag into her lip before she exhales. "We don't know for sure that it's related..." Harbinger's voice shrinks. "But your daughter's information was in the case notes for Raymond Reid."

The air is sucked out of the room. "The serial killer?" Mrs. Albrun whispers. Her head drops into her hands. Mr. Albrun looks distant, gaze unfocused out the window. Harbinger's fingers clamp together.

"I know it's not much reassurance, but there wasn't anything concrete. Just her file. No evidence, no interviews. Nothing like that."

Mrs. Albrun takes a steadying breath before she lifts her head again. Harbinger tries to be delicate when she asks her questions.

"Did the OID tell you anything about what they think happened?"

"No." Frustration laces through Mrs. Albrun as she stands, circling into another room to pull out a stack of papers. They're flyers with Evie's face and information, news articles of other missing girls or arrests. "They took our report. Sent out a detective. Before we finished telling him about the day she went missing, he started asking if she could have run away. Since then, nothing. No updates, even when I call. At first, they said they were following leads. Now, I can't even get a call back."

"The OID noted she could be a runaway." Harbinger's gaze lifts. "But you don't think she is."

"No." There's no hesitation. "She isn't."

The Albruns tell Harbinger all about Evie. Marching band practice that left her legs aching. An advanced statistics class she dreaded and excelled in. Her parakeet familiar that hasn't so much as chirped since she disappeared. None of her friends know where she could've gone. No nefarious secrets. Nothing looming over her.

Why would she leave? What did she have to run away from?

When they finish, the Albruns lean back against the couch, exhaustion threaded through their faces. The kind you can't sleep off, seeping into their bones every moment their daughter is missing.

Mrs. Albrun disappears into the kitchen and returns with a business card, one punch away from a discount. "This is where she was going that day after school." Mrs. Albrun holds it as reverently as she did the picture. "It never stayed in her purse. I always told her to keep it in her wallet, but it must have slipped out."

Harbinger's glove runs over the star-shaped holes centered over pieces of sushi. "Do you want me to read it?" Both Albruns stare before Harbingers explains. "I can see certain things through touch. Only the past. Only what happened while she had the card. But if Evie touched it, I might be able to get a glimpse of what she was doing that day."

"Yes!" Mrs. Albrun thrusts the card toward her. "Please. Anything."

Harbinger reels back in her seat, taking the card between her fingers. "Just don't touch me, please. During or after."

Mrs. Albrun steps back toward the couch. Harbinger pulls off her glove, fingers drifting over the card before they settle on the center punch.

All the threads stretch out in her mind, a tapestry pulled loose, bound with images of Evie's face. Rifling through her purse in school, laughing with a pair of chopsticks in hand, a petty argument outside the restaurant: teenager things. But the most recent touchpoints show Evie's mother pulling the card off the refrigerator. Trying to hand the card to a detective. And before that, slipping the card into Evie's hand as she hurried out the door.

Harbinger hones in on that memory. The last trace of Evie, copper strands pulled out to frame her smiling face. The card slips between her fingers as she presses her cheek against her mother's. It's like seeing a ghost, the last visage of someone so alive.

Then Evie's out the door. The card floats to the ground, forgotten.

It's a skill Harbinger hasn't mastered, pulling emotions from objects, finding anything more than location in time and space. But there isn't any doubt when she taps into the card's final memory of Evie. Harbinger pulls her bare fingers away from its surface.

"I saw her at the front door." Harbinger holds up the back of her hand. "Wearing a metal ring with a pattern cut into it. It was glowing."

Mr. Albrun nods with rapt attention. "We made that ring for her thirteenth birthday, to glow when she was near someone she could trust…" His throat tightens. "So she would always be safe."

What Harbinger can say is too simple, too meaningless in the face of everything else, but it's the one resounding certainty. "Evie was happy. She smiled after you when you went back in the kitchen that morning. You're right; I don't think she would have left you for anything."

Harbinger wishes she could give them more, give them anything real, but this is all she has.

The tremble in Mrs. Albrun's lip is too much to look at.

Harbinger averts her eyes, tugging her glove back on before she digs into her pocket.

"Here: text me your phone number. We'll keep you updated on what we find. Do you have a picture of Evie I could take with me? Something more recent."

Mrs. Albrun takes Harbinger's simple business card while her husband moves toward a hutch in the corner. He pulls out a school portrait with Evie's hair pulled away from her face.

He lingers on the picture before he hands it to Harbinger. She takes it between her gloves, careful not to bend the edges. "Thank you. I'll take good care of it."

He guides Harbinger back to the front door, and she gives a weak wave before she reaches for the knob.

"Do you think she's alive?"

Harbinger's hand hovers in the air. She turns back toward the living room, where Mr. Albrun's hand rests on his wife's shoulder. Dusk outlines the front window. Their home looks safe. Warm, despite the fog hanging over it. Like somewhere their child would want to come back to.

"I don't deal with this sort of thing often." Harbinger clears her throat. "I don't think anything I can say will help. But I want to find Evie. And I hope that she is."

It's the most she can offer. "I'll call you," she adds. "I promise. Every week."

Mrs. Albrun does her best to smile, but Harbinger knows that look. Like she doesn't believe it. Like she's been burned before. Harbinger can't blame her. She steps out onto the porch and pulls the door closed behind her.

Garden flora sways in twilight purples and pinks as Harbinger moves back toward the SUV. From a distance, she can make out Flint's massive shape and Agony's eyes floating in the backseat. She pulls herself into the passenger side, exhaling for what feels like the first time since she stepped inside the house.

Flint locks the doors and keeps his eyes on her. "How'd it go?"

Agony's silent, which is unnerving in its own right. Harbinger turns over the portrait of Evie, clicking on the overhead light so they can all see it.

"She was supposed to —"

"I recognize her."

Flint and Harbinger turn to the backseat. To Agony's gaze hooked on Evie's face.

"You do?" Harbinger's wary. Uncertain. But Agony's fingers curl around the bars on the cage, all his attention on the picture.

There's nothing malicious in his gaze. No wicked intent. Just a tenderness she hasn't seen from him.

"She likes sushi."

They both say it at once. Agony's eyes meet Harbinger's. Her heart thuds. "How do you know that?"

"I don't know." His eyes drift back to the picture. "But she was in the dream."

FOURTEEN

Harbinger

That's the most Agony can give them. *Evie was in the dream.* Anything more devolves into Agony's snarky remarks that he could see more if they'd remove his cuffs, followed by Flint's sharp refusal.

And that's not the only thing they bicker about. Once they pull into the next hotel, Flint cuts off the engine. "We think there's more to your connection with Agony than originally suspected."

Harbinger pinches the corner of Evie's portrait. "How would that work?"

They both shrug in sync. Flint glares in the rearview. "The connection must have forged like it would with any other living thing, even if he's not quite alive."

Harbinger scowls as the dashboard clock clicks to the next minute. "But I don't feel his emotions the way I do with yours. Even when you're both in the same room, I barely get anything from him."

"Maybe his emotions are different." Irritation cuts through

Flint's voice. "You said yourself that you could feel that he wasn't going to…"

Flint trails off. Agony blinks between them. "Wasn't going to what?"

Harbinger leans against the door. "When you put your cuffs around my throat, I could feel you weren't going to hurt me."

The shadowy flames on Agony's head heighten. He smooths them out, reclining in the seat. "Hate to break it to you, babe, but that's wishful thinking."

Flint keeps his eyes out the windshield. "Agreed."

Anger spikes in Harbinger, angled toward Agony. "Can you feel what I'm feeling now?"

He tilts his head. "Hard to say. Can you feel something strongly?"

"How strong are we talking?"

"Judging by the last time?" Agony stares straight into her. Faint heat settles in Harbinger's cheeks. "Pretty fucking strong."

"What does that…? Whatever." She massages into her eyelids. Her shoulders ache, neck heavy under thoughts of Evie. Flint can't feel any better. Even Agony is irritable. "We'll figure it out later. Let's get some sleep. We have to drive again tomorrow."

Flint takes first watch. Harbinger doesn't put up a fight, head pounding by the time she's out of the shower. She drapes a towel over her pillow, not giving her hair a chance to dry before she crawls under the sheets.

The Albruns bothered her more than they should have. She knows why, but when it crosses her mind, she buries the memory in the hole that was left for it and forces her thoughts in a different direction. The headache fades, but she knows she's asleep once she sees the house.

It's exactly as she remembers. Old-fashioned, split-level, blackout curtains pulled tight across the windows in her bedroom. The front door's ajar, as if someone's just stepped out…but Harbinger knows the truth.

She sprints away down the cul-de-sac, past other houses she's long forgotten, until the blur of garages and siding gives way to trees and the cold snap of air. It's an unfamiliar forest, but she recognizes the stone dais rising out of a lake. Water spills over its edges, a luminescent purple emanating from the darkness.

She turns back the way she came, but now, there's nothing but wooded night settling around her. White noise crackles in her ears.

"Someone's in a hurry."

She knows that voice. A wisp of smoke phases through the trees, less opaque than she's used to. Agony looks different here, body curling and coiling as his eyes and mouth stretch into jagged shapes.

Her heart pounds, but not from Agony. It's almost a relief to see him here. A reminder that none of this is real.

"Was that your house?"

So he saw it. Of course: this is all her imagination. A dream version of Agony that her mind supplied from the leftovers of the day. She breathes deeply. She shouldn't be tired. This is a dream. "No."

Agony's eyes narrow into slits. "You're lying."

"So?" She throws up her hands. "What, should I take your example and say 'I don't know' instead?"

"Mine's not a lie." Shadows shift, snapping him closer until he's a wall of smoke before her. "I *don't* remember." Then he scans the woods, circling her to take in the trees. "Is this part of your dream? With the stone slab?"

She ignores his question. The forest is murky, lacking detail, pine needles and a rush of chilly air. Nothing familiar. Nothing but the slab that she pushes deeper into her subconscious. "The forest isn't mine."

Agony moves toward one of the trees, lingering over a set of gashes in its trunk. His voice is muted like they're underwater. "Then maybe it's mine."

Long marks wrench through the bark, like someone clinging

to life. A cold snap darts up Harbinger's spine.

"Can you read them?" Agony asks. Harbinger lifts her hand to pull off her glove, but there's nothing there. She touches the tree.

"It doesn't feel like anything." Her fingers drum against it. "It's not really here."

There are more marks on the next tree. Agony and Harbinger follow them, winding deeper into the forest, pine needles slipping underfoot. The trees are endless, identical when Harbinger tries to look closer. As soon as she has a solid thought in her mind, the dream turns it to mush and clouds it with fog.

"There."

Agony points. Harbinger moves toward another tree with gouges, but it's the same tree as before. Impossibly, they've circled back to where they began. They turn in a circle, trying to find another path. There's nothing but cold wind.

"Forget it." Agony sinks onto the nearest rock, kicking a twig aside. It skitters across the ground with a hollow, echoing sound. "We can't go any deeper. Not like this." His wrists flex, but in the dream, nothing constrains him. No cuffs. No chains.

But they both know what's holding him in the real world.

Harbinger takes in the endless tree trunks again. "You made this?"

With a shrug, he rests elbows on his knees. "You said it wasn't yours."

Her fingers trace over a patch of moss. It feels strange, a sensation she'd nearly forgotten. That's how she knows she's dreaming; her gloves are off. She can touch things without a barrier, mind pulling on fuzzy memories to give her some semblance of reality. Bark and the leaves feel foggy, too long forgotten when her skin doesn't come into contact with such things any more.

"Why did you pick this?" she asks. "Why this place?"

"I don't know." The shadows of Agony's body billow higher until he sighs, leaning back against a tree trunk. "I know you both think I'm full of shit. That I'm lying. That I should be able to remember what Reid did, but it doesn't work like that."

"What's it work like, then?" Harbinger's careful not to let her eyes linger on the curve of his shoulders. The teasing curl of his shadows. The way he looks up at her.

"It's like blacking out. Wasted with no memory of it, until something reminds you of what you did. Memories come back. At least, pieces of them. Like déjà vu: a memory your mind can't place, but your body remembers. When it happens again, you know you've been there before, but you can't conjure it up on your own."

"So this..." She gestures toward the tops of the trees when a bird calls, distant and garbled. "Appeared. You made it because it's in you somewhere, but it's not something you consciously create."

He flicks a bug off his leg. "This is a facade. That's why we end up back here, in the same spot. Looks great, as long as you don't look too closely. I can only go so deep in the dream when I'm stuck in that physical form. What I don't understand is why I've only accessed this with you. When I try to find it myself, there's nothing."

Fading light shifts through the tops of the trees between clouds moving overhead. "Maybe you need a conduit" she murmurs. "A connection with someone that dreams, so you can project."

His shadows never stay in one place, surging and blending into the darkness around them. Her brow hikes. "Is this how you really look?"

Agony's smile grows inhumanly wider until her stomach twists. "Maybe. You like it?"

Thoughts run away with her. Trees glitch with static, shimmering into an image of shadows against her naked body before she jerks the forest back into place.

Agony doesn't miss it. "You couldn't handle the real me, *baby*." The word drips hot, a mockery of the way Flint calls her.

"I'd fuck with your mind."

"Like you've been doing for the past two weeks?" Her foot itches to step closer to the line he's drawn. To press right up against it and drive this dream to its limits. "I'm not afraid of you."

Darkness rushes past her. Agony's face jerks close enough to heat her breath with his horrifying mouth. Hundreds of tendrils brush over her bare arms, a threat outlined against her skin.

"You should be."

Shadows slip over her shoulders, dusting her collarbone, fluttering in the hollow of her throat. A reminder of the handcuffs there before. "No wonder Flint has a fit when you leave his sight." Tendrils curl around her neck. "You'd dive right into death if it gave you half a chance."

This isn't real...but it's Agony's world. What could a creature like that do in her dreams? In this world that belongs to him? Could he hurt her?

Could he kill her?

His shadows tighten around her throat. Enough for her to gasp, to bring that smirk across Agony's face once more, until her expression hardens. Until she speaks.

"I'm not afraid of you because you want to be bad. It's your very nature." Her voice is little more than a whisper when she leans into his grip. His gaze flicks down to watch the press of her skin against danger. "But that's just it. You *want* it. Because that's not what you are, is it?"

He's impossible to read. Impossible to understand, shirking any logic of the real world. Impossible to trust, because he doesn't care, doesn't cling to any human emotion. Agony does what he wants when he wants to, no loyalty to anyone or anything else.

She doesn't know why that makes her chest ache.

His teeth grit. "All I want to do is *hurt* things. Stoke the terror. See the fear..." Tendrils outline her lips. "Make you scream." Fury burns the depths of his eyes, but she catches that uncertain flicker. His mouth lowers until it nearly molds to hers. "I've killed people for less."

Her throat aches when she swallows. His grip bobs around it. "What the OID did to you wasn't less than this."

A line knits between his brows. And then it disappears, as if it hadn't been there at all.

"Careful, little death…" A strand of her hair curls around his finger, like a vine crawling toward the sun. "It sounds like you're making excuses for me, and Flint can't protect you from that." Shadows brush her jaw, sharpened to the point of a knife. "I could do anything I want to you in here."

"Then do it."

Warmth radiates from the gashes in his face. "I wonder about you, Harbinger. Because you say things like an invitation. Like you want me to show you what I'm capable of. Like you want to push me far enough to break you."

She squirms in his grip, but he doesn't mistake it for fear, his eyes flaring brighter when her thighs press together.

"*Is* that what you want?" He searches her face for an answer. She tries not to give him one. "What are the words? The colors?"

She barely breathes. "The stoplight?"

"Red, yellow, green." His eyes are ravenous. "And green means you like exactly what I'm giving you."

Every thud of her heart is a reminder of what she promised Flint. How she swore to be careful. To stay away from Agony. Instead, he bores straight into her soul.

"And what color are you, little death? Do you want me to tell you about yourself?"

Her traitorous mouth moves before her thoughts can reach it. "Green."

It's exactly what he wants to hear, shadows shuddering with delight. "You want someone to take a risk with you. That's why I felt your desire after the fire — because your man Flint was jealous. Possessive. A little mean."

The heat from Agony's mouth is secondary to the ache

between her thighs, flushing up her cheeks when his voice drags lower. "Because that's what you want, isn't it? What you've been waiting for: him to lose that perfect, practiced control. To stop holding you so gently. That's why you're here with me." Agony's gaze dips between her legs. "You want to use me to stoke his anger?"

"No."

Agony lifts his brows. Is this real? Is it a dream? Is it all in her head? She doesn't know the words. Doesn't know if they make sense.

"I don't want to use you. I want..."

But the thought is too perilous to consider, a want that could only sprout in a dream, absurd and futile.

I want him to give me everything.

I want you to fuck with my head.

I want Flint. And I want you.

Dangling over the edge of desire, baiting the monster to surge up to meet her. "Yellow." Her mind grapples for sense. "Red."

Agony fades back into the darkness, his whisper hissing louder until it's a scream.

"Then wake up!"

FIFTEEN

Flint

Things don't get easier.

The threat of Agony killing Harbinger lessens, but that's dangerous in itself, lulling Flint into a false sense of security. He can't let his guard down. He has to be vigilant. But it becomes more difficult the longer Agony is there, a third where it's always been the two of them.

The terror gets into debates with Flint about answers to the crossword, spinning theories with Harbinger about whatever show is on TV. It entertains her, at least. When the corner of her mouth ticks up after a long day of interviewing families, it eases a little of Flint's stress.

She takes it harder than Flint expected, sitting in those living rooms and gently rejecting the offered drinks, bringing a tiny spark of life back to what feels like a tomb. The families always ask the same question. No matter how long it's been since they last saw their daughter, no matter how faint the thread of hope may be.

Do you think she's still alive?

It's too much to put on Harbinger, too much to ask her to find a response. But somehow, she always does. She tells them all the same thing, and more importantly, she always means it.

I want to find her. And I hope that she is.

But none of them can deny the facts: probability and evidence and ticking time. Once Harbinger slides back into the SUV with the weight of each family on her shoulders, the ride is always quiet.

Flint wishes he could go with her. That he could carry this burden for her, but he's not sure how he would react. What feelings of his own it might stir up, talking through the worst moment of these people's lives, immortalized in the amber of their minds. Flint offers nonetheless, but Harbinger declines. Says it's something she has to do herself.

Each of the missing girls are different. Maybe not to the OID, who view them as a cluster of characteristics that lead back to Reid. Skin color, age, appearance: clues to why he chose them. But Harbinger finds the constellation of the girls' differences and paints them into galaxies for Flint and Agony. Mila was a cougar shifter intent on hiding it. Greer did her lipstick before drag races, like it was good luck. Isolde was starting to lose her deciduous faun horns when the girl next door shyly gave her a heart charm for her bracelet.

When Flint notices the girls share similarities with Agony, it's disconcerting at best. Evie's craving for sushi was first, but then one family mentions their daughter's affinity for puzzles. At the drive-thru, Agony requests an obscure soda; Harbinger pauses halfway through their order before she tells him it was another girl's favorite drink.

They don't know what the coincidences mean. Unsurprisingly, neither does Agony, but the pit in Flint's stomach sinks deeper.

The connection between Agony and Harbinger grows stronger. Flint would be lying if he said he wasn't concerned. What started as a strange quirk has turned into the two of them moving in sync, glancing toward the door at a sound. Laughing at the same joke. Shivering when Flint turns on the AC.

It's nothing like Flint's connection with Harbinger. Or, Harbinger's connection with Flint. Theirs only goes one way, funneling his jealousy and doubt straight into her. He does his best to control it, benefitted by gargoyle stoicism, but it's a constant open line between them. He can't imagine what it's like for her.

Until she tells him.

"We need to talk."

Her voice is thick with sleep. Anxiety curdles in Flint's stomach as he pushes his glasses back on his head.

"It's nothing bad," she adds quickly. "Nothing life-threatening."

Flint knows how very differently they quantify that. He turns in his seat at the table, eyes narrowing immediately to Agony across the room.

"What?" Agony tries to throw up his hands, stopped by the chains looped around his chair. "Why do you assume it has to do with me?"

"Because it always does."

"Our connection..." Harbinger cuts in, gesturing between her and Agony. "You said it seemed different than we suspected."

Flint keeps a tight grip on the apprehension threatening to leap out of him. Harbinger watches him like she can feel it anyway.

"It might be even different than that. More than Agony feeling me."

Flashes of the night after the fire burn through Flint, dark and slick with heat. Immediately, he douses his thoughts until all that's left is swirling smoke. It doesn't get past Harbinger and her lingering look before she continues.

"I don't know what I'm getting from Agony, but it seems like we're connected in my dreams."

What does that mean? What else can Agony do? Flint clears his throat. "How connected are we talking?"

"I don't think it's dangerous." Of course she doesn't. "But

Agony's able to see my dreams. To affect them. To shape them."

"Shape them how?"

"It's not in my control," Agony answers. "Sometimes her dreams are from her subconscious, but sometimes, they're from mine."

"Related to Reid?"

"I can't be sure. With these cuffs on — I *know*, they're not coming off — but I'm constrained. We're not able to dig deeper or change the location. We can't look closer at anything."

We.

Green acid eats away at Flint's stomach.

"We wanted to tell you," Harbinger rushes to add. "Because I thought I was just dreaming at first, but Agony's really there. I'm conscious. I'm lucid. And nothing *happened*." Her cheeks flare pink, avoiding both their eyes. Jealousy drives a spike through Flint's chest. "But with all of these connections, it complicates things. My mind and my body aren't just mine." Bitterness streaks across her face before it's gone again. "So we need to agree that if two of us know something, then we all know it. We share between the three of us. Anything that two of us do, the third has to agree first. At least until we figure out an alternative. We have to go into things knowing there are three people involved, in one way or another."

"You mean fucking?" *Gods*, Agony has no subtlety. He's practically salivating. "Trust me, you don't have to ask —"

Harbinger and Flint cut in at once. "Yes, we do."

"But not just that," she continues. "Agony and I won't do anything in the dreamscape without Flint knowing. Same goes for you two." Not like she needs to worry about that. Harbinger looks at Agony. "Do we agree?"

He nods. She turns back to Flint, and that's where her skepticism lies, brows lifted. "Can you handle that?"

No.

What would she say if that was his answer? He hates the

thought on principle, sharing anything with such an unknown creature. But she's right — there's no room for secrets. Not when the three of them are crammed into the smallest possible spaces: motel rooms, SUVs, Harbinger's mind. And if Agony can experience Harbinger's strong emotions, it's only right he has some say in it.

That doesn't make the pill any easier to swallow. "Fine," Flint grinds out.

Harbinger gives him a look. "Flint..."

"I said I can handle it."

"I can feel —"

"I know you have a sense of my emotions." He presses fingers to the bridge of his nose. "That they aren't aligning with what I'm saying. But that's how it has to be. I need you to take my word for it, even if you can feel the difference. I need you to trust me."

Like you trusted me?

She doesn't have to say it. Flint can't look at Agony. Only the gods know the new ways he plans to fuck with the tenuous intimacy Flint and Harbinger have.

"I'm gonna shower." *A cold one.* Without another word, Flint moves into the bathroom where he can finally breathe.

Anything involving the three of them is careless, a game they shouldn't even think of playing. But since the fire, Flint's mind wanders down roads it shouldn't. Perverse places he's ashamed of, twisted positions he never wants to put Harbinger in. Maybe that's why he hates Agony so much, for putting these contorted ideas in his head. Knowing that doesn't keep the thoughts at bay, slipping like water down Flint's neck.

Harbinger bent over Agony. That sickening smile curling beneath her, weaving filthy words against her chest while Flint drags his cock out of her. Flint's hand wrapped around Agony's throat to see if it thrills her. Forcing Agony to watch as Flint takes Harbinger apart on his tongue, Agony's smartass mouth telling her how delicious she looks.

It's dark. It's dangerous. It doesn't make any sense. It's nothing Flint can afford to give attention to.

Knowing that doesn't stop the ache through Flint's swollen cock. Harbinger appears in the bathroom at the sense of his arousal, and Flint tries uselessly to hide it.

"We can't leave him alone," Flint reminds her.

"I can see him." She sinks to her knees in the doorway, bare hands on his thighs. His dick twitches. She looks up at him beneath her lashes. "Color?"

It should be red. It should be *no, absolutely not, we can't trust him*...but it's not. She can feel that it isn't. And still, she waits at his feet, like she's giving him permission to want this. Like he isn't sick for thinking of it.

"Green," he finally breathes.

Harbinger glances toward Agony in the other room, his chains clinking in response. "Green, fucking..."

All their groans bind together when Harbinger wraps her lips around Flint, positioned so Agony can see. It's the sight of her perfect mouth and Agony watching her work that makes Flint come down the back of her throat.

Once should be enough. *More* than enough, but every day is a fuse lit by petty arguments, burning through them until they combust. Harbinger riding Flint in a dark parking lot while Agony curses from the backseat. Flint fucking Harbinger against the motel wall where Agony can only see their shadows. Flint eating Harbinger out until she has to shove him away as Agony begs for mercy.

Always, emphatically, it's *green* from all three of them.

It's hard enough for Flint to keep basic emotions from Harbinger, but now, his feelings don't make sense. There's a spike of jealousy when Agony grins at Harbinger, and then the thud of Flint's pulse when Agony turns that grin on him. Constant tension in Flint's body, prepared to slam Agony against the wall...and then the memory of Agony's tongue against his hand that swells heat in

Flint's stomach.

He refuses to look at it, focused instead on the countless dead ends they keep running into. After they talk with the families, they investigate the places the girls were last seen, the shops Reid frequented, the sporadic sightings that hold no real hope. Harbinger picks up plenty of information from different surfaces, but nothing that leads them any closer to the girls.

By the end of the second week, even Agony's cavalier attitude is flagging. The OID has gotten around Flint blocking their number. Now, they call from a new line each time, trying to track the three of them. Flint flips through the leads they've exhausted. Agony checks behind him, abandoning the oversized child's puzzle that Flint bought him as a joke.

"So we confirmed all the girls in this stack attended schools where Reid sold printers."

Flint glances up from his own pile. "Right."

Agony searches for a sticky note. "And the ferryman from the Break called back. Said he recognized Reid from his younger days, when Reid got caught sneaking into the Break to hunt animals?"

"Correct. Every area — city, township, whatever — has its own governing body. And that body works out protections for its community. The OID oversees investigations throughout those areas, especially when a crime crosses multiple regions, but the OID loves to overstep."

Sarcasm drips from Agony's tone. "Sounds shockingly familiar."

"They insert themselves in community issues so often, any 'help' they give is more of a power trip than any real investigation. But the Break's governing body — the Conclave — would remember Reid from his past. He wouldn't be welcome back in the Break. At least, not openly."

Agony's fingers drum on the table. "Still no word from the Timbers, though."

It's strange, hearing Agony talk about things he's learned from

Flint and Harbinger. "No. Reid's hunting history might be a longshot, but we should at least look into it. After that, though…" Flint surveys the files they've picked through more than once. "We're running out of leads."

Harbinger rubs her temples when she leans back from the table. She's been silent all evening, enough that both men pause to watch her now.

"If we can't think of anything else…" She grits her jaw, like she's not sure she wants to finish. "I have somewhere we can go."

She waits for one of them to offer an alternative. Unfortunately, Agony is hideously fascinated by her pain, and Flint will be damned if he cuts her off now that she's finally sharing something.

"If we've run out of trails to follow…" she starts again. "We could try the Convent."

Agony blinks. "What's a Convent?"

"It's where banshees go once our abilities initiate." She sinks down in her chair. "A religious school where we live together. Follow the tenets. Strengthen our skills."

In the early days of their partnership, Harbinger mentioned the Convent. It's never been a bright spot of conversation, but Flint knows enough. It's the place where Harbinger spent a portion of her adolescence, and not somewhere she's keen to go back to.

"We don't have to go there," Flint counters. "We'll find something else. We can try the schools again —"

"We've tried them. Twice already."

They all fall silent, racking their brains for another option. Harbinger looks wearily to the ceiling.

"I want to do it before I talk myself out of it. Rip the bandage off."

Flint waits to see if she'll change her mind. Instead, the phone rings. Harbinger checks the screen.

Unknown number. *OID*. Again.

She tosses the phone back on the table. "At least the Convent has no cell service."

SIXTEEN

Flint

It's the furthest they've traveled yet. Red dust billows out behind the SUV as dusk falls over the desert. They're closer to Faerie than they have been in a while, but it's little more than clouds in the distance. Harbinger directs Flint with a grim expression, past the wooden sign erected by the road.

Shrine of the Sacred Oracle.

The rock formation towers over them when they pull up. Holes cut into its face for windows, fitted with an amalgam of stained glass. Flint carries their luggage in one hand as Agony's eyes catch on stars pricking through the darkened sky. The three of them stand back from the heavy wooden door, Flint and Agony watching Harbinger from either side.

Another minute passes. Agony shifts in the dirt before he leans forward to look at her. "Are you gonna knock?"

Harbinger's gaze stays narrowed on the door. "They know we're here."

And with that, the door creaks open, revealing a tunnel lit by torches and an older woman with the same skeletal markings as Harbinger.

The woman's loose black robes brush the dirt as she walks, stopping before them with a dour expression. Unlike Harbinger's fingers, this woman has black marks scorching in and around her eyes. No one speaks. They stare at each other until Harbinger breaks first.

"You don't look surprised."

The woman doesn't look happy, either. "We knew someone would disturb our peace." She lifts both palms toward her eyes, bringing her hands down to her mouth where she fans her fingers forward. "So say the Oracle."

Harbinger's mouth twitches like she's biting something back. Resisting words. Resisting the gesture.

The woman's scowl deepens. "Why are you here?"

Harbinger's boot scuffs against the ground, grinding the ball of her foot into the dirt. "I'm working a case. We're..." she gestures beside her. "Working a case. I need to speak with some of the Seers."

"We don't allow outsiders."

Harbinger's mouth pulls into a reticent smile. "That's not true."

The woman's eyes harden. "We don't allow outsiders with no respect for our purpose."

For a moment, Flint expects Harbinger to turn on her heel, to flip both middle fingers as they head back to the car. Instead, she inhales. "We're talking about death, Auspice —"

"That's *Diviner Superior* to you, little girl." Diviner Auspice's expression sharpens, honed on Harbinger like a blade, torchlight flickering behind the weight of her voice. "Have you forgotten our customs so quickly?"

It's enough. Flint moves to pull Harbinger away, to find another way of doing this — but Agony's stops him, chin jerking toward Harbinger.

She doesn't retreat. Doesn't ask Flint to step in. And something about that wounds him. He settles back when Harbinger speaks again, her voice softening the same way it does after she visits with the families.

"We're looking for young girls. Dozens of them, probably dead. We need to find where they are to give their families some peace. That's what you do here, isn't it?" Gloved hands clench at her sides. "Use the Oracle to help people who need it?"

Even with the two women at odds, their similarities are as distinct as their contrast. All black, catsuit leather clashing against humble robes. Diviner Auspice's defiance fights past her reverence while Harbinger struggles not to give into ingrained deference.

The prodigal daughter returned.

One thing is clear — no matter how Harbinger tried to escape this place, she hasn't gotten out unscathed.

"We do not use the Oracle," Diviner Auspice corrects. "The Oracle uses us." But she looks over them for a long moment before she continues. "The others are in their rooms for the night. You may stay in the guest quarters until tomorrow, and if the Seers have time, you may speak with them."

Then she turns, not waiting for them to follow.

Inside the rock formation are catacombs, tunnels dug into stone that lead past walls of skulls and bones. Agony edges closer to Flint. Flint pries Agony away, but he can't deny the eerie feeling lingering at his back. Hanging torches guide them through twists and turns large enough for Flint to fit through comfortably. The Diviner Superior brings them up a set of stone stairs to a landing with smaller wooden doors.

"Breakfast at dawn. You may eat after our students have finished."

Harbinger presses open one of the doors. "I remember you treating guests with a bit more hospitality."

"Those patrons honor the Oracle." The woman eyes Flint and Agony as they enter.

Harbinger's laugh is brittle. "And I guess we're fucking spitting in her face."

Red flares up the woman's neck. Flint wraps an arm around Harbinger's waist. "Thank you for your generosity." Then he tugs her back into the room and swings the door shut.

He and Agony hold their breath until a flurry of footfalls disappear, and Flint releases Harbinger's tense body from his grasp.

"Someone's the black sheep of the family." Agony sprawls out on the mattress on the floor, swimming among woven blankets. "Is that, like, your grandma?"

"No." Harbinger pops open her suitcase, rifling through it with no purpose. "None of us are related. She's one of the leaders, the head of all the Diviners. The *Superior*. They bring banshees here when they get their curse."

Flint tracks her movements: sharp angles, rigid legs, haphazardly discarding things. "Curse?"

"Abilities. Powers. *Whatever*." Harbinger knocks the lid shut, tossing a nightshirt onto the bed. "I'm gonna shower."

She strips out of her catsuit, leaving it hanging open around her waist as she disappears through an open doorway at one end of the room. Agony watches her go, but as Flint scowls, Agony turns back with a derisive look.

"Seems *homey*."

Flint sinks into a large cushion on a rock seat curving out from the wall. "She told me about it, a little. But I didn't know it was this...charged."

Agony pushes up to rest elbows on his knees. "What did she tell you?"

"She came here when she was young. Twelve, I think. The timing is different for each of them, but that's when it started for her."

Harbinger keeps parts of her past close to her chest, sharing just enough that someone won't pry for more. So Flint didn't —

something he hadn't realized until Agony shined a light on it.

"I don't know exactly what happened here" Flint adds. "Or what happened before. She's always seemed conflicted when she talked about it."

"What did she mean by 'using the Oracle' to help people? What's the Oracle?"

"Not sure." Flint scowls at the way Harbinger phrased it. "The Convent hosts people in need. People who can benefit from a banshee's abilities. People who need help communing with the dead or reading auras or anything else banshees can do."

"So they aren't all like her?" Agony's head tilts toward where the shower kicks on. "They don't all 'read' things?"

"No, every banshee is different. Their commonality is they all access things that aren't in the physical world."

"Like me."

Flint huffs a laugh. "Sure. Actually, one of the girls Harbinger went to school with traversed through dreams."

Agony perks at that. "Really?"

"Yeah." Flint stands. "Pretty sure Harbinger hated her."

Agony sneers as Flint moves toward the bathroom, leaning against the doorway as steam rolls out. Past the stone wall of tile, a strip of Harbinger's skin is visible, pink from the heat and her insistent scrubbing.

"We don't have to stay here," Flint reminds her.

Harbinger scrubs harder. "We do if we're going to figure out where the girls are."

Flint's rarely seen her do it, scouring her skin like a punishment to further irritate her ability. "Harbin..." His voice is barely louder than the water against the tiled floor. He steps closer until she stops the assault on her arms. "I know you want to help those girls and their families, but it's not worth hurting yourself to do it. I know we disagree on that, but we can find another way. We always do."

Of that, he's certain. Water splashes against her chest, the hand that had scrubbed so vigorously falling back to her side.

"I didn't think coming back here would make me so…"

The thought trails off. Agony appears in the doorway.

"If it helps, I'm pretty sure your presence was enough to work the stick up the Diviner Superior's ass straight into her tonsils."

Harbinger laughs. "Yeah, they're pretty precious about their Oracle."

Agony leans against the other side of the doorframe. "Why is that?"

Flint's prepared to tell him to knock it off when Harbinger lathers gently over the curve of her hip.

"For devout believers, it's their god. They worship the Oracle. They think it's a being, or a consciousness, somewhere between life and death. The Oracle 'blesses' banshees with their abilities. In return, banshees are supposed to use those abilities to honor the Oracle. To be mouthpieces for it. That's the line the Convent gives, anyway."

"Honor it how?"

"By staying in the community. Giving thanks for whatever 'gift' you've been bestowed. Providing services to acceptable outsiders, often for a generous donation."

Agony's eyes narrow as Harbinger rinses her hair. "But you don't think that."

The water shuts off. "If it's true, the Oracle can kiss my ass."

Flint hands her a towel to dry off. Hair hangs damp against her skin, streaks across the hollows and bones her chest, one strand curving over the top of her breasts.

"You're staring."

Flint jerks his eyes up, but Harbinger isn't looking at him. At least, not only at him. Her gaze cuts between the two men with a hint of amusement.

Flint prickles. "What?"

"Didn't expect to see the two of you not plotting ways to piss each other off."

Both Agony and Flint lean against opposite sides of the doorway, a foot of space between them, waiting for her. They both straighten at once, which widens Harbinger's grin before she passes between them.

Flint clears his throat, nudging Agony out of the way as she moves back into the room. "So what's the plan? Should we prepare for tomorrow?"

"Oh, there's no way to prepare you for what you're about to experience." Harbinger catches his eyes in the mirror across the room, smirk settling on her face. "The Seers are gonna eat you alive."

SEVENTEEN

Flint

The Convent awakens before the first light of dawn. Harbinger doesn't seem to have slept at all. Her leg jiggles beneath the casefiles in her lap as Flint finishes his morning routine. They all make their way down winding rock corridors to a room near the center of the building. It's carved with vaulted stone ceilings and skylights that look down on long, wooden tables. On one side, a kitchen bustles with activity, utensils scraping through any remnants of sleep. The sounds are less harsh than the look the Diviner Superior gives the three of them as they linger near the back of the room.

"The students eat first." Harbinger scuffs her boot against the ground. "We wait until the end of the line. But head's up, they're all going to stare at you."

And stare they do. The youngest come first, filing into the dining hall with excited morning chatter. Heads whip toward Flint and Agony, followed by whispers and giggles. It's far from the first time Flint's been stared at, but it is the first time it's done by lines of girls with skeletal faces. He can't help the twitch of a smile at the tiny fingers waving in his direction.

Harbinger shifts her weight from foot to foot, but it doesn't do much to quell her anxiety. This must be what she looked like all those years ago, rebellious teenager following the Convent's strict rules only as far as she had to. Flint lowers his mouth near her ear. "Do you want to leave?"

"Can't. We need their help. It's just..." She shuts her eyes, trying to breathe through her nose. "This place has the most people I've ever touched. And they're all getting closer at once."

The line of banshees changes to older children, then teenagers, then adults. That's when the stares begin to shift. They still catch on Flint and Agony first, trying to work out what the massive gargoyle is doing next to the cuffed shadow, but then their eyes land on Harbinger. Recognition crosses their faces. Some pinched expressions fall while others' jump in surprise, but one redhead actually rushes out of line.

Skeletal markings on her body contrast with her bright clothing, pops of vibrant color in dizzying patterns. Her shirt sits off both shoulders, cropped over her stomach as she pushes giant floral sunglasses back into her curls. All her energy seems ready to burst, and Flint shifts closer to Harbinger, but the woman doesn't reach for her. Instead, she stops, weight rocking to her toes in glee.

"What are you doing here?" The woman's voice shifts in an impressive imitation of Harbinger. "I thought you were only coming back *'over my freshly murdered corpse. Or yours.'*"

"You should get back in line." Harbinger keeps her eyes on Diviner Auspice's scowl. "*Her Divineness* doesn't like anyone acknowledging us."

Air blows between the woman's lips. "Please: she's not gonna say shit." Then she turns with a brilliant smile, waving across the dining hall. Diviner Auspice huffs, turning back to ladle food to a table of younger banshees. The redhead leans close to Harbinger again. "She's given up the backhanded comments about my clothes. I'm gonna have half the kids wearing them."

Harbinger's tone is flat. "That's 'cause you're fucking weird."

The woman isn't deterred in the slightest, finally tipping her smile toward Flint and Agony. "Hello. Do you shake?"

She extends her hand. Flint mirrors her, enveloping most of her forearm as delicately as possible.

"I'm Portent," she curtsies. "You can call me Poe."

Flint remembers that name. One of the few Harbinger brought up over the years of their partnership, scrawled on postcards or motel stationary before Harbinger dropped them in the nearest mailbox. Poe reaches for Agony. He makes a disgruntled sound when Flint pulls his shadowy arms back.

"I'm Flint. This is Agony."

Poe's smile slips into a smirk. "I know who you are." She holds out the crook of her elbow to Harbinger. "You can sit with me. I won't make you talk to Herald."

"Thanks," Harbinger answers dryly, and to Flint's surprise, slips her arm through Poe's. The line of banshees has petered out, so Poe leads them to an empty table on the far side of the room.

If the banshees weren't staring before, they certainly are now. Flint can't be sure who it's directed at. He tries to find some tell in Harbinger's body, but there's only tension. Poe chats until she finds a space big enough for all of them, and Flint's prepared to squeeze into the bench when Poe turns to him.

"Do you prefer a chair or a floor pillow?

"Uh..." He blinks. "A cushion is fine."

From a corner of the room, Poe presents a giant floral pillow and sets it at the head of the table. "I made this after a troll visited a few years ago. It suits you."

"Thank you." Flint guides Agony into his chair before he takes a seat. Most of the attention from the other banshees has died down, but a small cluster of Diviners shoot narrowed eyes toward their table. Harbinger does her best to ignore them.

"Seriously, what made you come back?" Poe reaches for a bowl of rolls, voice lowering. "And with two men, no less. Omen's gonna be jealous."

Agony's smile slips across his face. Harbinger rests her forehead in her hand. "We're not…" But she doesn't finish. "We're working an investigation. I need some help, and I thought with some of the Seers' abilities…"

"Yes!" Poe claps her hands against her cheek. "We would love to! What are you investigating? Is someone missing?"

"They're dead."

It lands with a weight it hasn't possessed before. Poe stills. Chatter from the rest of the room circles around them. "Girls," Harbinger finishes. Poe's mouth molds into a thin line, fingers resting against Harbinger's glove.

"Ok. Of course we'll help." Poe inclines her head toward Harbinger, voice so soft Flint can barely hear. "Pick it up. Then put it down."

Poe doesn't remove her hand from Harbinger's, peppering Agony with questions as they eat. Harbinger doesn't attempt to move food around her plate. Her hand clenches once around Poe's, and Poe squeezes back, but otherwise doesn't let the smile on her face falter.

At the front of the room, Diviner Auspice steps up onto a platform, waiting for the banshees to shush each other. It doesn't take long before the dining hall falls silent, and she begins to speak.

"A surprise storm will roll in tomorrow, so take advantage of today's weather while you can. The Diviners have seen the prank Year Nines are planning next week, so don't bother." A round of groans rises from the other side of the room. "Seer Herald is offering extra oneironautics practice next week. If you are interested, please bring your own dream journal to the Seer Suite after dinner. And a reminder: no one should traverse the Veil Chambers on the lower level without a Diviner escort."

Harbinger's fork scrapes against her plate. Poe keeps a hold of her hand.

"And finally..." Diviner Auspice's eyes land on Harbinger, Agony, and Flint. "Rumors have circulated about our current guests. I can assure you that none of them are true."

Flint doesn't know what the rumors might be, but from the way the Diviner Superior glares, he's not sure that she doesn't believe them. She makes the same gesture as the night before, bringing hands down from her eyes to her mouth, passing on a message. "So say the Oracle."

A chorus of banshees respond. "So say we all."

Poe mouths the words. Harbinger's lips don't move. Diviner Auspice steps down from the platform, and Flint leans to gather their dishes.

"Seer Portent?" A younger banshee stands near Flint's elbow at the table, watching Poe. The girl tries and fails to keep from blinking towards Flint. "I can take your dishes for you, if you want."

"Aren't you sweet..." Poe slides the tray toward the girl. "With no ulterior motives. Make sure you get Mr. Flint's cup."

The girl holds out the tray, and Flint sets his mug in an open place. "Thank you."

She's too shy to look at him any longer. "You're welcome." Then she scurries away with a blush, rushing back to a table of clamoring girls.

Harbinger scoffs, pushing up from the table with the others. "You have people waiting to clean up your dishes now?"

Poe waves off her concern. "If I'm gonna be up at night helping with puke or bad dreams, I'm gonna reap the benefits." She turns to Flint as they walk. "They'll be talking about you for weeks. Most of the visitors we get are boring and don't know how to dress."

A smile flits across Harbinger's face. It tugs at Flint's own, until Agony has to speak.

"Do all banshees have ominous names?"

"Banshees choose a new name once they cross over." Poe gives him a conspiratorial look, but there's something heavier behind her sunglasses. "Better fits the 'aesthetic,' don't you think?"

"And are all banshees girls?"

"Mostly." Poe shrugs. "No one knows why. There are plenty of theories."

Harbinger's voice sours. "Easier to take advantage of."

Poe nudges her with a hip, but doesn't contradict her.

They follow Poe through more tunnels, past carved classrooms where Diviners clap for attention. Children scamper to and from the dorms with things they've forgotten. A few teenagers wait for the Diviners to herd stragglers away before they slip down a hidden corridor. The stone stairways are vast, molded between stalagmites as sunlight filters through patterned windows.

Up they go, away from the dining hall, until the bustling sound of classes fades in the distance. They come to a landing a few stories up, cozier than the larger arched corridors. Flint ducks to follow. Small windows dot the wall between mismatched curtains, hallway curving toward an open seating area.

Poe gestures toward the piles of cushions and couches. "I'll see who else is around. I know a few of them are making house calls."

"Seriously?" Harbinger asks.

Poe holds up her hands with a quirk of her lip. Clearly a conversation they've had more than once. "I told him."

Sun winks off Poe's jewelry as she moves down the hall. Agony picks a lumpy sectional and flops down.

"What is this, VIP?"

"Seer Suite." Harbinger moves in front of a mural on the wall, a mixture of styles and names interlocking. Animal bones, colorful chalk outlines, pressed flowers and abstract shapes and poems. "Once you graduate, they put you in one of these coteries with people around your age." She makes her way to a corner littered with spikes and flaming skulls, smiley faces blooming between. Three signatures weave beneath them, as distinct as the artwork: *Omen. Poe. Harbin.*

"If you stay?" Agony adds, waiting for her confirmation.

Harbinger presses fingers against her name. "If you stay."

Boots scuff along the corridor. A banshee enters the lounge draped in black jeans and a t-shirt, feathered white hair swept back from his face. He breaks into a grin.

"How's our favorite capitalist pig?"

EIGHTEEN

Flint

How's our favorite capitalist pig?

Even Agony blanches, but Harbinger rolls her eyes, letting the other banshee scoop her into a hug that she doesn't take part in. Still, there's warmth in her voice. "You're so annoying."

The man sets her back on the ground, chucking under her chin. "Don't sweet-talk me."

"Thought you were making house calls."

His smile sharpens. "Had to reschedule. I could use a hundred bucks, though."

Harbinger gapes. "For what?"

He inclines his ear toward her, covered in a smattering of piercings. She flicks one, unimpressed. "A hundred bucks for that?"

"It's contraband!" Then he turns back to the room. "Hey — oh. You're Flint." The banshee winks at Harbinger. She blushes as he extends his hand to shake Flint's. "Heard so much about you. All good. Great, really." Then he turns toward Agony. "Don't think I've heard about you."

Agony musters a charming expression. "I'm new. Agony."

The man acts as if a name like that isn't shocking. For them, maybe it isn't. "Omen."

"Oh." Agony catches Flint's gaze. *Oh.*

Omen lifts his brows until Agony provides an answer. "Poe mentioned you'd be jealous of us showing up here with Harbinger."

"Ah." Omen clicks his tongue. "Well, I was Harbinger's first..." A smile drips across his face. "*Kiss.* Poe was her second. She's the one you really need to look out for."

Before Flint can consider what that means, a dozen banshees bustle down the corridor in a flurry of shouts and squeals. Most keep their distance from Harbinger, but a few grip her arms and circle closer.

"Oh my god, what the fuck?" One holds Harbinger out to give her a once over, curlers spilling out of her hair. "Literally, *what the fuck?*"

Another toys with Harbinger's braid until she recognizes the pained grit of Harbinger's teeth, the strain at the sudden swell of others' emotions. Wincing apologetically, the closest banshees release her. "Sorry, sorry..."

"We're still missing a few." Poe shouts over the din, standing on an ottoman. "They should be back tomorrow."

Agony drifts closer to Flint at the far edge of the crowd. The outer ring of banshees murmur, but once the inner circle turns away from Harbinger, the whispers hush. They take in Flint towering near the entryway, Agony a flaming shadow next to him.

The banshees make no attempt to lower their volume.

"Oh *fuck*, he's hot."

"What is that? Is that a shade?"

"They're with *Harbinger*?"

Heat spreads into Flint's cheeks. Harbinger shrugs through the sea of hands toward him, voice tightening. "Okay, calm down.

We're here for work. This is my partner, Flint. And this is Agony."

Flint bows his head in greeting. Agony lifts chained wrists and waves. Voices crescendo again.

"Is he *handcuffed*?!"

"Wait, your *partner*-partner, or, like —"

"The cuffs are a sex thing. One hundred percent."

Agony points toward the final speaker. "That one is true." Harbinger shoots him a glare. Flint runs a hand down his face.

Poe leans in from the side. "Forgive them: no one cool ever visits us."

Flint almost gets lost in the chatter, but Poe slows the banshees down, introducing each one in turn. Despite their similar skeletal patterning, their clothing and hair are as varied as their personalities. Very few have Harbinger's black marks creeping up their fingertips. Some have the marks — Veil marks — across their eyes, dripping from their ears, spilling from their mouths. Some have no black marks at all — at least, not where Flint can see — but all the marks tie to their abilities.

Eventually, the banshees sprawl across cushions and dilapidated couches, forming a semi-circle in front of their guests. Wrapped in throw blankets, hugging pillows, perched on the arms of chairs as Harbinger speaks.

"There's a man who's killed young girls. He's been arrested, but we need to find out what he's done with their bodies. We've tried using my ability, but we keep coming up empty. If you all agree, we want to see if you can find anything. Only if you want to," she adds, pain wedging into her voice. "It's your choice. I hate to ask, but it's pretty dire."

A banshee with black marks bleeding out of their ears cuts in. "Who are you thinking to help?"

"Bodie, of course. You." Harbinger's jaw clenches. "Herald. Maybe Augury? I'm not going to turn anyone down who wants to try." She looks toward Agony. "And Agony is a night terror. He was extracted from the killer's mind. He's..." Harbinger struggles for words, none of which are true. *Harmless. Not dangerous.* "Fine. You may be able to use him with your powers, but keep your distance. Don't touch him, to be safe."

A few banshees' mouths drop open before they volley Agony with questions, undisturbed by any danger he might pose. *So that's where Harbinger gets it.* Agony basks in the attention as the banshee voices topple over each other.

"We should get the candles. For crystals, do you think moldavite or..."

"Maybe I could hear something. Yeah, I *know* she said don't get close."

After a few minutes of planning, a handful of banshees wave their goodbyes. Other Seers disappear to gather supplies, and the final few linger on the edges of the room, offering suggestions that Poe makes note of. Omen turns to Harbinger from his perch on the arm of the couch.

"You know I want to help..."

"I know," she answers. Omen's blackened hands flex. "I know it doesn't work like that."

Poe directs Agony to sit on a coffee table facing the entrance of the room, fluffing a cushion for Flint close by. Seers move in and out of the room, shutting curtains and squealing at Agony's glowing smile. One of them offers slices of toast with jam. Flint declines, but Agony scarfs it down.

"His aura's intriguing, actually." A banshee with deep blue hair traces Agony's shape through the air. "I expected it to be murkier, but it's actually quite clear."

Agony rocks forward. "What color is it?"

She holds her fingers up like she's looking through a camera. "Orange and yellow. Very vibrant. Scintillating. Full of life for someone who...isn't."

Flint disguises a laugh before the banshee turns to him. "Yours is very good, too. More muted: green and blue and brown. Earthy. Solid. A nice contrast to his, so say the Oracle."

Another banshee inclines their head toward Agony. Harbinger leans over their shoulder. "Do you hear anything?"

The banshee shakes their head. Flint keeps a firm grip on Agony. Agony leans toward him, pressing the warmth of his mouth against Flint's ear. "You're squeezing a little *tight*, Jasper dear."

Flint's scowl deepens. He loosens his fingers — but only marginally. The banshee sits back on their cushion, tugging at their bun as they think. "I do hear *something*, but it's a lot of whispers." They look between Harbinger and Flint. "About you two."

Agony narrows his eyes. "What's your superpower again?"

Harbinger tenses. The banshee snickers at her, tilting their head toward Flint. "You want me to listen to him too?"

"You've heard *quite enough*." Harbinger grips the banshee's elbow, ushering them away as Poe stands in front of the table again.

"We're going to set up the séance. Bodie's going through the information you have to see if any of it sparks something. We'll keep Agony here, in the center, to see if he can bring any spirits in. We need you to focus on the girls, ok? Any memory you have of them." Poe rests her hands on Agony's shoulders. Flint fights the urge to rip them away.

Bodie perches in a windowsill, sorting through the photographs and knick-knacks from the case files. She keeps a small pile to the side, one hand hovering over it before she touches the black marks spilling from her mouth.

Half-burnt candles and crystals line the room, blues and purples and whites on every available surface. "We need you two to stay still, ok?" Poe reminds Agony and Flint as the Seers close the rest of the curtains. "Don't want you slipping through any gaps between the Veil. It's a nasty recovery process."

Around Agony, incense curls toward the ceiling. A bowl of oil passes between them as the Seers take their seats around them. Flint watches the others before he follows suit, smearing oil against his pulse points.

Firelight flickers off of Bodie's face, the missing girls' names carved into the candles before her. *Greer. Rachel. Effy...*

"The spirits that find me are usually stuck before trauma, days or hours or minutes before the inciting incident." Bodie braids her hair methodically, a ritual in its own right. "It's often hard for them to focus on the details of what happened. It may take some time, and it may be painful. Is everyone prepared for that?"

It's quieter than the chaos of before, something otherworldly settling between them. Hands link around the circle, weaving connections until Harbinger's hand settles into Flint's. Her reassuring smile through the dark is one last bit of comfort before the banshees cross beyond the Veil.

It's amplified with so many of them here, a dull buzzing that shifts when Flint turns his head. What starts as the low croaking of a thousand voices becomes the vibration of tectonic plates. But when Flint looks around the room, it's eerily still. No motion. Not a breeze. Liquid ripples in nearby glasses.

Flint focuses on the girls. Even Agony doesn't move, brows knit as his eyes press closed.

"One of them is here."

Bodie's voice is little more than a breath. Ringing starts in Flint's ears. Everything is silent and still, connection too tenuous to risk frightening the specter away.

Bodie's head bows. She doesn't lurch or scream as Flint feared she would, rattled and shaken by whatever exists on the other side of the Veil. Instead, it looks more like an agreement. An offering. Bodie extending herself as a mouthpiece to whomever wishes to speak.

Silence stretches through the room. Maybe the connection's lost, gone wrong on the other side. But finally, Bodie lifts her head, blinking as if she's woken from sleep. Her fingers tighten in the hands holding hers, breath evening as she stares into the middle distance.

"She's young in her lifespan. Late adolescence." Bodie's fingers lift toward her cheek. The motion jolts in Flint's stomach, but he tamps it down. *Focus.*

"What's her name?" Harbinger murmurs.

Bodie's head shakes once, as if the spirit speaks rapidly. "She was doing her hair. Getting ready for something." Bodie's fingers linger over her braids. Her voice is weary. "She felt beautiful."

Flint pages back through through the stories they know. Zavi missed her soccer game, Evie had a date with her friends, Greer was prepping for an art show...

"She wasn't supposed to go. Her brother told her not to."

Flint's talons dig into his palm.

"Who had a brother?" Harbinger whispers. "Zavi, Mila..."

"There was a man. He was nice." Bodie's voice drifts as if she's mourning. Reid's face flashes in Flint's mind. "He was nice when she went with him. He told her they understood each other."

Flint's eyes meet Harbinger's. "She knew him?" They'd found nothing to suggest the girls went with Reid willingly. That he groomed them. A cold chill darts through the room. Flint tenses to keep from shivering.

"But then he was cruel." Bodie reaches over her shoulder, along her back, as if something protrudes — but there's nothing. Then she covers her mouth. "Oh no."

"What?" Poe asks. Bodie presses her chin down to her chest, sucking in a breath.

"I don't want to say it."

Omen ducks closer to her ear. Bodie tightens her fingers in his, color draining from her face as if she's going to be sick.

"He —" Bodie shakes her head. Nausea rolls in Flint's stomach. Harbinger sucks in a breath. "After — her wings —"

Bile rises in Flint's throat. His tongue is heavy. Tingling. He can't find breath to force the words out.

"Wings?" Harbinger murmurs. "But that's not..."

Flint's voice crackles like static. "It's not them."

Bodie hisses in pain. Omen wraps both his hands around one of hers. She clutches tighter, gritting her teeth. "It's so much. It's like she's been waiting so long…"

Flint's head swims like he's there again, torn between before and after, her reflection in the mirror with hair falling down her back. Those same strands wet with blood, spilling out around her, as dark as a hole dug straight into the ground.

"Stop." Flint breaks the grip Harbinger has on him, pushing to his feet. The candles flare. "It's not one of them!"

Patches of black throb in his vision. He can't breathe. He reaches for the wall, hand slipping when he tries to steady himself.

Someone calls his name. There's a tunnel with Bodie at one end, her eyes locked on him for the first time. The look splinters his chest the same way it did all those years ago, worn by someone else. Her voice is small through the dark room.

"You watched her die?"

NINETEEN

Harbinger

Fear hits Harbinger first.

Of course this spirit is scared, fury splitting the atoms of her despair. But then there's guilt. A heart-wrenching ache that leaves Harbinger clutching her own chest. Only then does she realize these emotions aren't coming from the spirit at all.

They're coming from Flint.

He stands so tall above them on the floor, but the look on his face is distant, pulled so taut that Harbinger could almost see straight through him.

Candles scatter under his feet, light spilling across the ritual when he bursts out the nearest exit. The spectral dome over the group shatters. Bodie swipes at her face, returned from between the Veil as Omen smooths a delicate hand over her hair.

"I'm sorry —" Bodie bursts into tears. Every inhale is a shudder. "It never gets easier."

Harbinger's legs won't stay beneath her. Emotions flood from all the corners of the room as she tilts, trying to stand. The floor rises up to meet her —

Shadowed arms loop over her head and catch around her waist. Her head spins. "Sorry." Agony shushes her. Poe's face appears before them, a reassuring grip on Harbinger's hands.

"You don't need to apologize," Poe assures them. "It was an accident, but it wasn't a mistake."

She urges them toward the open door, out to a balcony that wraps around the rock face. Stairs lead down each level toward the ground, but a flap of wings descends beneath them.

Harbinger squints against the sunlight. "He shouldn't fly like this."

"Come on." Agony's voice cuts through the daze. "I've got you."

Breaking the Veil's connection so abruptly leaves her reeling against the emotions pouring into her. Agony loops her arm around his neck, guiding her down the stairs as she tilts to catch sight of Flint over the ledge. Agony's grip tightens around her waist. "Will you *please* let me lead?" She leans her weight against him until there's solid ground beneath their feet.

There's one rock big enough to hold Flint. His elbows press to his knees, head resting in his hands as he swallows a deep breath and holds it. The sight breaks open a part of Harbinger's chest. Flint looks up when they approach, rising to his feet, but it lacks the brusque certainty he always carries.

"Shit. I shouldn't have left you with him…"

"It's fine." Agony perches Harbinger on the rock before he draws his bound hands back over her head. "I didn't even try…"

But he trails off. It's too close to home, too raw. Flint's stony presence is fragile, a hairline fracture waiting to shatter.

"The girl Bodie spoke for…" Harbinger presses her gloved hand down against the boulder. "You know her."

A dust storm kicks up in the distance. Questions batter at Harbinger's lips, but she keeps them at bay until Flint's voice finally comes. It creaks before he clears his throat, rusty through disuse.

"It was my sister."

His emotions claw at her chest as if they were her own. Loss and remorse like the dry ground beneath them, desperate for a drop of water.

"Sidi. She was a kid. Old enough to think she knew everything."

His eyes slip closed. Everything in Harbinger is amplified.

"A man started stopping by work to see her. I told her from the start. *'There's a reason a grown man's paying attention to a child. It's nothing good.'*" Flint shakes his head. "She said she would stay away from him. That there was nothing going on."

His mouth twitches, the barest flicker of a smile blooming like flowers in Harbinger's chest when he touches his cheek. A memory faded from his skin.

"She told me I worried too much."

Then his face falls. The petals drown in a deluge of pain.

"I should have done it differently. Said something else. Changed my tone. Should have just *stopped* her...but I didn't. I knew when she was late coming home that night that something wasn't... She was always late, but it was different. By the time I realized she'd gone to meet him..." Flint's claws dig into his skin. "I barely made it to her before she was gone."

Storm clouds hang on the horizon. Thunder rumbles. Harbinger's legs are jelly. "You never told me that."

He sucks in a breath. "I hate remembering it. For years after, my family was never the same. We splintered. I'm not proud of that point in my life."

"Why?" Agony's voice is soft. Flint closes his eyes again. There's a pang at the memory playing out behind his eyelids.

"Because I killed him."

Lightning flashes in the distance, but it feels like it strikes straight between them. Flint won't look at her.

"He wasn't hard to find. Or maybe it's easier with enough *motivation*."

Restrained rage boils inside of Harbinger, but she's not sure what's hers and what's Flint's. Agony's the one to find words. "But he deserved it."

"Maybe he did. But I didn't do it for protection. I did it out of anger." The tension in Flint's shoulders finally sinks, like he can't carry the weight any more. "It didn't bring her back. It didn't make me proud of myself." His claws have left marks in his palms. His fingers flex as he stares at them. "It didn't make me someone she would be proud of."

That's where Flint's grief is. What hurts the most, fathomless and raw, a gaping wound Harbinger doesn't realize sends tears slipping down her face.

"That's why the OID warns you away from me." Flint's hands drop between his knees. "They were investigating him, a serial rapist. Sidi was his first murder. If they would've caught him sooner —" But Flint doesn't let himself follow that thought, a path already worn down from constant travel. "They said they didn't have enough evidence, so I used it against them. Didn't leave anything they could pin to me. They know I did it. They just can't prove it."

He won't look at her. Harbinger pulls off her gloves and reaches for him, pushing to teetering feet, the bare skin of her hand pressing into his. Feelings avalanche through their connection. She tries to keep her head above them, fingers curling in his sleeves, trying to pull him closer. His weight sinks down against the rock, jaw in her hands until he finally meets her gaze.

His eyes are dull, numb and glassy. She wishes she could take it all, that her power would let her bear the weight of his pain instead of just *feel* it.

"I never wanted to have to tell you..." His jaw clenches. "I didn't want you to think of me like..."

Nothing she says will be right. *I'm so sorry* begs to slip off her tongue, but it won't bring his sister back. Won't leech away the guilt. Won't withdraw all the swords left in him.

"None of it changes us, ok?" She smooths out the tension of his jaw with her fingers. "I need you to know that. We're still partners. I still trust you. *Shh*, yes, I do. It doesn't change how I feel about you." Heat pricks behind her eyes. "I'm just...so sorry you didn't feel like you could tell me. That you've been holding it all by yourself."

Flint's exhale is long and deep, like the first breath he's truly taken. Harbinger's thumbs stroke over his cheeks. "Is that why you didn't want to take this case?"

His voice cracks. "They all look *just* like her." A tear slips down beside his tusks, tracking through the dust on his cheeks. "They've barely lived. None of them were thinking about the end. None of them should *have* to. They should have...*so much* time left."

Harbinger wraps around his neck, pulling him into her like it might protect him. They stay like that until his breathing evens, and he lifts his head enough to look at her.

"I can't bring her back. I can't bring any of them back. But I can protect *you*." There's pain in him she can't understand, even as she feels it, a fear that makes it hard to breathe. "That's why I'm here. Why I need you to stay safe, because I can't..."

His head rests heavily against hers. One hand cups her cheek, his thumb brushing against her pulse, hectic and alive. "I can't lose someone that important again. I can't lose you."

"You won't."

It chills her that it sounds like a lie. Because everything she's done up to now, all the thoughtless situation she's put them in, could have made a liar out of her. Could have hurtled Flint into danger they couldn't find their way out of.

And she can't imagine the gaping hole that losing him would leave in her.

Weary lines fade into his face. "It got to me more than I wanted to admit, the shooting at the restaurant."

The shooting Harbinger led them into. The one Flint had to protect her from. Guilt twists in her stomach.

"I haven't been dealing with it the way I should," Flint murmurs. "I haven't been dealing with it at *all*."

"You don't have to carry it all on your own. You can tell me when something's eating at you, even if it's just a feeling." Harbinger swallows. "Even though I haven't been very receptive to what worries you..."

Flint's wet laugh breathes air into the space again, his palm smoothing down Harbinger's back. Sand drifts over the cooling ground as her fingers drift through his hair.

"You never talked about Sidi before. Not even stories before it happened."

Flint watches a cacti flower shiver in the wind. "It's been a long time. I was still a kid myself. And it's hard, having to think about how I've become someone she'll never know. Everything I did for a while felt pointless, because she wasn't here to see it. To experience it. All the milestones felt empty. Now, I never know what's gonna set me off. I'm never fully prepared."

Harbinger swallows around her heart in her throat, nodding as she stares across the plain. "Grief has a funny way of showing up at the most mundane opportunities. But you should talk about her anyway — if Sidi comes to your mind, you should mention her. Any time."

A smile drifts across his lips when he hears Sidi's name again.

The weight becomes a little easier to carry.

TWENTY

Agony

The pain is...confusing.

Even after Flint and Harbinger pull apart, a weary gravity in their bodies, Agony can't place the feeling he has. Once Harbinger gives him a quirk of her brow as they make their way back to the guest quarters, Agony realizes he hasn't spoken for the better part of an hour.

The séance should have been a feast for him. All that delicious pain and terror, a nightmare taking shape in the physical world. And yet, Agony feels nothing.

Not nothing: nothing *good*.

No delight or satisfaction or contentment the way he should have. The way he *used* to. Instead, he feels strange. Queasy. Some other emotion he's never experienced.

So he stays silent, watching, observing, the same way he had after the fire. But this time, there's no horrifying fascination. There's something else. Something quieter. Something softer, like wind drifting through a window, soft and yearning.

It makes him sick.

Because the closest thing he felt to thrill was after the séance, when Harbinger leaned her weight into him and let him guide her.

When she took Flint's face in her hands as if she could take his pain. When Flint and Harbinger wrapped their arms around each other, foreheads resting together, murmuring until thunder drew closer.

Flint's the strongest creature Agony knows, and still, that rock armor was no match for the mere mention of a spirit. Invisible, yet effortlessly decimating.

What emotion could do that? What feeling has that power?

It's dark before Flint sits up in bed, bleary from the stupor he fell into after the séance. "We're supposed to leave today. The Diviner Superior said —"

"She's not gonna do anything." Harbinger eases him back with a hand on his shoulder. "Better to ask forgiveness than permission. And we're not asking forgiveness, either."

Poe brings dinner with a few low words to Harbin before Poe departs. Agony's stomach — or where it might be — growls, and he's not even sure he needs sustenance. The three of them eat before Harbinger jolts Agony from his thoughts.

"You've been quiet."

He looks up from the brie halfway to his mouth. She and Flint are watching him. Agony smooths out his expression and shrugs. "You two have been loud."

It's silent until Harbinger gives a tired giggle that reaches into Agony's chest and twists. Flint's smile lifts as he butters his slice of bread. "Well. Thank you for being less of a bastard than usual."

Agony drops a grape into his mouth. "Regular operations resume tomorrow."

They turn in for the night, awoken hours later by a rap on the door: more work with the Seers. Omen leads them back to the suite where Herald waits, tucked beneath the sheets of her bed.

Her Veil markings spread like a lightning strike, outlining cerebral connections across her shaved head. Indigo candles line her headboard between pictures of the girls. Herald stares into a mirror as the three stand awkwardly in the doorway until she finally acknowledges them.

"I use this as a test of reality." She sets the hand mirror aside. "To be sure I'm awake when I think I am. In my dreams, I have no reflection. I am not present. I am an observer. Unlike Harbinger, my skills extend much further beyond the Veil. The Oracle rewards my dedication."

Harbinger rolls her eyes. Herald doesn't notice.

"Dreams show everything: past. Present. Future. Things that will never come to pass. Mundane objects. Impossible phenomena. The trick lies in determining which is which. I will focus on your question: the location of these girls. I will sleep for a period of time. Long enough to reach the stage of dreaming, after which, my timer will pull me out of sleep." She points to Agony. "You should stay in the vicinity. My room or the lounge is fine. You may try to see if you can enter my dreams, but in either case, I will share what I find when I wake."

It's a meticulous process. The leftover scents from Herald's bath are overwhelming, potent combined with the oil she smears onto her hands. "100 passes," she murmurs as she rubs it into her skin, "not a stroke less." There's no light in the room, curtains pulled tight, leaving the space cool and dark. Herald turns onto her side in the bed, and Harbinger sticks out her tongue until Flint nudges her with his hip.

Agony sits at the foot of the bed, eyes closed, trying to focus on Herald twitching in her sleep. A whisper cuts through the darkness. "Anything?"

One of Agony's eyes cracks open. "Not if you keep *interrupting.*"

"She's been asleep for two hours," Harbinger hisses. "If it hasn't happened by now…"

Flint shushes them. Herald rolls over but doesn't wake. Once her breathing evens again, Agony hones all his attention on her. Not a blip for him to grab onto. No dreams. Not even a hypnic jerk.

"Nothing." Agony leans back against the wall. "I've got no idea what she's dreaming about."

"She should be in REM by now, yeah?" Harbinger checks the timer. Herald starts to snore. A nagging feeling eats in the back of Agony's mind, frustration he's never had to contend with.

Flint moves out of the doorway. "Maybe she'll have something when she wakes up. We can check back in a bit."

They move to the lounge to wait. Flint finds a deck of cards and offers to teach them a game he and Sidi used to play. There's that feeling again, the warmth that sparks in Agony as soon as Flint mentions her name. Flint catches him staring; Agony tries to bury it behind the cards in his hand.

He picks up the rules quickly. Flint swears he's cheating. Harbinger actually *is*, but they've just discovered her secret stash of cards when Herald's timer chimes.

She's upright in bed as they enter. A notebook lays open in her lap, full of scrawls and scribbles, diagrams and drawings. Her fingers rub over a pearly blue stone, waiting until Harbinger breaks the silence.

"So...did you see anything?"

"Yes." There's a smug sense of satisfaction as Herald says the word, turning her notebook to face them. They lean over the page for a long moment.

"It's..." Agony blinks. "It's illegible scribbles, right? That's what we're all seeing?"

Flint clears his throat. "It's..."

But Herald isn't offended. "This is your Reid." She circles a shape with her finger, pronounced in the center. "And these..." She taps the smaller identical sticks at the base of the drawing. "Are his greatest desires."

Harbinger's eyes narrow. Agony glances at Flint. Finally, Flint asks the question. "...what are they? His desires."

"Followers." Herald gestures, as if it should be obvious. "It's his greatest goal, to build a community that worships him. Acolytes that share his ideals."

"O*kay*," drawls Harbinger. "Is that it? You saw what he wants to do? What about the girls?"

"I do not choose which threads to follow."

Harbinger groans.

Agony leans over the paper. "What is that over them? Is that a giant leaf? Are they *fanning* him?"

Herald gestures to the drawing again. "The Oracle provides what is needed. You will find the answers you need here, so say the Oracle."

"Except we didn't," Harbinger snaps.

Flint mutters her name under his breath. "Thank you for sharing what you saw," he tempers. "But is there any chance you can go back? Have another dream? Maybe there's more to it than we understand right now."

"I can try." With a flip of her notebook, Herald sinks beneath the sheets, immediately back to business.

They wait through another cycle. And another, until Harbinger begins to nod off as sunlight peeks through the windows. The vision is always the same: Reid standing above his desired groupies. No girls. No location. Just crude stick figures.

"This is what the Oracle wants you to see." By this point, Herald's irritated. "Perhaps it is not what you seek, but it is what you need. This dream comes to me over and over. It's clearly important."

"Well. *Thanks*." Harbinger's lip curls. "We'll keep it in mind."

Flint sounds more sincere. "Thank you. Is it all right if I keep the picture? Just in case?"

Herald tears the page from her notebook before she escorts them out the door. It closes a little harder than necessary.

Harbinger's fists ball at her sides. "What the fuck? What are we supposed to do with that?"

"She can't control it. You said so yourself." Flint folds the drawing into his pocket. "Maybe it'll make sense as we get closer."

"We're not going to..." But Harbinger trails off as Bodie

approaches, apologetic smile on her face. "Oh no," Harbinger breathes. "You couldn't get anything either?"

"I'm sorry, I tried. Sometimes a group is too powerful, so I tried reaching out to the girls on my own." Bodie shakes her head. "I couldn't find anyone, not even the spirits that are usually around." At their crestfallen faces, Bodie cringes. "I'm really sorry. I wish I could choose who the Oracle lets through."

"I know." Harbinger shoots a guilty look toward Flint. "She only lets you see what you need."

Harbinger thanks her and moves away to gather the casefiles. Agony follows, but Flint stops Bodie around the corner.

"I wanted to know..." His voice strains. Agony lingers on the other side of the wall. "If you might help me, just the two of us. Maybe we could reach..."

"I'm sorry." Bodie's voice is soft. "I looked for your sister, too. Yesterday was just too traumatic for her. Sometimes spirits need to rest after making contact." She considers her words before she finishes. "And your sister's been trying to get in touch with you for a long time."

Neither of them speaks for a moment. Across the room, Harbinger stacks the folders. Agony strains to hear Flint.

He sounds deflated. "I understand. Thank you for all your help."

Agony isn't fast enough. Flint turns the corner, catching Agony by both arms to keep him from stumbling. Flint's brows knit. There's a weary weight that doesn't leave his eyes as he stares into Agony's.

Harbinger appears behind them. Flint releases Agony before he turns to make his way back down the corridor.

And there's that fucking feeling again.

TWENTY-ONE

Harbinger

Flint stops Harbinger outside the guest quarters. Agony raises his brows, but mercifully, leaves them near the staircase. It's been a long night of back and forth. Harbinger's body is rusty and worn, focused on the bed waiting for her to crash into it, but Flint's concern rouses her drowsy mind. "What is it?"

Pressure constricts through Harbinger's chest. Being back here, at the Convent, leaves her on edge, but it's left an imprint on Flint, too. Suddenly finding — then losing — a connection with his sister has taken a toll, but there's more to it. Harbinger doesn't need her ability to name the tension the two of them haven't addressed. The things they aren't saying. The topic neither of them have been brave enough to breach.

"After yesterday…" Flint runs a hand through his hair. "I need to ask. I need to know where we stand."

She knows what's coming. What they should have addressed the first night. What she's been avoiding for months. It doesn't make Flint's words land any easier.

"Are you only sleeping with me because you have no other options?"

Her head jerks. It's not what she expected him to say, wrong enough to throw her off-balance. She grapples for an easy answer. "You asked me that before."

"And I'm asking you again. Now that you've had some time to think about it."

His gaze levels on hers, a question she isn't escaping. Inside herself, she reaches for the tap of his emotions, to get a feel for where he's coming from — but there's nothing there. No flow. Not a drip.

He barricades his emotions from her, locking them down and shaking his head. "Don't use that."

Her jaw clenches. She hates that he knows that's what she reached for, that it's the first thing she tried. That she'd cheat to make this easier, use her powers to an unfair advantage. Her tongue runs over her lip and comes back tasting salt. "Are you serious?"

"You don't want to go back to your exes, so there's no one else who can touch you like I can. I'm not blaming you if you are. It's fine." It doesn't *look* fine, from the steel rod through his spine. "Just want to be on the same page about what we're doing."

Her mouth is dry. "Why would you think that?"

His laugh drives a spike through her chest. It's barely a breath, like he can't find any humor for it. Like she should know the answer. "Come on, Harbin."

Of course she knows. She's been careful with what they share, what they do, always pulling back before they talk about what they are. But a different guilt gnaws at her chest, a different fear she's not ready to face.

"No, you're not — the only option. That's not *why*." It's like she's sliding down a cliff face, grappling for a handhold. "Do you want more than what we're doing?"

"This isn't about me."

Now *she* laughs. "Of course it is! We're both a part of this, aren't we? I haven't been fucking myself for the last four months."

He averts his eyes while her mind flips back through their encounters. Her tugging on his belt, her undoing both their buttons, her...

It dawns on her in a flare of embarrassment. "But I always initiate it." Breath scrapes out of her. "Do you not want to do this?"

"No! No, that's not what I'm saying. I —" But he cuts himself off, as he always does. "I want whatever you want, Harbin. Whatever you need. I can do that for you."

And there it is: that valiant propriety, the chivalry that fell on its sword. It rolls in her stomach, remorse bubbling in the face of all his noble sacrifice.

"That's not...I don't want to *use* you. I don't want this to be about *me*." Her hands run down her face before she turns back to him. "You're always so fucking worried about me, wondering if I'm in the barest hint of danger. If you're putting the *slightest* pressure on me. What about what *you* want?" She throws out her hands. "Ask for it! Take it!"

There's fire in Flint's eyes, like he might do it. Reach across the space and tell her what she knows he's hiding. But then he shakes his head, voice heavy from the weight of all he refuses to spill. "I can't do that to you."

"I want you to!" She closes the space, gripping his sleeves, searching his face for a hint of what he's feeling. "I know you're doing your job —"

"This is not just my *job*."

"— but you don't have to safeguard me from your emotions. You're allowed to *feel things*. You're allowed to *want* things. It doesn't always have to be good; it doesn't have to be selfless. I'm not *precious*. I'm not breakable."

Flint's fingers close over her arms until they're engulfed completely in his hands. "But you are...*so fucking breakable*, Harbin." Emotions swell past the wall he has around them, squeezing through the cracks with anxiety and fear. "I don't know why you don't realize it. I don't think you want to. But sometimes, the things you do...it's like you want to get hurt. Like you want to lean as far over the edge as you can, and then push a little further. Like you want to..."

He doesn't finish, but they both hear the word drop between them, lead that echoes.

Die.

Flint hesitates. "Is that what you want?"

The word buzzes through her brain, rattling her thoughts. She can't look at him. "I need a minute." Her boots thunder down the stairs, not slowing until the sound of him calling her fades in the distance.

Of course it's not what she wants. It's ridiculous. But each step she takes is a fight against fear. Has it been seeping through her body without her realizing? Has she been hurtling toward an end without looking where the signs pointed? Has the thing she swore she hates had its claws in her all this time?

It's not what I want...is it?

She's afraid of the answer.

It was easier before. Before Harbinger and Flint talked about things outside of where they were stopping for dinner. Before she caught him staring at her bare face for a fraction too long. Before she knew the comfort of his arms closing around her, the low rumble in his chest as he assured her everything would be fine.

Before Agony crawled into her mind, under her skin, finding pieces of her past that she thought she'd buried. Before his cuffs against her throat got her pulse racing. Before the flicker of his eyes offered some reckless promise, that ledge she wants to step out onto.

Her feet carry her without thought. All these years later, it's muscle memory, escaping the Convent's oppressive presence through the caverns to...here. Her eyes slip shut.

"Rough day already?"

Omen's voice startles her. Right: she's not wearing her helmet. Easy to forget how comfortable she's gotten, keeping the visor between her and the rest of the world. Shielding her face, her expressions, her feelings. There's no barrier now, but there never has been between them.

She averts her eyes. "Need some space."

"Well, you came to the wrong place." He elbows Poe's door open in invitation. Harbinger can't fight the twitch of her lip as she enters.

He's right; the banshees have never had enough space between them. Crammed into dormitories, bodies draped over each other, clothes strewn across someone else's bed. Harbinger learned quickly what touching someone else meant for her, but there were accidents over the years.

Touch is something she's avoided for so long, but with Poe and Omen, it's a comfort, a feeling she adjusted to long ago. While others are a thudding reminder inside her, these two glow like embers, candles to guide her way.

"Found a stray," Omen calls as he pulls a joint from his pocket, flopping down onto the bright orange couch. Poe glances up from her sewing machine, beaming as Harbinger sinks down next to Omen. Her knee knocks against his. He returns the gesture. Harbinger's head falls back to stare at the ceiling.

"Don't tell me we're better company than the bedmates you brought."

"They're not..." But Harbinger's voice trails off under a confusing swirl of emotion. The feelings are all her own, untainted by anyone else's. In the distance, Flint's uncertainty muddles with Agony's probing. Harbinger should feel more from this room. She reaches for her connections with Poe and Omen, but they're placid as a lake, showing Harbinger her reflection.

Her eyes narrow. "Still pulling that shit?"

Poe readjusts the fabric she's working on. "Sometimes you need it."

It's a trick they learned a long time ago. A way to force Harbinger to examine her feelings, walling off their emotions with a mirror that amplifies Harbinger's own emotions back to her. In the early days, it was the only way to get Harbinger to acknowledge what she felt.

"Is it working?" Omen holds out his hand with the rolled Seelie Bark. Harbinger takes it and presses it to her lips. She inhales, staring across the expanse of her feelings until she takes one slow step into their depths.

"Maybe." She exhales smoke, shivering even with morning light through the windows. Omen tugs a woven blanket off the back of the couch. She bunches it around her. "You live like fucking bats here."

A laugh trickles from Omen before he reclines against the arm of the couch, crossing his ankles in Harbinger's lap. "So above it now, huh, Big Shot?" He plucks the joint back from her as Poe inspects her fabric. This is how it was in the years before Harbinger left — smoking things they weren't supposed to, talking shit and laughing about whatever new rules the Diviners initiated.

Poe's eyes flick over the seams of her garment. Her voice is low, like she's trying not to spook an animal. "They're good for you, Harbinger."

"And how would you know?"

Poe doesn't rise to the bait. Harbinger's frustration reflects off of them until she's forced to recognize who she's actually upset with.

Like looking in a mirror.

Poe wets the end of a thread between her lips. "Flint watches you like he'd lay on the ground and let you walk across him if it would make things easier for you."

"That's the problem." A pang drives deep into Harbinger's stomach. "And Agony would try to kill me."

"And you still look at him like you want to see what else those handcuffs are good for."

Omen takes another hit from the joint. "Freaky bitch."

Poe snips a thread with her scissors. "You always liked to live on the edge."

"Oh my gods..." Fingers massage into Harbinger's eyelids. Despite her best efforts, there's still a smile tugging at the corners of her lips.

Poe's room decor is the same, but there's more now. Shitty paintings by Omen, clippings from contraband magazines, photographs Harbinger wasn't present for. She can't get comfortable here, not just because of the cold. The Convent is full of such contrasting feelings, warm and cold fronts clashing until they whirl inside her.

A chill follows the Diviners wherever they go, guiding students through dark corridors, ushering them into deeper rooms, and locking them in the Veil Chambers...

But then there's this: the warmth of Poe's smiles. The weight of Omen's legs across her lap. The same things Harbinger clung to back when they tucked into matching beds, legs stretching toward footboards as they giggled in the dark.

Now, those memories stretch over her like an old favorite shirt, worn and soft, but not somewhere Harbinger can fit again.

"Why couldn't I be happy here?"

The sewing machine clacks, but they're listening. They always are.

"You were never meant to be here, Harbin." Poe slows the pedal. "Not forever. You were never gonna stay."

"How do you know?"

Poe taps the Veil marks around her eyes before she extends both middle fingers, dragging them down to kiss. She raises them proudly in a bastardized version of the holy motion. "So fuck the Oracle."

Omen and Harbinger follow suit, the way they have a thousand times. "So fuck we all."

Rolling back in her chair, Poe drapes the garment over a flat surface. "You told me not to tell you," she reminds Harbinger. It's an agreement that's withstood the test of time, sworn after the first vision Poe had of her.

You should eat something light today. Poe leaned over Harbinger's shoulder in the dining hall. *You're going to be sick later.*

Harbinger was surly then. Well, surl*ier.* *Don't tell me anything you see about me.* Spitefully, she reached for the greasiest thing she could find. *Even if I'm dying. Especially then.*

She spent that night vomiting after another banshee accidentally knocked against her bare hand. Poe held her hair back, careful not to touch Harbinger's skin, even though they were already connected.

"I didn't need the Sight to tell me that you would leave." Poe bunches the fabric, pins peeking out between her lips. "You were never happy here — not like you could be. Not like you are now."

TWENTY-TWO

Agony

Agony didn't mean to overhear...this time. That's the thing with him and Harbinger. He's not sure if it's the connection or intuition or doors that are too thin, but he knows something's up when Flint returns to the guest room.

Yesterday wore on him. After the last month — phoenix-fire burns, the near-loss of his partner, Agony's irritating presence — a séance was the thing to catch up to Flint. He drops the casefiles on the dresser, sinking down on the end of the bed.

Agony should leave well enough alone. But when has he ever?

"Did you fight?"

"Eavesdropping?" But there's no fire in Flint's tone. He doesn't have the energy to bite back at Agony as they always do, not when everything's coming undone around him.

Agony leans back in the desk chair, propping his legs on the top. "Over-protective?"

Flint pinches the bridge of his nose. "How do you know that?"

His irritation is different. Not directed at Agony for once, but at Flint himself. It must be frustrating, how someone new sees what Flint can't after he's spent so much time thinking he knew Harbinger. Thinking Harbinger knew him.

Or maybe that's Agony's wishful thinking. He shrugs. "She's telling you exactly what she wants."

Flint undoes the top button of his shirt. "Then why am I struggling to do it?"

"Because you don't trust her."

"I trust Harbinger with —"

"Your life, right?"

Flint's eyes narrow.

Agony nods. "Exactly: that's not the most important thing you could trust her with."

A scoff escapes Flint. "What could be more important?"

"You trust her with your life. Do you trust her with *hers*?"

The muscle in Flint's jaw tenses. His gaze dips to the ground.

"I know you're not big on putting faith in other people." Agony presses a sarcastic hand to his chest. "Present company excluded. But it's more than people you don't know. You don't trust Harbinger to understand her abilities. To tell you when something's too much. To ask for what she needs. What she wants. And I don't think you trust yourself to give it to her, either."

"And why is that?" Derision laces Flint's words, but at least he's asking.

"Because everything in you screams to protect her. It's your nature. It's your job."

Flint's eyes roll. Agony drops his feet to the ground. "All those years sharing the same cramped car, and you still don't understand each other."

"We understand each other," Flint grumbles.

"You know how to work together. How to keep each other alive. But how close have you actually let each other get?"

The séance proved that with the massive weight Flint was carrying without realizing. Every move he makes happens in the shadow of his sister's murder, echoing through Flint's every action. How much of his hypervigilance has to do with Harbinger, and how much has to do with Flint himself? The man has never learned to put something down just because it's heavy.

And Harbinger's not innocent. Even if Agony doesn't know what her dreams mean yet, that house and the stone slab aren't nothing.

"You could predict almost anything Harbinger does — how she'd look if you held open her car door, what condiments she uses at every restaurant — and she could do the same for you. But neither of you know why. Why you react the way you do. Why you keep butting heads any time there's a hint of peril. Harbinger's not the only one holding back."

Flint rubs his jaw as bitterness slips into his voice. "Must be nice getting all that insight from one touch. Being connected to her. Seeing things I've apparently missed for years."

Agony shakes his head as he tilts the chair back on two legs. "You have a connection with Harbinger — one that magic can't replicate. But you don't trust it enough. You don't trust *yourselves* enough."

Flint doesn't look at him. Keeps his eyes on his flexing fingers, gaze tracing over his palms. Agony sets his chair back on the ground.

"Is it because of that man?"

Flint doesn't answer.

"It wasn't wrong, you know," Agony supplies. "Killing him."

"And you're the expert on that."

"I'm a pretty good authority on what *is* wrong."

There's no arguing that. When Harbinger explained it to Agony, it made sense. It seemed simple. But Flint doesn't see it that way.

"Why do you feel guilty?" Agony tries.

Flint considers the answer. Considers not responding. His eyes dart toward the doorway, as if chasing Harbinger down would be far better than this conversation. But then, his fists drop between his knees.

"It didn't feel good. It didn't make me feel better. It didn't make a difference."

"You stopped a bad person from doing bad things to someone else. I'd say that makes a difference."

A biting laugh scratches Flint's throat. "And how do you know killing him didn't make me a bad person?" The words stick on his tongue. Agony tilts his head.

"When I killed people, it felt good."

"Why?"

It's the first real question Flint has asked him. Agony stares up to the ceiling. "It felt good giving back what I was getting. Revenge. Returning the favor." Agony rolls his head to look at Flint. "Have you killed other people?"

"Yes."

"For the same reason?"

"Similar."

"But you wish you hadn't?"

"No." Flint lays back across the bed, hands resting on the curve of his stomach. "There were no other options. I'd do it again to protect Harbinger. To protect other people. I don't regret what I've done, but...killing people isn't nothing to me."

"So you need a guard dog."

Flint lifts a brow toward him.

"You're defense," Agony explains. "The armor. The wings to escape. You need someone to play offense. To get their hands dirty. You protect Harbin, and your guard dog attacks."

Finally, there's a shred of humor in Flint's smile. "And that's gonna be you?"

"Maybe."

You can't protect her everywhere...but we could.

"See..." Flint hisses a skeptical breath. "I can't tell if this is a game to you. If it's a fun way to fuck with us. Get as close as you can before you kill us and everyone around."

"You wouldn't believe me if I tell you I won't."

"No."

Agony shrugs. "For the best. Not sure I could give you an honest answer."

"We know next to nothing about you." Flint follows Agony's gaze toward the ceiling. "What you're capable of. If you can circumvent Harbinger's abilities. Place false emotions and thoughts in her head. Put up a wall to hide the truth."

"You want the truth?"

Flint's hands lift, like he doesn't expect it to come either way. Agony reclines in the chair.

"Harbinger wants you to fuck her brains out. Decide what you want and take it. Push her body to the brink until she begs you to stop." His knees fall open, draped over the chair. "Quit worrying if it's too much, too vulgar for you to want. You have this idea of what it means to be good; you're either valiant, or you're villainous. Chivalrous or corrupt. But it's not like that."

Raw heat flares in Flint's eyes. It stokes the coals deep in Agony's stomach, not a leftover flare of Harbinger's arousal. Flint's mouth forms around the words. "What's it like, then?"

"You can make her choke on your dick and hold her after. Make her work for it and then take it away." Agony leans forward into his knees, grin melting as slow as butter. "You can be as mean as she's begging you to be, *Jas*. Promise she'll think you're a saint."

Flint doesn't look away. Doesn't blink. Agony aches to be free of these cuffs, to snap across the room and find out how Flint's mouth tastes when it's not trying to be good. His voice rumbles through Agony.

"You sure seem to think you know what you're talking about."

"I could show you a thing or two."

Flint keeps Agony pinned under his gaze. "That requires trust."

Agony exhales, sinking back in his chair. "That it does."

TWENTY-THREE

Harbinger

You were never happy here. Not like you are now.

Harbinger knows it's true. No matter how many good moments she had at the Convent, the comfort she found with the others, it wasn't enough to drown out everything that happened.

"You could leave, too," she murmurs. "Come with me."

Omen's lips quirk behind his joint. Poe doesn't look up. Guilt sticks Harbinger as sharply as embarrassment.

"You *could.*"

"Yes," Poe agrees, "technically, we could."

"What does that mean? 'Technically'?"

"It means we're not fit for the real world!" Omen nudges her with his foot, but there's austerity in his tone. "We were here a while before you came along. No matter what we did, the Diviners always had the biggest problem with you."

Harbinger remembers her first day at the Convent. Glowering to hide her fear as she stood at the dorm entrance, a lanky preteen who recoiled whenever someone got close. She still looked almost human at that point, circles darkening under her eyes, but she couldn't stop staring at two of the others her age. Patterned like skeletons, watching her and whispering.

Poe and Omen knew every secret tunnel of the Convent. The ways to tilt their heads and smile when a Diviner grew suspicious. *We barely remember anything before the Convent*, Poe and Omen told her. Harbinger said that was sad. They thought the same thing about her.

"I would help you," Harbinger says now. Omen shakes his head as he laughs. Poe cringes.

"No offense to your nomadic lifestyle, but I don't want to live in various motel rooms with you and your boyfriends. It's not for me." It takes a moment for her eyes to widen toward Harbinger's glare. "Totally appreciate the offer, though!"

Giggles spill from all three of them, encouraged by glimpses at each other, the same rolling laughter that got them into trouble in the back of classrooms. Harbinger takes another hit from the joint, coughing until Omen pats her back and takes it from her.

"You know they do it on purpose, The Diviners." Harbinger's voice seems to echo. "They don't teach us about the rest of the world. They keep us helpless so we'll stay. They make the Convent the only place we can survive."

"Well, it's working." Poe aligns her garment before she stops, fingers curling into the fabric. "You remember what you said? How it's strange the Oracle never seems to 'bless' anyone with a happy family? I met my first one this year. Talking about her parents, how excited she was to write them, and the Diviners were already doing it. Telling her she'd be *very busy* with her lessons, that she should focus on her gift, that keeping attachments to her 'old life' could keep her from being able to pierce the Veil. I took over after they left. Made sure she got plenty of stationary to write her letters, but I could see it starting." Poe waves a weak hand in front of her eyes. "The doubt."

In her mind, Harbinger stands in front of her house again. She boards it up until she can breathe.

"Maybe we do need to leave," Omen murmurs. Sunlight reflects off the shattered glass hanging from strings near the window, broken beer bottles repurposed when he returns from house-calls. "Maybe we keep holding on, hoping this place will feel like it used to, but it won't. It's not easy when the Convent is everything. We didn't have lives before this. We've been here longer than we've been anywhere else. This place tore us apart..." He flicks a piece of glass above his head, and they all tinkle together. "But it's also the thing that brought us together."

They sit like that for a while, under the whir of the sewing machine, until Harbinger exhales. "I wish it was as easy to start something new with Flint and Agony as it was with you two."

The whirring stops. Harbinger doesn't get a chance to glance toward them before they burst into laughter.

"What?"

"It wasn't *easy* with us! You don't get to rewrite history now!" Omen throws a pillow toward her. "Revisionist."

Harbinger ducks under the pillow and gapes. "What do you mean?"

"You fought us every step of the way!" Poe gestures. "By the time you left, I still wasn't sure if you actually liked us or tolerated us."

A delinquent grin creeps across Harbinger's face.

"I knew you were soft." Omen rummages through the basket of snacks on Poe's coffee table. "The letters were further confirmation."

Harbinger sits up straighter. "You got them?"

"Of course." Poe pulls her foot off the pedal. "You kept writing not knowing if anyone read them?"

Harbinger picks at the fuzz pilling off the blanket. Omen digs his heel into her thigh. "Told you she was sweet on us."

Writing to the two of them was like a diary, no chance of their reply when Harbinger never stayed in one place for long. Detailing the rough nights, the good days, the familiar pangs from their connection when uncertainty overwhelmed Poe or Omen was numb with grief.

"We had dramatic readings of your letters," Omen says as Poe pulls out a stack of pages from her desk drawer. She smooths them out, tapping the bottom of the stack until it's even.

"*Got shot at last week.*" She tosses her hair over her shoulder. "*Also accidentally touched Flint, but that hasn't been all bad.*"

Omen leans closer to Harbinger. "This is my favorite part."

Harbinger shoves his face away. Poe continues.

"*Turns out he's talented at more than business and security. It was so much better than the fantasies.*"

Poe squeals. Harbinger wraps the blanket over Omen's head as the room dissolves into giddy laughter. It's as warm as the first memory of Flint touching her.

By the time Omen wrestles out of Harbinger's grip, she combs hair back into her braid.

"You're happy with them." Poe slips the letters back into the drawer, pressing fingers to her lips then down to the paper where Harbinger sealed them. "How much have you told them?"

It's tempting to lie, but Harbinger doesn't. "Not enough."

"I know it's hard letting people close. Showing them what made you. Things that happened that you'd rather forget. But keeping your back to those things doesn't make them go away. It doesn't make them hurt less. You picked them up, but you have to put them down."

Harbinger hangs on the memory of a much smaller Poe clutching her gloved hands, both of them quivering outside the guest chamber doors. It's the way they survived the expectations of their gifts, seeing and hearing and feeling things through the Veil that they were never prepared for.

Pick it up, and put it down. Use your powers, but don't let them control you. Don't carry the weight of what you see. You have to release it. You have to let it go.

"Flint's been with you for, what, seven years?" Poe continues. "And now you can see inside his heart. The least you can do is share a fraction of yours with him."

"And what about Agony?" Harbinger worries teeth into her lip. "He's already gotten inside my head in ways Flint can't. In ways I've never let him. That's fucked up."

"So?" Omen rests an arm against the back of the couch. "People are different. Relationships are different. It doesn't make one less than another."

"And do you think, *maybe*," Poe stretches the word, "you let Agony closer because Flint is with you? Because you feel safe enough to open up when he's there."

Even when things with Agony didn't make sense, even when Harbinger learned the OID had tricked her, Flint was beside her no matter what. They would always figure it out together, whatever that meant.

"And —"

But Poe stops. Her lip quivers, eyes darting toward Omen. He gives the smallest shake of his head. Words beg to spill — something Poe's seen. Something the Sight gave her. But Poe keeps her mouth clamped shut.

"Just consider removing Agony's cuffs," Omen supplies. "You can't keep him chained up forever. Unless it is a sex thing."

Poe's smile is watery. "You have a new family, Harbinger. You're always welcome with us, but this isn't where you're supposed to be."

It's that ledge Harbinger's always inching toward. Dark enough that she can't see over, a place to step out without knowing where she might land. It would be easier to stay here, even as she knows it would destroy her. A place where she knows what to expect. Where the people have lived the same lives. Have seen her through dark times. Know her trauma without Harbinger having to say a word.

Her lip trembles. "But I'm happy with you."

"You're happy with us," Poe agrees. "But don't pretend you're happy *here*. Don't let the Convent take anything else from you. It's not your home any more, if it ever was."

Omen's hand finds Harbinger's, squeezing as tightly as he can. He and Poe let their emotions through the reflective surface, turning into a warm and sticky mess that Harbinger can't avoid. She sinks back and lets it wash over her.

"It was."

The bind around Harbinger's chest loosens as she descends from Poe's room, mulling over the truth she's avoided since she left this place. Children scamper down the great staircase, scurrying to their new classes.

"Harbinger."

The thought of Poe or Omen following makes her stop. But when Harbinger turns, she's met with black robes and clasped hands.

Auspice. *Diviner Superior.*

"It's *Seer* Harbinger." Malice laces Harbinger's tongue. "Or have you forgotten our customs?"

"Those titles are reserved for those that remain within our practice." Auspice drifts closer. Harbinger's head aches, fending off the drip of Auspice's emotions inside her. "But we could make an exception. It could be your title again."

The bustle of class changes fades in the distance, conversations and footsteps dying as doors close, leaving the two of them alone.

"What are you talking about?"

Auspice keeps her chin raised, looking down at Harbinger to bestow a glorious purpose. All these years, and it's still the same; Auspice's curtailed emotions prod through Harbinger's skin. She hates the feeling. Hates feeling *her*.

"The Diviners have discussed it. We could accept you back into our fold and provide you with housing among the other Seers. Despite the way you left, it has been decided that we will allow you to return to the Convent...under a few conditions."

A disbelieving laugh tugs on Harbinger's lips. "Are you joking?"

"There's plenty of use for your power here. Our patrons would benefit from your gift, and it would be a wonderful way for you to give thanks to the Oracle. To express your gratitude for what She's given you."

Rage lights a wick inside of Harbinger. "I'm not coming back here again. *Ever.* I shouldn't have come this time."

Auspice clucks her tongue. "Divine purpose has chosen you. You've known that since you were a child. There's no glory or grace in resisting for the sake of rebellion."

Fury floods half a smile onto Harbinger's face as she tries to keep her voice even. "If you think some childish rebellion is what keeps me from coming back here, you're kidding yourself."

"Look at the creatures you've made acquaintances with." Auspice's voice lowers, body looming over Harbinger. "One of them is in *handcuffs*. It's not the first time we've aided — troubled visitors, but you won't find virtue there. You're squandering your glorious gift following treacherous roads. They are not the paths to righteousness. The Oracle does not reward reckless charity."

She plucks a worn spot on Harbinger's suit. Harbinger smacks her hand away. "Don't touch me."

There's pity in Auspice's eyes. "I know we've had our differences. But your gift is too important, your value too great. Don't let all you've been given go to waste."

Harbinger descends the stairs as Auspice calls after her.

"If you insist, we could create a new position for you. One that allows you to travel and spread the Oracle's word, giving your gift to the community. But you would have to return to the Convent —
"

"I'm not coming back here!"

Every time, Harbinger gets sucked back in: the arguments, the guilt, the rules and regulations, the strict guidelines of what's acceptable. The reminders of how lucky and useful she is. The whole suffocates the individual, worship over all. Even now, as Harbinger knows she shouldn't, she whirls back up the steps.

"I don't want to do this! I didn't ask for this! None of us did!"

"You're the only child that can't give thanks for the blessed talent the Oracle has given you."

A nasty laugh escapes Harbinger. "No, I'm not. You just don't see. You don't *look*. For all that extra sight, you ignore everything in front of you."

Auspice is unyielding. "You're being selfish. Think of all who could benefit from you, everyone you could help."

"What about *me*?"

The crack in Harbinger's voice stops them both. Exposing a chink in her armor, a fracture in the waver of her lip spreading like the hot pain edging behind her eyes. It's an echo of Harbinger before, small and scared without the words she needed. Without anyone to hear them.

But that was someone else. Harbinger's not that girl anymore; she lost her.

"What about *us*?" Harbinger's hand thuds against her own chest. "We're right here. We aren't just an extension of some holy purpose. We're *people*. We were *kids*. Some of them still are!"

Auspice snatches Harbinger's wrist with a tide of anger. "Lower your voice."

Harbinger rips her arm away. "Don't *touch* me! Do you know how much I saw? The things no one — no child — should have to, all because you wanted to use my *gift*? You made me rifle through every object you chose, no matter where it had been. No matter what had happened to it. Horrible things I could never prepare myself for. That I shouldn't have *had* to."

Memories still cling to her like cobwebs, visions that won't wash away. Tear-stained cheeks, broken bodies, gore and death and everything worse. Secrets darker than the shadows hiding them. Pain that can never be put into words. Ugly truths the

Diviners didn't want to hear.

That's not what we asked. Find what they're looking for. The Oracle will lead you where you need to go.

Then why had she led Harbinger here?

"You had no idea what you were asking me to see. You never let me stop. You connected me to people, forever, because you said I should be grateful. I should be *happy* I was chosen to carry this burden of a blessing. Well, I'm not!"

When Harbinger steps forward, Auspice steps back, alarm radiating through her.

"You make Bodie relive the most traumatic events of people's lives. You make Omen spend his days at graveyards and funerals, digging through grief to find people to bring back to life. But they're never the same. *He's* never the same. And we all do it because you trained us to. To be selfless. To give up parts of ourselves to serve everyone else, all because of your devotion to something you don't even know exists. But *we* exist. We're *right here*."

All the steam slips out of Harbinger in one shaky breath. All her anger, fear, and pain won't leave her when the words run out.

This means nothing.

This does...nothing.

Harbinger takes another step down, legs trembling. "The worst part is, it doesn't matter if you understand. If you hear what I say, for *once*." Distance returns to her eyes. "The harm is done. You left your mark. You destroyed the person I could have been. You made my father do what he did."

Auspice has the decency to lower her gaze. Harbinger doesn't.

"You made us like this. You made *me* like this."

Keeping the world at arm's length. Skirting close enough to the edge to plunge over. Looking for any part of herself that's worth more than a blessing she hates.

A door opens down the corridor, overflowing with children's voices. Harbinger winces away from the sound.

"No matter what you do, we'll always be collateral damage in the holy war you waged."

TWENTY-FOUR

Flint

Omen comes to the guest rooms with lunch before Harbinger returns. "She'll be back," he assures them. "Give her an hour. She has to talk herself into it."

Talk herself into what? But Omen waves to Flint and Agony as he disappears, leaving them to wait in stilted silence. When the door finally creaks open again, it's Harbinger in the doorway.

Flint swallows roughly. "Are you ok?"

"Yeah." She sets the cell phone on the dresser. "Updated the families on our progress. Had to drive for a bit to find a signal. The OID tried calling again." She doesn't look at either of them, pulling the keys from her pocket and tossing them as well.

"Is something wrong?" Agony tries.

"No." But she pauses, fingertips pressed to the top of the dresser, like it's holding all her weight. "...Yes."

Flint rises from the bed. Uncertainty scrawls across her face when she looks at him.

She has to talk herself into it.

"It's kind of...always been wrong," she finishes. "I need to show you something." Her gaze flicks to Agony. "Both of you."

They follow her out of the guest chambers, sound echoing through the hallways and fading the deeper they go. Winding through tunnels embedded with skulls and bones, down hundreds of stone steps. Soon, trickling water blurs out the other sounds, leaving the corridors humid and cool.

Even this deep within the caverns, torches burn bright. The three approach a spider web of corridors, lined with wooden doors backlit by emanating colors. Harbinger keeps an eye on the rooms they pass. Never looking back at Flint and Agony, making turns until they're far from the sound of anyone else.

The door she stops in front of looks exactly like the others. Wooden slats beneath a heavy metal handle, the faintest purple illuminating its edges. She looks like she wants to run. Flint reaches for her, but she pushes into the room.

Bioluminescence clings to the ceiling of the dark room, a stream weaving along the back wall. It flows into a larger pool, then back out the other side, past a stone slab standing in the deepest water. The slab seems to float above the surface, attached to the floor by stalagmites.

Harbinger doesn't take her eyes off it. Flint looks at Agony, but he's staring too, as if he's seen a ghost. Harbinger's chest rises and falls, bones pronounced as Flint pulls the door shut. All three of them breathe in time, as if their bodies are connected.

"You told us about your sister." Harbinger's teeth almost chatter. Flint's never heard her so small. "About what happened to her." In the dark, Flint can make out the murky white of Harbinger's eyes, the shape of her lips as she speaks. "It's time I tell you this."

She turns to Agony. One look is enough to send a tremor through Flint at the openness in Harbinger's gaze, the puzzled knit of Agony's brow as he absorbs her emotions. There's no denying the connection.

She turns back toward the pool. Her features are soft against the purple light: the slope of her nose, the pull of her lips, the angle of her jaw.

"You don't have to share anything you don't want to." Flint doesn't cast a shadow in the low light, no hulking reminder that he's there. The stony gray of his skin and the darkness of Agony blend into the walls until Harbinger stands at the water's edge, alone.

"I wasn't always like this." She gestures to her face, bones protruding through her skin, sunken hollows beneath her cheeks. "I looked human. I *was* human. I could touch whatever I wanted: any thing, any person...I was normal."

A mocking smile twitches her lips. "The Diviners say we shouldn't question when the Oracle calls, but that's an excuse. They don't know what provokes it. Can't predict who or when it'll happen. Once a banshee triggers, they bring you back to the Convent. They don't tell you what happens after."

Every line in Harbinger's face hardens, eyes on the pool like it might boil under her gaze. "These powers can't run on nothing." Her tongue lashes over the words, ingrained countless times. "*It's an exchange. The Oracle has given you a beautiful gift. All she asks in return is your devotion.*' But there was no asking."

Her gaze is distant, lost somewhere in time, somewhere that isn't here. "But this gift takes everything: the way you look. The way the world sees you. Every memory from before the change... It eats them, one by one, cleansing the vessel for divine duty. A blessing you have to suffer for. I guess that's how they justify it. Now *that's* divine."

Her voice is almost casual, so simple it breaks Flint's heart. "I don't remember my old name. That's usually the first thing to go. It's why we choose a new one, so we don't forget our purpose. So we focus on the reason we were chosen, to share our gifts without getting bogged down with our old lives. With human ties. Why would you need your own name when you're a mouthpiece for someone else?"

Agony steps closer, frantic energy through his body — the need to move, to do something to make this right. "Let's go back upstairs. We'll make the Diviners tell you." Fingers clench below his cuffs. "*I* can make them tell you."

Harbinger smiles, but it's not right. Not happy. "I don't want to know. Think it would be worse to hear my old name and feel...nothing. No connection. No memory. I don't know if I could take that."

Something in Flint strains to reach her, stretching to cover the gaping hole inside him. She inhales to keep her breath even. "The Convent sees it as the beginning of a beautiful new life: new body, new powers. But they don't care about what's ending." Her eyes are glassy. "No one crosses the Veil for free. Do it once, and you won't live to tell about it...unless you're not alive."

Flint's pulse thuds. "Harbinger. Did they —"

"Once the Oracle chooses you, that's it. Your bones protrude. Your skin sinks in, all that divine power eating away at your body. No living thing could handle it; it's a matter of time. So the Diviners bring you to one of these rooms." Harbinger's voice barely rises above the sound of water. "Doesn't matter how much you cry and plead. How you tell them it hurts. They lock you in, alone, and you wait for the sacred rite."

Agony stares at the slab, eyes flaring with heat when Harbinger lifts her chin toward it.

"That's where I died."

Words spill from her like a flood. Unstoppable, held behind her teeth for so long. "They say it's a gift for loyal service. You die, but the Oracle rewards you with eternal servitude. You'll live forever — at least, until someone kills you. It has to be intentional. Your body decayed once; you can't die naturally again. No accidents. No sudden illness. And you can't kill yourself." Harbinger's smile sharpens, wet and bitter. "The Oracle doesn't appreciate people returning her gifts."

Flint sucks in a breath, stinging and cold. "Harbin —"

"I don't want that to be what I remember. This place has taken everything from me." Fear wells in her eyes when she turns to face them, fighting to pull back from the ledge she's always racing toward. "I want to take something back."

She tugs at the buttons on her catsuit, stripping it down over the bones and hollow places of her body, braid unraveling in her hands. "I want you to make me forget all the bad things that happened here." Every inch of her is lit by thrumming purple light, her carnal hunger as sudden as her confession, wild and alive. "I don't want to be holy or precious or divine; I want to be desecrated."

There's no hiding how Flint's throat bobs. Where his gaze goes, a red glow over Harbinger's body, tracing the curve of her hips.

"We have to agree," she breathes. "All three of us."

Agony meets Flint's eyes. There's a pull in Flint to resist, but he's been denying for so long. Denying himself. Denying his pain. Denying what Harbinger needs.

They both nod. Harbinger doesn't wait any longer, following the steps down into the pool until she disappears beneath the water. Flint undoes the buttons of his shirt, working the fabric off his shoulders, illuminated by a sudden yellow light.

Agony doesn't look away. Not when Flint reaches for his buckle, zipper rasping as he tugs it. He works his trousers down over the wide stretch of his thighs until he's as bare as both of them. He doesn't need connection to place the want radiating off of Agony, flames atop his head flaring higher in the darkness. There's so little space between them, a few feet Flint could close in seconds if he just...

Harbinger surfaces, pulling herself atop the slab, flinching at the memories passing through her skin. The dais is pristine, clinical, no trace of what happened here. An insult to the memory of how much it changed her.

Flint's wings expand to both sides of the entryway. Harbinger doesn't hide her desire when he steps down into the water, sinking until he's up to his hips. Water displaces over the rim of the pool, splashing against Harbinger's fingers clenching the edge of the slab.

Rivulets of water slip down her body, curving around the edge of her breast. When Flint approaches one of the shorter ends, she presses her foot to his chest and drapes back along the slab. Flint aligns himself, tracing a claw around the curve of her thigh before he grips her hip in one hand. She looks back over her shoulder.

"I want you here."

Flint lifts his eyes to Agony still on the bank, watching them both like a predator in the darkness. Only once Harbinger hisses does Flint realize his claws have pricked her skin, but she looks no less wanton.

"Please," she breathes. Want rises in Flint, but Agony doesn't move. He waits, shadows undulating in the darkness until Flint finally nods.

Agony sinks down into the water, submerged until the ripples on the surface finally still. There's a moment when Flint wonders if Agony will use this chance to try to pull Flint under, but Agony surfaces behind Harbinger, pulling up onto the slab and dripping water onto her face.

"This close?" he purrs. Droplets slip filthy across her lips. Flint has to bite back a groan when Agony lowers his mouth to hers. Flint doesn't stop him. Doesn't want to stop him. Harbinger sucks in a breath — but when his eyes light her entire face, Agony stops himself.

"You can't have that yet, little death."

TWENTY-FIVE

Flint

Flint drags his ribbed tongue against Harbinger, large enough to cover her entire cunt. Her eyes roll back, hands gripping for his horns, Agony's shadows rippling when she clenches.

"You want him to do more?" Agony asks. Flint makes sure she can't think straight, curving his tongue against her clit, rolling it between his lips until she shudders. Agony rests his chin in his hand, staring down at her like she's the only one melting into a slick mess. "Then tell him."

Her body seizes, engulfed by sensation. Flint moves slow. Purposeful. Tusks brushing the juncture of both her thighs, toying with her clit. Agony's expression is unmoved, but his fingers grip the edge of the slab, shadows shuddering with the movements Flint makes — because Agony can feel them, too.

"I want more," Harbinger grits. Agony hovers over her, breaths ghosting each other's mouths as Flint swirls his tongue between her thighs.

"That's all you've got?" Agony clucks. "Not very persuasive."

He turns apathetic eyes up toward Flint. "She wants a little more. Not too much. I don't think she can take it."

Harbinger writhes beneath him "You fucking b-"

But Flint stands to his full height, water slipping down his body. Harbinger sucks in a breath when he aligns their hips — before he parts her legs over his thigh.

Agony laughs. Harbinger gapes up at Flint like he's torturing her, and that brands heat straight into his gut. "What?" He lifts his brows, guiding her to grind against the thick trunk of his thigh. "I thought you wanted more."

It's not enough. It's barely anything, but she's needy, desperate, teeth digging into her lip as she circles her hips against him. His cock is *right there*, hard and ready, brushing the outside of her thigh. She reaches for it —

And whimpers when Flint wraps his own fist around it. Both Agony and Harbinger curse, his head falling to hers as they try to compose themselves. Flint mocks the rhythm Harbinger tries to set with her hips, teasing his head with his fist until both she and Agony are captivated.

"This is what you want?" he asks, precum beading on the tip of his dick.

"*Yes,*" Harbinger strains, but Flint keeps himself out of reach.

"Show me, then. Show me why I should fuck that tight little pussy instead of my hand."

Frustration arches through her body. "Fucking..." But she keeps circling her hips, chasing his skin against hers and lifting onto her elbows. It makes Flint's dick twitch. That same determined look she had their first night together, trying to envelop him completely before he'd even spread her over one finger.

"Aw, he's making you work for it, huh?" Agony coos into her ear, but she grits her teeth, focused on the tight circles her hips are making. It's the unstoppable force of Harbinger's need meeting the immovable object of Flint's determination.

He could keep her there for hours. Make her beg. Make her *sweat.*

A whine builds in Harbinger's throat. She's slick against him, frantic for friction, grinding out her desire while Agony laughs in her ear.

"You're making a mess," Flint chides. The words tighten the circles of her hips.

"I want your *dick,*" she growls, but there's so little fight in it when she keeps working herself against his thigh.

Agony leans closer. "I don't know if you want it bad enough. Maybe he should make you get off on his thigh and never let you have it."

"That's right, baby." Flint's eyes meet Agony over Harbinger's body, Flint's palm spreading over her chest, giving her another shot of contact. "Show me how bad you want it. Show me the *thought* is enough to make you come."

She doesn't slow, reaching back to grip the slab and fumbling for Agony's hand. There's a flicker on his face, desire to twine their fingers together, but he withdraws. "Don't touch me, baby," he murmurs against her neck, eyes cutting to Flint as Harbinger cries out her frustration.

"You're almost there." Flint drags his hand down to her waist, tilting her up toward him. When the angle shifts, she groans, finding more leverage she can chase against him. Flint's voice never changes. Never grows louder, a low rumble as she spirals. *"Convince me."*

That's when she breaks. When the tight groans slip between her lips, hips stuttering out of time, only getting what she's after because Flint holds her against him. Her legs give out, but Flint keeps giving her what she needs until she comes apart, nails digging into his fingers.

"So good." Agony mouths the curve of her shoulder. "That's it. Let it out." Harbinger gasps through her orgasm, sounds swallowed by his mouth. The sight of them together stokes heat in

Flint's stomach.

"Good girl." He rakes claws gently down her chest while she writhes against him. "Such a good girl for me."

"So good I get what I want?" Harbinger stares breathlessly up at him. With a talon, he circles her nipple, humming in thought.

"You want me to take that pussy raw?"

Even as Harbinger groans at the filthy way he says it, anxiety spikes in Flint's chest — until he looks at Agony. Those eyes beside Harbinger's head, next to the pitiful need on her face, and Agony nods once.

Reassurance.

"If I do," Flint's claw dips around her navel, "you have to be *so good* for me. Let me take care of you. Do exactly as I say."

Agony sucks in a skeptical breath. "I don't know if she can do it..."

"Fucking bastard." She grits her teeth, a feral flare in her eyes. Her hips rock closer to Flint, her eyes glaring up at Agony. "I can be good."

Flint huffs a laugh. "So good when you want something, huh?" But he slides the pad of his thumb against her entrance, drawing slow circles as she gasps. "But we don't have any lube."

"Like hell we don't." She almost tips off the edge of the dais, kept out of the water by Flint and Agony's hands. She reaches for the closest edge of the pool, a metallic pitcher sitting next to a matching bowl.

"Holy oil?" Agony shakes his head, but he moves through the water to retrieve it, returning beside them with a grin. "We're definitely going to hell now."

"Worth it." She reaches for the pitcher before Agony swats her hand away and pours it into the bowl. Harbinger dips the black tips of her fingers inside, but then she stops, looking up at Flint beneath her lashes.

"Can he help me?" Her fingers glide over Flint's cock until his eyes slip shut, slick and hot and tempting all his control. After a moment, he nods, trying to focus past Harbinger's fingers around him.

Agony hesitates. But he trails his fingers through the oil, dipping both palms into the bowl, smearing them together until there's no mistaking the slickness. Then he reaches his cuffed hands to meet Harbinger's.

The first touch makes Flint twitch. His mouth presses in a thin line as Agony's eyes flash up to him, Harbinger's teeth digging into her lip. They both work over Flint, cock slipping between their fingers, so thick they barely make their hands meet on either side. The sight is risky. Perilous. Enough to drive Flint to distraction as he grips the edge of the slab, fighting the urge to fuck into their fists.

"*Gods*, it's so fucking big," Agony breathes.

Harbinger stifles a laugh. "Don't make his head any bigger."

There's the smallest lift of Flint's lips, gripping her thigh to pull her closer, pumping his hips into their hands. "You'd still take it."

Agony and Harbinger clench their fists tighter when they groan, ragged breaths slipping past their lips. Flint's eyes glow like a poker. Then Harbinger guides Agony's fingers between her thighs, glancing between the two men as he slips against her center.

Agony's voice is rocky, gaze following his fingers. "That's not what good little acolytes do." Harbinger tilts her mouth toward his, using his fingers to circle her clit.

"Have to make sure it's wet enough." Her breath hitches dangerously close to Agony's mouth. "Right?"

Shadows dip between the skeletal pattern of Harbinger's skin. The spring in Flint's stomach coils tighter. When he lifts his gaze, Harbinger's watching him.

"Have to," he rasps. Agony keeps his eyes on Flint, trailing his hand lower, circling Harbinger before he dips one finger inside.

She gasps, gripping his wrist, clenching her other hand around

Flint's cock as her hips rock to take Agony deeper. All three of them fill the same space, so close they're sharing air. So close they could —

"Now behave," Agony murmurs against her temple. With a final glance toward Flint, Agony withdraws, pulling back to hover behind Harbinger's shoulder.

Harbinger doesn't pull her eyes from Flint. Like she knows something, sees something, *feels* something through their connection. Flint won't acknowledge it, easing her back against the slab. Everything between her thighs is slick. Flint doesn't waste it, rutting his cock between Harbinger's folds but never inside.

"Come *on*," she whines. He drags the ridge of his head against her clit, over and over, until she squeals.

"Don't think you're wet enough yet," he teases.

"I fucking beg to differ." She grinds her desire along the bottom of Flint's shaft, but he doesn't give in. Instead, he finds Agony's eyes behind her. Somehow, Agony knows, reaching for the pitcher of oil and tilting it over Harbinger's chest. Drizzling over her breasts, oil slipping into the hollow of her throat, dripping down her ribs.

Oil pools on her stomach, and Flint massages it up her thighs as Agony does the same with her shoulders. Her eyes shut, and finally, she gives into them kneading memories out of her muscles. Working down her calves and biceps until she's wet enough to reflect the small bit of light in the room, skin awash with purple and the vibrant mixture of Flint's and Agony's eyes mingling over her like they've painted this masterpiece.

Flint's hand spreads across her stomach. "That's so nice, baby. Now you're wet enough for me."

He notches himself against her, biting back a sound at the first stretch of her over his head.

It ignites in her. Hot and fast, like matches and gasoline, both Agony and Harbinger groaning at the contact. The first time there's nothing but Harbinger wrapping around Flint's cock, no barrier to help him keep a hold of his emotions. Every feeling flows between them, Flint's arousal flaring bright as it spills into Harbinger and further into Agony.

She tries to get closer. To take all of him at once, but Flint digs his claws into the rock beneath her when he cages her stomach.

"Look at him." Agony guides her eyes to Flint with hands on her cheeks. "He wants to watch you the first time."

When Harbinger meets his eyes, something greater than desire swells in Flint. He sinks deeper, enough to make her gasp, eyes rolling back. It's the first time they've been this close. The first time his bare cock is buried inside her, enough to make her tremble.

She slips through the oil on the slab, reaching back for Agony as Flint pauses to let her get her bearings. She can't keep her mouth closed, pulling Agony closer when her fingers find her clit. "*Green, green, green,* yeah, *green!*"

Flint's halfway inside her, but the oil and her desire have him sinking until his hips rut up against her. Until she tightens her thighs to keep him there. *"So fucking good,"* she moans. Already, she works herself against him, the bulge in her stomach visible when she twirls her hips.

"Take your time with it." Flint tries to think past the wet heat wrapped around him, letting Harbinger grow bolder, pulling back as much as she can before she takes him completely again. "That's it. That's what I want, baby."

He could watch her like this for hours, bathing in both their pleasure, worshiping her body...but he remembers what they said.

I don't want to be holy or precious or divine.

You can be as mean as she's begging you to be. Promise she'll think you're a saint.

"Lift your hips for me, baby."

Harbinger does as Flint asks. He grips beneath her waist, flipping her until she's on her hands and knees, bracing herself against the ridge of the slab. Agony floats in the water before them, eyes following Flint's fingers as they grip into Harbinger's hair. As his arm wraps around her waist, pulling her back up against his chest until he can murmur against her throat.

"You know I won't let you fall, yeah?" His tusks scrape her neck. "So take it from me; that's how you're gonna be good for me. I'm not gonna fuck you with it —"

She whines. Flint's fist tightens in her hair.

"I'm gonna let you fuck me. And you're gonna thank me for it, like the good girl you are. Aren't you?"

TWENTY-SIX

Agony

It's not meant to be divine.

They're doing the furthest thing from holy, but Agony's never seen anything as sacred as the two of them. Flint's claws in her hair, his body blocking out everything behind her, keeping her kneeling on the altar above Agony. Harbinger's dazed eyes and panting chest flood under purple light, celestial and transcendent.

Even with Flint sunk to the hilt inside her, Agony's graced with the spectacle of them. Flint's wings spanning the pool, Harbinger's dips and curves...Agony wants to paint them. To lie on his back and fill a chapel with their image. To humble himself at their feet, wretched creature that he is.

Flint's finger dips against her clit. Harbinger bucks. It rocks through Agony like a shockwave, desire pulsing when Flint lowers her hands back to the slab.

She's right in front of Agony. Teeth digging into her lip, eyes staring dazedly into his, the heel of her palms pressed against the rim of the slab. Agony doesn't need instruction. He holds her wrists, bracing at the same time she widens her knees to keep her in place.

"Good girl." One of Flint's clawed hands splays beneath her stomach, keeping her from slipping. "Now take it like you want it."

It's a hypnotizing motion when she works back over Flint, ass grinding as she pants for breath. Agony's mesmerized by the heat in her eyes. Arousal floods from Flint behind her, her body rocking forward with each thrust.

"Just like that, baby," Flint hisses as he watches where they meet. "Work your hips on me just like you like."

It's captivating, but Harbinger starts to get lost, emotions whirling as the slab smears memories against her. Agony presses up into her space.

"You like that, don't you?" Agony squeezes tighter around her wrists, grounding her. "Of course you do. He fucks you *so good*, doesn't he?"

She tries to let her head fall, but Agony doesn't allow it, gripping back in her hair. "Ah, ah: you're gonna let me see it. You're gonna tell me how good his dick is in you."

She rocks forward, so close to his mouth that he could taste it. Could take her lips against his, tease her until her arms are shaking. But still, he looks at Flint. And with Harbinger working over him, Flint nods.

Something wedges into Agony's throat. He doesn't focus on it, lifting out of the water to tip into Harbinger's space.

"You want me to kiss you?" The sight of Harbinger aching is enough for Agony to lose control, but he doesn't touch her yet. Keeps rocking back out of her reach. "You want me to lick every holy word out of your mouth until all you taste is blasphemy?"

"Fuck."

She lowers her head to fuck back harder, but Agony keeps her upright with a finger under her chin. Breath cascades over her lips. She surges forward to meet him, but it's too slick. Flint grips her tighter. Agony pulls back on her hair.

"That's not what a good girl does." Agony's eyes scrape over her. "*Gods*, look at you."

Humiliation tinges his words just enough to sting. He extends a hand toward Flint. Flint meets him, letting Agony guide Flint's fingers over Harbinger's shoulder. Flint retracts two claws as Agony presses Flint's fingers against Harbinger's lips. Flint hesitates — but Harbinger whines, opening her mouth to take them. It's sloppy, messy when his fingers stretch between her lips, leaving both of them groaning.

I want to be desecrated.

"So fucking full of him, stuffed from both ends. What a precious little offering." Agony pats her jaw roughly, squeezing her cheeks where Flint's packed between them. Flint withdraws his fingers, spit dripping down Harbinger's chin as Agony sneers. "Such a good girl. Such a *filthy fucking martyr.*"

She surges toward Agony's mouth. He pulls back just in time, pressing on her shoulders to sink her back until Flint moans. Agony squeezes her cheeks in his hand again. "Bet you wish my tongue was on that clit, don't you?" Her hips move faster in response. "That can be arranged."

He doesn't move. Just lets his mind play out the thought of him crawling beneath her to lave his tongue against where she and Flint meet. It jolts through her, body spasming at the feeling he places into her head, toying with their connection.

"How —" she gasps. Agony doesn't stop, dropping another image into her mind. That same tongue working past her navel, splitting and curling around both her nipples. He doesn't need to move to make her feel it. She arches, trying to get closer to his mouth, but nothing's there.

"Pitiful baby," he teases. The sound of skin slapping grows louder, echoing off the walls. Agony toys with her mind until her arms and legs wobble beneath her. Until she feels Agony's tongue gliding over the most sensitive parts of her.

"Please," she begs.

"You've got it, baby." Flint guides her hips against him. "Keep using me."

She groans at every inch she takes, whimpering for more, but Flint doesn't give her an inch. When her slick hair whips over her shoulder as she tries to find his eyes, her head dipping down toward the slab. "Flint, *please*. Please fuck me. Please give me more than —"

"So polite when you're after something." There's no denying the restraint Flint's barely holding onto. "You want me to give it to you? Is that what you want?"

"Please!"

Tears edge into her eyes. Flint strokes a hand through the hair at the base of her neck. "Then thank me for letting you use my bare cock."

"*Thank you.* Fuck!" She keeps working back against him, fingers sloppy against her clit, ass bouncing with each motion. "Thank you. Thank you, *thank you, gods*, just *please* give me —"

Flint's claws dig into the back of her neck. "You're so fucking good for me." Then he fucks her faster than Harbinger could muster. Her head dips forward onto Agony's shoulder, arms slipping out from under her, but Agony keeps her upright. Muttering in her ear, his hand meeting Flint's buried in her hair, their eyes locked as Harbinger screams toward the peak.

"Let me feel it," Agony growls. "Everything he's giving you — I want it *all*."

She crashes against Agony's lips, their moans melding between their mouths as she comes apart. It's euphoric, emotions ripping through Agony as he curls his tongue against her lips, swallowing her sounds. Kissing her like it's his last chance.

And then Flint curses. Agony's eye peeks open enough to catch Flint watching their mouths meld together. Flint grips Harbinger's hips, claws digging into her skin as he spends himself inside her.

Harbinger can't form words, panting against Agony's shoulder, both of them struggling through her release.

"Congratulations." Agony's tongue glides along her lips, drawing out her shiver as cum and holy oil drip from where Flint meets her. "You're sacrilegious."

TWENTY-SEVEN

Harbinger

It's some time before they leave the Veil Chamber. Prior to this, Harbinger wouldn't have spent more than a few minutes there, and not by choice. But now, when the water drips off of them, and she gets her wobbly legs under her, the room echoes with quiet laughter.

There's an accomplished tenderness in all her muscles that accompanies sex with Flint. But now her mouth burns too, blush creeping up her neck when she remembers Agony against it. Dipping his fingers between her thighs, guiding Flint's hand, that slash of a mouth swallowing her sounds.

She stumbles in the corridor. Two sets of hands catch her waist, Agony's mouth hovering over her shoulder. "You act like you've never been fucked in your death room before." As they reach the ground level of the Convent and pass the staring banshee students, she realizes she's grinning.

Once they're back in the guest quarters, Agony flings himself onto the bed. "How is it you two have fucked me no less than seven times without touching me?" He nuzzles into the pillow. "It's like being edged for weeks."

It only takes the lift of Harbinger's brows to have Flint strip down with her in the shower, angled to keep an eye on Agony. Flint eases her thighs apart, letting the warm water wash away any remnants of him.

"You feel ok?"

"Sore and perfect." She tilts a smile up to meet him, but it pulls tighter at the ends. They both recognize it. Something's unfinished…or on the precipice of starting.

"I didn't have any idea what you went through." Flint's talons brush along her clavicle, outlining the bones pressing through her skin. "I wouldn't have…" He tries to rearrange the words. "I hope you don't feel like you had to come back here just because we didn't know what happened."

She averts her eyes to scrub along her arms. "I don't."

"You understand my concern…" His hand closes over hers until she meets his eyes again. "Since it wouldn't be the first time you've suffered for someone else's sake. Put yourself in danger to get answers for someone."

Her eyes drop again. Flint returns to soaping her body. She chews the inside of her cheek.

"You know when you live with something for so long, you almost start to believe it's normal? That you're exaggerating what it did to you. How it shaped you."

Flint rinses soap down her arms. "You try so hard to leave it behind, you don't realize it was on your back all this time, weighing you down."

"Yes," she breathes. He runs both hands down her arms, engulfing her biceps with his palms.

"We've both been holding onto things while we were trying to ignore them." He brushes a strand of hair off her shoulder, letting it slip down her back. "Maybe we have to let them exist. Admit they changed us, so we can live without them ruling us. So we can make them light enough to carry."

Prickling heat presses behind her eyes. Flint goes back to work on her body. Agony's dark shape lies across the bed, both hands propped beneath his head.

"Didn't know he could sleep," Flint chuckles.

"After that?" Harbinger hums into a smile. "Maybe he learned. If he felt a *fraction* of what I did…" Her toes curl at the memory. "But I wonder if it works the same."

"What do you mean?"

"We know he can pick things up from me, but my ability's supposed to let me feel other people. I know he's different, but I might be able to feel things from him in the same way. If someone touched him…"

Flint's hands slow. She presses further.

"Every time he's experienced heightened contact, so have I: the first night. During the fire. The extent of our connection is muddled. But if we tested it…"

Flint's fingers curl gently around her throat, where Agony's chain was all those weeks ago. Her eyes slip shut. Flint moves onto her chest.

"Do you ever wonder…"

Her eyes blink open under the spray, water trickling down her face. His hesitance tugs on her like a tide, the same thing that's kept them both from truly talking to each other. But this time, Flint finishes what he started.

"Do you think you're only attracted to us because of the connections?"

She takes the time to consider Flint's question as he works suds down her stomach. "No," she answers finally. "I was attracted to you before we touched. But I don't think I would have done this with either of you if we weren't linked."

Flint kneels to work soap over her thighs. There's that uncertainty again, but Harbinger cups his face until he lifts his eyes to her. Her thumbs smooth against his cheeks until he says what he's thinking. "You were forced to connect with both of us. You didn't have a choice. And I hate being something else inflicted on you."

Sometimes she forgets what her ability means for other people. She's the one that has to bear the connections, but Flint didn't have a choice in sharing what he feels, either. He has to make a constant effort to keep a wall up between them, but that isn't foolproof. He can never keep any of his emotions to himself. Can never struggle without Harbinger knowing it. Can never experience anything fully for fear it'll overwhelm her.

"You didn't have a choice, either." Her fingers curl under the broad line of his jaw. "It was forced on all three of us."

Flint moves down her calves, cleaning her feet one by one. Words weigh down her tongue before she says them, fast, as if she might not work up the courage again.

"Agony understands something about me. Some urge."

Flint slows his motions. There's a prickle of jealousy from him, but it merely surfaces above his own swirling confusion. "I'm glad he can do that for you," Flint says finally.

"He does something for you, too."

Flint watches her warily, rising back to his full height.

"Like you can loosen up," Harbinger continues. "Let go. Try things you won't with me."

Flint's mouth presses into a tight line. He's tempted to deny it, to make some excuse for why it can't happen. *Too dangerous. Too reckless. I have other things to worry about.*

"I can feel how you want him," Harbinger murmurs. "You won't let yourself. Do you want to know what I feel, when you're fighting it back?" Agony doesn't stir in the bedroom. "It's like the start of a wildfire, spreading before you can get a handle on it. Before you can control it. Then you snuff it out just before it rages. Throw water until it's out, cover it with sand, but the signs are still there. The scorch marks. The smoke. The hiss of what almost was."

"That's very poetic." Flint turns his face up toward the water, but his body's tense.

"You've always been so dedicated to me." She takes his hands in hers. "Making sure I get what I want. But you can't neglect yourself." Her fingers wrap between his and squeeze. "I need you to speak up for what you need, even if it's hard or uncomfortable. You can't...*I* can't do this if you're suffering to make sure I'm happy." Her voice catches in her throat, gaze some place along the tile. "I don't want you to sacrifice anything for me, especially yourself."

Flint traces the pad of his thumb under the hollow of her eye. "Ok." She leans her face into his palm. There's the rush of his emotions, swelling tightness in her chest. "I understand."

"And I will be more careful," she promises. "Start listening to your worries. Stop taking unnecessary risks."

"Thank you." Flint's eyes find Agony. "Maybe you should meet him in the dream. See what else you can find."

She presses her lips against Flint's palm. "My connection with him does not mean I want you any less."

They dry off after the shower. Dinner hasn't passed yet, but both their bodies drag with exhaustion.

"Can we both sleep?" Harbinger crawls under the blankets at the far side of the bed. "One night. You can stay between us."

Flint examines the space. Then he sighs, eyelids drooping, laying down to face Agony. Harbinger leans up to whisper in his ear. "I won't tell if you cuddle him."

Flint swats at her. "Shut up." But there's warmth in his smile again.

In the dream, she wakes on the stone slab. It's brighter this time, bioluminescence bathing the room in light. Familiar jagged eyes watch her from the far side of the room as she slides down into the water. The slab turns to dust under her fingers...for now.

"That's one mystery solved." Agony emerges from the shadows, extending a hand to greet her at the top of the stairs. His gaze rakes down her body, and she realizes she's naked, heat spreading between her legs. When she meets his eyes again, she's clothed, his gaze drifting over her shoulder. "Gonna tell me why you keep coming back here?"

She doesn't have to look. It looms behind her, the same house stretching like a funhouse mirror until its shadow mingles with Agony.

"You know..." She moves toward the tree line, leaving the house behind. "I liked you better when you tried to kill me."

Agony follows with a grin.

They don't get far. Same untrodden path, delving deeper into the forest until slashed trees become visible. Same markings. Same feeling. Same circle they make through the trees, returning to the claw marks again and again.

"Still can't get anywhere." Agony slumps down against a tree, flexing his wrists.

You can't keep him chained up forever.

Harbinger sinks beside him, trying to pick at a strand of grass, but the definition's off. Fuzzy and wrong, like her eyes can't focus.

"Were you actually sleeping?" She looks at him skeptically. "In the guest room?"

A smug look crosses his face. "Resting my eyes."

"Mmhmm." She tosses the plucked grass at him.

Agony shields himself from it. "I like listening to you two talk. It sounds nice." He seems surprised by that. "And I wanted to give you a chance, in case..." He rests his head back against the tree, staring off through the woods.

"In case what?"

"In case I did something I shouldn't."

Her eyes skate over his lips, flaring at the memory. "You didn't."

Agony doesn't seem convinced. They wait for a bird call, a frog croak, *something.*

"Does he hate me?"

Harbinger's head jerks toward Agony.

"Don't act surprised," he admonishes. "He did at one point."

Her mouth twists in consideration. A way to assuage Agony's fear without discussing what Flint hasn't said. Hasn't admitted to himself.

"He did," she agrees. "But I think he doesn't hate you anymore. And I think he hates *that*."

Agony keeps pulling blades of grass as they crumple under his fingers. "Everything he does is so…"

"Good?" Harbinger finishes.

"Yeah."

"When this first started, Flint was right; I was drawn to you because it was reckless. Perilous. I don't know. But now…"

Agony doesn't move. "Now, what?"

"Now, I'm so used to feeling other people and dealing with their emotions, but you feel *me*. You understand me in ways no one else can. I thought it was impossible to experience that. To find anyone that would 'get' the connection. But you do."

Agony won't look at her, head shaking, gaze on the ground. "That's a mistake. You were right before; it's reckless." His voice drops like the thud of her heart. "Sometimes I want to hurt something."

It shouldn't surprise her, given what she knows. What Flint's been trying to instill in her for weeks. Agony trails his fingers closer to her leg, walking a knife's edge.

"Doesn't mean you're bad." The words stun her, but she doesn't retract them. "You could hurt bad people."

Agony's smile wavers. "Making excuses for me again?"

"That's what Flint's done." That stops Agony, his hand hovering off her leg. They both stare at it, breath caught in their throats, waiting. "Hurt bad people to keep them from hurting someone else. Hurt bad people for good reason. Hurt bad people if you have to."

Agony's fingers flex over her leg. The forest quiet grows so loud.

"Better be careful." His fingers meet her ankle, a brush of wind against bare skin. "Keep sweet-talking like that, and I'll think you want to keep me."

"Maybe I do."

She's on her back before she realizes, wind knocked out of her. Agony hovers over her, a hand around her throat. Neither of them moves, chests rising and falling in tandem. Agony's eyes follow his thumb across her lip, the gentlest touch he's ever given her. "That's a bad idea."

"Why?"

"You can't want that." His gaze is still honed on her mouth, like he can't believe himself. Like the words are coming from somewhere else. "You can't want both."

"I do." There's no hesitation. It thrums through their connection, a convoluted emotion, a complex feeling. "I want you both."

"You don't know what you're asking for."

"I *do*."

"Do you?" His mouth twitches in pain. "You want a guardian to ruin, and a monster to keep. Do you really think that can work?"

Not a monster, she thinks. *My monster. Mine.*

Agony shudders like he hears her. She stays back from the cliff's edge, but she stares down into the waves crashing against her desires.

"This is a dream," she breathes. "Anything's possible."

Agony smiles sadly. Fingers trail down her throat before he sinks back into the shadows, one thought echoing through the forest.

It's not just a dream to me.

Then Agony's glowing face snuffs out.

TWENTY-EIGHT

Agony

Flint can rarely be considered soft. Even in his calmest moments, his body is a fortress, strong and sturdy with a chest like a castle battlement. But when he looks at Harbinger, it's a contrast, eyes open and vulnerable while his body wars with itself.

Agony never thought he'd understand it. But when he returns from Harbinger's dream, floating and hazy, there's something soft against his back. Heavy warmth drapes across his chest until he's conscious enough to recognize it.

Flint sleeps on his side behind Agony, the swell of his stomach nudging Agony's back with his breath. Flint grinds his teeth, arm draped over Agony like a stuffed toy cradled against him.

It's enough to make Agony chuckle. That jerks Flint out of sleep, pushing up in the bed and blinking to place the sound before he realizes.

Agony rolls onto his back, stretching hands behind his head. "Comfy?"

Flint tugs back the blanket. "Making sure you didn't try

anything."

"Seems like *you* were trying something." Agony shoots a grin at Harbinger sleeping on Flint's other side before he's struck by how...right it is.

Flint won't look Agony in the face. "It wasn't like that."

That digs into Agony's chest, but he keeps his face aloof. "You're bad at this. Lying."

When Flint's weight shifts, Harbinger stirs. After the dream, Agony's not ready to face her. Not ready to deal with anything that isn't antagonizing Flint, so before Agony's pulled in by her sleep-softened face, he makes his way into the shower just to see what it's like.

By the time he's done, they're packed and ready, carrying their bags back to the Convent entryway. Poe chatters with Harbinger while Omen lugs a picnic basket over his shoulder before they meet the rest of the Seers at the main doors.

"You should go see the rabbit," one says, distracted by the parchment in their hand. It's covered in abstract shapes and colors, painted in an altered state. They check a small notebook from their pocket. "At least, I think that's what it means..."

The three of them pile into the SUV, waving to the Seers gathered in the dust as Diviner Auspice's scowl burns after them. Agony glares back.

At the first gas station they cross, Flint pulls over, filling the tank while he presses the cell phone to his ear.

"Do you want anything?" Harbinger asks Agony in the mirror.

Yes. Your mouth.

"From inside," she adds, as if she knows what he's thinking.

"Hmm...I want something I have to work for. That I can crack open. Messy." He smiles. Gods, he's irritating. "Sunflower seeds. Do you think they have that??"

Harbinger doesn't reply, but when he looks toward her, she's watching him.

"What?"

She doesn't blink. "That was one of the girls' favorite —"

"Gods…" Agony shuts his eyes, head knocking back against the seat. For the first time, the coincidence is polluted, turning his stomach. "Don't tell me."

Flint spares the rest of that conversation when he hoists himself back into the driver's seat. "That was a message from the Timbers. Lev."

Harbinger's brow quirks before recognition dawns on her. "Mm: the rabbit."

"Guess what creature just got taken down in the Break in a grab for power."

"What?"

Flint cranks the ignition. "A phoenix."

They head across the desert, radio signal flickering in and out. *Well, if there's no fucking background music…*

"Why'd it take so long for the Timbers to get back to you?" Agony rolls down his window. Heat wafts up from the ground.

"Most technology doesn't work in the Break." Harbinger pulls a bread roll from the Convent's parting picnic basket. "When Faerie withdrew from the continents years ago, it left behind residual magic. Created the mountain ring around the Break, sapped this area until it became a desert…" She gestures to the dry land stretching around them. "The ferry's the only approved way to enter the Break, so the ferryman relays messages through the mountain pass. The Break has its own mail system to carry letters, but it takes some time with the terrain and the distance."

"So how did packs end up in the Break in the first place?"

Agony tugs up on the window switch. Flint's glare flicks to the rearview.

"They say Faerie caused that too." Harbinger takes a bite of her roll. "The area was uninhabited until Faerie left. Once the mountains jutted up and the canyon formed, people just…appeared. Fully adult, a variety of species, no recollection of lives before. Like magic. Teleportation. Time travel. Not even they knew where they came from."

"Interesting," Agony manages. But it's not half as interesting as the crumb on Harbinger's cheek, her throat extending when she swallows. He presses down on the window button so hard his finger cramps.

"Can you not?" Flint snaps. Agony ignores him under a flare of heat.

"Then how does the OID oversee the Break? It's part of Orena, isn't it?"

"The OID tends to stay away from self-contained entities like the Break. And the Convent." Harbinger's mouth tightens. "Don't want to get involved as long as controversy doesn't spill out. But there are still plenty of disputes about it, when crimes cross area lines or the OID gets that insatiable urge to insert themselves."

Agony tugs up on the button until his window closes again. Flint flips the child lock into place.

"You're full of questions this morning." Sunlight glints off the hood of the car and across Flint's jaw.

Agony stares. "Nothing else to do." *Except think about your dick in both our hands. How warm you are when you're asleep.*

Romance: disgusting.

It's the most awkward day they've had, so naturally, they spend it crammed in the same car. There are minor reprieves at meals or when they have to fill up the tank, but those stops aren't safe from the weird cushion between them. Invisible padding that keeps them shifting around each other, so they don't have to acknowledge the very profane way they fucked in a holy room.

It's uncomfortable, but doable. The night's motel, on the other hand, presents a problem.

"Sorry," coughs the wizened satyr at the front desk, "only one bed. It'll be a tight fit, unless you want another room?"

Flint's jaw clenches. "One's fine." But he takes the keys so abruptly, he nearly elbows an elk centaur waiting in line behind them.

The three of them unpack, making the bed with Harbinger's sheets, looking for excuses in the bottoms of their bags until Agony tries the TV.

It won't cut on. Flint jumps at the opportunity. "I'll ask the front desk about it."

"Actually..."

Both men turn toward Harbinger, who's flicking the zipper on her pack. "There's something we need to figure out. Probably best with no distractions."

The room is deathly still. Her eyes roll. "Gods, it's not that big of a deal..."

Flint and Agony speak at once.

"I don't know if now is —"

"It's probably not —"

Harbinger cuts in. "We need to see exactly how deep the connection between Agony and me goes."

Oh. Flint and Agony don't move. She scowls. "We know he's connected to me — that he can visit my dreams, that he can feel some of what I do — but we don't know about my connection to *him*."

Agony watches her warily. "How would you want to test that?"

"Flint can do something to you, and we'll see how much of it I can feel. He'll hold back his emotions. I'll go into the bathroom so we know I'm not responding to any other stimuli. And Flint's not going to risk hurting us, obviously..."

"Obviously," Flint clips.

Harbinger's gaze drifts. "So it would make sense..."

Flint's eyes narrow until she confesses.

"If you two agree, I think you should have sex."

Agony chokes. As soon as Flint looks toward him, he smooths his features into nonchalance. "I don't think your bodyguard's gonna stick his dick in —"

"Fine," Flint answers.

Agony does nothing to hide his offense. "*'Fine'?*"

"If it's the only way to test it —"

"It's not," Agony splutters. "We could, I don't know, stick me with a pin or —"

"It needs to be strong enough that I can feel it." Of course Harbinger has an answer for everything. "Like the night after the fire."

The room is sweltering. Agony fans himself. Does he even sweat?

"If you don't want to do it —"

"I didn't say that," Agony snaps. Flint holds his hands up in surrender. "Fine," Agony mimics before he turns to Harbinger. "Let's do it."

"All right. I'll get comfortable." She moves toward the bathroom, leaving Flint and Agony standing awkwardly by the bed.

"Clothes stay on," Flint insists.

Agony fights a shudder. "You know that makes it filthier."

The bathroom door cracks open. "It'll be a lot easier if you stop acting like you don't want to!"

"Who asked you?" Agony calls back. The door clicks shut.

So maybe he's thought about it. Multiple times. And since last night — Agony's hands slick around Flint's cock, Harbinger dragging his fingers between her legs — gods, has he thought of anything else?

The question isn't if Agony wants this. It's how badly.

Ignoring self-preservation, he hoists himself onto the bed, reclining among the pillows. Flint's gaze follows him until he realizes and jerks it away. Agony tries not to let it sting.

"You shouldn't force yourself to fuck someone you don't want to." Agony crosses one leg over the other. "I'm sure she'll understand."

Flint scrubs a hand down his face. "I don't *not* want to fuck you."

"A ringing endorsement."

"Look, I don't get it. And I don't relish the thought, but it is what it is." Flint reaches for his belt buckle. Agony holds up a hand.

"No, no, no."

Flint pauses. A smile cracks across Agony's face. "If we do this..." He settles back against the pillows. "I want to hear you say it."

The rim of Flint's eyes spark like an ember. "Say what?"

He knows. He knows exactly. And Agony will be damned before he lets Flint take the easy way out. "I want you to tell me *explicitly* that you want to fuck me."

Flint could crush Agony's head between his hands and shut Agony up in a second. Instead, he clenches fists around the ends of his belt, hating that he loves every second.

"I want to fuck you," he finally grinds out.

Agony's head tilts. "Details."

The look on Flint's face is bitter regret, but the hard bulge in his trousers says differently. Agony can't take his eyes off it.

"I want to make you shut the fuck up," Flint says.

"More."

Acid laces Flint's expression. "I want to see what it's like when you can't find some smartass comment. When you're the one who's fucked up. When you both are."

Flint halts, burning like there's a thought he's not sure he should share. That he almost feels guilty for. Agony sits up sharply. *"Tell me."*

"I want to fuck with both of you at once. I want to tease until your eyes roll back, and she's crying for me to touch her. I want to overstimulate you, and I want to edge her, until you're both begging by the end."

There's the Flint who's been hiding. Too scared to come out to play, too worried he'll break Harbinger and leave a mark on her...but he doesn't have that fear with Agony.

A shudder ripples through him. "Put your hands on me."

Flint slips his belt from the loops and rolls up his sleeves.

"Stalling," Agony yawns. Then there's a hand around his ankle, yanking him toward the edge of the bed. Flint hovers over him, shadow making Agony's eyes brighter.

"Good luck to you," Agony breathes in the space between them. "I've got a filthy mouth on me."

"You don't have to tell me."

Then Agony's facedown on the bed, held in place by a firm hand that wraps around his entire waist. Flint's voice comes from behind him. "You remember the safewords?"

Agony arches his ass back. *"Green."*

Claws prick into Agony's sides. He curses against the sheets.

"Do you know what kind of things you like?"

"No." Agony squirms, but Flint keeps him in place. "To be honest, I'm not sure how this is gonna work."

"That's comforting."

"Do things that she likes." Agony turns enough for Flint to see his smile. "But maybe a little harder."

He writhes out of Flint's grip, cuffs clacking until he's on his knees on the bed in front of Flint. They watch each other like circling creatures, unsure who's predator or prey. With his fingers, Agony unclasps the front of Flint's slacks. "You'll use the colors too?"

The zipper slips open. Flint stiffens. "Yes. Don't take them off."

"Yes, Sir," Agony hums, reaching for the belt loops. Flint grips his chin.

"Say that again."

"Yes," Agony drawls, tongue brushing Flint's thumb. *"Sir."*

Flint simmers before he releases Agony with a jerk that stokes heat in his stomach.

"Hear something you like?"

Flint doesn't respond. Just shoves his pants down enough to fist over his cock, stroking to the head until Agony shivers.

"See something you like?" Flint mocks.

Agony understands the urge to shut Flint up, to make that

snarky mouth fall open until he can't form anything coherent. So Agony does, lunging forward to take Flint into his mouth, but Flint catches him by the back of the neck.

"Aw, come on." Agony's mouth is hot, bright against Flint's cock, tongue lying flat when his gaze flicks up to Flint's. "You don't want it? At least make me believe it." Agony's poised on his knees, ghastly smile carving into his face. Flint tightens his claws in the shadows.

"Ask nicely."

It's tempting to fight it. To draw Flint to the edge, to get him frustrated enough to rough Agony up, but Agony takes a different tack.

"Please." As soft as a whisper. Agony plays his part, dragging cuffed hands up the slacks pulled tight over Flint's thighs. "I can make you feel good."

Flint's dick twitches. Agony smirks, but Flint doesn't let it linger, burying himself into Agony's mouth. He takes all of Flint, moaning around him, nuzzling the base of his cock before Flint pulls out with a curse.

"Are you fucking with me?" Flint pants, unnerved. Agony's the same size as Harbinger. There's no way someone as big as Flint should fit so easily. Agony gives a satisfied lick of his lips.

"I can make room. Could make more room if you took these off." Shadows quiver under his cuffed wrists. "Scared you're gonna hurt me? I'm only solid in the most ambiguous sense." Agony leans forward to take him again, but Flint keeps his hand in Agony's flaming head. Agony jostles in his grip.

"You can fuck the back of my throat as long as you can take, and it won't leave a mark. Not like with sweet little Harbinger."

Flint's fingers clench. Agony rests back on his heels, innocence paired with the vulgar way he talks. "You don't have to be gentle. Use me like your little *fucktoy*, Jas. Lose control a little. See if she likes it."

There's a battle in Flint's eyes, thoughts darting to where

Harbinger waits. It's instinct to keep his body still. Mind conscious, focused on not giving her too much, but Agony stokes something deeper. Darker. A dangerous thing that Flint's long tried to keep buried.

With a hiss, Flint slots deep into Agony's throat, shadows stretching to accommodate. Flint flinches, prepared for the inevitable singe of Agony's heat, but it doesn't come. There's the lift of Agony's brows, a siren call tempting Flint toward the edge.

But Flint goes slow. Bottoming out until Agony's tongue drags along the underside of his cock, spurring Flint to pump harder.

A whimper comes from the bathroom.

TWENTY-NINE

Agony

Flint pauses before he thrusts slowly again, fucking Agony's mouth as Agony relaxes his throat. Helpless sounds spill from the other room, as if Harbinger can feel it. As if Flint's using her too.

There's a mental block, Agony knows. Flint's never thought of her that way. Could never use her like that. Never do anything to harm her, but the sounds she makes through the wall drive his hips faster. In Agony's mind, she's between them. Letting Agony guide her mouth over Flint, showing her how to take him deep while Agony whispers filth into her ear.

Chest heaving, Flint pulls Agony off of him. Agony's head swims with want. "Not so bad letting go, huh?"

Without warning, Flint turns Agony and smears him face-down against the comforter. "How about you take this dick like I told you too?"

Harbinger's groan echoes Agony's as he grinds his ass back against Flint. "Yeah, that'll fucking do it..."

But Flint hesitates, hands hovering over Agony's body.

"Where do I..."

Agony's a mass of shadows in the shape of man with no clear place for Flint to sink into — but Agony's also impatient. "Pick a fucking place; I'll make room. Put it anywhere you want, just *put it in me.*"

There's a little vengeance when Flint thrusts forward, bottoming out between Agony's legs, all three of their groans filling the room. Agony grips the sheets, winding back against Flint's hips. Flint can't help himself.

"Aw, it's not that big." He grinds into Agony, stretching Agony's cunt around his shaft. "Don't tell me it's too much for you."

Agony clenches around him. "I never fucking said that." The headboard creaks under Flint's hand, threatening to splinter, but Agony's goading him. Always searching for more, reaching back to dig his fingers into Flint's hips.

"Fuck me like you hate me, if you're so sure of it."

It shouldn't be a challenge. Shouldn't give Flint pause. Flint should hate the risk Agony presents, the person he was pulled from, the danger lurking beneath his surface. Being together like this is reckless for Flint, but when their eyes meet, memories come to Agony in bursts.

Pointing to Harbinger's sooty helmet in the yard. Catching her around the waist when Flint couldn't. Crushing their mouths together when she came apart atop the dais.

Flint should hate Agony. So when Flint bears down, Agony lets the lie hang between them, his teeth tearing into the sheets as he takes it.

"Gods..."

Both their eyes flash up to Harbinger, catsuit undone to her hips like she might combust. Flint slows the roll of his hips, hand tight in Agony's hair. "You're supposed to — "

"It worked." Her chest heaves, fingers gripping the wall like she can't keep her legs under her. "It fucking worked, ok, I'm telling you, so can I —"

She moves toward the bed, but Flint is faster.

"Stop."

She freezes. Panic rushes through Agony as if Flint might pull out, send them to three separate corners of the room to consider what this means. But Flint's jaw sets.

"Sit down."

It surprises Agony. Harbinger blinks. "Are you —"

"I said..." Flint's voice is low and controlled. Agony gives a muffled sound when Flint drags in deeper, never dropping Harbinger's gaze. "Sit your rebel ass down."

It knocks her off her feet, stumbling back to the TV stand, lifting one boot to perch against it. Blackened tips of her fingers trail down the skin of her chest.

"Don't touch yourself."

She gapes. Agony chuckles at Flint's command, until Flint stirs his hips again. Harbinger looks like he's smacked a treat from her hand.

"What?" Flint taunts. "Not used to being denied anything?"

"Not by *you*."

But she shudders like she enjoys it, fingers digging into the wood grain, desire overpowering anything the object gives her. Then Flint pulls completely out of Agony, and both he and Harbinger protest.

"Shouldn't need to touch yourself." Flint stirs a claw into Agony's back, dipping past the barrier of shadows. Beneath him, Agony shudders. So Flint does it again, raking down until he reaches the place between Agony's legs.

"How much can you feel, Harbin?"

She turns a shade of petrified, fingers jumping and desperate to touch. "I don't —"

Her words bind up in a curse when Flint draws experimental circles against Agony, mimicking the motions he's made against Harbinger. "What if I put this right here?" Flint winds his thumb against Agony, finding both their clits. Harbinger's legs clamber like they don't know where to go.

"Oh, she likes it," Flint purrs while Agony buries his face in the sheets. Three pulses of desire come from each new movement. There's the feel of Flint touching him, the wanton look on Harbinger's face, and their connection firing her arousal back.

"What if..." Flint stretches Agony to fit around his finger. "I slide in here? What if I take my time?" Harbinger can't keep her eyes open. Agony writhes in pleasure. "Is that good?"

Flint doesn't give them time to recover. "What if I curl my fingers like that? You feel it?"

Harbinger nearly knocks the TV off the stand. Agony tries to escape, but there's no pulling himself from Flint's grip.

"Does that feel good?" Flint's voice is so casually cruel when Harbinger whimpers. "Yeah? I bet it does, baby."

Then Flint dips the rest of his hand inside of Agony.

Strangled screams come from both their throats. Harbinger's thighs clench together, desperate for a modicum of friction. Flint presses Agony's face to the bed, sinking past the wrist and winding them up. "Does that hurt? What's your color?"

Flames on Agony's head flutter and jump, voice rasping. "No. *Fuck*, it feels like *green*."

"Harbinger?" Flint twists his arm until Agony and Harbinger bite through curses. "Tell me."

"It's green. It's like —" Her hand knocks the picture above her head askew. Fingers dart between her legs.

"Don't touch."

"Flint," she sobs.

"Tell me."

Her squeal steeps in frustration. Her hand jerks back, cheek pressed into the wall like it's too much. "It's like you're filling me up. Like you're in my fucking throat. *Flint*..."

"Good?"

"It's so fucking much. *Good*." Spiteful words spill out of her.

"Asking *'Is it good?'* while you've got a fucking *forearm* in me. In *us*."

Agony strains, trying to break out of the shape he's trapped in, cuffs draped over the side of the bed. Flint keeps eyes on him. "Still green?"

"Yeah. *Fuck*. Ah — yeah. It's fucking *green*, old man."

Retracting, Flint smirks before he buries his cock inside again. Agony's cuffs bounce against the side of the bed with each thrust.

Harbinger seethes. "Let me touch myself."

"You have absolutely zero manners."

"*Please* let me fucking touch myself, Flint!" Her fingers drag along the TV stand, nails digging in as she tries to obey. Flint considers it a moment longer, unbothered, winding her up.

"Fine."

Her hand darts between her legs, but it can't be that easy. "With me," Flint instructs. "No faster. No slower." His hips keep working into Agony as he adds a thumb into the shadows above. "Touch yourself like I'm touching him."

A groan stifles between her teeth. "I can't reach —"

"Do it, Harbin."

She obeys, sinking three fingers deep inside her pussy and grinding the heel of her palm against her clit. She's hypnotized when Flint rocks forward as she wets her other fingers in her mouth. Pitiful. Pathetic. But she follows Flint's command, dragging her slick thumb beneath her ass, whining when she rocks into both holes.

Flint hums. "That's a good girl."

A thought crosses Agony's mind. A product of him or Harbinger, he doesn't know, but with Flint grinding into him, Agony's voice takes a wicked tilt.

"Call him 'Daddy'."

Harbinger shudders still. Flint grips the back of Agony's hair. "Are you fucking..."

But Agony doesn't miss the way Flint's body tenses. It takes a moment for Harbin to recover, but she notices, too. How Flint hasn't moved, sweat slipping down his throat.

"Do you like that?" she asks. Flint doesn't respond. A slow grin creeps up her face, eyes meeting Agony's. *Organized sabotage.* Agony makes a figure-eight with his hips.

"Is it green, *Daddy*?"

For a moment, Agony wonders if he got it wrong. If this will make Flint pull away and leave space between them. Instead, Flint shuts his eyes. Grits his teeth. *"Yes."*

"I need to hear the color, *Sir*." Agony stirs his hips until Flint's claws dig in.

"Fuck."

"That's not a color."

Flint tries to retract, but there's no chance now. "Tell me, *Daddy*," Agony purrs. Flint jerks Agony's head back until his throat is bared to Flint's mouth.

"It's *green*."

Harbinger whines, trying helplessly to fuck herself on her fingers.

"You need more, baby?" Agony pouts. "Then tell Daddy all about it."

Whimpers fall from her mouth, body arching and desperate, and Agony wants to run his tongue over every inch of her. She's close to slipping off the TV stand, needy for it, teeth scraping her lip as Flint tries to regain control.

"Look at me," he demands.

She can't keep her eyes open, torn apart with moans.

"If you look away, I stop."

That gets her attention. Agony's already groaning at the stillness of Flint's hips.

"Gods, *please* look at him," Agony begs. By some divine fortitude, she meets Flint's eyes until he starts fucking into Agony again.

"Take your hands away," Flint adds cruelly. It pains her to

obey. "Good girl. So you do know how to listen."

Harbinger curses under her breath. Flint slams into Agony. "I don't even know if he can come." Flint turns Agony's face in one hand. "Can you, little terror?"

Right now, Agony can't do anything but groan. Flint smirks. "You might not get to come, Harbinger. Might edge both of you."

Pitiful sounds split her lips. "Gods, *please* don't..."

"Then beg me."

She's a sloppy mess across the room, squirming like she wants to crawl out of her skin. "Please, Daddy, I need to touch —"

Flint sets a pounding rhythm into Agony. "Why does that sound so fucking *good*?"

Neither of them answers, Agony drilled into the mattress as Harbinger begs nonsense until Flint turns Agony onto his back. The sight of Flint's face above him, rife with pleasure, threatens to send Agony over the edge. Then Flint's wings spread.

"I'm not pulling out."

Being fucked between the two of them is more spiritual than anything at the Convent. Agony's emotions shred with Harbinger's, both of them staring up at Flint like he's the only thing that can save or destroy them. His wings pump, lifting him off the ground and rocking him deeper into Agony.

Every thrust moves Agony across the bed. He wrestles the feeling begging to rip through him, trying to prolong this, but he can't hold it off. Not with Flint dragging every last ounce of desire from them.

There's no word for when Agony breaks. Shadows threatening to shatter, flames flaring higher, a string of curses caught in his throat. Harbinger amplifies everything. Her cry tears through him, blazing a thousand times hotter.

His ears ring like being caught in phoenix fire again, decimated and razed to the ground. When his eyes finally open, Flint holds himself off the bed, chest heaving as he looks at the TV smashed on the floor.

Agony doesn't try for words. Harbinger can't open her eyes, hand resting where the TV had been. "Shit," Flint pants, head dropping closer to Agony, exhausted laughter mingling between them. "We're gonna have to pay for that."

"Broken anyway," Agony croaks.

"Worth it," Harbinger breathes when Flint pulls out of Agony. Between Agony's legs, Flint's cum mixes with a slick coating that glows the same color as Agony's eyes.

"Is this...?"

"Fuck if I know," Agony puffs. "Was that coming? It felt good. Very good. Like holding in a sneeze."

"I don't think that's quite..." But Harbinger gives a furtive glance to Agony's cuffs. He rolls onto his side to face her.

"What was it like for you? Did you come"

Her head tilts back against the wall. "*Yes*. It was like he was fucking me. *More*. Like he was inside me. Like I was you." She looks toward Agony. "Or in you. Or you were in me."

Harbinger wraps an invisible hand around their connection, pulling closer to Agony.

"And was it ok? For both of you?" Concern is back on Flint's face, but they don't give it a second thought.

"So fucking good," they groan, staring at the ceiling like it might crack open and whisk them away. "I like it when you lose control," Harbinger murmurs. "When you don't hold back."

It's the first time they've spoken about it in front of Agony. Flint's shoulders are stiff, but he lets the tension out.

"I don't want to hurt you."

"You *won't*," she laughs. "Flint, you're the most cautious person I know. Definitely in this room." Agony grunts in agreement. "I want to do this with you *because* I trust you, but you get so caught in your head. I know you're worried, but it's so obvious that you're distracted. Like you're inside me and thinking about what could go wrong, or who could show up, or if I know how you feel. Remember when you made me hold the headboard still? And you knew I couldn't?"

Heat twinges in Agony's stomach. Fuck, *he* wants to remember that.

"Like that," Harbinger finishes. "I want that, when you act like the fucking know-it-all that you are. When you patronize. When you're a little mean. When you give us more than you think we can take and trust us to tell you if it's too much."

Us.

Even lying between them, being fucked between them, it's the first time Agony's been a part of it. There's a new softness to Harbinger's face. When Agony turns his head, Flint's looking at him, too.

"It helps when he's here," Flint murmurs. "Feels less wrong, somehow."

That unnamable emotion swells in Agony's chest. He buries it behind a cocky grin. "You just want to fuck somebody you don't mind roughing up."

Flint looks away. A knowing smile settles on Harbinger's face. "That's not it."

THIRTY

Flint

All three of them crowd into the motel bed. "It makes more sense for you to be on one side," Harbinger mutters to Flint. It's unfortunate that she's right, because pressing up against Agony seems like tempting fate, forcing Flint to look at exactly what's stirring in his chest.

Harbinger slides between them, her back against Flint's chest, breath evening as she drifts off. Exhausted from an orgasm wrung out of her through Agony, who's staring at Flint over her hair. Flint scans the wall for anything else he can focus on, counting patterns on the wallpaper.

"That's one of the weirder ones."

Agony's voice is an intrusion. Flint follows his eyes to the picture hanging above the TV stand, still crooked from Harbinger. It's a mountainous landscape, vast and open with no other sign of life. No birds. No deer. No people.

"Kind of ominous."

Harbinger rolls over with a snuffling sound, nuzzling her back into Agony's chest. He lifts his hand to the side of her face, brushing a strand of hair behind her ear.

"I won't hurt her." Agony's voice doesn't tilt with a sneer, soft against the back of Harbinger's hair. There's something impossibly fragile about the sight of Agony curved around her, her peaceful face beneath the curl of his fingers. "And I won't hurt you, either."

Flint's lip quirks, voice as low as he can manage. "I'm not too worried about you getting through the rock armor."

Another tendril of Harbinger's hair slips through Agony's fingers. "I don't mean like that."

Watching Agony and Harbinger's breaths slip into sync, it's too easy for Flint to fall asleep. Much harder to wake with his arm and wing draped over both of them, foreheads pressed together. He maneuvers out of bed, leaving the two of them entwined, and realizes for the first time in months that there's no leftover tension in his neck.

The three eat lunch at the ferry dock, passing time as the sun blazes overhead. Harbinger props their cell phone against her cup, switching it to speaker. "We'll be out of cell range, but I'll call once we're back. No more than a week." She rifles for fries in a paper bag. Agony threatens the gulls circling overhead.

"Ok." Evie's mother closes a cabinet door on the other end of the line, oil sizzling in the background. "We'll do some spells for you tonight: discovery, protection…" One of her children asks for their lunchbox. She points it out with fond exasperation.

Harbinger smiles. "Thank you. We appreciate it."

As soon as the call ends, the phone rings again. *Restricted number.* OID. Harbinger declines it, taking a long swig from her cup. Her throat's surely raw from the last two hours of talking. Flint and Agony had their turns as well, but with one phone, calling families was a lengthy process.

"Last call?" Flint asks. Agony offers barbecue sauce across the picnic table. Harbinger dips her fry in as he coats his chicken nugget in mustard. Flint scoffs his distaste. "That's disgusting."

They take identical bites and moan. Flint rolls his eyes toward the station clock to hide his smile. "Ferry should be here in a minute."

They clean up their trash as the boat pulls up to the dock. The ferry's built to fit a couple of cars, but as the only passengers, their journey's particularly cozy. As the ferryman chats to Flint about the Break's latest news, Agony and Harbinger set out to determine who's the better cheat at Sidi's card game.

Once they land in the Break, they take the SUV through winding hills up to the base of a mountain. A range extends around them, but the Timber Pack resides on a slope, nestled between pine trees and a lake. The air stings with cold. When they pull up, Agony hoists himself out of the backseat to help Harbinger into an oversized jacket. Flint tugs on a knit sweater.

The Timbers' main building looks like a small ski lodge with wooden A-frame cabins dotted around it. Despite the cold, wild blue iris blooms, vibrant against the dark earth.

Flowers like that spilled out of Sidi's hands once. She maneuvered for a vase in the kitchen, leaving Flint to recover stray petals. And later, her cold fingers curled around those flowers pressed against her chest, eyes closed...

"Flint?"

Agony and Harbinger watch him from beside the car. Flint considers not saying anything, shaking off the thought as he always has and sinking back into stoicism. But he peers at the blooms once more. "Sidi liked those."

Wind rushes through the tops of the trees, rustling leaves beginning to die. Agony and Harbinger stare solemnly at the patch of color before Agony plucks two stems from the ground. He extends the flower to Flint, the smallest bow in his posture.

It's far more earnest than a simple gesture. The flower fits in Flint's hand, small and delicate when he closes his fingers around it. With a far grander dip, Agony turns to Harbinger. "M'lady." She shoves him with a smile, tucking the flower into the helmet cradled under her arm.

"Wait." Flint steps forward, wrapping his fingers around the chain linking Agony's hands. "Before we go in..."

Harbinger's eyes widen before she nods. Keeping Agony contained was necessary to avoid collateral damage, but it's long past time to admit he isn't the depraved creature Flint expected. And with all this open space, Agony could make a break for the horizon and never encounter another person.

With a claw, Flint slips beneath the cuffs, metal groaning as he slices through. The chains thud to the ground, and Agony becomes nebulous, rubbing his wrists incredulously.

"Requires trust, right?" Flint murmurs.

He resists the urge to pull Harbinger toward him, but Agony doesn't move, shadows shifting like sun dappling through trees. "You seem surprised."

"I kind of thought..." Harbinger eyes him. "You might leave."

In a flash, Agony curves around Harbinger's back, striking panic in Flint's chest — but Agony just leans his wicked smile against her cheek. "You're gonna have a harder time getting rid of me."

It doesn't sound like a threat. It sounds like a promise, and Flint wants to see it through.

Then the front door of the lodge opens to screaming.

The three of them streak across the grass, but the wererabbit in the doorway is unphased. Exhaustion seeps into the bags under her eyes as a harpy struggles with her bindings inside.

"Uh, Lev?" Flint clears his throat, but he's not looking at the leporine woman. Instead, they watch the harpy, wings beating as she snaps at the werecreature trying to feed her. "Is this a bad time?"

"Lately?" Lev knocks the door the rest of the way open, ushering them in from the porch. "It's always a bad time."

They follow her into the open kitchen, keeping their distance from the squalling harpy. "Pheir," Lev gestures by way of introduction, but the other woman pays them no mind.

Harbinger stares. "Should we —"

"She's fine." Lev leans elbows onto the counter, ears drooping. "She likes to act like we're torturing her."

"Fuck you." Pheir jerks against the chair, clawing at anything within reach. "As soon as I get out of here, you're gonna wish —"

"Okay!" Lev's rising shout gets tangled in Pheir's diatribe, both their voices clamoring to be heard. "Put the muzzle back on her — "

"When Vesta gets her talons —"

"— back to her cabin. Clearly —"

"— fuck you up —"

"— not interested in eating!"

The other werecreature fumbles with Pheir's muzzle, narrowly avoiding her teeth before he gets the strap around her head. Pheir's screams echo as he pulls her out the doorway. Agony leans toward Flint. "Somehow, I don't think they would have cared if I was still in cuffs."

When the commotion finally fades, Lev slumps back in a bar chair. "Sorry." She presses fingers to her temples. "Usually, Aren and Caius keep a better handle on her, but even they need a fucking break from...*that*."

Agony's head tilts with intrigue. "Are you holding her hostage?" Harbinger gives him a narrow look. "I'm just *asking*."

"It's complicated. She's a danger to herself and others." Lev plucks a piece of hay from a bowl on the counter. "The Conclave decided it was best to pair her with a strong pack to keep her in check." The hay sticks out of her lips like a cigarette. "You can see how that's going."

"Sounds like something the Conclave would do," Flint murmurs.

"They're the governing body of the Break, right?" Agony looks at Flint like he's waiting for a gold star. So he has been paying attention to the investigation.

"Yes, we are." Lev isn't thrilled by the reminder. "We deal with the Break's internal disputes on our own, setting rules and guidelines for the packs to follow. But since there are so many members from various ways of life, The Conclave rarely makes any decisions unanimously."

"You said there was an issue with a phoenix recently." Harbinger props her helmet on the counter. "Is that related?"

Lev jerks her chin toward where Pheir disappeared. "It's why we took so long getting back to you. The phoenix was Pheir's Alpha. Vesta was killed last week in battle when it all came to a head."

"Shit." Harbinger sinks into one of the chairs. "So we can't talk to her?"

Lev shakes her head.

"Do you have anything of hers? A feather, a scrap of clothing..."

Lev tugs on her necklace, a vial dangling from the end. "Ashes?"

Harbinger's mouth twists. "Not enough surface area."

"Then I'm afraid not. And Pheir won't be much help to you, either. The Vestals were mindlessly loyal to their Alpha. Interrogation does nothing."

Flint and Agony find their own seats. "What happened at the battle?" Flint asks. "How'd it get to the point of cremating her?"

As if a weight is finally settling, Lev's shoulders sink. "There's been a lot of unrest recently, and I'm afraid it's not over. Vesta was always overly-ambitious. Power hungry." Her eyes shift a shade darker, gaze sharpening to glass. "The Conclave was able to keep her in line for a while, but years ago, she disappeared off the map. I thought we'd heard the last of her, but a year or so ago, rumors started. A new pack gaining traction, poaching members from weaker groups, decimating smaller factions until the Conclave had to take notice. By then, the Vestals were a lot stronger than the Conclave predicted. They weren't going to surrender."

Agony frowns. "What does that have to do with Raymond Reid?"

"I don't know." Lev's arms fold across her chest. "Flint said you're looking for a place he might have buried girls. Wondering if he was involved with a phoenix. I don't have any specific evidence for you, but I wouldn't put either of those things past Vesta."

"But why?" Harbinger tugs at her gloves "What would she get from Reid killing girls? Why would he come out here?"

"It's remote. Lots of land, not a lot of people asking questions. He might have thought it was some lawless place, but if most of the packs in the Break found out what Reid was doing, he would have begged for the OID to take him instead. If it was Vesta, though..." Lev stares out the window as light begins to fade. Upstairs, other pack members move about, calling down the hallway. "I don't know for sure, but there are ways she could have used the girls to strengthen her pack. To make herself more powerful."

Harbinger stops picking at her gloves. "How?"

"There are a few ways. None of which are looked upon highly. Techniques to forcibly bind someone to your pack, to force a sense of loyalty. New members tend to make a pack stronger, and a stronger pack means a stronger Alpha. Vesta may have compelled the girls to join her pack when Reid brought them around."

"Wait, so the girls could still be *alive*?" Agony leans forward, earnest hope on his face. Lev sees it and winces.

"I'm afraid not. Especially after the battle..." She shakes her head. "But your girls weren't there. At least, not the ones Flint described."

"Then what would Reid get out of it?" Frustration edges into Harbinger's voice. "And wouldn't members dying weaken the pack?"

"No, actually." Lev plucks the strand of hay from her lips. "Like I said, there are a few different ways to make a pack stronger. One is adding new members — it takes time for the pack bonds to make room and solidify around another person. But if they kept the girls alive long enough for that, losing those members would strengthen the pack at an exponential rate."

Unease creeps up Flint's neck as Lev speaks. "If a member withdraws or dies, it's like a muscle tearing to become stronger, scar tissue forming over a wound. The binds of the pack cinch tighter and bring the remaining members closer together. That's what happened with the Vestals. They lost most of their members in the battle, so the bond tried harder to knit them back together. It's a painful process. A *terrible* process," Lev amends. "Especially if an Alpha were doing it on purpose, killing people to make the pack stronger."

A side door bursts open. The three of them jump, but Lev is unperturbed, waving the other Timbers through the door. Harbinger stares into her helmet on the counter. Agony scowls. Flint finds some words. "Thank you, Lev. That's very helpful."

"You're welcome to stay tonight." She pushes up from the counter. "I don't advise driving back down the mountain after dark. We have plenty of room in the smaller cabins outside. Most of the right row should be empty."

A feral screech comes from outside. Lev rolls her eyes, swinging the chain of ashes to her back. "Dinner's in an hour. Help yourselves. And let me know if you need anything else."

THIRTY-ONE

Harbinger

Harbinger's dead on her feet, so Flint and Agony leave her to pass out in one of the extra cabins. It's hard to get comfortable, even in a bed big enough for multiple pack members to pile on at once.

There are ways Vesta could have used the girls.

If a member of a pack dies, it's like a muscle tearing, scar tissue forming over a wound.

Harbinger scowls against the pillow, trying to tie Vesta and Reid together before her thoughts overflow into the well of her dreams.

Flint drives the SUV. Agony's in the backseat, but not the Agony she's used to. Not the real Agony, just a figurehead of her imagination, fading into the background as the radio changes stations on its own.

It takes a few moments to recognize the street. As if her brain is blocking it out, trying to protect her, but familiar dread seeps in as soon as Flint pulls up to the curb. She wants to lock the car doors. She reaches for the button, but her hand doesn't obey, gripping the handle and pushing the passenger door open.

This isn't like her dreams with Agony. She can't make her body react. Can't stall her feet. Can't open her mouth to tell Flint to stop. Instead, she follows Flint up the front steps where he rings the doorbell.

"I'm sorry this is hurting you."

His voice surprises her. He doesn't look at her, as if they're continuing a conversation from Harbinger's head.

"It's fine. It's not hurting me."

"It *is*," Flint insists. "You're stuck with this." He rings the bell again. "You have to feel what I'm feeling, forever."

Nervous energy crawls up Harbinger's spine. Hands wringing together, rocking on her heels, glancing between Flint and the door.

She knows what's coming. She doesn't want to go inside.

"It's ok. Flint, *please*." Desperation stretches her voice like taffy, molding it into the words she didn't say back then. "It's ok that you touched my skin. It's ok! I can deal with it."

Flint shakes his head. There's a strange quality to it, distinctly not-Flint. It's his body, his voice, but the way he moves isn't right.

She recognizes it.

Flint rings the bell again.

"I have to. I'm hurting you."

"You're *not*." Harbinger wills her hands to reach for him, to pull him back, but they don't move. "It's ok. I promise it's ok."

Suddenly, Flint turns the knob and pushes into the house. "I have to do it."

She scrambles to follow, but as soon as she steps inside, he's gone. She knows she won't find him, and still, she moves from room to room on the ground floor.

There's nothing. No trace of him.

Her feet stop in the living room. In the corner is an old recliner, discolored from years of use, a pattern worn into the fabric. Two lines against the leg rest, one on each arm, a patch rubbed raw against the back.

As if someone was just sitting there.

Darkness shifts in the corner of her vision. She can't look right at it. It's not supposed to be here. Shadows don't quite take shape, peering in from a distance. Watching.

Harbin.

Upstairs, the house creaks. Wind batters the walls until they sway. Harbinger clings to the doorframe, staring at the darkened stairwell, afraid to blink. Afraid her feet will take her there again.

Harbin, you're dreaming.

All the noise cuts off. The house is drowned in silence. Everything is still.

Then Harbinger screams.

Phantom pain rips through her. Her knees hit the carpet, scream echoing until it boils out of her in the real world, sending her shrieking up in bed.

The sharp pain is gone, but the hole inside her throbs, rubbed raw at the reminder — like stitches torn open. One of the Timbers rushes up to the cabin, but Harbin holds up a shaky hand. "Sorry: it was a dream. I'm sorry."

Aren's lynx ears twitch. "Should I get Flint and — your other partner?"

Harbinger breathes through her nose, inhaling until it burns. "No, it's ok. I'm fine."

His eyes narrow. Still, he steps down from the cabin, ushering away the other Timbers approaching.

She needs air. Fresh, not the stale remnants of her house, so she finds her way out to the lake. It's so dark she can hardly make out the opposing bank, but on this side, a small fire burns in the center of a loose circle of empty seats. She drops into a chair, fighting not to shiver against the cold.

Before she sees them, she feels them. The buoys of their presence bob to the surface of her mind. Flint comes with a steady gravity of emotions. Certain and strong, never overbearing, a solid rock beneath the waves. What he lets her feel is the tip of the iceberg, but she can make out the massive expanse beneath.

Agony's harder to pin down. A drifting dreaminess that tickles her senses, déjà vu slipping from her grasp. Feather-light and teasing, a flutter of eyelashes or rustling leaves before it vanishes again, leaving her reaching for something she can't quite get her hands around.

"Bad dream?"

Flint and Agony cast dark outlines against the sky, wings blocking out starlight next to a pair of incandescent eyes. Feeling swarms Harbinger's chest, ruffling everything in its path before she tamps it down.

For a moment, it seems normal, as if Agony was always with them. As if they weren't thrust together through some weird hand dealt by fate. Agony sinks into the chair beside her. Harbinger tears a blade of grass between her fingers. "Believe it or not, my body's already gotten used to cramming into the same bed."

Flint drapes a blanket around her shoulders, taking a seat on the bench to her other side as Agony grins toward her. "Can't sleep without me?"

She flicks the shredded grass. "Either of you."

The blanket warms her, but not as much as them being here. Tension eases from her chest before there's a shout and a round of laughter from the pack house.

"They're so fucking *loud*."

Smiles stretch across their faces as Agony reclines in his chair. "I take back what I said about motel life. Even it's calmer than the Timbers."

It's true. But the Timber compound is infused with community, knit together and looking after each other. A family they've found. A family they've created.

"What did that dream mean?"

Sweat beads on Harbinger's neck. They watch the water of the lake. She can't keep it from them — not after everything.

"I didn't tell you everything about it before." Harbinger tucks her knees to her chest beneath the blanket. The firepit flickers and shivers like Agony's hair. "About my dad."

"You told me your parents were gone," Flint adds softly. "You never told me how."

She remembers that conversation in the early days between them, when Harbinger still sunk into surliness at the slightest provocation.

We could take a weekend off cases, Flint murmured. *Visit your family.*

Harbinger shook the ketchup bottle harder than necessary. *They're gone. No one to visit.*

Flint didn't press further. Maybe that was so Harbinger wouldn't ask about his.

"My mom left when I was young. I don't remember her. But my dad and I were complicated." Harbinger twines a blanket thread around her finger. Her father always felt like a missed connection, like he wanted to care, but couldn't. Wouldn't. When Harbinger pushed back, he gave up. Left space between them for weeks on end, locked away in his room to the sound of clinking bottles. She settles on the easiest description. "He was there, but I was alone. And when the banshee change happened, it got worse."

Her eyes shut against the memory. Screaming out of sleep in the middle of the night, crashing to the floor, trying to escape the feeling of *everything*. Memories soaked into her from her sheets, her clothes, her carpet, unyielding and overwhelming and terrifying.

"My dad was the first person to touch me. He didn't know better. He was trying to help, but that was it. We were connected. It was the worst thing I've ever felt." There's the barest hint of a smile, but it's twisted and pained. "Well...until that point. I was sick for days after. I'm sure he thought I was dying. *I* thought I was dying, sweating and puking and screaming until the Diviners showed up."

Sour taste seeps into her mouth, the same way it had then. "It didn't take much for them to convince him that the Convent would be better for me. After that, I hardly saw him. The Diviners wanted me to focus on my ability, and to be honest…" Her lip wobbles, teeth digging into it. "My dad and I didn't want to be around each other."

It was hard enough before the connection. But after, even when he wasn't within a hundred miles, he was a pounding reminder inside her. Constant. Exhausting. "When we did see each other, I felt so embarrassed. Humiliated at what a fucking mess we were. We didn't know what to say. It amplified how much everything hurt."

"You were a kid, Harbin." Agony's voice makes her want to cry. "That's not something you could have prepared for."

"I was such a *bitch*." Breath hisses through her teeth. "We kept doing that for years, until…I shouldn't have told him. The Diviners kept saying he was a distraction, hindering me from my purpose, and they were telling him, too. Blaming him, saying my 'earthly connections' kept me from fully appreciating my *gift*."

She tightens the string around her finger. "I was overwhelmed. But if I blame them, then I have to blame myself. He came to visit me, but I was over it. Tired of dealing with the Diviners, tired of dealing with him…I was angry, and I was scared, and I was tired of acting like there was any sort of relationship between us. That we'd ever been any sort of family."

Her voice wobbles. "I wanted to hurt him. Wanted to abandon him as much as he had done to me. I told him how much I hated it. Seeing him, feeling him, all of it. I told him not to bother coming anymore…"

"Hey, hey, hey." Flint kneels beside her when her voice cracks, wrapping fingers around hers.

"That's why you can't put me above you." She desperately finds his eyes, squeezing his hand tight enough for the skin to lighten. He doesn't pull away. "That's why you can't focus so hard on me that you don't take care of yourself —"

"Ok," Flint soothes. Agony lifts her braid off the back of her neck, pushing the blanket down her shoulders until she can breathe.

The air is cool and crisp, but she still feels suffocated. "I didn't know what it was then, but I felt it. Something pulled so tight inside me until it snapped. All his emotions, his feelings, the constant reminder of his presence, just...vanished."

THIRTY-TWO

Harbinger

Breath swirls into Harbinger's lungs, ballooning to fill the empty spaces in her chest, but the hollow is still there. She tugs on the front of her suit. "I told the Diviners I needed to go home. They wouldn't allow it, so Omen and Poe got us out."

She doesn't know how they did it. Harbinger could barely move, gasping in pain at the invisible wound in her chest. Poe and Omen carried her weight for miles before they found a ride to the train station. It was another hour before the train ran. Hours more before they arrived in Harbinger's town, but Poe and Omen never took their hands off her.

"It was quiet at my house." Details stay ingrained in her memory; the neighbors' flowers bloomed early that year. A kid left their scooter in the front yard, covered in weeds. "Our front door was cracked, like someone was running inside. Like they'd forgotten something. Like it would just be a minute."

Agony's eyes burn against the back of her neck. She can't stop now. If she does, she won't say it. "I asked Poe and Omen to wait outside. I don't know why. I guess I knew..." Heat pricks the back of her eyes. "I checked the rooms downstairs, calling for him, looking in the closets twice even when I knew he wouldn't be there. I couldn't go up the stairs. I knew. I knew when I couldn't feel him."

It happened so quickly. So slowly. All at once. She's not sure where the gaps in her memory come from; her mind trying to protect her, or the Oracle stealing one more thing. In Harbinger's memories, she can see the room. The things he used. But her father isn't there, a blurry outline that she, mercifully and agonizingly, can't conjure.

She begged Omen to bring him back. It didn't matter that he couldn't. She pleaded, desperate and screaming, but Omen just held her while she sobbed.

In the end, maybe it was an exchange, Omen's power bringing Harbinger back from the brink instead.

Agony drifts beside her. Flint sinks low enough to look at her, and she feels as small as she was back then. "That's not your fault, Harbin."

Tears slip when her eyes squeeze shut. "I can't let someone love me like that again. I can't take someone else dying to protect me. *Killing themself* to make sure I'm ok. I can't live through that again. I can't carry another hole. I *can't*." Sharp grief blades through her chest when she looks at them. "Please don't make me."

Flint's arms encircle her, pulling her down into his lap, Agony pressed against her back. Fear escapes her in the tears pressed against Flint's chest. He and Agony cover her with gentle words, soothing circles against her skin until her jagged breaths have slowed.

"That's why I don't think about it," she whispers. "What could happen to me. It's why I've been reckless, taking risks because I hate what happened. What becoming this has caused." Her forehead presses into Flint's shoulder, and she tries to breathe. "So much of life was out of my control, but diving headfirst is one thing I had a say in."

"You have a say in things now," Flint murmurs. "Or you should. I know I've been overbearing..." His head tilts back at the realization. "I've been trying so hard to protect you, I didn't recognize it was stifling. That it was hurting you."

She swipes at her face. "You didn't know."

"But you tried to tell me."

She sucks in a shaky breath, sinking back against Agony. Shadows weave through her hair, unbraiding it until the pain in her skull eases. They probably look ridiculous, the three of them on the ground next to the fire, half-wrapped in the blanket, but she can't bring herself to care.

"That's something else the Oracle takes." Her fingers trace the knit outline in Flint's sweater. "I didn't keep anything of his, because one day, I won't remember him at all. I'll see a picture of him, and I won't know who it is. I won't know anything about him. Nothing except —" Tracks of tears dry on her cheeks. "The hole he left."

Agony's mouth presses to her temple. "How do you feel about him now?"

"I don't know. Conflicted. Angry. Guilty...sad, but more for the things I can't do now. Confronting him, or telling him how much he hurt me, or repairing what was there. Maybe those things never would have happened, but now I know they won't. It feels wrong to love him. I don't know if I do, but why would it hurt like this if I didn't? And then I wonder..." Another shaky breath escapes her. "Did he care about me? If I was important enough that he wanted to stop hurting me, why wasn't I important enough for him to stay? Why wasn't I important enough for him to try harder?"

Agony brushes through her hair.

"I wish it were simple," she murmurs. "That I felt one thing about him. That I could mourn the loss without lightness. Without being glad that I don't have to hurt like that anymore. It's a different hurt now. Relief that's unfinished. I can never close the wound. I don't know if that's better or worse."

Agony's chin rests on her shoulder. Harbinger's lulled by the rise and fall of Flint's chest until Agony speaks again. "Do you think you became who you are *because* of your father, or in *spite* of him?"

Agony doesn't look at either of them, gaze cast across the water. She can make out his face next to hers, blending into the dark, shadows shifting around the light of his eyes.

"I'm not sure. A lot more of him worked its way into me than I wanted to believe. I thought I was living in spite of him; I was still here when he wasn't. I didn't leave like he did."

Emotions swell from Flint and Agony, twining together to reach the empty places within her. They don't fill the hole her father left, but for a moment, they cover it, a layer of reminder that the three of them exist. That the hole is not the only thing there is.

Her laughter is wet. "I went against everything the Convent tried to instill in me. Every rule they made, I rejected, because of what they did to me. What they did to him. But now..." She tilts her head back against Agony's shoulder. "I'm realizing that every choice I made specifically against the Oracle, I made because of them. They still had a hand in things I didn't want them to be able to touch. If I did it to spite them, I still did it because of them."

Agony still doesn't look at her. She probes their connection and reaches something like shame. His question seems less about her and more about something else.

"It doesn't have to be like that, though," she murmurs. "You don't have to let the past hold onto you. At least, I fucking hope you don't."

Agony's grin presses to the side of her neck. It tugs on her own, and when she lifts her eyes, Flint's watching them both with that soft expression he's only ever reserved for her.

There aren't words for it: the complexity, the delicacy, the intricacies that don't make sense. The steady thrum of contentment coming from both ends of her connections. A steady spark with her as the conduit, linking the three of them until the presence of their emotions is no longer a burden. It's a comfort, a reminder of the things she's carried and where she's safe to set them down.

"We should head back." Flint twists a strand of her hair and Agony's shadows around his finger. "Agony has something to show you."

They pull themselves off the ground, making their way back to the cabin where Agony leaves them on the deck. On the field in front of the pack house, the Timbers play a pickup game that mostly involves tackling each other to the ground.

"You remember at the Convent..." Wind ruffles through Harbinger's hair. "When you asked if I'm sleeping with you because I have no other options?"

Shame surges through their connection. "I shouldn't have —"

"You asked the wrong question."

There's temptation to keep her lips clamped shut. To avoid putting this into words, but she doesn't want to be that any more. Doesn't want to avoid this. Doesn't want to lose anything else to the walls she built to keep loss away. If the walls prevent her from getting close to someone else, keep her from experiencing this, she wants to tear them down.

"You were asking if I would have chosen to make the connection. I'm telling you that I choose it now. I choose *you* now." She meets the tender look on Flint's face with the certainty of her own. "I would choose to feel both of you, forever, if it means keeping you. Even knowing that there's no going back. Even knowing how complicated this is. It was an accident, not a mistake. I would choose this connection a thousand times over not having you." It's a relief to say it. A smile tugs across her lips. "After everything it's taken, this power has finally given me something good."

Flint sweeps her into his arms, kissing her deeper than he ever has, mouths molding together and pressing out a sigh when her fingers knot in his hair. When he finally sets her back on the ground, her knees are weak.

"You said you wanted me to tell you what I want." Flint's hand comes up to cup her cheek. It makes her stomach flutter. "I want more from you. Not just sex. I want us to call this what it is." His fingers brush her skin so gently, but the heat of his eyes is enough to melt her. "I don't just want to be your partner anymore."

Her teeth dimple into her grin, pressing her cheek into his palm when she inclines her head toward the cabin. "You want more from him, too?"

Flint follows her eyes with a sigh. "Yes," he admits. As if he hasn't said it to himself, shoulders rising like a weight has finally lifted. "I don't know how it's possible. How it could work." There's a pining glint in his eyes. "But I do."

THIRTY-THREE

Agony

Freedom is a funny thing. Agony spent so much of the past month considering what it would take to get it, and now that he has it, he stays still. There's no urge to escape. No desire to run. He's content to remain kept by the very hands that freed him.

Getting out of the cuffs was nice, though. No longer constrained to one physical form, Agony expands his shadows and stretches the tendrils across the cabin bed.

His connection with Harbinger grows stronger by the day. If he's honest, sometimes he presses his ear to their bond to feel the vibrations of Flint and Harbinger. It's less about the words they say and more about the tender lilt in their voices, the quiet crush like velvet before they come back into the cabin.

Harbinger scans the mass of his body. He's amorphous, spilling off the side of the bed, undulating like an open portal. "You look so different."

"Hardly recognize me, huh?"

A little smile comes to her face. "Not that different."

Agony's shadows flutter.

"You were going to tell us about the dreamscape."

Flint's voice makes him jump. "Uh, right. Yeah." Flint smirks behind Harbinger as Agony explains. "Now that I'm not constrained, we can get more from the dream. Find more landmarks, follow the trail further. Go deeper."

He expects her to jump at the chance, but she looks to Flint. "What do you think?"

"It's a risk." Flint rubs his beard. "But anything new is. We've exhausted everything else. You've read every surface we could find, spoken to the girls' families, pierced the Veil with the banshees. If you and Agony are able to get more from the dream, then I think it's our best option."

"Agreed." Harbinger kneels on the edge of the mattress, staring down into the swirling mass of shadows.

"It'll be different," Agony warns. "More real. You don't have to fall asleep to enter, but that means we have to pull you out when we're done." This time, Harbinger's willingness isn't spurred by reckless desire. Still, Agony meets her eyes. "I won't let anything happen to you." He glances to Flint. "I promise."

The certainty in Flint's gaze makes the shadows ripple. "I don't doubt that."

Harbinger situates herself over Agony, prepared to dive into the pool. "Ready?"

"With you?" He cranes up to reach her, stopping short of her mouth. "Always."

Tendrils outstretch, encircling her waist and pulling her into his depths. With one last look to Flint, Agony dives in after her.

Air rushes past them, wind growing louder as Agony tightens his hold around Harbinger. It's a freefall, endless and impossible, forcing their eyes shut until the roaring settles to a breeze. When they land on the ground, it's in the same clearing of clawed trees they've grown so familiar with.

Harbinger whispers, as if something might hear them. "This is it."

A shudder darts through Agony. She's right; it's the same dream as before, but the details are clearer. It's colder than the Timber compound, dead leaves already scattered on the ground, frogs croaking in the woods around them.

It's *real.*

Agony lingers behind Harbinger, breathing against her ear until the tension loosens from her shoulders. She reaches toward the claw marks on the trees, fingers shaking. Agony laces shadows between them, and they touch down against the bark.

"...nothing. I still can't feel anything."

But the other trees are still gouged with marks, a jagged trail leading deeper into the darkness.

I wish Flint were here.

Agony hears her thought and squeezes her bare hand.

He's close. I'm here. You're safe.

Her breath is so loud. Her fingers tighten against Agony before she lifts her foot and takes one step forward.

They move through the brush, stepping over a fallen tree, pushing back branches as Harbinger's boots crunch over acorns. Snow lingers under the layered canopy of evergreens, bushes and saplings and mighty trunks towering toward the sky. Soil gives under their feet. Not frozen. Not compact. A woodpecker jabs into a tree above them until the sound is drowned out by a blue jay chased by a squirrel.

A strange smell lingers in the air. Dust kicks up where they step. Agony peers through the shadows cast by the trees until he spots a patch of fading light ahead.

There.

Twilight paints through the gap in the tree cover. The evening grows dark around them, but the clearing they move toward swallows up any remaining light. It's impossibly black, ground covered in darkness. Harbinger kneels at its edge, pressing her fingers to the dirt. They come away darker.

"It's burnt." She rubs her fingers together. The dirt drifts away, ash in the wind. Agony remembers that smell, wafting off of Reid's house in plumes.

"Phoenix fire."

Someone laughs in the forest. A cruel howl back in the direction they came, followed by a shriek that makes Harbinger grip Agony's wrist.

"Is that him?"

"I don't know." Agony is dipped in molasses, as if any swift motion will give them away.

Harbinger's voice is tight from the cold air in her chest. "He's not real, is he?"

"No," Agony answers immediately. But then, he stops. "I'm not sure."

It's a dream. It should be fake, manufactured, but Agony's real. Able to speak. To touch.

To harm.

His grip tightens on Harbinger's hand. "We need to leave."

Her heels dig into the earth. "But what if we can find more? What if we follow him, find a sign post, something?"

"Harbin." Agony grips both her hands in his. "I promised."

I won't let anything happen to you.

They move away from the path. Mounds of leaves rustle as they tramp deeper into the forest. Behind a pair of entwined trees, Agony rests his head against the trunk. "*Fuck*, I can't move you in here." His shadows try to extend, to pull Harbinger inside, but he slips over her body like a smoke circle.

A branch snaps behind them. Footsteps thud along the trail: rhythmic, like a heartbeat, weighed down.

Carrying something.

Harbinger sucks in a breath.

The footsteps pause.

Agony pulls her back into his chest, gripping a hand over her mouth as he presses his mouth to her temple.

Stay still. Stay silent.

Her breath tremors against his hand until a bird flies off in the forest. The footsteps pick up pace down the trail again.

They wait until the footfalls change, muffled as they step into the ash. There's a singular thud, much heavier than the others. Agony's stomach sours. Then glass shatters, followed by a rush of wind and heat. Rainbow colors flicker off the forest around them. Agony grips the backs of Harbinger's arms.

"Run."

It's a dead sprint through the forest. Her boots catch on rocks and roots, kicking up debris as they run from the raging phoenix fire. Agony stays behind her, trying to get a glimpse of the person behind them, but there's a thousand shadows against the flames.

Then he hears the footsteps. Running toward them, far faster than they should, covering ground and eating away at the distance between them. Agony shoves Harbinger in front of him, breaking through the trees until they stumble back to where they started.

"Flint!"

Agony shoves Harbinger up the trunk of the first tree. Her fingers strain for the first branch, closing around the air beneath it, just out of her grasp.

"Flint!"

Agony heaves Harbinger with his shoulder. She leaps, digging her nails into the bark, snapping the lowest branch in half.

Footsteps shake the ground behind them. Agony's body rattles.

"Flint, *take her! Pull her out!*"

A clawed hand appears above them, gripping Harbinger's wrist and yanking them both off the ground. They come gasping back into the real world, Flint's eyes skirting over both of them for any sign of trouble.

"I'm fine." Harbinger collapses onto her back on the mattress, reaching for Agony's hand. He takes it, both of them staring at the ceiling. "Holy fuck."

"What the hell happened?"

"He was there," Harbinger pants. "Or someone was. And I think they were — burning a body."

Flint does his best not to look distraught. "But it wasn't real, right? It was a dream. A memory."

"I think so." Agony turns onto his stomach. "But I didn't want to risk it. This is all uncharted territory, and since Harbinger couldn't wake up..."

There's a moment of hesitancy before Flint sinks into the mattress between them. "Did you find anything?"

Harbinger runs a hand back through her hair, trying to shake the daze of the dream world. "Nothing definitive, but we have a better idea of the landscape. Someone familiar with the area could give us an idea of where to start."

"I'll get Aren."

The werelynx returns with Flint, standing next to him with the same stoicism as Harbinger and Agony describe the dream.

"It has to be somewhere close," Aren agrees, furred arms folded across his chest. "One of the other elevated territories. From the landscape, it sounds like higher ground, somewhere across the pass."

"What's the best way to get there?"

Aren tilts his eyes toward the ceiling, running mental calculations. "We can escort you — sometime in the next few days."

Flint waves off the offer. "That's not necessary. You've already been more than generous."

One of the harpy prisoner's screams pierces the night air, followed by a torrential string of curses. Aren rubs the bridge of his nose while Flint fights a smirk. "And you have your hands full already."

"Who should we talk to?" Agony asks. "Who knows the area there?"

"Start with the Conifers and Broadleafs." Aren pauses. "But be aware, there's been a lot of turnover within packs recently. It's tenuous."

"Lev mentioned that." Harbinger crosses her legs. "Were those packs involved in the last battle?"

Aren shakes his head. "The Conifers were, but some packs didn't want anything to do with subduing the Vestals. The Broadleafs are a lot smaller and weaker. Their Alpha, Diction, was having enough trouble preventing infighting. Even his beta was struggling. We offered to help, but the Broadleafs are very independent. They don't love visitors, but you can tell Diction that you came from here. He and Lev are old friends."

Flint sees Aren to the door. Aren gives Harbinger a look with raised brows before he steps off the porch.

"Sweet dreams this time."

THIRTY-FOUR

Harbinger

After the dreamscape, they should be exhausted, unconscious at the earliest opportunity. But when the rest of the Timber compound settles to a low hum, Harbinger can't sleep. The slash of Agony's eye peeks at her from the other side of the bed.

"You either?"

She shakes her head. Flint's voice rumbles from the chair across the room. "You two are supposed to be sleeping." Moonlight glints off his glasses, nocturnal vision pouring over the casefiles to keep from disturbing them.

Harbinger flops onto her back. "I'm not tired."

Agony bounces on the mattress. "And I *can't* sleep — literally."

Shadows spill around his body, falling across Harbinger's legs before he pulls himself closer. She twirls a tendril around bare fingers, lit by Agony's contented gaze half-closed like a cat.

"I'm sorry we kept you in cuffs for so long," she murmurs. Shadows slip around her hand like smoke.

Flint's guilt matches hers, but Agony teases against her cheek.

"It was for the best; I did entertain the thought of killing you for fun. Plus..." He inclines his mouth against her ear. "The cuffs were kind of kinky."

Her fingers dip into Agony's darker shadows until he shivers back into an almost-human form. "Is it different?" she asks. "Being free?"

Agony expands out of shape and back again, like a balloon. "The cuffs are limiting." He lifts his hand in front of his face, and the light of his eyes passes through it. "Like something in me's always straining to get loose."

Harbinger understands that. The yearning to push limits, to rush right up to the edge and jump over. Shadows lick along the skin of her wrist. Hesitant, unsure if he should continue. But then, his eyes lift to Harbinger. "I can do a lot more like this."

Her heart trips in her chest. Flint's attention rises in her, but she doesn't look away from Agony. "Sounds dangerous."

In a surge of darkness, Agony's face hovers before her. "You like dangerous." His touch is magnetic, dusting over the promise that pulses in her neck. Tendrils curl under her chin, turning her to face Flint. "Does he?"

Flint could deny it. Say he hates the thought of risk so much that he'd keep Harbinger locked away rather than let her close to possibility, but it's not that simple. Not anymore. Not when the deadliest thing either of them have ever met touches her more softly than even Flint can. Agony stretches to extremes, suffocating darkness that becomes as gentle as wind across skin. Powerful enough to swallow them whole. Dreamy enough to slip past Flint's armor.

Arousal streaks through Harbinger, but not just from her. Flint tries to hold onto it, to contain it, but there's no disguising it when Agony's sultry smirk presses to Harbinger's jaw.

"Maybe he should watch." Agony breathes against the side of her neck, the buttons on her suit popping open one by one. "Make sure you don't get into trouble. Make sure you're safe." His mouth drifts down her bare shoulder. "Until you're so strung out, you'd promise him anything. Swear to be a good girl."

Thrill thrums through her veins. Holding Flint's red gaze is like touching a hot stove, but he makes no move to stop them. Harbinger bears her hand down until it sizzles. "That's not gonna happen."

"Ooh, someone's big and bad." Flint sets aside the files, knees resting open, dress shirt and pants pulled taut over his body. Broad chest, rounded stomach muscles, thick thighs that leave Harbinger's mouth watering. He lifts one hand to rest behind his head, pulling his shirt tighter. "Let's see how brave you are, then."

Desire throbs straight to her clit. It's the closest Flint has let her get to risk. Agony's mouth slots against hers, pulling her attention with the hot slide of his tongue.

It reminds her of dying. Sinking so completely into darkness, giving herself over to shadows that engulf her. This time, though, beneath it all is wanton need, slow and teasing before it disappears.

She tries to keep Agony close, to get her arms behind his neck, but he vanishes in smoke. Frustration sears into her before Agony appears solid again. "So fucking spoiled, aren't you?"

She chases his mouth with bared teeth. "You're one to talk."

"Let's see what Daddy wants to give you." Agony looks over his shoulder to Flint. "What do naughty girls get?"

"They don't get this."

She can't see through the darkness. When Agony lifts his eyes toward Flint, she can make out the sight of him fisting over his cock. Harbinger tries to move off the bed, but Agony holds her fast, laughing and plunging Flint back into darkness.

"It's been ten seconds, and you're already folding!" Harbinger strains toward the ground, but Agony yanks her back underneath him, hovering weightless off her chest. "You're not gonna try to hold out?"

Her head tilts backward off the bed, keeping Flint's eyes in her sights; they're all she can find in the dark. "*I* think bad girls should get that."

Flint shakes his head with a chuckle. "That's not how this works."

"It could be." She struggles against Agony's restraints, but when she shakes off a tendril, two more replace it. Blood rushes to her head. "It'll feel *so good*."

"Yeah?" There's a slick sound, like Flint circling his fist over his head. Her thighs clamp together. "Better than you behaving?" He lifts his head, as if he might give her what she's after. "Show me where you want it."

No hesitation: she lays out the flat of her tongue. Flint presses up from the chair, and her body strains toward him before he sinks back down. "I'm not falling for that."

Her whine crushes into a groan when Agony retakes his firm shape, grinding between her thighs. As soon as she tries to meet him, the weight is gone, leaving her aching for friction.

"She's been asking for more for months, hasn't she?" Agony tilts his head, observing her like a specimen when Flint answers.

"She has."

Agony's eyes slip shut at the depth of Flint's voice. Contained. Vaguely threatening. Harbinger tries to clench her thighs together again, but Agony keeps her knees pinned apart.

They interact like she isn't there, like she has no control over what happens here. So reminiscent of the rest of her life — but here, between the two of them, it's comfort. Desire. Darkness she wants to step into with both their connections alive inside her.

"We should give it to her." Agony teases her lips as she reaches for him, but he lowers his mouth to her throat, swirling his tongue in sinful patterns. "Everything she asks for." He trails down to her open collar. "So much she can't ask for anything else."

Flint hums a delicious sound. She knows there's a stern knit in his brows; one that says she owes him. That she's going to pay. "Is that what you want, Harbin?"

It's the same careful question Flint always asks, dipped in something molten and dangerous. She fights to get her thighs against Agony's hips, to work herself against him, but there's no moving when he has her pinned. He jerks her chin to face him. "Daddy asked you a question."

White-hot desire twists in her stomach. Through the darkness, she tries to find Flint, but he doesn't give anything away. No swell of his emotions, no flicker on his face, just level silence that stokes the flames of her want.

Can't you just trust me?

"Yes." Her heart thuds. "That's what I want."

Flint gives a pitying click of his tongue. "I don't think you know what you're asking for."

She can't see him. Can't tip her head back, can't make out his body through the darkness. Can't find anything but Agony's face. She writhes under his tendrils until she snaps. "Then *show me!*"

Shadows flip her to her hands and knees, tendrils pressed to her back and wrapped beneath her, teasing through the catsuit. "Have you ever been patient?" Agony presses the words behind her ear. "Since you're so certain, I'm gonna give you exactly what you've been begging for. I'm gonna push your body to the edge, and *Daddy's* gonna tell me exactly how to do it."

Harbinger's knees tremble against the sheets. A tendril flicks against her clit, and her eyes squeeze shut.

"Keep them open." Flint's voice is stern. She forces her eyes open again, finding burning red through the darkness. Then, Flint's voice softens. "I want to see you."

Pitiful sounds claw out of her. She's helpless, trapped in the dark with the two of them to guide her. But she trusts the shadows, the two pairs of glowing eyes showing her only enough to make her want.

Agony slips her out of her suit, mouth dragging along her spine. "Ask Daddy how wet I should make you."

"I want —"

Her head jerks back. Agony's fingers curl tighter in her hair. "I didn't ask what *you* want." Every word is punctuated by a circle against her clit, dragging slick through her desire. "*Ask. Your. Daddy.*"

She can't speak. Can't *think* past the shadows teasing against her, dipping inside before they dart away again. Still, she tries. She *tries*.

"Daddy..."

There's no disguising Flint's groan, his eyes slipping shut at the pitiful, needy scrape of her voice. Never before has she felt so much like prey, on display as Flint's eyes rake over them. Harbinger's hungry for him, but Agony keeps her in place, squeezing her cheeks to make her talk.

"Daddy..." she tries again. Agony can't fight his hiss at the sound. "How wet should he make me?"

Flint's eyes lock on Harbinger's. When he speaks, her mouth waters.

"As wet as you can get."

THIRTY-FIVE

Harbinger

Agony's voice curls against her ear, shadows slipping around her throat. "You heard the man." A thousand tendril kisses trail over her skin. "Do you want me to fuck with your head?"

She wants to sob at the thought of being taken apart, pushed to her limits, truly wrecked. Reaching the line Flint's been too afraid to cross, but now, he eases her over it.

"Yes."

Agony does as he's told. Breathing visions into her head, sensations she's not sure exist. Spilling through their connection until everything feels slicker: his tongue against her neck, the smear of tendrils on her clit, his cock stretching her around him.

Her body bucks, taking him deep enough in her cunt that they both groan. It's an accident. So easy for him to slip inside, no resistance with desire dripping down her thighs. Impossibly wet, as if Agony made her mind believe it until it was true.

He rocks into her, cursing at the filthy sound. "You're gonna soak the sheets." Then he presses her face down to the bed. All she can see are Flint's eyes across the room, little more than embers in the dark, but the heat they give off makes Harbinger sweat. There's the barest hint of jealousy, but it's overcome with so much more. All the walls Flint erected turning to fire, desperate to keep Harbinger blazing inside them.

But not just her. Flint's eyes scorch over Agony, leaving his mark on them both. Branding them. Claiming them with the flicker of Agony's shadows doing Flint's bidding over Harbinger's body.

Agony whispers into the depth of her mind, touching her in places only Flint's emotions have. "Now let me hit that spot." His mouth trails down her back as he rocks inside, wet and messy. "Let me do it for you." A tendril drags through her desire, slipping down her legs before circling against her ass.

Her eyes roll back. *"Shit —"*

"You want me to fill you up?" Agony teases.

"*Yes*, gods..."

He angles her face toward the chair. "Then ask."

Her pleading eyes find Flint. While her emotions ricochet inside her, Flint is calm, rising from his seat across the room. He approaches, reaching down to brush her lips with his thumb. "Color?"

She strains to get closer. Agony keeps her back.

"Green."

She waits for Flint to hesitate. To put an end to this, to tell her it's too far. Instead, Flint flicks his dark gaze toward Agony. "As much as she can take."

It barely registers before Agony eases shadows into her, filling both her holes. It's bizarre. Overwhelming. Inundating her past the point of thinking until all she can feel is the flutter of shadows stretching her.

They twist deeper until Harbinger can't lift her head. Can't work herself back any more. Her arms shake, trying to keep her upright as another shadow circles her clit.

"So fucking *good* when you've got my dicks inside you." Agony holds her down against the bed. "Is that what you need to behave?" Then a dark look takes his expression. "Or do you need three?"

Her voice pitches to a whine. "Agony, *please* —"

"Tap the bed twice if you want to stop. Show me."

Her fingers tremble as she does as she's told. Agony lets his shadows spread until another tendril dips between her lips. It fills her mouth, muffling her moan before she digs her teeth into him. Agony laughs, squeezing her jaw with fond aggression. "Little *brat*."

All his shadows expand, toying as he leans over her shoulder, illuminating Flint's heavy cock in his hand. Harbinger tries for it again, but Agony pins her wrists to the bed.

"You don't have a hole left for it." Humiliation burns hot along Harbinger's skin, and Agony follows it. "You said you couldn't be good, didn't you? This is the price you have to pay. You can't do anything but take it."

He presses against her — her back, her thighs, her stomach, enveloping her in shadows until there's nowhere he can't reach. The slightest motion drags her against him, teasing her nipples, the apex of her thighs, the seam of her ass —

But it's his voice that destroys her.

"That's it..." An undercurrent trembles through their connection, like Agony can feel what he does to her. Wrapped around her, delving inside, finding the filthiest desires of her body and sucking them to the surface like bruises.

"Shh," he soothes, dragging his mouth along her throat. "You're doing so well for me."

Every nerve is stimulated, vibrating through her until Flint guides her chin up with his hands. She floats between the nebulous pleasure of Agony and the grounding touch of Flint, whimpering when he lowers his mouth to hers. Agony doesn't remove his tendril, and Flint doesn't ask him to, tracing his tongue against the bottom swell of Harbinger's lip.

She groans at her mouth stretched over Agony, swollen where Flint sucks her lip between his, tracing his tongue over the place where Harbinger and Agony meet. It's as filthy as if Flint had laved against where Agony grinds inside her cunt.

Flint knows what he's doing. His eyes hang on Agony as he gives another slow swirl of his tongue. Agony shivers inside her, swelling deeper at the sensation, and then Flint pulls away.

Nearly distracting enough for Harbinger to escape, but Agony keeps a hold on her, muffling her scream.

"You like watching me fuck all her holes at once?" Agony's grin grows wicked against Flint's cock, close enough that Harbinger can almost taste it. "Sorry: *your* holes."

Then Agony drags his tongue over Flint, making all of them moan as Agony swallows him deeper.

"Yes," Flint grits as Harbinger whines around the tendrils. Frustration slams her hips back against Agony. He meets her, dragging against the spot deep inside when Agony pulls his mouth off of Flint's cock.

"Fuck, *just like that.*" Tendrils wind tighter in her hair. "Don't stop." The tendril on her clit shifts until it suctions against her. Harbinger shudders at every unpredictable shift in Agony's body. He keeps her close, planting his mouth against the sweat-slick line of her hair. "You've got it. Let go for me, baby."

She whimpers around the tendril in her throat, legs trembling as heat coils in her stomach.

"You can do it." Agony snaps his hips into her, suction honed on her clit. "You know how to do it. Let me feel it."

Frenzied pressure trembles through her. Flint holds her chin in his hand, but he won't come any closer. Won't let her look away. "Good girls come for Daddy." He drags his thumb along her cheek. "Come on, baby: you know what I want."

Her orgasm tears through her, a scream wrenching from her mouth when Agony removes his tendril. She's a mess of shudders in Flint's hand while Agony holds her tight, murmuring against the back of her ear. "So good. *So* fucking good, baby, there you go..."

His moan is breathless, biting teeth into her shoulder as they wind down together. Luminous strands from Agony's release stick to the inside of her thighs, lambent through the skin of her stomach. "You're glowing," he murmurs. A laugh shivers through all three of them.

She can't keep herself upright, easing down to the sheets as Agony withdraws. She's never been filled like that. Never been touched so much deeper than any person should be able to — any person besides the two of them.

Her eyelids sink, sleep finally tempted to find her. There's a low rustle of words she can make out through the haze.

"Wasn't so bad, was it?"

There's cheek in Agony's tone, but it's hesitant, an olive branch toward Flint. Harbinger clenches her body, holding her breath.

"It wasn't so bad." Flint's agreement holds a waver of uncertainty, but there's acceptance in it, the breath of relief he's been holding. He loosened the wall around Harbinger, and she survived, because Agony was with her, covering her when Flint couldn't. "Almost makes me want to trust you."

She's sure she heard Flint wrong. Certain he couldn't have said that, but the silence that follows says she hasn't mistaken a word. She wants to pry her eyes open. To see the look on Agony's face, the look on *Flint's*, but she can't bear the thought of obstructing this.

Agony's voice is so low, she almost loses it to the wind blowing against the cabin. "I want you to do more than trust me."

Her fingers tighten against the pillow. Her lungs burn from lack of air.

"What do you want me to do?"

It's not a simple question. Not with doubt tearing through Flint's voice, under the fear he hasn't set down for years. But Agony tries to take it. To shift the burden onto his shoulders, so it's easier for Flint to carry. When Agony's answer comes, it's raw and terrifying and beautiful.

"I want you to fucking *love me.*"

Their emotions collide inside her. Crashing, shadows slipping against stone, filling in the cracks until Harbinger can't find where they split. The whirlpool of Flint and Agony swirl inside her until all three of them are bound up together, impossible to untangle.

Her body is a vessel, a citadel, a temple for this. For the three of them. For what she wants to worship more than anything.

She pushes up from the bed. Flint and Agony are lost in each other, lips melding as Flint clutches Agony closer. There's a cinch in Flint's brows, but Agony's shadows wrap around him, engulfing them both until Flint releases the worry. Until he gives himself over to it. Until he chases Agony's mouth as hopelessly as he wants to.

Then they see Harbinger. They move like the same being, same body, same desperate pulse thudding through them. Flint's hand closes around Harbinger's throat as Agony pulls her in, drawing her up to meet them. Against her skin, shadows lace between Flint's fingers, sending her eyes fluttering shut.

They're both so gentle with her life in their hands. That's the only place she wants it. The place she knows it's safest. The place she trusts to hold her breath more than her own lungs.

Flint kisses them both like he wants this. Wants *them.* Agony doesn't flinch from the demand of his mouth, an assurance that he'll meet Flint's every expectation. And Harbinger surrenders to it, giving all she can, promises merging between their lips. It's sacred and slick and hungry, until she can't tell them apart. Until there's nothing but *them.*

THIRTY-SIX

Flint

They leave the Timber compound when the sun peeks over the horizon, SUV jostling toward the distant crop of mountains. The vehicle creaks and sighs over the rocky terrain, but the inside of the car is comfortable in a way that it hasn't been before.

Harbinger's helmet rests on the floorboard, scenery passing out the window as she watches with a dreamy smile. Flint's thoughts drift back to the way Agony looked at him last night. What Agony asked for. How Flint reached for him without hesitation, and how Harbinger fit perfectly between them...

The SUV dips into a pothole. Flint tightens his grip around the steering wheel. In the rearview, Agony's coy smile does more to Flint's stomach than the road's hills and valleys.

After a few hours, they begin their ascent through the mountains. The dirt roads become less pronounced the higher they climb through the trees.

"No wonder they don't have visitors," Agony mutters. He rolls down his window, resting his chin on his forearm and searching the ground beneath them. "Did you do something to the tires?"

Flint tenses. "What do you mean?"

"They look a little flappy. Something's grinding out here." Agony points toward the front driver's side tire. "Think it's that one." Then he peers at the back wheel. "Oh, that one too."

Flint eases the car toward the side of the road and climbs out to inspect the tires. Harbinger leans out the driver's side window, next to Agony in the back.

"Flat. Both of them." Flint kicks a limp tire with his foot. "Should have known better than to take a chance off-road. We should have waited for the Timbers to bring us."

"What now?"

Flint turns a discerning eye to the sky. Despite the complication, the sun is shining, a cool breeze rustling against his back. "We should be close enough to fly, but without taking the roads, I'm not sure exactly where we're headed."

"You carry Harbinger, then." Agony slips out the window, disappearing between pools of shadows before he reappears. "I'll start that way." He points toward the jagged rock faces in the distance, a lush forest expanding beneath it. "You two fly in the other direction, and Harbinger and I will see if we spot anything familiar."

"Patch of charred earth." Harbinger stuffs her helmet under her arm and pushes open the door. "How hard can it be?"

Flint lifts Harbinger in his arms, gaze lingering on Agony. "Use the connection if you need to get in touch."

Agony melts back into the shadows, but not before appearing between them, tickling with his tendrils before he darts away.

"Insufferable," Flint grumbles fondly. Harbinger crosses her ankles where they drape over his elbow.

"You're like one of those dads who says they don't want a pet before they end up doting on it."

Her laughter turns to a squeal as Flint takes flight, soaring up toward the mountains.

Finding anything recognizable is more difficult than they thought. Tree lines roll over hills between the base of the mountains, and after a while, Flint's wings ache from the effort. Harbinger inclines her head to see the ground below them.

"Look: Broadleaf compound." Between the trees, there's a clearing where smoke curls from a chimney. "We can break and talk to them."

The pack house is a lot smaller than the Timbers', a three-story cabin surrounded by muddy tire tracks on an open field. Harbinger dons her helmet once they land, flipping her visor up as Flint knocks and steps back off the porch. When the door opens, a birdlike woman wipes claws on an apron, adjusting blue feathers back on her head.

"Pardon our intrusion." Flint gestures beside him. "I'm Flint, and this is Harbinger. We're coming from Timber territory. Our car broke down a few miles away, but Lev told us Diction might be able to help us with an investigation."

"An investigation?" The woman folds her arms across her chest. "About what?"

"No one's in any danger," Flint assures her. "But we think an outsider may have used a part of your territory to hide something."

The woman scoffs. "Trust me, we would know if somebody was in our territory. They wouldn't be hiding anything for long."

Flint doesn't belabor the point. "That may very well be our mistake. Would it be ok if we came inside? I don't mean to intrude, but we'd love to ask Diction some questions to see if he can point us in the right direction. Maybe toward the Conifers? Their territory butts up against yours, doesn't it?"

The woman gives them a long look before she steps back from the door, leaving it open for them to follow. She calls over her shoulder as she makes her way into the kitchen on one side of the open floor plan. "Diction's out right now, but he should be back in two shakes." From the fridge, she pulls out a large pitcher of lemonade, pouring two glasses as Flint and Harbinger wait beside the counter.

"Sorry I'm not the most welcoming." She averts her gaze with a nervous smile. "We don't get a lot of strangers up here, but if Lev sent you, then we'll do our best to help." One of her yellow wings sweeps toward the long dining table, fitted to seat fifteen people. "Have a seat. I'll see if I can answer any of your questions."

Harbinger and Flint sink down on the bench facing the kitchen. The woman deposits the glasses on the table and places a hand on her hip. "Now, what's this about someone hiding something?"

"Was your pack familiar with the Vestals?" Harbinger asks. "Lev mentioned you weren't involved with the recent revolt."

The woman's eyes narrow, but she forces a tight smile. "We had some other things to deal with. Interpack conflict."

"But you knew about them?"

The woman laughs as she moves back to the kitchen. "At the end? Every pack in the Break knew about them. They didn't exactly go about things quietly."

"So you know their leader was a phoenix."

The woman nods, washing her talons and drying them on a dish towel before she reaches for a jar of beetle snacks.

"Are there any other phoenixes in the area?" Harbinger asks. "Or any place known for storing phoenix fire?"

"Not that I know of." The woman flours the counter, plopping dough before she rolls it out. "They aren't common creatures. And phoenix fire isn't easy to get a hold of." She takes a bite of a beetle and glances toward Harbinger. "Aren't you thirsty, sweetheart?"

With a clap, the back screen door swings open on a massive white werebear who drops keys in the bowl on the end table.

"Oh, Char!" The woman sets the rolling pin aside. "I was about to come looking for you."

Char scuffs his feet on the mat. "Yeah? For what?"

"We have visitors." She gestures to Flint and Harbinger. "These two are doing an investigation. They want to meet with

Diction."

Char looks up from the mat. "Oh, yeah?" As he moves into the kitchen, he pulls a brown bottle of alcohol from beneath the counter. "What are you investigating?"

"Phoenix fire. Do you know of anywhere nearby that might show signs of it being used?"

With a slow sip, Char leans back against the counter. "No. But, maybe... Can you —?"

"Already on it."

The woman bustles out of the kitchen as Char takes a final swig. "Hold on. We might have something for you."

He follows the woman into the foyer. Harbinger pulls off her glove and presses bare fingers to the table.

"What is it?" Flint asks. She shakes her head, trying to follow the threads in her mind.

"They switched seats?"

Before Flint can ask what she means, there's movement out the window. A toady woman and an elk centaur scurry around the side of the building. They seem...familiar. Flint pushes up from the table to get a closer look before his eyes catch on a crack in the chimney beside him. Memory guides his hand toward the misshapen brick, claw digging behind one corner until it clatters to the ground.

Trinkets spill into his hand: charm bracelet. Lipstick tube. Concert wristband. Beaded friendship bracelets and brooches and lanyards with bright pops of color.

Trophies of the girls they're looking for.

"Har-"

Flint's neck pricks — three times. He swats it, scattering metal darts tipped with blue and yellow feathers. Harbinger slumps against the table, hand falling from her neck as her voice slurs.

"Ru..."

Flint stumbles back toward her. His legs give out, sending him crashing to the ground, table screeching across the floor. He tries to pull Harbinger from the bench, but his arms lose strength, sprawling her across the ground.

She's out of reach. The room spins, colors morphing and blurring until her catsuit looks like fading gray skin. Flint strains toward her, but his claws only scrape her boot. A looming figure appears above them, toeing Harbinger's helmet, dart gun swinging by her leg. The woman's face swims in Flint's vision. Darkness swallows him whole, drowning him in panic and the last of her voice.

"We've been waiting for you."

THIRTY-SEVEN

Harbinger

It's not quite a dream.

Somewhere between waking and sleeping. Living and death. But it's not like the others. All the colors are too bright, swirling with sickening speed, a carnival ride Harbinger can't get off of.

Something dark prods at the edges, swooping in and out of her mind. She can't keep her thoughts straight long enough to discern what it is.

Harbin.

Harbin!

Let me in!

Her name sounds frantic from a great distance, echoing like two fists pounding on a door. She reaches for the voice, but her arms won't lift. They're too weak, dead weight dangling from her shoulders.

Then the voice slips from her grasp completely.

She tries to wake up. Over and over, sitting up in bed, checking the time on her phone. But it's another dream, an endless loop keeping her trapped, broken by a hard surface beneath her cheek.

Where did they stop last? Another motel? No, the Timber compound. They should be in the cabin. Where's the bed? There are no warm bodies beside her. The room sways — or is that all in her head?

Are her eyes open? She blinks slowly, barely able to pull her eyelids apart. It's pitch black. Her head pounds, fingers curling into dirt. There are weights around her wrists, clinking when she tries and fails to get her arms to respond.

Everything is cold. She remembers the night the Convent torches ran out of oil, corridors chilly and damp and impossible to see through.

Bugs skitter through her mind. Worms and ants and centipedes making her skin twitch until she lifts her bare cheek from the ground. Her helmet's gone. She's pinned on her stomach, limbs chained to the ground. Her head's too heavy. It drops back to the earth and floods with memories again.

There's a hulking shape in the far corner of the room. She can make out its outline seated upright against the wall. "Fl..." Her throat's too dry to produce any sound. She swallows to wet her tongue. "Flint."

The shape doesn't move. She tries to crawl closer, but all it does is clink her chains together. Dirt dilutes her senses.

How did they get here?

The Broadleaf house. They'd been inside. Harbinger strains to get free, but she can barely lift her head. In the corner, the shape rustles. A twitch of wings, a low groan, and finally, glowing red eyes.

"Oh, thank the gods. Flint?"

His eyes blink, body shifting in the dirt until he finds his chains as well. They sound heavy. Much heavier than hers.

Fuck.

"Harbin?" His voice is thick. Chains rattle as he tries to pull free.

Nothing.

"Fuck," he groans. "Are you ok?"

"I'm fine." She writhes to get a look at the cuffs around her ankles. "You?"

"Enough."

"Can you see me?"

"Yeah." His throat sounds stuffed with cotton — or her ears do. "Chains staked into the ground around your wrists and ankles. Don't see your helmet anywhere."

"Figures. The rest of the room?"

His eyes swivel, wincing when they twist too far. "A dirt cellar. Tree roots in the far corner. Concrete stairs a few yards in front of you, to your right. Couple of support beams throughout. Shelf near the stairs. Walls look like rock."

Harbinger's gloved hand slaps the ground. *"Fuck!"*

"We need to —"

The footsteps above quiet them. Her heart pounds as locks and chains shift at the top of the stairs, scraping against the metal double-door before it swings open. Harbinger squints against the light. It doesn't reach far, but she can make out Flint's face in the corner, caked with something dry and brown...

Blood.

Her fingers clench into the dirt.

"They're awake," Char calls back up the stairs. He flips a switch on the wall, casting dim light through the room from one naked bulb. "How was your rest?"

"Fuck off."

Char clicks his tongue. "Touchy."

The woman descends the stairs behind him. "No service on the phone, but we'll take it and the vehicle to Conifer territory to set the scene."

Harbinger's stomach sinks. Poe and Omen won't expect to hear from her for a while. The Timbers are busy with their own issues. It'll be weeks before the OID catches up to them, if ever.

There's no one looking for them.

Except —

She makes a panicked grapple toward Agony's connection, but her head swims when she gets close. Whatever toxin the woman injected them with fucks with Harbinger's head, overwhelmed by the flood of information from the dirt.

"Sorry about the darts." The woman doesn't look sorry at all, feathers ruffling. *So that's where they came from.* "But you weren't drinking anything, and we made that lemonade *special* for you."

"How could you have known we'd show up here." Dirt scatters from Harbinger's breath. "*We* didn't even know."

"Let me rephrase; that batch is for *any* visitors." The woman's cold eyes linger as Char moves toward Harbinger. "But we knew you'd end up here."

"How does that —"

Another dart pricks into her. Flint fights his chains as the room tilts around her, and Char's face contorts into a smile.

"That's enough questions for now."

Then he flicks off the light, plunging them back into darkness.

Harbinger goes to the clawed forest again, but it's wrong, dimensions skewed and colors painted where they shouldn't be. She can't keep her eyes on anything.

Harbin! Tell me where you are…

Her mouth opens, but only foam comes out, drifting to the tops of the trees. She tries to scream, but all she hears are bubbles popping in the distance.

Waking is as bad as the first time. Groggy, head lolling, thoughts scattered to the wind. Red eyes watch her from across the room.

"I can't reach Agony." Her forehead presses to the ground. "My head is all —

"Harbinger."

Flint's voice sinks like lead into her stomach. She knows what that voice means. He's bracing her for the worst. Her breath puffs dirt against her face. "What?"

He doesn't respond.

"What is it?"

"There are horns behind you. From someone's head."

Bile rises in her throat. "Where?"

"Behind your right foot."

"Is that it?"

Silence is the only answer.

"Flint."

"They look like a faun's. Bloody. There are other things scattered in the dirt. I can't tell what they are."

Harbinger's face scrapes the ground, trying to focus on cold air filling her lungs. "Can I reach them?"

"What?"

"The horns: can I reach them?"

Flint inhales warily. "Harbinger…"

"Can I reach them?"

"Maybe. If you really stretch."

She extends her right calf as far as she can before she brings her foot down. It strikes something hard. She fights the nausea, stretching further, curving her foot along the ground. With a grunt, she sweeps the dirt up toward her glove. "Did I get them?"

Flint hesitates. "You kicked one further away."

Harbinger curses. Pressing the toes of her boot against the ground, scooting the hard formation toward her. She stretches her hand back toward her leg.

"You're gonna make yourself sick," Flint murmurs. She doesn't stop. The hard shape shuffles closer. She kicks until her hand touches down on something smooth.

Thank the gods she can't see. Still, she shuts her eyes, sucking in a breath before she presses the horn to her cheek and gags.

"Harbin…" Flint's tone is a warning.

"It's just — jarring. The last thing that happened. The first thing I see."

She swallows the vomit creeping up her throat, returning the horn to her cheek and sinking into the vision.

There are far fewer threads than she's used to. So much less time than she normally sees. It clenches in her stomach, but Harbinger rushes past the end and reaches back for the beginning.

The horn chipping during a softball game, its tiny owner sobbing, mollified by the game-winning ball in her hand. A cold rush of wind against the horn, two giggling girls running down a snow-laden street, a beanie tugged tighter against the chill. Lips pressing softly against the horn, a mother's whisper above a smile tucked into bed. Hundreds of memories, bright and beautiful, spanning the girl's life —

Until its sickening end.

The horn jamming into the trunk of a car. Scraping tallies into the wall of a dark room with no windows. Dragging across this cellar floor, a voice screaming to escape. Horrifying crunches as blood splatters and the horn snaps from the girl's head.

"It's one of ours," Harbinger gasps. "One of the girls."

"Who? Isolde?"

An ache runs rampant in Harbinger's chest, flooded with the girl's final remnants. Anger. Panic. Pain. *Fear.* So much fear pounding through her body, covering a tiny shard of hope.

"Harbin." Flint's voice reaches her through the sob threatening to break through her lips. "Harbin, tell me —"

"Give me something else." She opens a palm on the ground, clutching the horn in the other. "Give me something else I can read."

Flint rummages around him as far as the chains allow. "I'm going to throw it near your left hand." The object clatters through the dirt. "If you stretch your fingers a little further, you should reach it."

Harbinger strains until she gets her gloves around it. "What is it?"

"A necklace. It was caught in my chains — prepare yourself," Flint reminds her. She takes a steadying breath and touches the necklace to her skin.

Memories engulf her. She dives through them, trying to make sense of the visions, but there's no mistaking what happened. Her voice croaks out, fingers tightening around the pendant.

"Diction is dead."

THIRTY-EIGHT

Harbinger

The necklace leaves an indentation in Harbinger's cheek. "This was Diction's. The pack chained him up down here, because..." She plunges back into the memories, translating to Flint as scenes stampede past.

"Are you out of your mind?" Diction drapes the necklace over his head, turning away from his dresser. "You caught a man burying bodies in our territory, and you just — let him go?"

"He made an offer." Something acidic eats away at Char's expression. "If we let him use our land, he'll bring the girls alive, so we can bond them —"

"I don't care what his offer was! That's grotesque." Diction shakes his head, avoiding Char's gaze. Avoiding the root of the problem. "Don't mention this again. If anyone finds out...if he comes back, we have to turn him into the Conclave. Understood?"

There's so little power in it. Already, the cracks begin to show. Char doesn't respond, pushing off the doorframe and slamming the door behind him.

Harbinger surfaces from the vision. "That's what Lev meant about the pack conflict. Diction didn't tell anyone, because he was ashamed. They had problems before, but he never thought they'd actually…"

Her mind darts out to catch another memory.

The necklace bounces off Diction's chest as he bounds down the back staircase. A hush falls over the Broadleafs gathered near the distant tree line, resentful eyes and hardened jaws as he approaches.

"What's this about?"

There's no answer.

Diction raises his voice. "What's —"

"You know what it's about," Char spits. "We want to take the offer."

It's unbelievable. From the house, the final pack members follow: Diction's beta. His mate. The rest of his inner circle. The few people left with any sense of morality.

"We discussed this, Char." His feet grind into the dirt. "We're not getting involved with a murderer."

"Our pack is small. Weak." Among the majority of the pack, Char looks eerily in control. "You've gotten by being a shitty leader, but the Vestals are getting stronger. It's only a matter of time before they come for us. Either we're strong enough to fight them off, or we join them. It's time you start thinking about the pack you claim to hold in such high regard."

"Char." Hair lifts on the back of Diction's neck. Behind Char, the pack members begin to circle. "We will not take part in it. That's final."

Claws flick out on Char's hand, echoed by every Broadleaf beside him.

"We'll see about that."

"So they killed their own Alpha?" Flint tries to fit the pieces together. "They cannibalized themselves?"

Harbinger dredges herself out of the bloody clash. "They got rid of anyone who disagreed: Diction, the beta... They trapped them all down here and gave them a chance to flip. When most of them wouldn't..." She rests her head against the ground. "That's why they're so chaotic; there's no one in charge."

It's why she'd thought they switched seats upstairs. The table showed her Diction at the head, until suddenly, Char was there instead.

What the fuck have they stumbled into? Harbinger grapples for Agony again, but the connection is submerged, only bubbles screaming to the surface.

"It wasn't Vesta's pack using the girls to get stronger," she pants. "It was the Broadleafs. We have to get out of here."

"Harbin..."

Sensations pound through her. Every part of her is trapped: her body, her mind, her senses, forced to reckon with new horrors and haunting memories.

"Harbin..."

She jerks against the chains. Panting, straining until her body gives out under the reality of where they are. What this means.

What happens next.

"I'm sorry..." A tear slips down her cheek, splattering against the dirt. "I made us do this. I should have —"

"Harbinger." Flint's voice is the only steady thing she can cling to. "You are not going to die here. We will get out. Agony will come."

She wants to believe it so badly, to trust that they'll make it as they always have. All that reckless energy burns straight out of her at seeing Flint trapped like this. She wishes she could reach him, slip her hand in his, squeeze him tighter than she ever has. Desperate for the weight of his body against her, his solid pulse under her fingers. "How can you know that?"

There's a long moment before Flint answers. "Because I trust him. And I trust you."

It must be night by now. Every passing moment makes her shiver, cold seeping into her bones as the chains jitter. Above them, the lock clinks against the doors. Harbinger digs her fingers into the dirt and tries to stop her body from shaking.

A shadow appears. Harbinger's heart leaps — but it's just Char with a lantern, clicking on the cellar light again.

"Rise and shine! Hate to cut this short, but..." He tugs a tarp from the corner shelf. Harbinger's stomach turns. "We've got other shit to do."

"Killing more girls?" Flint's tone has no levity. It doesn't stop Char's smile as he deposits the tarp next to Flint.

"If it makes you feel better, *we* weren't the ones taking them."

"That was Reid's contribution, huh?" Harbinger fights down the fear souring her stomach. "I don't get it. You have such a hard on for power, and this is the best you could come up with?"

"It worked, didn't it?" Char yanks another tarp from the shelf, nudging it toward her with his foot. "This way, we all win."

"Except the fucking *girls*." Harbinger's chains clink as she struggles. "Except Diction and every other member of your pack that didn't get on board with *murdering* people. *Children*."

Char stops rolling out the tarp beside Harbinger. "You know about that?" He considers it, setting a vial of phoenix fire on the shelf. "So they were right about your little power."

His grin crawls under Harbinger's skin. "Who's 'they'?"

"The Broadleafs he sent to keep an eye on us." Flint's voice is dark. Char unrolls the tarp past Harbinger's body. Her mind whirs, but Flint looks certain. "You set Reid's house on fire."

"We should've done it sooner." Char lifts Harbinger's torso as he tugs the tarp beneath her, avoiding any attempts to land her teeth in him. "The OID had already cleared the house when we got there. We knew they'd fuck up the investigation, but they kept eyes on Reid's place for a couple months. They didn't find anything with their tools, but then they called *you* in as reinforcements."

The tarp beneath Harbinger extends in all directions. Char catches her looking. "For the spatter," he explains.

Flint fights against his chains. They don't budge, kicking up dirt around him.

"Those held an Alpha," Char calls over his shoulder. "Don't think you're getting out of them."

The tarp crunches under Harbinger, a new layer of cold that makes her teeth chatter. *Where is Agony?* Her bare face touches down against the tarp, a memory spreading out before her.

"I'm just a little confused." Reid stands by the stairs in the cellar as Char packs tarps onto the shelf. Dust stirs at the movement. Reid cleans his glasses on his shirt. "You said if I brought the girls, I'd be your new Alpha."

"And you will." Char doesn't bother to look at him. "But we have to get the pack in fighting shape for you. Just keep doing what you're doing. Bring the girls, we'll bond them, and once the ties are solid, you can kill them. You get to satisfy your urges, and we get a stronger pack. Everybody wins."

A girl screams inside the house.

"Trust me." Char's fangs flash in a smile. "Building the pack is boring. Ruling is so much better."

"Hey!" Char nudges Harbinger's chin, prying her skin from the tarp. "Stop spying on shit. Is that what you're doing?"

"Is that what you promised Vesta too?" Another memory slips from Harbinger's grasp, but she catches its tail. "If she gave you phoenix fire to hide the evidence, you'd support her rebellion. You'd join her pack."

Char's jaw twitches as he glares down at her. "...gods, you're a nosy bitch." He turns to surround Flint with more tarps, always keeping himself out of reach

"But you were never going to let either of them take over the Broadleafs." Harbinger squirms in her chains. If she makes her hand small enough... "You wanted the title for yourself, but you're not the Alpha."

Char turns dark eyes over his shoulder. *"Yet."* He flattens out the last of the tarp, pushing back to his feet. "Vesta didn't care what we were doing, as long as we were strong enough to serve her. Reid was perverse. There wasn't a reason; he just liked killing girls. We're the ones who gave those girls a purpose."

"That's not their fucking *purpose*." Harbinger's chains scratch the tarp as she fights. "They aren't there for you to *use*."

"But we did." Char towers over her. It's dizzying how small she feels. The distance between them stretches, so nauseatingly familiar she wants to retch. "They helped the greater good. Otherwise disposable. Forgettable. Easy to use. Easy to kill. I hardly remember any of their faces."

"Girls are the reason we found you."

The corner of Char's mouth quirks. "And look where that got you. All this for nothing."

"*You* were nothing. You needed *them*."

His eyes narrow. "They were weak. Barely put up a fight."

"Those claw marks in the trees say differently."

He blanches. It's a small hit of satisfaction, pulse thrumming in Harbinger's ears. Char exhales, turning away from her. "You know, this whole thing would've taken a lot less effort if you would've died in the fire. But what can you do?"

Then he moves toward Flint.

Harbinger scrabbles against the ground. Her boots scrape the tarp as Char draws closer, lifting his hand, claws flicking out of his paws.

She screams. Char's hand slams into the stone of Flint's shoulder.

"Fuck!"

Char cradles his paw, bent at a wrong angle. He slams into

Flint's armor again, feral sounds filling the cellar as stone chips away near Flint's throat. It barely leaves a dent. Char pants for breath, wild and incensed before he whirls back to Harbinger.

"No!"

Flint shifts out of his armor. Char's arm cocks as Harbinger buries her face into the ground, braced for the paw snapping into her leg. Bone crunches. Blood pumps through her ears, drowning out Flint's roar as pain throbs through her.

Every new hit Char lands against her skin floods her with his emotions. Carnal rage. Vicious hatred. Horrifying apathy. Darkness surges in the edge of her vision, a copper taste pooling in her mouth. Chains clank across the room, but not enough to break free.

Another blow lands in her back. Blood splatters her face, scream cut short as she gurgles for air. Trying to remember any moment before this. Anything but mind-numbing pain.

Everything is slick. Each hit sends her body slipping through blood gathering beneath her. She can't feel her fingers. Can't tell if she's numb from cold or pain — or if her hands aren't there anymore.

She wants to sleep. To close her eyes and sink into darkness, into the dream with Agony, where she doesn't have to feel this. Doesn't have to feel anything.

The tarp is dark with her blood. That can't be the last thing she sees. It has to be Flint, beautiful and happy, arms curled around her. It has to be Agony, his grinning whisper in the dark, a candle in a darkened window.

Rhythmic thudding starts. Maybe it's her pulse, but it's too fast and wet and sickening. Through the blood-slick hair over her eyes, she sees Char's claws slam into Flint's flesh.

She reaches for him. She can't lift her head. Can't blink. Can only stare at the ground beneath the shelf, toward the glow that emanates from the darkness.

Agony?

But it's too small. Not shaped like his face. Her vision blurs and doubles, but she thinks it's...a ring.

It glows around people she can trust.

New wetness slips down Harbinger's cheeks, mingling with her blood. Flint's connection begins to dry up inside her. Harbinger remembers what this is. Remembers her last breath on the stone slab, liquid sloshing against her the way it does now. Her eyes slip closed, pain shutting down the lights in her mind until all that's left is the single ring.

That...that can be the last thing she sees.

THIRTY-NINE

Agony

Something is *wrong*.

Agony knew hours ago when his steady connection with Harbinger suddenly spiked before it vanished. He stopped behind a tree in the forest, tugging on the link as he would Harbinger's sleeve.

There's nothing.

Through the shadows, he found their broken-down car again. No sign of Flint or Harbinger. Agony scoured the skies from below, looking for anything flitting past the clouds.

Nothing but birds.

He tried to trace the route they'd taken, but flying moved them so much further, leaving no crushed branches or footprints for him to follow. The trail went cold — but the connection with Harbinger stirred again. Agony strained to reach her, but her mind was slurry, dragging her away from him until she slipped out of his grasp.

Then it was silent again. Murky, as if she was dreaming. Agony raced through the forest as night fell, multiplying the places he could slip through.

It never brought him any closer to finding them.

He won't stop looking. *Can't* stop looking, even when fear surges inside him, the lingering trail of their connection fading fast. He's not used to this. Being free, slipping through shadows, covering so much ground in such little time. Tendrils of his being waver, flickering like candles about to be put out as exhaustion sinks into his limbs.

Harbinger's mind sends up a flare. She's desperate, clawing for Agony, clawing for *anyone* — then the connection clangs with impact that knocks him off balance. Pain screams through him as he fights to stay on his feet. It slices through his connection with Harbinger, over and over, until it hangs by a thread.

There's a cabin in the distance.

She's there. He knows she's there. His teeth grit, pushing past the fatigue radiating through him. He dives into the shadows, whizzing past movement in the house and down into a darkened cellar. He pulls his aching body from the darkness to the sight of Harbinger's bloody body splayed on a tarp.

Agony grapples for her hand, slipping through the blood beneath her. "Harbin!"

Her eyes tilt in her head, voice slurring, hand limp in his. Life drains from her body. He can feel her leaving, room spinning as Agony presses to his feet.

A bear creature hunches over another broken body. *Flint's* body, his head slumping, face covered in blood. The creature above him blinks, face streaked with surprise under the splatter. "What the fuck?"

It takes nothing for Agony to slam him back against the wall. Nothing to leave an indentation in the rock as the creature claws to escape. Nothing for Agony to crush the air from the beast's lungs as he lowers his mouth.

"Now I know how agonizingly to kill you."

Agony knows his namesake. He understands *rage*. How it

overpowers the weariness within him. How it gives him a glimpse at what created him.

The hate that lay dormant in Agony has finally found an outlet, splitting his body into shadows that rip the creature in every direction. Fury pours from him, so loud he barely hears the footsteps thudding down the stairs before he catches a feathered woman. Her legs spasm as Agony crushes her skull into concrete, reflected in the bleeding gashes of her eyes.

He billows up the stairs, bursting into night air and surging into the cabin. Dark strands snap around every creature that springs to attack. They're nothing. They do *nothing*. Agony barrels through them all, flinging bodies through windows, breaking every limb, filling their noses and throats with darkness.

The vengeance in him is louder than their screams. There's no sense of time, nothing but shadows destroying all they come across. Seconds tick by to the sound of bodies slumping to the floor.

Seven.

Eight.

Nine.

Silence. He listens for more, but there's only the slow trickle of blood from the chandelier — until something creaks in the attic. Agony flashes toward the sound with the last bit of his strength, flinging open a closet where a girl screams.

She doesn't ask for mercy. Agony won't give it, reaching to yank her from the depths when matted ginger hair falls over her eyes. Her hands tremble to cover her face, thick lines of dirt curving around one finger, leaving a pale band of skin.

...one of the girls had a ring. Which one had a ring?

"Evie?"

Her frantic gaze darts toward him. "Y — you know —?"

"You're alive?"

Her eyes are glazed, bruise forming around one. "Are you..."

Agony sinks to his knees.

Her fingers press to her lips. "Are — are they all —"

He nods. Evie covers her face, breath hiccupping like she can't get enough of it. He brushes a tendril against the top of her head. Her body jerks away before she sinks into it, cradled against his chest.

"It's ok now. It's ok. I've got you." He holds her cheeks to face him. "I'm going to get you out of here, but I need your help. You can heal, right? You're good at healing magic?"

A shudder wracks through her before Agony pulls her gently from the closet, blocking the carnage on the staircase with the power he has left in his shadows.

"I'm going to take you downstairs. There's a lot of blood, ok? Close your eyes."

Agony slithers under the door, breaking the chains on the other side before he dodges corpses and guides her down to the cellar. Blood is ripe in the air. Agony shatters the lightbulb where it hangs, guiding Evie to Flint in the dark.

"They won't hurt you. I need you to heal them." His eyes light the rivulets pouring down Flint's face. "I haven't seen him move."

Evie kneels shakily, reaching a tentative hand toward the side of Flint's neck. She's silent for a long moment — so long a wail rises in Agony.

"He's there." Her voice is hoarse. "It's faint..."

"Please help him," Agony whispers. "Please. Anything you can do."

She presses the palms of her hands across a gash in Flint's throat. Agony darts across the room to lift Harbinger's limp body into his lap.

Shadows trace her hairline, drifting over blood streaked across her face. How much is hers? How much is Flint's? Agony closes his eyes, resting his head against hers. "Come back."

Her mind is tattered and torn, shredded like a canvas. Agony reaches for her through the holes, through the dreamscape, into the woods they've been searching for months. Past claw marks in the trees, charred ash drifting through the wind, pinpricks of stars overhead.

No banshee.

"Harbinger!" His voice blends with the sound of the forest, whispering winds and croaking bullfrogs. Static grows louder through it all, white noise that drowns out every other sound.

The end. The last note before silence.

Agony darts through the darkness, combing for any trace of Harbinger, forest blurring past him — until he spots her.

Little more than a ghost, body slumped beneath the trees, a haze that threatens to flicker and vanish. Agony sinks to his knees, but his shadows pass through her, like she's going somewhere even he can't reach.

"Harbin..." He covers her body with his, trying to wrap her in him, to keep her here. "Please don't go. Please."

A sound racks through him. He doesn't know what it is, a low moan in his chest that pricks behind his eyes. "*Please*. Please come back. Please stay." A glowing tear slips down onto her face. "I can't carry this hole, *please,* I can't carry it..."

Weight settles into his arms. Agony pulls back as color returns to her skin, gravity settling back into her body. He surfaces from the dream, back to the cellar. Evie sits in the dark before him, hands gripping Harbinger as the blood seeps back into her. Soaking up from the tarp and slipping back into her veins as skin and bones knit back together.

Liquid splashes onto Harbinger's skin, sparking before it vanishes. Evie wipes a drop from the corner of Agony's eyes. It fades gold on her finger. "I think you're crying."

"Is she ok?"

Evie's lip trembles. "I don't know." Blood coats her hands in the dim light of his eyes. "I tried. I'll keep trying..."

Agony leaves Harbinger in her hands, shifting back to Flint. His labored breathing breaks Agony into a wet laugh, burying his face against Flint's shoulder until he stirs. Blood cakes his tusks.

One's broken off at the base. Agony dazedly cradles Flint's jaw in one hand. "You're missing a tooth."

Flint blinks back to consciousness. "Where's – Harbinger?" He tries to pull himself to his feet, but the wounds take their toll, body still struggling to heal.

"We're taking care of her." Agony's hand eases against Flint's chest. "I need to get you out of these chains."

Exhaustion sits heavy in Flint's bones. Agony's tendrils spread, weaving between the links in the chain before he squeezes and shatters them. Metal falls away, and Flint struggles to his feet until he can move in Harbinger's direction. Agony hovers beside him as Flint falls to his knees. "Is she…?"

"I don't know." Tears slip down Evie's cheeks. "I tried."

Agony curls between Evie's fingers, wrapping his other hand around Harbinger's. Flint presses her palm to his lips, squeezing his eyes closed.

Please don't leave.

There's a raspy breath. Agony's eyes shoot open, the shallow rise of Harbinger's chest illuminated in their eyes. Agony buries his face against her hip, and Flint mutters a prayer into her hand.

A light hovers on the shelf, swirling and flickering through rainbow shades. Then Agony sees the arm extended to it, the bear creature stretching toward the vial of phoenix fire with his final breaths. He tips the glass from the shelf, smashing it to the earth and engulfing the stairs in a roar of color. Evie's panicked eyes light with the flames. Flint shields her from the heat as Agony breaks through Harbinger's chains.

"Come on!" He expands his shadows, straining against collapse. Tendrils flicker and threaten to fade. "I can do it." He bares his teeth, screaming until the shadows spread, fire clamoring around them. "I have to fucking do it!"

Evie stumbles into him as Flint lifts Harbinger in his arms. Agony envelopes them all, flames eating away at the shocked bear's face as they disappear into the darkness.

They emerge into open air, away from the carnage and smoke and horror, collapsing onto the ground. Agony is barely more than shade, shadows shriveling on a patch of grass as he struggles to catch his breath. Harbinger slumps in Flint's arms. Evie clutches at a tree trunk, staring into the distance.

Dying leaves blow in the breeze, forest waking in the first hints of sunlight. Agony isn't sure where he dropped them. It's calm, dew still wet on the grass.

Flint leans against the sturdy tree beside Agony. "Did you think we left you?"

It takes a moment for Agony to find his voice. "After the dick I gave you two last night? Nah."

His laugh sounds more like a sob. Flint lays out his palm beside him, and Agony slots his fingers inside. They stay like that for a long moment, until Harbinger stirs against Flint's chest, blinking through the streaks of blood and the darker hollows under her eyes.

But she's *alive*.

Flint gathers her up, tightening his arms around her as Agony does the same.

She mumbles against Flint's jaw, groggy and confused. "I need my helmet. They took it…"

Flint eases her back down. "It's gone."

"But we brought you something better," Agony adds.

Harbinger's brows knit until she sees Evie staring at them through the gap in their arms. Flint sets Harbinger back on the grass. Breath works weakly in her lungs.

"You're alive." Her gaze skirts over Evie. "Are you ok?"

Evie hesitates before she answers. "I don't think it's hit me yet."

"I saw your ring. In the cellar. I thought you were…"

Evie twists her fingers around the place it had been. "I left it yesterday when they took me down there. I was the last one. They were going to…" Dread flashes in her eyes. "They kept us in the attic. When they took a girl downstairs, she never came back."

Her lip wobbles, adrenaline finally waning. "There were things in the cellar. In the dirt. Pieces the other girls left, clues for somebody to find. I rolled one of my rings under the shelf, but Char took me back upstairs. I didn't know why. I saw —"

Her eyes drift over Flint and Harbinger. "I saw you on the floor of the cabin. I thought maybe you were there to save..." Her voice is tiny with disbelief. "But hours went by. And then the *screaming*."

Agony shrinks back beside Flint, but Evie takes in his shadows with admiration. "Thank you."

He's too stunned to speak – and then his eyes catch on a tree over Evie's shoulder. A stripe of claws dug into the trunk, jagged and rough and smeared with dried blood.

"It's from the dream." Harbinger tries to stand, but Agony pulls her weight against his body. They move toward the tree. Harbinger removes her bloody glove before she places her hand against it.

A low hum vibrates out from her touch. Harbinger's brow knits before she pulls away. "It was Mila. The shifter. They thought they killed her in the cellar."

Evie rises on wobbly legs. "Did she make it out? Did she get away?"

An ache cuts through Harbinger, her gaze slipping away from Evie's. "I can't tell from this."

But they all know the answer.

Evie tries to steady herself. Flint offers his hand, but she presses into his body instead, trembling until he lifts her off the ground. She looks so small cradled against his chest that Agony has to look away.

They follow the claw marks down the trail. This forest is different in morning light, birds hopping between branches and squirrels skittering through leaves.

The smell of smoke is the same. Agony sees the dark earth

from a distance. Each step feels heavier, weight pressing down through his feet. There's the twin trees Agony and Harbinger hid behind. The path the creature chased them down. Ash dusting along the ground.

When they reach the charred earth, Flint sets Evie back on her feet. They can all hear it, whispers like steam rising in the air. Agony wonders if he imagines it, but the others hold their breath too, staring out across the ashes.

The Veil has parted here. Not enough to cross. Not enough to reverse what's been done. Only enough for the voices of the dead to find living ears and tell stories of the man that captured them one by one. How he drove them into the wilderness. How the pack trapped them in the cabin, the girls' entwined hands the only thing keeping them alive. Voices rise from every end met in that cellar, the pieces of the girls left behind, and the fire that took everything else.

Harbinger's arms tighten around Agony's neck. She buries her face in his shoulder when Evie falls to her knees in the rubble.

Her scream rips to Agony's core: the most wounded, heart-wrenching sound he's ever heard. It scatters birds from trees, drawing Flint closer as Evie's hands crush into the scorched debris.

She screams until green tendrils sprout from the earth, blooming where her tears fall. Petals of every color, poppies and orchids and daisies forcing their way through the ash until Agony can't see the ground any more. She doesn't stop screaming until every inch of dead earth is covered in flowers, vibrant and alive, and she can't scream any more.

FORTY

Flint

Everything passes in a blur.

Once their bodies recognize the threat is gone, Harbinger gets sick, overwhelmed with new sensations. Trying to heal through the sudden attachment and amputation of Char's emotions, amplified by her new connection to Evie.

Flint flies them as far as he can, terrifying the grocer at the Conifer Outpost when they approach, bloody and broken. After that, they're passed through different hands — pack members rushing to contain the blaze, sending urgent messages across the Break as the poor grocer finds some way to feed them all.

One of the Timbers arrives to escort Evie to her family, but Agony and Harbinger have a hard time letting her out of their sight. It's all Flint can do to keep his eyes open, jaw aching and head pounding, but his thoughts revolve around the two hands in his.

They made it out.

They made it out.

It's days before they manage to get to the OID offices, despite the non-stop phone calls. Once Harbinger manages to make it through the night without vomiting, they drive back to the building where this all started.

"You should stay out here." Flint looks at Agony as he unbuckles his seatbelt. None of them have fully recovered, Agony's shadows a much paler shade as they spasm and quiver. "I don't want them trying anything with you."

"I'm coming with you." Agony props his chin on Flint's shoulder, but there's no disguising the effort it takes for him to smile. "Promise I'll be sneaky."

For a creature that started intent to escape by any means, the knowledge of the girls — and what Agony's creator did to them — weighs heaviest on him.

They wait in the same conference room, but everything feels different. The fluorescent buzz is little more than background noise, a pitcher of complimentary water at the center of the table. Harbinger's backup helmet rests on her head, currently pressed to the table as she breathes through the pain. Flint soothes a hand over her back. Dark tendrils squeeze her fingers where Agony hides in the shadows under the table.

They all flinch when Tamneth bursts in, frustration etched into his brow as armed officers flank him. "Where's the night terror?"

"Elsewhere," Flint answers.

Tamneth's teeth grit so harshly they clack together. "That's not going to work."

"It'll have to." Shadows brush Flint's knee as he leans back in his chair. His broken tusk still throbs, but the rest of him is numb. He doesn't give Tamneth a reaction. Flint enjoys the calm before Tamneth finally takes a seat.

"So." Tamneth tries to contain his temper. "What the fuck happened?"

Flint massages his eyelids. How many times have they told

this story? "Reid struck a deal with the Broadleafs. The pack forcibly bonded the girls and then let Reid kill them to make the pack stronger. It's a lengthy process; that's why Evie's still alive."

"Then where is this 'pack'? There was nothing but ash when we got there."

"Dead, I assume. We were trapped in the cellar. One of the pack members set the cabin on fire so none of us could escape."

"Then how *did* you escape?"

Flint and Harbinger shrug. Tamneth fumes.

"Evie is telling a very different story. She says..." His mouth twists, unable to comprehend it. "That the night terror killed the pack and pulled you out of the burning house. Why would it do that? Why would it save you?"

Flint's lip twitches. "Maybe he's sweet on us."

Harbinger snorts beneath her helmet.

"This is a matter of national security," Tamneth snarls. "Who knows what you've unleashed on the world? If that night terror is capable of slaughtering —"

"It was a little *traumatic*." Flint presses his palms into the table. "Excuse us if we don't have a perfect recollection. All you need to know is the Broadleafs were in bed with Reid. He started this on his own, but working with the Broadleafs meant things could happen faster. Everything incriminating stayed with them."

"Then where are the girls' remains? That's what you were supposed to find. That's what we hired you to do."

Flint gives a ruthless laugh. "Are you upset we uncovered an operation your team didn't catch a whiff of? The girls were cremated with phoenix fire. They're gone. Have some fucking care when you talk about them."

Blood rises in Tamneth's face. "Quite a mess you left. Now there are no witnesses —"

"Besides Evie."

"— no evidence, and an entire new fucking crime scene that spans miles of the Break. How the hell are we supposed to explain that? We have nothing!"

Harbinger slams her gloves down, spilling water across the table. "Should we have let them beat us to death so you never would have found *anything*? So Evie never would have seen her family again? So more girls could've been killed? I swear to *fuck*, you blame everyone but yourself. *You* messed up. *You* fucked up the investigation. Now you're embarrassed you have to answer for why you couldn't figure any of this out."

The guards by the door keep their eyes on Tamneth. His jaw tics with the cruel expression he's always regarded Flint with, waiting for the chance to put him in his place. To make him pay for what he did after Sidi's death.

"Because of what *you* did…" Tamneth's pinpointed with rage. "Reid is going to walk free."

Harbinger makes a strangled sound. "Are you fucking *joking*?"

"There are no suspects. No evidence. No remains. What the hell is the OID supposed to do with that? Reid looks like a choir boy after your screwup."

"But Evie can identify him!"

"For kidnapping," Tamneth snaps. "He'll probably get time served. Evie never saw him harm anyone else."

Flint gapes. "So he's gonna fucking *walk*?"

"His lawyer's already negotiating a deal with him in the room next door. Thanks to you."

"This is not our fault."

Even as Flint knows the words are true, guilt rips through him. Everything the girls went through, every moment of suffering, every second of torture because of this man — it was all for nothing.

Harbinger grips the edge of the table. "That's not — there has to be a way."

"You know what?" Tamneth pushes to his feet. "How about you two take some time in a cell to think it over. Maybe you'll come up with some brilliant new plan to recover all the evidence you lost us."

Flint pushes out of his chair, edging in front of Harbinger. "You can't be serious."

Tamneth jerks his chin toward her "Make sure you strip-search her. Can never be sure what she's hiding under there."

"You will not *fucking* touch her." Flint's snarl rattles the table. The guards tighten their hands around their weapons. Flint grapples for something to make this stop, but they're as trapped as they were in the cellar. "This is an abuse of power. You're retaliating."

Tamneth tilts his head as the armed guards move around him. "And who's going to believe you?"

Flint replays it later — over and over, looking for something that he missed.

The lights go out.

Agony's eyes appear next to Harbinger's, tendrils ghosting across her cheek. "You have to keep going, little death." His voice is little more than a whisper, lost in the sound of guns cocking. Harbinger's eyes reflect Agony's light before he turns to Flint. Wisps drift weakly from Agony, his expression faltering until his shadows give one final flare.

"Jasper."

And then he vanishes.

Flint knows with one word. The same way he can read Harbinger with a look, Flint translates Agony's wish into movement.

Gunfire pelts Flint's rock armor the second he turns his back, clutching Harbinger to his chest. Bullets chip away at him, ricocheting off walls and paintings, shattering glass in the frames.

Someone runs shrieking into the hallway.

"He's convulsing! Someone, hurry, get him out of his cuffs!"

It only stops the gunfire for a moment, but that's enough.

Drywall crumbles as Flint smashes through the wall. Tamneth shouts. Flint doesn't look back, barreling down the corridor with

Harbinger.

It's chaos. Reid writhes on the floor, foam spilling from his mouth, body jerking at impossible angles. OID officers scramble to subdue him, but something supernatural flails in his body. Flint can only imagine what he sees; the terror he inflicted, his worst nightmares crammed repeatedly into his mind.

Screams fade as Flint ducks around a corner, the footsteps behind him growing louder. Harbinger clutches at his arm. "Agony." Her eyes widen. "He's — no!" She tries to pull out of Flint's arms. "We have to go back! *We have to go back!*"

Flint presses down the pain in his chest and holds Harbinger closer, darting around another corner. He needs an exit.

"Flint! We can't —" she gasps, pressing her hand against her chest. "I'm —"

Boots thunder around the corner behind them. Flint's tail whips into a room, yanking rows of shelves across the hallway. He shifts out of the armor on his wings, feet cracking the tile floor as he sprints.

A window —

There.

"No, please! He can't do this! He's going to —" Tears streak down Harbinger's face. Flint wishes he could spare her. Save Agony. Keep her from feeling every second of it.

Flint crushes his arms around her, bursting through the glass, sending shards raining to the street below. His wings carry them skyward, straining to arc them back over the building, dodging gunfire as his rock armor shifts away.

Then Flint feels it — a taut line severed inside him, recoiling like a cut thread. He's never known pain like that. Not since Sidi, light fading from her eyes. Flint can't escape it now, the candle snuffed out, leaving a wisp of smoke in Flint's memory.

It's nearly enough to take him out of the air, the hole inside him growing. Harbinger wails like she's dying herself. They both know it now.

Agony is gone.

FORTY-ONE

Harbinger

Harbinger doesn't dream any more.

When she reaches for them, there's a void. Cobwebs that slip through her fingers. Emptiness. She wakes groggy and delirious before the crushing reminder sinks into her chest.

Flint does his best. He's the only thing keeping her functioning. The only thing keeping her *alive*, but his worry is too strong for him to tamp down on. It swells when he returns to the motel room, keycard plinking down on the table. Harbinger's in the same place he left her, curled on her side, staring numbly at the motel painting.

Agony brought it to life. Agony, the not-quite-living thing that tried to kill her, managed to make something as abysmal as motel art magical. With him, dreary paintings provided an odd sort of comfort.

Now, every piece is as lifeless as he is.

As lifeless as *she* is. A carcass of reminder, her body a tomb for the loss, hosting a hollow gap in her chest where Agony had been.

Living feels like reaching for a step that isn't there, stumbling in the darkness when she tries to put her foot down on something solid.

Like the hole her father left. Overgrown after years of vacancy, but when she reaches into the crater of Agony, it's the same shape. Jagged edges like something ripped out of her, connection vanishing, leaving her raw and open. The place Agony once filled is still tender, painful to the touch, but she knows it'll harden the same way her father's has. Growing wild with disuse, turning into calluses and gnarled roots until Harbinger is able to forget the ache from time to time. To make it through a single day without the debilitating pang as a reminder — until her curse takes it all away for good.

She cries when she thinks about it. Because losing a fraction of this pain means losing Agony all over again.

For a week, she hates Agony. Hates that she met him. That he made her feel anything. That Flint let this happen. In her darkest moments, she wants to punish them. Wants Agony back so she can make him suffer the same loss...but the anger turns to heart-wrenching sorrow when she looks at Flint.

He feeds her. Eases her into the shower when it's been too many days since her last. The TV is a steady hum in the background, one small way for Harbinger to pretend she has social interaction. Until a rerun plays — one she and Agony made commentary about — and she's dropped back into that hole she can't climb out of.

After they escaped the OID, she and Flint holed up in the quietest motel they could find. They didn't touch the money in their bank accounts. She only knows time is passing from the news Flint shares with her. Omen took a few others to the charred patch of earth where the girls were burned. With the banshees' abilities, they recovered some form of remains for the families. The Break is in turmoil after word got out about the Broadleafs. Lev's been trying to get in touch with Flint and Harbinger for days. The OID is looking for them, too, but the partners are laying lower than they ever have.

Slowly, Harbinger starts to dream again. She never goes back to the forest. Now, it's always the same story on different backdrops that leave her feeling like she hasn't slept at all.

Always looking for Agony. Borne into the dream with one purpose, searching desperately for him, even before her dream-self realizes he's missing. Sometimes Flint is there, asking anyone they pass if they've seen a dark shadow. Sometimes it's only Harbinger, walking through the hallways of the Convent, sprinting down endless motel corridors, crawling along the bloody dirt of the cellar.

At first, Harbinger searches calmly, pulling aside curtains and opening drawers, shifting her body to cast a shadow and hoping a disembodied smile will appear. Then she grows agitated. Furious. Tearing tarps from shelves and shoving pitchers off of tables, bursting with frantic energy that yanks her out of sleep.

Under the weight of her own grief, she forgets that she isn't alone in it. It's another week before she pulls her head out of the fog long enough to see Flint staring out the window. The breakfast he made sure Harbinger finished sits next to his, still untouched. That's when she notices the dark circles under his eyes, fatigue draped heavy over his shoulders. While she's been suffering through dreamless sleep, Flint hasn't slept at all.

She pulls herself out of bed and into his lap. He tightens his arms around her and buries his face against her neck.

They trade places in the weeks after. Harbinger does up her catsuit with purpose. One button after another. One step at a time. She kisses Flint's temple as he stares at the newspaper.

"You see this?"

He lays out the front page for her to read, splashed with a picture of Tamneth holding a tense press conference.

Orena Investigative Division Faces Charges for Gross Criminal Negligence and Misconduct.

"'Bout time." Harbinger tugs on her gloves before she sinks her backup helmet over her head.

"Where are you going?"

Even in his suffering, Flint worries. Her fingers trace over his jaw, gentler still around his broken tusk.

"I'll get breakfast. Feels like I need to look someone else in the face. Make sure I have any interpersonal skills left."

Maybe it's his grief, but despite everything, Flint does his best to ease off of the protective circle he wants to draw around her. He presses his lips to the inside of her wrist. "Get more than varying shades of beige, please."

She tucks away her keycard. "If I'm feeling generous." Then she slips out into the crisp morning.

Cars hum along the highway. Across the parking lot, a diner welcomes its morning patrons. The sight of so many people makes Harbinger's chest tight.

Her gloves cling to the motel doorknob. She can turn back. She's only a step outside. But she lets the cold air swell into her lungs with icy pinpricks, a reminder that her chest is not a hollow place. She'll try the gas station today. With that small comfort, Harbinger stuffs hands into her pockets and starts down the stairs.

It's tempting to stay in the fog that traps her, but Harbinger reminds herself to look both ways, waiting for the *Walk* symbol to light. The sun's still lazy, not yet catching the grays and blues of fuel pumps as the convenience store door dings.

Breakfast sandwiches are tempting — so Harbinger doesn't resist. Still, she juggles a small fruit salad in the crook of her arm, adding a packet of baby carrots to the pile. *Better than beige.*

It's enough to make her feel like she's earned the largest drink from the fountain, so she fills her cup with dark soda while Flint's coffee brews.

"Excuse me?"

Harbinger turns blankly to the girl behind her. "Yeah?"

Harbinger's eyes narrow before it dawns on her. She barely

recognizes this girl without blood caked to her face. No wild fear in her eyes, bones no longer protruding…

Evie.

FORTY-TWO

Harbinger

Liquid seeps into Harbinger's sleeve. Only then does she realize the soda's overflowing.

"Oh, shit. Hi. Sorry." She pulls back her drink, fumbling to clean the mess off the counter. By the time she tosses the wet napkins, a customer huffs behind them. Harbinger navigates Evie around him to the chip aisle before she takes her in.

In the midst of the cloud around Harbinger's mind, she hadn't noticed Evie's emotions growing closer. Hadn't realized how near they were to Evie's town, as if something had drawn them there.

There's an awkward length of space between them. The bruise has faded from around Evie's eye. At sixteen, she's taller than Harbinger, teal jacket hanging off her shoulders. Seeing Evie here among bright plastic packages, her sneakers shiny and new, makes Harbinger's heart twist in her chest.

"Hi," she breathes again.

"Hi." A wrapper crinkles in Evie's hand. Sunflower seeds.

Harbinger nearly bawls.

Evie glances uncertainly at Harbinger's helmet. Harbinger pushes back the skull, opening the visor so their eyes can meet. It's the first time someone new has *relaxed* at Harbinger's skeletal face.

"You got your bird," Harbinger manages. The parakeet looks like a different animal on Evie's shoulder, nuzzling her cheek and chirring as she laughs.

"Yeah, he's doing better. I'm sorry — I don't know your name. I never got it during...everything. And the OID wouldn't talk to me about you all after."

"Harbinger."

Evie's lip quirks. "Harbinger," she repeats. "Of good things."

Harbinger's throat is tight. "You'd be the first person to think that." She fights down the pricking feeling behind her eyes.

Evie rocks on her feet. "I never got a chance to thank you..."

"It was nothing."

Evie slows as she blinks. "You got trapped in a cellar. And tortured. And the house burned down."

A laugh croaks out of Harbinger, the first real one she's given since... "Ok, maybe it was something."

Evie's laugh is musical, dimpling her cheeks before she presses her lips together. "I wanted to thank the others, too. The gargoyle, and — the night terror? Are they here?"

Pain surges inside of Harbinger, a tap turned sharply to full blast. "Um. Flint — the gargoyle —" She clears her throat. "He's back at the motel. And Agony..." Her voice wavers. She tries to hold it steady. "He didn't make it."

A cloud falls over Evie's face. Her gaze skirts to the ground. "Oh. I'm so sorry."

Harbinger doesn't know what to say. Evie's toes press together, eyes glassy and distant.

"He...when I first saw him, I was so scared. He looked like he could rip me apart. But once he recognized me, everything changed. The air around him..." She gestures with her hands. A tiny smile forms on her face. "Everything felt safe. Good. For the first time in a long time."

Harbinger tries to swallow the lump in her throat. "He'd be very happy to hear that."

"At night, when I can't sleep..." A heavy laugh bubbles out of Evie. "Which is every night. I try to imagine the dark like his darkness. It wasn't scary. Better than the light. He was warm. Quiet. I don't know if that's a good coping mechanism. Should probably tell my therapist."

"Therapy..." Tears threaten to slip down Harbinger's cheeks as she nods. "I should probably try that."

Evie extends her hand, but stops herself. "You saved my life. If you hadn't shown up, I would have..." Evie shakes her head, darkness crowding the edge of her eyes. "Thank you for coming. For not giving up on me."

"We couldn't have gotten out without you." Harbinger reaches her gloves for Evie's fingers and squeezes. "I'm really glad we found you."

They stay like that for a moment. Then Evie pulls away, stepping back toward the end of the aisle. "I should go. My parents barely agreed to let me come in by myself. They're probably freaking out."

Her bird trills as she gives a final wave before she disappears out the door. Across the parking lot, she lifts the packet triumphantly in her hand before her father curls his arm around her and presses a kiss to the top of her head.

Back at the motel, Harbinger empties her pockets of food. The smile stays on her face, an unfamiliar guest Flint notices immediately. His lips quirk to match hers. "What?"

"I saw Evie at the gas station. She says thank you."

He softens. "How is she?"

A disbelieving laugh pops out of Harbinger. "She's good." Warmth spreads across her chest, the ember of Evie's feelings a reminder that she's alive. "I think she's gonna be good."

"And what about you?"

Harbinger doesn't reply, condensation forming on the outside of her cup.

Soon, it's been a month without Agony. The hole tunnels deep inside her, past the clutter of everything else she's touched. There's not "nothing" where he once was. There's a pit. No matter what grows over it, one wrong step and Harbinger sinks right back into his absence. Grief has taken up residence where he once was, and it refuses to leave.

Her dreams change again. It feels wrong for her mind to sink back into something that resembles "normal," but Harbinger still suffers in the mornings when she wakes. Any time she lets herself fall into the trap of forgetting that Agony's gone, the wound tears again when she opens her eyes.

There's a nagging in her dreams as she moves from one loop to another. Thrust back to the Convent, having a sleepover with Evie and a female gargoyle that looks like Flint. In another dream, Poe and Omen hang glass windchimes above motel doorways. Everyone in her dreams is out of place, crossing over where they shouldn't be, but someone's always missing.

The real world isn't better. She and Flint get sucked into the trial for the OID. It's tempting to duck and run, to take cover from the very people who got them into this. The people who left Evie and the other girls on their own. The people who tortured and killed Agony. Who tried to kill *them*. But Flint reminds Harbinger that if they can stop this from happening to someone else, they owe it to all of them to try.

Every morning is a game of roulette, waiting to see if they'll be called, until the day they are. Harbinger sits on the witness stand, wringing her gloves and staring fixedly at Flint. It takes more than one reminder from the judge for her to remove her helmet. She keeps it clenched in her lap.

Tamneth glares bullets from the defense table. The OID attorney approaches the stand. "Now, Ms…"

"Harbinger."

The attorney checks his notes. "Is that your real name?"

"It's the name you're going to call me."

Cross-examination goes about like that. Days later, when Flint and Harbinger are finally free, it doesn't feel like victory. It doesn't feel like anything.

Harbinger shrugs out of her coat in the motel room. It's already dark outside, the cold chill of fall kicking dead leaves across the half-empty parking lot. She doesn't bother stripping out of her suit, flopping onto the bed with a heavy sigh. Flint tosses his wallet onto the table. "You want dinner?"

"No." She stares at the painting above the bed and wonders what Agony would have seen.

Flint's keys clink against the table. "I guess in a few days, we'll be out of here."

It's what she's been dreading. The final day of their testimony, the only thing keeping them in one place. They haven't taken a job in two months. They hardly get out of bed most days. The finale of all of this means they have to move on. Get back to a life she can't imagine any longer.

"Do you just feel aimless?" Her gaze stays on the ceiling. She's too afraid of what will break in her if she looks at Flint. Before he speaks, she feels his answer.

"...yes."

"Like everything is purposeless," she murmurs. "Like, what's the fucking point?"

Flint sinks down on the edge of the bed, elbows resting on his knees. "Yes," he murmurs. "I feel like that. Wondering if it's possible to be happy again. If that was the happiest we'll ever be,"

Heat pricks behind her eyes when she looks at him. He's so lost in his own way, unsure how to protect her from this. How to bring her back. How to bring *himself* back. She reaches for his hand. "I don't know what to do. I don't know how to keep going." Her lips tremble. "I'm really sorry things aren't how they used to be."

Flint guides her into his lap. His chest against her makes her sob.

"You don't have anything to apologize for." He brushes claws through her hair. She curls her fingers into his shirt so tightly that it hurts. "Things aren't the same. It's not wrong to feel that. It's not wrong to recognize it."

He holds her face in his hands, swiping at tears slipping down her cheeks. "It doesn't mean I won't stay here. I would still choose this — choose you — every day. Even if it's hard right now. Even if it hurts. I would rather miss him with you than forget him anywhere else."

Her tears soak into his shirt. He lets her cry against him, smoothing a hand over her back.

"I know it's what you were scared of," he murmurs finally. "Someone else dying to protect you. And I'm sorry..." Flint's voice grows tight. "That it happened that way. That it hurt you again."

Harbinger takes a shaky breath. "I hate it. But I don't..." Her eyes slip shut. "I don't want to be angry at him. Or you. I don't want to hold onto that again. I know that you did it because..."

But she can't say the words. Flint presses her palm to his chest, forehead resting against hers. Calm from both of them settles inside her. "We'll figure it out. Together. And we'll keep a place for him while we do. But we can't keep him buried like we did with my sister. With your dad. Ok?"

Harbinger pulls back to look at him. Exhaustion creeps into his eyes, an ache etched into the knit of his brow, a timeline of all the pain he's tried to protect her from. Worry he tries to hide from her. Fear that she'll slip back into her old ways, hurtling headfirst into death in the hopes that this time, it'll stick.

"I don't want to be anywhere without you." Her fingers trace his jaw, warm beneath her hands, blood pulsing and promising not to leave. It's the first time in so long that she's said it. Never to her father after her change. Not even to Poe and Omen. Never to Flint, before today. But she squeezes tighter. "I love you. And I want to stay with you. Until the end."

Flint's kiss is like relief. Murmuring the words against her mouth until they become as necessary as air. *I love you, I love you, I love you.* Like he finally sees light in her eyes. Like he finally trusts her to stay. She doesn't know how to do it, how to live for something rather than in spite of it. How to live for some*one*. For Flint, and Agony, and herself. For hope that one day, they'll have something better than life has given them.

Face puffy and Flint's body warm against hers, she finally sinks into sleep.

She returns to the forest — the one Agony brought her to — but nothing is the same. The trees are still marked, but they've grown over their wounds, scars preserved inside as they form new branches. Clover and wild berries sprout around their roots. The grove no longer smells of ash. It's fragrant with flowers, blooming and flourishing across the field in the distance.

Harbinger doesn't visit where the girls were burned. They're gone now, resting somewhere safe. Instead, she hikes up a hill, far away from the cellar that haunts her. She keeps walking until she no longer recognizes anything, passing brush and streams that guide her toward an unknown destination.

She's not sure how she knows when she's there, but the earth is familiar beneath her feet. This is where Agony was the day of the cabin, where he realized something was wrong. She searches the ground for footprints before she realizes her foolishness. As if he would leave any. As if he would still be here.

She crouches to the earth, running hands through the cool grass. Blades slip between her bare fingers, wind rushing through the reeds. It's warm. Serene. A place she wouldn't mind staying. Even if it's all in her imagination, she clings to the thought.

Birds fly off from a nearby tree. Harbinger wanders closer until she comes to a hole dug into the dirt. It's almost tempting, comforting, like she could cover herself with a patch of wildflowers and fall asleep.

It's Agony's grave. Harbinger sinks to the edge, dangling her legs into the depths. She can't see the bottom. The wind tosses her voice. "Sometimes I wish I could crawl in there with you."

Maybe this is how she heals. Saying goodbye. Laying Agony to rest. Finding a place for him in the dreamscape where she can visit. He isn't there, but she can pretend.

She's been pretending she can hold it together; she'd rather pretend this.

Come on. I wasn't even that good.

A wet laugh slips out of her at his voice in her head. She can still picture him over her shoulder, tendrils draped over her neck.

"You were good to me," she murmurs. "And Flint. And Evie. And my friends." She swipes at a tear with her sleeve. "The list is getting longer. You're in danger of losing your horrific reputation."

There are worse things.

Harbinger swallows. She knows there are; she's been through them. She's living them. But mercifully, Agony's voice takes a different track. *I was only good to Flint for you.*

Laughter bursts out of her. "You're a fucking liar."

There's a grin in Agony's voice. *Yeah.* Then it grows silent, and she thinks she's lost him before he returns quieter than before. *Does he miss me?*

A sob rips from her throat. "Yes, you *fucking* jerk."

How do you know?

"Because I *feel* it." Her eyes squeeze shut. "Every day. Every time he turns out a light, or sees a puzzle, or looks in the backseat. Every night when he can't sleep. There's not a moment he's not thinking about you."

Agony's voice draws nearer. *And do you miss me, little death?*

"*Yes.*" She keeps her eyes closed, clinging to the darkness, willing herself to sink into it. "I don't know how to do this. I don't know if I want to."

You do. You have to. She can almost feel the flutter of his body.

This is no place to live. No place to die, either. Trust me, I know. The real world is better. There's a kiss of shadows against her cheek. *It brought me to you.*

Tears slide down her face. He tries to catch them, but there's no end to them, every drop disappearing into the grave.

"Is this the last time I'll see you here?" She tries not to let her voice break. "Are you going to leave for good?"

Maybe. He dries her eyes as the forest thrums around them. *If this is the last time...if you could only wish for one thing, anything, what would it be?*

It's not a question. She's known since the second he left. She doesn't open her eyes, too scared of what she won't see. Too scared to leave this world behind.

"I want you back. I want you alive — *real.* I want you with us."

Tendrils pull tighter around her. She can almost feel them. Almost believe they're more than her mind. More than Flint's arm draped over her. More than wishful thinking. She curls her fingers into one.

It squeezes back.

Wind rushes past her until Agony's voice is a shout in her ear. "Then *wake up!*"

FORTY-THREE

Flint

Flint didn't realize how heavy his grief was until he finally sat down with it and found he couldn't get back up.

He'd kept himself busy by keeping Harbinger alive, but the pain was always there, waiting for the right moment to drag him back beneath the surface.

His dreams take him back to the cellar. Watching blood seep out of Harbinger's broken body, her hand straining toward him until the life drifts from her fingers. Sometimes she becomes Sidi, fading in Flint's arms far more slowly than she did the first time. Other times, he can do nothing to reach either of them. Without fail, he wakes to the burning pain of chains digging into his wrists and that serrated feeling in his chest.

Most often, though, it's Agony. Not bloody. Not beaten. Just dissolving into shadow, leaving no trace, as if he'd never been there at all. That makes it harder, having nothing to show for him. No body or ashes or trinkets, just memories imprinted in Flint's skin where Agony found cracks in Flint's armor and slithered inside.

Flint doesn't know why he could feel the very moment Agony died. Doesn't know if something forged between them that night at the Timbers', when their bodies were knit and melded together, Agony no longer constrained to a physical form. But it means the wound his absence leaves is almost too much to bear, embedded in a part of Flint that he can't reach. If he feels like this, he can't imagine how Harbinger manages the empty sockets left in her.

Dreams are the place he finds Agony. The place where, if Flint is lucky, Sidi lives as vibrant and vivid as every day before the last one. The place he can take those waking moments when he finds a crossword in the newspaper, and his fingers flex to hand it to Agony. When all these years later, the fleeting thought still passes through Flint on the most mundane whims. *I should tell Sidi about that...*

Muscle memory.

Too bad his body couldn't remember anything useful to save either of them.

Tonight, he can't find Agony or Sidi, even in sleep. His mind is dreamless darkness, a void without the broken pieces he seeks. He drifts in and out of consciousness, lulled by Harbinger's chest rising and falling against his side.

Her gasp jerks him awake. A sound that's almost strangled, ripping Flint from the place before sleep that reminds him most of Agony: shadows pressed against his eyelids, hazy and intoxicating. Harbinger topples off the foot of the bed. Flint lunges to his feet, rushing to separate her from the figure she's tangled with, but Flint's hand disappears into shadows.

Harbinger buries her face against it. Flint can't move, blinking, disbelieving, certain he's sunk into another of those hopeless dreams where Agony promises, *I'll look after her*. Flint's never sure which 'her' Agony means: the living Harbinger or the ghost of Sidi.

Glowing eyes turn to Flint now, matching jagged mouth stretched into a smile. Shadows extend toward Flint, brushing his jaw. His eyes slip shut.

Agony's voice is clear and absolute. "You *did* miss me."

Flint sinks to his knees, cutting through any remnants of sleep. Harbinger holds Agony back from her, shaking fingers slipping through his shadows. "How…"

"I told you I'd come crawling back." Light casts across her face when Agony leans close. "You're stuck with me."

He looks like Flint's dreams, but this Agony doesn't vanish. Doesn't rip away as soon as Flint reaches for him. Tendrils twine around Flint's hand. He flexes his fingers, trying to make sense of it. "Is this a dream?"

Agony squeezes between Flint and Harbinger, nuzzling into Flint's neck. "Been dreaming about me, huh?" But Agony already knows the answer, pressing his forehead to Flint's. Firm. Solid. "I told you I'd take care of her."

"That was really you?"

Agony's breath is warm against Flint's lips. "You think I'd pass up an opportunity to annoy you?"

Flint tightens his arms around Agony, too afraid of him slipping away. "How?"

"Trial and error." Shadows flare as Agony lifts his arms. "I didn't even have *this* for a while. No body, no form. I barely existed. Couldn't fathom my own exhaustion, because I was nothing. But I had one thought. One purpose. The thing that kept me going." His hands find Flint and Harbinger's faces. "To get back to you."

Her cheeks are sticky with dried tears. Agony wipes the fresh ones away. "Hey, I'm here now."

But as he soothes her, there's strain on his face, fatigue worn around his eyes and tension in his smile. No matter how he assures that he was always going to return to them, there's despair that he very nearly didn't.

"How did you find us? After Reid —"

"I couldn't see anything." Agony brushes Harbinger's hair back. "Couldn't feel anything. Couldn't find anything. Just kept trying to crawl out of the darkness into something real. I couldn't get back to the real world. It took weeks to find your dreams, and even then, I couldn't get close enough before you drifted away. But you..."

He lifts Harbinger's chin, tracing the carved line of her jaw. Flint's never seen Agony look at anyone like that. Like he would kill and die for her, over and over.

"You found that place in your dreams between life and death. You held the Veil open for me."

It's the first time Harbinger's powers have done something for her. Given her something. Her breath trembles. "But that should be impossible."

"Come on: you didn't think something as small as death would stop me." Agony nudges his nose against hers. "Not when I have you."

Everything she's been holding onto breaks. Shattered and splintered at finally, *finally* touching Agony again. Her mouth hurtles against his, desperate to be closer, to make sure he's real — and Agony holds her together. Reassembling the broken parts, engulfing her until her skin is drenched in shadows.

He's perfect on her, draped around the thudding pulse in her neck, the swell of her chest, the v of her thighs when he hoists her into his arms. His shadows blend into the hollow parts of her body, knitting into every crevice until neither are whole without the other.

Impossible. Inseparable. Breathtaking.

Flint could watch the two of them forever, chasing each other on a razor's edge, but then shadows find Flint and hoist him back onto the bed where Agony appears above him.

"Don't fucking hold back any more." Agony clutches the back of Flint's head, pain daggered through Agony's voice. "I didn't know if I'd ever see you again." Their breaths mingle until Agony's snarl reverberates through Flint's body. "I want *everything* you never gave me."

This is what Flint's been hopeless to get back to, the feeling he wasn't sure he could find again. Emotions he can't keep at bay send him running, sprinting, diving headlong into the rush.

Now that he has it, he never wants to stop falling with them.

Flint pushes against Agony's hold, and Agony's surprise morphs into a grin. "You love me, then?"

It clenches in Flint's chest. He's always had doubts. Always questioned himself, his judgments, his choices — but he doesn't doubt Agony. Doesn't doubt the emotion that saturates every moment with him.

"Yes."

Agon doesn't get closer. Doesn't give Flint the touch he craves, but Agony's smile illuminates the darkness. "Yeah?"

Flint's growl drags against Agony's mouth. "Yes!" His claws dig into tendrils, keeping Agony as close as he can. "Don't leave us without you."

Agony licks the words from Flint's mouth and swallows them whole. Buried deep inside him, a promise embedded in the lining of Agony's skin until Flint has to come up for air. Only then does Agony pull back enough to speak.

"Show me."

FORTY-FOUR

Flint

Agony doesn't release Flint. But he makes room for Harbinger to slide between them, her back to Agony's chest, thighs on either side of Flint's. She's all bare skin now, proud and perfect as Agony works Flint's sweats down enough to take him in hand. Harbinger presses her palms to Flint's chest, searing over the thud of his heart.

"You're gonna give us everything," Agony instructs. He tilts her forward toward Flint, almost close enough for them to kiss, until Harbinger gasps against his mouth. Agony drags his tongue over her cunt, trailing back against her ass, working her open as gold drips from his mouth.

She clutches at Flint like she wants to be under his skin, closer than this world allows. Agony pulls back enough to meet Flint's eyes. "Everything you feel, I want you to share it. All your pain, all your pleasure: right now, it's *ours.*"

There's a flicker of hesitation in Flint. At the thought of overwhelming Harbinger, of letting every emotion spill into her.

But all his restraint is subdued by the glassy want in her eyes, pain and joy and relief.

So Flint lets go.

The room fills with gasps. Harbinger grips Flint's shoulders, burying her face against his neck the same time Agony's shadows ripple. Flint lets everything flow through their connection, a swirling cocktail he can't put words to. Emotions threaten to burst out of him, spilling into Harbinger, into Agony, until there's no question how Flint feels about them both.

A drop falls onto Flint's chest. When Harbinger pulls back, tears drip off the line of her jaw. He tries to staunch the flow of his emotions, to wipe the remnants from Harbinger cheeks, but she shakes her head.

"It's good." Her laugh shudders into a breath, hands holding Flint's face like that day in the desert. "It's green."

Then she kisses him with everything he gave her. He doesn't need a connection to know exactly how she feels. It's evident in the shift of her hips. The insatiable drag of her mouth, drinking from him fully for the first time, lips swollen and reaching for more.

Agony pulls her back upright, tendrils framing her breasts while his mouth trails over the pulse in her neck. Both her holes are sloppy and slick, Agony's spit leaving glowing tracks down her legs.

"You ready?" he breathes. Shadows curve against her hairline, Agony's mouth against her ear when her eyes roll back. He toys with her head, tendrils teasing her clit until her desire drips onto Flint's cock. He does his best not to rut up against her.

A shadow drags through her folds before it dips between her cheeks, making her arch in Agony's grip. He works into her ass, spreading her over his shadow, plying her mind with want until her body relaxes around him. She's supple and pliant in his arms, a heady smile on her face before she rocks back against him.

Agony presses a curse to her neck, tightening his circles against her clit until she squirms. "You take it so good for me, baby.

Like I was made for you."

Harbinger grapples for his tendrils, for Flint's chest, but Agony doesn't stop driving her toward the peak. "Come for me once. Come for me, and Daddy will give you more."

And Flint gives her a taste of it, the sight of the two of them burning into arousal that slips through their connection. When her orgasm crests, Agony fights to keep himself from following her over, and Flint grips under her thighs to pull her to straddle his mouth.

"Let me taste that pussy while it's coming."

She whines as soon as Flint gets his mouth on her, shuddering as the waves crash. His tongue spreads over her cunt, reaching back to where Agony's shadow works into her ass until Agony jerks at the contact. Flint doesn't stop until Harbinger pries herself off of his mouth, and Agony's entire being shivers.

"That's fucking *it*." Agony pulls her back against his chest, her eyes dazed and hot where they meet Flint's. Shadows flutter over Flint's body, stroking his cock before Agony sheaths Flint completely.

They both groan, Flint's hips rolling into Agony's grip as other tendrils withdraw from Harbinger. There's not an inch of Flint's dick that isn't covered by Agony and his perfectly-molded shadows. Agony tries to center Harbinger over the two of them, but Flint pulls his own hips down, fucking shallowly into Agony's sheath until Agony's eyes roll back.

"You tell me when," Flint murmurs, his eyes on Harbinger. She circles over both of them, brushing the shadows covering Flint's head. Agony smears a groan against her neck at the sticky mess he's made between her legs, hot and waiting.

"*Please* let him put it in," Agony begs. Harbinger hums, swirling her hips in torturous patterns until finally, *finally* she nods.

Carefully, Flint guides them both into her ass. The pleasure is mind-numbing, Flint fucking into the tight hold of Agony, working them both into Harbinger. His cockhead barely fits past her tight ring, but she's already rocking her hips for more. Her body yields under the tricks Agony played with her mind, the overwhelming slickness of his mouth, the taut velvet of his shadows.

Flint tries to keep his mind straight, but the sight of her head falling back against Agony's shoulder is beyond words.

"I know, Daddy." The corner of her lip twitches as she presses her weight onto Flint's chest, working back against them both. "I know it's good."

They work her down with slow pumps of Flint's hips, his thumb against her clit until she sinks as far as she can. Stretching over both of them, whining when more of Agony's tendrils meld her hands to Flint's chest until she can only take what they give her.

"That what you want, baby?" Agony murmurs. Her thighs tremble against Flint's. Agony coils her hair around his fingers, lifting the sweat-slick strands off her neck. "I know it is. And we'll always give it to you. Because good girls get everything they need."

She swirls her hips, taking them deeper, all their bodies shuddering at the pleasure. Flint splays his hand over her stomach, slotting fingers between her breasts as he grinds up into them.

"You're going to open up for me." He rolls into her, intent to draw out every sound, and not just from Harbinger. Agony's eyes burn into Flint's with each thrust, with every word Flint speaks. "I want to know you. Every inch." Flint's hand shifts down to Harbinger's hips until he can grip her and Agony at once, working them in filthy rhythm over his cock. "Let me see it."

Agony and Harbinger dissolve into needy whines. Her nails dig into Flint's stomach, Agony's teeth in her neck when Flint's tail snakes up behind them, curling tight around both of their waists. Binding them together until Flint doesn't even have to move. He lifts Harbinger and Agony with his tail, bringing them back down against him until they're a mess of whimpers.

He can't look away from them, Agony's shadows and Flint's

tail draped across Harbinger, as close as their bodies can get.

But not closer than their minds. Not closer than the connections woven between them, tangled and entwined, past the desire and swells of emotions. Agony presses his mouth behind Harbinger's ear, loud enough for Flint to hear.

"Let me take care of you." *Both of you*. Agony eyes lock on Flint's, branding him with intention. "I don't want anything but this. I don't dream of anything but you."

Flint surges up toward them, holding them in place with his tail until they're both grinding down into his lap. Harbinger's a mess of gasps, stammering against Flint's mouth, fighting and failing to find words.

"Go on, baby. Tell us. Tell your men." His mockery is pure heat. "I know it's good."

She clenches around both of them, helpless against Flint's lips. Agony grips her chin, turning her toward him, her expression exposed. "You want to come again? Yeah? Show us how badly. Show us how much you fucking need it."

It's a demand for more. More than this world allows, a way for all of them to be melted down and melded together until there's no prying them apart again. Harbinger's delirious, gripping back for Agony's shadows, whimpering where she clutches Flint's shoulders. Her legs quiver when Agony pumps them both into her, gripping her hair and arching her back so they can sink deeper.

"There you go. Good girl." He presses kisses to her forehead as she spirals under pleasure. "Give it to us just like that."

Flint's never seen Harbinger like this: mindless, wild, free. And he's never seen Agony so desperate to be close, to be a part of something. A part of this.

Their scattered breaths are all Flint can hear when he pulls Agony in, too frantic to do anything but drag together, desire ripping through them as they race toward the peak.

Their mouths collide, filthy and open, moans binding together. Flint doesn't stop his fingers against Harbinger's clit as

Agony quivers.

"You're about to come all over Daddy's dick, aren't you?" Every rush of want pulses through them when they both clench around his cock. "Go ahead." Flint soothes their whimpers, tightening his tail until they can't get any closer. "Make a mess for me."

Harbinger tries, filled to the brim with them both buried inside her. Flint's tail and Agony's shadows cross over her chest, her throat, her clit, grinding her against them. They're shivering and sweat-slick as they thrust together, slow rolls so decadent and sinful, moving in perfect sync.

Groans splice every sound until Flint pulls them both into a kiss. Raw and messy and real, just like this. Release rushes through him faster than ever, crashing and overlapping and colliding as they all shatter together.

Shadows surge, spilling over the bed, engulfing the room in darkness. It coats the walls, the windows, the floor, until the only things left illuminated are Flint and Harbinger's awed faces.

There's no part of them that doesn't touch. Legs and tendrils and hair draped over each other, air shared between their lungs. Even when they finally pull apart, they're closer than they've ever been, inextricably tied to one another.

EPILOGUE

Agony

"No fucking way."

Agony flourishes the newspaper onto the table as Flint adjusts his glasses. "Wow."

Harbinger steps out of the bathroom, naked and dripping save for the towel around her hair. Shadows whip toward her thighs, and she smacks them away, leaning over Flint's shoulder as he reads.

"'The Orena Investigative Division has been disbanded after twenty-one counts of criminal negligence and misconduct.'"

Agony sidles up behind Harbinger, pressing his mouth against the droplets on her neck to listen to them sizzle.

"Holy shit." She squeezes Agony's arms tighter around her stomach. "I didn't think they'd get charged with anything."

"Evie's testimony was a big factor." Flint looks up at her. "And yours."

His smile makes the coil in Agony's stomach tighter, but Harbinger sighs. "They're not the only organization like that, though. There are still others."

Agony lifts her over his shoulder, tilting her onto the bed where he chases her breathless laughter. "Not the only one..." He laps at the water collecting against her sternum. "But they're the first to go."

She squirms against him with a grin, but Agony wrestles her into submission.

"If you two keep that up," Flint flicks to the next page, "we're not gonna leave on time."

"Oh, Mr. Killjoy," Agony's mouth drags down Harbinger's stomach until he settles between her thighs. She wastes no time hooking them over his shoulders. When Flint's eyes slip to them behind the frames of his glasses, Agony pouts. "We'll be so much faster if you help."

The warmth of Agony's tongue finds Harbinger's clit until she groans, and that telltale muscle in Flint's jaw flexes. She grips the top of Agony's head, rocking against his mouth.

"Because if you don't help..." Agony swirls his tongue in slow circles until Harbinger's heels dig into his back. "I'm gonna tease her. And you don't want a keyed-up, deprived Harbinger riding shotgun for the next four hours, do you?"

She scrabbles to get a better grip on him, but Agony shifts his shadows out of reach.

"Like she wouldn't convince you to fuck her halfway there," Flint scoffs, but his gaze hooks on both of them.

"*Please*, Daddy." A grin slices across Harbinger's lips. "If you don't put us in our place, how will we know to follow the rules?"

Flint fights a smile before he pushes to his feet, muscles in his bare chest shifting as he unbuckles his belt to wind around Harbinger's wrists. With one hand on the mattress, he bends down to meet her lips. "You don't follow the rules, anyway."

Their kiss is slow and filthy, branded deep in Agony's stomach. Harbinger's already working on Flint's zipper, bound hands be damned, when Flint lifts Agony's chin to face him. "You're a terror."

Agony's grin blooms. "You love it."

They don't leave on time, but Flint planned ahead for that. He knows their rhythms well by now. Agony pulls open the passenger side door and shifts in shadows across the seat to pop open the driver's side as well.

"You gonna do that every time?" Flint huffs as he climbs inside, but a flush creeps up his neck.

Agony settles in the small middle seat. "As long as you'll have me."

"It really does fit you." Harbinger pulls herself into the passenger seat, noting the heightened ceiling to accommodate Flint's size. A suitable automobile was the first and only big purchase they made with the remaining OID money. Flint flexes his wings enough to stretch them.

"It was a sound investment." He cranks the ignition. "And with the travel trailer, we can save some money on food and motels."

"Might not have to worry about that, if the court decision's any indication." Agony sinks back in his seat. "Might have OID settlement money coming in soon. I bet the girls' families will, too."

"Let's not get ahead of ourselves," Flint chides, but Agony's smile deepens. He has plenty of creative ways to ensure they all get a hefty payout.

Flint's brow lifts. "Do I need to put the cage up around the backseat?"

"Ooh, please." Agony snuggles his head against Harbinger's shoulder. Flint shifts into reverse, resting his hand behind Harbinger's headrest to back out. Agony sucks in a breath at the sight. Harbinger sighs in agreement.

Flint shifts back into drive. "Got the directions?"

"Yep." Harbinger finishes setting their course. "This camping lot should be close enough that we won't have far to go in the morning."

"How many girls have gone missing from this town?"

"Seven. I could hardly find any news coverage. It's like nobody cares, except the families."

Flint guides the SUV onto the highway. "Not for long."

These are not the first girls they'll search for. They won't be the last. Agony stood between Harbinger and Flint at the first memorials, hands intertwined as they mourned the girls they couldn't save. The sister Flint lost so early. The pieces of themselves that didn't make it out unscathed.

From time to time, Flint catches himself wishing he could share this life with Sidi. Harbinger suggested he write to her the way she writes to Poe and Omen, always traveling too much to worry about a reply. In the evenings, the three of them crowd around the table in their camper, pens and paper scattered among envelopes. Flint writes to Sidi. Harbinger writes to her friends. Agony writes to the families of the girls who still twinkle like stars inside him, monuments he treasures.

The banshees asked if they wanted to try to reach their families through the Veil, but Flint and Harbinger declined — for now. If things go right, they've got all the time in the world. Maybe even for that therapist Evie keeps hinting at.

A twin of her remade ring hangs from a necklace around the rearview mirror, swinging with the sway of the car. Her letter's tucked away in the trailer, worn from three sets of hands holding it close.

So you always know who you can trust.

Between the three of them, the ring never stops glowing.

* * * * *

THANK YOU for reading *Inextricably Tied*!

Want more Flint, Harbinger, & Agony? Sign up for my NEWSLETTER to get an exclusive bonus epilogue!

AVEDAVICE.COM/NEWSLETTER
AVEDAVICE.COM/DISCORD
PATREON.COM/AVEDAVICE

About the Author

Aveda Vice is the author of sinful stories and infernal paranormal romances. In her books, you'll find a weakness for monsters and polyamorous pairings. She researches true crime, decorates every day like it's Halloween, and is going to hell.

AVEDAVICE.COM

Sign up for Aveda Vice's NEWSLETTER and PATREON to stay up-to-date on new releases, special offers, and bonus content.

Follow @AVEDAVICE on TWITTER and INSTAGRAM for sneak peaks and promotions.

Join the FANGS WITH BENEFITS FACEBOOK READER GROUP for community chats and posts.

Leave a review for this book on AMAZON and GOODREADS.

Acknowledgements

When I began publishing, I started with the shortest of stories, because I didn't think I could pull off anything longer. I moved onto the smallest novellas, because a full novel seemed out of reach. Once I wrote a full novel, I kept the plot simple, because anything more than that intimidated me...but with *Inextricably Tied*, I went for it.

I'm so proud of this story and so grateful to the people who made it possible. My beta readers were phenomenal and truly helped shape Harbinger, Agony, and Flint's romance into what it is. For *Skin*: Freydís, Michael, Purabi, and Steph. For *Inextricably Tied*: Amanda, Amy, Gab, Steph (again, my love), and Whitney. Your input and support were invaluable to this process. A special thank you to Ames for leading me toward the title of *Inextricably Tied* and grasping Agony's voice so readily. And shoutout to Jacque for using the term "freelance forseer" in a post about *Skin*, because it's one of the best descriptions of Harbinger's work that I've seen.

Rabbit, erotic monster romance is a bit outside of your wheelhouse – but worldbuilding is absolutely within it. Thank you for creating the original map of Orena and helping me expand the Fangs With Benefits universe. I love (working with) you, and I can't wait to see how much better all of my worlds become with you in them.

A massive thank you to my Coremata tier patrons who were with me just after my first novel released. I truly could not do this without you, and I am so thankful for you every day. Ally, Amanda, Amanda, Angelicque, April, Ash, Ash, Becca, Carrie, Elle, Elley, Janla, Jessy, Katie, Kristin, Lauren, LB, Lexi, Lindsay, Maggie, Mari, Nicole, Nova, Piper, Sadie, Samantha, Shonna, and Whitney – you have made this story, and so much more, possible.

Finally, thanks to you, reader. I hope this story makes you feel as much as I felt writing it. I also hope it makes you cry. <3

Printed in Great Britain
by Amazon